"With haunting prose, Sherri Wood [...] in a small southern town a generatio[...] are filled with joy but with secrets buried deep in their souls. Bethany and Reana Mae, no longer children but not yet women, are tied together by bonds of kinship and friendship that help them survive challenges they don't understand. *Prayers and Lies* is a rich story of the triumph of love and decency."

—Sandra Dallas, author of *True Sisters*

"From the first sentence, the voice of the narrator, Bethany, rings true and never falters. *Prayers and Lies* is the story of a family that knows how to love and forgive and get on with life."

—Drusilla Campbell, author of *Little Girl Gone*

"*Prayers and Lies* is a sweet, revealing tale of family, friendship, long-held secrets and includes the all-important ingredients of forgiveness and love."

—Kris Radish, author of *Tuesday Night Miracles*

"When I was reading *Prayers and Lies,* the voice was so genuine, so sincere, I felt like Bethany was standing right before me, barefoot, earnestly telling me her story, alternately laughing, crying, wondering, confused, and scared. I was on the edge of my seat, listening, every scene coming in to full, bright, Technicolor detail as one prayer was heard, one lie was shattered, one family's raw, haunting life laid bare. I loved it."

—Cathy Lamb, author of *A Different Kind of Normal*

"Prepare to stay up all night reading! Sherri Wood Emmons perfectly captures the devastating impact of family secrets in her beautifully written—and ultimately hopeful—debut novel. With its evocative setting and realistically crafted characters, *Prayers and Lies* is a must read for fans of rich family drama."

—Diane Chamberlain, author of *The Good Father*

And praise for *The Sometimes Daughter*

"With strong Oprah Book Club vibes, *The Sometimes Daughter* is a pleasant, touching read . . . Emmons knows how to write women, capturing the nuances of ordinary life in such a way that her characters become people that you want to know."

—*NUVO Newsweekly*

Books by Sherri Wood Emmons

PRAYERS AND LIES

THE SOMETIMES DAUGHTER

THE WEIGHT OF SMALL THINGS

Published by Kensington Publishing Corporation

The Weight of Small Things

SHERRI WOOD EMMONS

KENSINGTON BOOKS
www.kensingtonbooks.com

KENSINGTON BOOKS are published by

Kensington Publishing Corp.
119 West 40th Street
New York, NY 10018

ISBN-13: 978-0-7582-8043-5
ISBN-10: 0-7582-8043-2

First Kensington Trade Paperback Printing: April 2013
10 9 8 7 6 5 4 3 2 1

Printed in the United States of America

For Chris, my favorite husband

1

Corrie lay beneath the delicately flowered sheet, her eyes squeezed shut, hands flat on her belly, listening to her husband's regular snores. The cramping increased, signaling another period, another failure. No pregnancy, no baby, just another month of wasted time.

She rose quietly and went into the bathroom for a tampon and some ibuprofen. Staring at herself in the mirror, she let the tears drip down her face and into the sink.

It wasn't fair. Everyone else could get pregnant. Little girls who were too young and didn't want babies got pregnant. Older women with grown kids got pregnant. *Why, God? Why not me?*

But she knew. Somewhere deep inside she knew why. She didn't deserve a baby.

She walked down the hall and opened the door to the nursery, sat down in the padded rocker, and stared around the room. Jemima Puddle-Duck, Tom Kitten, and Peter Rabbit gazed back at her from their frames on the walls.

She shouldn't have decorated a nursery before she even got pregnant. Everyone had told her so. And everyone had been right. But, God, she and Mark had loved picking out the crib and changing table, the wallpaper border, and the framed prints. Of course they'd get pregnant right away. Why shouldn't they? They were happily married, had a nice home and good jobs. Their friends were having babies. It was time, after all.

Instead, they'd endured two long, emotional, roller-coaster years of trying and hoping and despair.

Dropping her head into her hands, Corrie cried softly.

"Honey?"

Mark stood in the doorway, rubbing sleep from his eyes.

"Are you okay?" he asked.

She shook her head, not meeting his eyes.

"Cramps?"

She nodded.

"Oh, Corrie," he said softly. "It's okay, honey."

She rose and walked into his arms.

"I'm sorry," she whispered. "I'm so sorry."

"Don't say that." He stroked her hair. "It's not your fault. It's just . . . well, it's just not our time yet. But we'll get there."

He raised her chin to look into her eyes.

"I promise, Corrie, we'll have a baby. One way or another, we'll have a baby."

She nodded, willing herself to believe him.

"Come back to bed," he said, leading her out of the nursery by the hand. "Get some sleep. You'll feel better in the morning."

He kissed her forehead and pulled the sheet over them both.

"I love you," she said.

"I love you, too."

A few minutes later, Mark was snoring again. Corrie stared at the ceiling fan spinning slowly above the bed, wondering how he could go back to sleep so easily. Didn't he even care? Or was he just tired of the baby quest, the doctor's visits and hormones and endless disappointment?

But it had been his idea to have a baby in the first place. Mark wanted children; he'd said so from the start. He loved his nephew and niece. He was so good with kids. He would be a great dad.

Only she couldn't give him that. She couldn't give him the one thing he wanted most in the world.

She curled herself around his sleeping back, felt his heart beating beneath her hand. *Why, God? Why can't I get pregnant? I'm so sorry for before. Please don't punish Mark because of something I did.*

She held her breath and waited, as she always did, for some kind of reply, but the only sound in the room was Mark's breathing. After a long time, she rose again, went downstairs to the kitchen, and made a cup of peppermint tea.

"Oh, honey, you worry too much." Patrice sank into the faded red recliner, balancing a coffee mug in one hand, the TV remote in the other. "You've always worried too much, ever since you were a little girl." She sighed. "Just like your father."

Corrie's spine stiffened, her jaw clenched as she shoved the dust rag furiously across the coffee table. Why did she bother telling her mother anything? Why did she always expect that Patrice would suddenly be different? She sighed and walked to the kitchen, swiping the rag across a countertop.

"Mom?" she called, glancing at the empty coffeepot. "Where's the coffee?"

"Oh, I haven't made any today," Patrice called back. "I'm having tea."

Corrie held her hand over the stove's cool burners, then looked into the sink and the trash can for a teabag. She sighed again and walked back to the living room.

"For God's sake, Mom," she said, eyeing the mug Patrice held to her lips. "It's not even noon."

Now Patrice sighed loudly. She sipped from the cup and set it on the coffee table. "It's five o'clock somewhere," she said flatly.

Corrie stood a minute, waiting for her to say something else. But Patrice simply dabbed at her lips with a napkin, picked up the mug, and sipped again.

After a long minute of heavy silence, Patrice said, "I don't know why you come over here, if all you're going to do is lecture me."

"I came to help," Corrie said, waving her hand around the cluttered living room. Stacks of magazines covered the end table. Unopened mail, some stained with coffee, lay on the desk. A plate with something dried on it peeked from under the couch. "If I didn't come, you'd drown in filth."

Patrice leaned back in the recliner and rubbed her temples. Finally, she sighed deeply.

"I know you come to help, honey," she said. "And I appreciate the help, I do. But can't you keep your negative comments to yourself, just for once? Can't we have a nice visit without you nagging, nagging, nagging me? Can't you ever just . . . relax?"

Corrie bit her lip hard, feeling the bile rise in her throat. Her mother's mantra, ever since Corrie's father had died, had been the same. *Why are you persecuting me? I'm just a poor widow. Don't judge me. Stop worrying so much. Everything will work out . . . it always does.*

What Patrice never acknowledged was that things worked out because Corrie worked them out. She always had, even as a child. When the electric bill went unpaid, it was Corrie who called to plead for more time, before they turned the electricity off. When her little brother needed cleats for soccer, Corrie spent her babysitting money to get them. When her mother fell asleep on the couch after dinner, Corrie made sure her brother and sister finished their homework and brushed their teeth before bed.

And Patrice always smiled and said, "There, you see! It all worked out just fine."

"Sure, Mom," Corrie said softly in reply. "Whatever."

"Why do you let her get to you?" Bryn sat at Corrie's kitchen table, a glass of merlot in her hand, watching as Corrie shredded a paper napkin. "You know how she is. Patrice is just . . . Patrice."

"I know," Corrie said, rolling the last of the napkin into a small ball. "I just worry about her. I mean, it wasn't even noon and she was already into the gin."

"She's a drunk, honey. You know it, I know it, everyone knows it. Probably even Patrice knows it. She's an alcoholic, and there's not a damned thing you can do about it."

Corrie rubbed her hand across her eyes. "She wasn't always this way," she said quietly.

"I know she wasn't," Bryn agreed. "But she has been for a long time. God, Corrie, she's been drinking for as long as I've known you."

Bryn and Corrie had met their first day of college, assigned roommates at first, then friends, now more like sisters.

"At least she's a fun drunk," Bryn continued. "I mean, at least she doesn't get mean or anything."

Corrie simply nodded. That was the consensus among her friends. Her mother was a fun drunk, the life of the party. She was always ready with a joke, always flirting with her daughters' boyfriends, always dancing around the house in her short red kimono robe, swaying to music that no one else could hear.

But even Bryn didn't know the whole truth—that Patrice was fun until she hit a wall, and then the fun could suddenly turn to mean. Corrie had a long scar running down her thigh to prove it, evidence of the time Patrice had thrown a pan of scalding water at her because Corrie had refused to drive her to the liquor store when she ran out of gin.

"Before my dad died—" Corrie began.

"I know," Bryn interrupted her. "Before your dad died, everything was perfect. He was perfect, your mom was perfect, Maya was perfect, and Caerl . . . well, at least Caerl wasn't a complete asshole, like he is now."

Corrie's initial impulse to defend her little brother passed as quickly as it had risen. Caerl *was* an asshole. There was no denying it. Even as a kid, he'd been mean, stealing money from Corrie's drawer, teasing Maya mercilessly, lying to get what he wanted. Yet Patrice continually made excuses for Caerl, even as she neglected her daughters.

Poor Maya was only six when their father died and their mother retreated into an alcoholic haze. Corrie could still picture her small face, eyes wide and trusting, trying hard not to cry as Corrie bandaged her knee when she fell off her bike the first time.

"But your dad did die." Bryn's voice brought Corrie back to the present. "It sucks, but it happened. And your mom didn't have to . . . She could have made different choices back then. Hell, she could still make different choices. But she doesn't. And that's not your fault, Corrie. That's on her, not on you."

She reached across the table and took Corrie's hand. "You are not responsible for your mom or your siblings," she said firmly. "You just concentrate on taking care of yourself for now. Maybe you should take a break from going over there for a while."

Corrie smiled at her friend, staring so intently at her from across the table. Bryn's dark eyes never wavered from Corrie's, those eyes so big in her pale, heart-shaped face.

"I can't do that," Corrie said, pulling her hand from Bryn's. "She needs me."

"Honey, she's always going to need you," Bryn said. "She's going to need you until she realizes she has to take care of herself."

Corrie rose and carried her wineglass to the sink. "Do you want another glass?"

"Better not," Bryn said, rising as well. "I've still got work to do tonight. But thanks for dinner."

"I'm glad you could come," Corrie said, hugging her friend lightly. "I hate eating alone."

"Well, make that husband of yours come home for dinner some-time," Bryn said, grinning.

"He's really busy right now," Corrie began. "It's a huge project and . . ."

"It always is, right?" Bryn said. "But hey, I'm not complaining. I got a free meal out of it."

After Bryn left, Corrie poured herself a second glass of wine. At least she could have wine now, knowing she wasn't pregnant . . . again. She sat in the dark living room, her bare feet curled under her on the white leather couch. Maybe Bryn was right. Maybe she should take a break from her mother, just concentrate on herself and Mark and . . . She leaned her head back and let the tears come, the ones she'd been fighting all day.

If they had a baby, maybe Mark would stop traveling so much. Maybe he'd come home for dinner sometimes. Maybe Patrice would fall in love with being a grandma and cut back on her drinking. Maybe . . .

She shook her head sharply and swiped her eyes with the back of her hand.

No maybes. It is what it is.

She switched on the lamp, reached for the TV remote, and saw the invitation on the coffee table. Picking it up, she read it for the hundredth time. *Please join Middlebrook University's Class of 2001 for our ten-year reunion!* Could it really be ten years since she'd graduated? It felt like so much longer, like a whole lifetime ago.

She leaned back and closed her eyes, remembering her first day at the university, the day she met Bryn, the day she met Daniel . . . the day everything changed.

"Hey, I'm Bryn!"

Corrie had stared at the girl with short, dark, spiky hair standing in the middle of the dorm room, holding a curtain rod in one hand and a hammer in the other. She didn't look old enough to be in college. She hardly looked old enough to be in high school.

"Well hello, Bryn!" Patrice said, smiling widely. "I'm Patrice, and this is Coriander Bliss." She waved at Corrie. "It looks like you two are going to be roommates."

"Coriander Bliss?" Bryn repeated, staring at Corrie.

Corrie felt her cheeks redden. "It's just Corrie," she said, staring steadily at the floor.

"Oh all right, just Corrie," Patrice said, laughing. "If that's what you really want."

She turned to Bryn and smiled again. "I don't know why she doesn't love her name. I think Coriander Bliss is beautiful, don't you?"

"Um, sure," Bryn mumbled. "I guess so."

"And Bryn is an unusual name, too," Patrice said. "Is it short for Brenda?"

"No, just Bryn."

"Well then, just Bryn, you and just Corrie should get along fabulously."

After Patrice finally left, Corrie sat on her bed, watching Bryn hang dark purple curtains that matched her black-and-purple bedspread.

"Hope you don't mind it dark," Bryn said, stepping back from the window to admire the curtains. "I like to sleep late."

"It's okay," Corrie said. The black and purple contrasted oddly with her cream-colored quilt, delicately embroidered with tiny pink rosebuds. Corrie had made the quilt herself. She had embroidered sheer curtains to match, but they were still folded neatly in the sweater box now stowed under the bed.

"Is your name really Coriander Bliss?" Bryn asked.

"Yeah," Corrie said, blushing again. "My mom was on an Indian cooking spree."

"Could be worse," Bryn said, grinning. "She could have named you Galangal."

Corrie laughed. "I guess."

"So, where are you from?" Bryn asked, flopping onto her own bed.

"Here," Corrie said. "I mean, Middlebrook. I grew up here."

"So how come you're living on campus?"

"I had to get out," Corrie began. "That is, I . . ."

"Oh, I get it," Bryn reassured her. "I wanted out, too. That's why I came here instead of going to Butler or IUPUI."

"So you're from Indianapolis?" Corrie asked.

"Just north of there. My folks live in Carmel." Bryn glanced at Corrie to see if she had registered the name of the expensive Indianapolis suburb. She was relieved that Corrie didn't react.

"So, will you be going home much?" Bryn continued.

Corrie hesitated, then nodded. "Probably," she said. "My mom needs help with my brother and sister."

"What about your dad?"

"He died," Corrie said softly, "when I was twelve. He had a heart attack."

"Oh, I'm sorry. That's tough."

Corrie nodded. "He was a professor here," she said. "That's why I can afford to be here."

"What did he teach?" Bryn asked.

"History," Corrie said. "Mostly he focused on East Asian history."

"Cool. Is that what you're majoring in?"

"I don't know," Corrie said. "I haven't decided. How about you?"

"Art," Bryn said firmly. "I want to be a graphic artist."

"Wow," Corrie said. "I wish I knew what I wanted to do."

"Oh, you'll figure it out," Bryn said. "Meantime, are you hungry?"

* * *

They walked into the crowded, noisy dorm cafeteria, filled their trays, and looked for a place to sit.

"There," Bryn said, pointing to two seats at the end of a long table.

"Oh, hey," she said, smiling at a redheaded guy who took the seat opposite them. He was tall and lanky in an Atlanta Braves T-shirt and jeans.

"Hey," he said, setting his tray on the table.

"I'm Bryn and this is Corrie. We're freshman. How about you?"

"Yeah, me too," he said. "I'm Daniel."

He smiled briefly at the girls, then began eating his hamburger.

"Where are you from?" Bryn asked.

"Atlanta," Daniel said, pointing to the T-shirt. "You?"

"Indianapolis," Bryn said. "Corrie's from Middlebrook."

"Cool."

Daniel kept eating, so Bryn turned her attention back to Corrie. "So, what's fun here in Middlebrook?"

Corrie thought for a minute. "Well, Kendle Street is fun, lots of shops and restaurants from all over the world. And there's a movie theater on Fourth, and the mall is on Second."

"How about clubs?" Bryn asked. "Any good clubs?"

"Well, I've heard Ike's is good," Corrie said. "But I haven't actually been there. You have to be twenty-one."

"Or," Bryn said, grinning, "you have to look twenty-one and have a good fake ID."

Corrie stared at her, and Bryn laughed.

"Oh, come on," she said. "You don't have a fake ID?"

Corrie shook her head.

"Well, we'll have to get you one," Bryn said. "How about you?" She nodded in Daniel's direction. "Does Mr. Atlanta have a fake ID?"

Daniel stopped chewing and looked at Bryn for a moment before answering. "Nope," he said. "No club-hopping for me. I came to learn, not to get drunk."

"Well, excuse me," Bryn said, her eyes widening as she turned to Corrie. "Heaven forbid anything should get in the way of your *learning*."

"What are you studying?" Corrie asked.

"Political science and sociology," Daniel said.

"Very marketable," Bryn said, laughing.

"The goal isn't to make money," Daniel said, smiling now. "It's to make a difference."

Bryn laughed again and began talking about where to find a fake ID for Corrie. Corrie sat half listening, watching Daniel tackle his salad.

"What do you mean, make a difference?" she asked when Bryn paused for a breath.

Daniel set his fork down and leaned his elbows on the table. "I want to make a difference in the world," he said. "Not just earn a paycheck, but make a real difference in people's lives."

"You mean, like a social worker?" Corrie asked.

"Maybe," he agreed. "But I'd rather work on a larger scale, maybe lobbying in Washington for a higher minimum wage or for workers' rights . . . stuff like that, you know?"

"Oh," Corrie said. "That's . . . impressive."

Bryn laughed, watching Corrie with raised eyebrows.

"It is," Corrie insisted. "It's impressive to know what you want to do, and to want to help people. That's . . . impressive."

"Thanks." Daniel sounded skeptical. "How about you? What are you majoring in?"

"Graphic design," Bryn said. "For me, the point *is* to earn a big, fat paycheck."

"What a surprise," Daniel said, laughing. "And you?"

"Oh, I'm not sure yet," Corrie said. "Maybe history or literature or . . . I just don't know."

"Well," Daniel said, pushing his chair back from the table and rising, "you've got some time to figure it out. See you later." With that, he picked up his tray and walked away.

"Well," Bryn said, watching him. "He's pretty much full of himself."

"Maybe," Corrie said. "But it's nice he wants to help people."

Corrie smiled, remembering that day fourteen years ago, at how naïve she had been, how naïve they'd all been. She'd been awed by

Daniel, right from the start. How could he know at eighteen what he wanted to do with his life?

She stared at the invitation in her hand. Would Daniel come to the reunion? Would she still feel for him the way she had all those years ago?

Headlights swept through the picture window. Mark was home, and he'd be hungry.

Corrie crushed the invitation in her fist, dropping it into the trash can on the way to the kitchen to fix a plate for her husband.

3

"This one is from us."

Mark smiled as he handed the package to his parents. He turned to Corrie and winked as he said, "I guess you'll know who picked it out."

Grace carefully opened the wrappings and laid them aside. She looked up before opening the silver box and smiled. "Well, if Corrie chose it, I'm sure it's perfect."

She lifted the lid from the box. "And I was right. It's beautiful."

She raised the crystal bowl for everyone to see. "It's the one we saw at Macy's, Tom. You remember, the one I liked so much?"

Tom leaned over and kissed Corrie's cheek. "It's beautiful, honey. Thank you."

Corrie felt a quick rush of relief. She had known Grace would like it, but she was never sure about Tom. In the six years he had been her father-in-law, she'd never learned to feel comfortable with him. He was an imposing man, tall and broad-shouldered, with a regal bearing, as if he owned the world. Corrie felt like an intruder in the family when Tom was around. Mark always laughed when she said so. Then he would kiss her forehead and say, What did it matter, anyway, what his father thought? He loved her, and wasn't that enough?

Grace was opening another gift. Corrie rose from the couch and walked into the kitchen. She'd seen Ian heading in that direction, walking with a studied casualness she knew meant mischief. She opened the kitchen door and, sure enough, there he was, standing on a stool by the counter, dragging his fingers through the white icing on the huge anniversary cake.

Standing by the stool was his sister, Laurel, two years his junior. Ian was passing fingerfuls of icing to her. Both children had mouths full of the sticky sweet stuff.

Corrie stood in the doorway for a moment watching them, smiling. Her nephew was such a handful, always thinking up schemes that seemed well beyond the scope of a five-year-old. Just now, he was using a spoon to smooth icing over the bald spots he'd left on the cake.

Corrie put on a serious face and let the door swing shut. Both children spun around. Ian nearly toppled from his perch. Then he climbed down and stood behind Laurel, saying brightly, "Hi, Aunt Corrie. We were just looking at the cake."

He nudged Laurel and they both moved away from the counter. "We weren't having any." He smiled sweetly, exposing a gap where his top front teeth had fallen out.

"I think you'd both better go back out and watch Grandma open her gifts. You'll have to wait till later for cake."

The children ran past her to the living room. Corrie smiled again. She picked up the spoon and began smoothing the icing, finishing Ian's job.

"Couldn't wait?" Sarah was standing in the doorway, laughing. "I saw the kids come out of here and thought I'd better see if the cake was still standing. I see you beat me to it."

"I probably let them off too easy," Corrie said. "But they were so sweet."

"Oh, they have their moments." Sarah smiled as she eased herself onto one of the stools. "Last week, Ian decided on a new name for the baby," she said, patting her pregnant belly. "He thinks Obo would do just fine."

Corrie laughed. "That'd be . . . different. Have you and Kevin thought of a name yet? You've only got a couple months left, you know."

"Well, actually we have. If it's a boy, we'll call him Thomas Carl," Sarah said.

"That'll make Tom proud." Corrie grinned. "But what a moniker for a little boy to live up to."

Sarah paused and looked at the floor. "Corrie, if it's a girl, I hope you won't mind if we name her after you—Corrie Ann."

Corrie felt tears sting her eyes, and she stood still for a moment, saying nothing.

"We can come up with something else. I mean, you might want to use it yourself someday . . . for your daughter. I just . . . I'd like my daughter to be named for my best friend. But, honestly, just say the word if you don't like it."

Corrie wrapped her arms around Sarah and hugged her. Her voice trembled as she said, "I think that's the sweetest thing I've ever heard. Of course I don't mind. I'd love to have a namesake. I'm just glad it's Corrie and not Coriander."

"You're sure?" Sarah asked.

"Yes, I'm sure." Corrie dabbed at her eyes with a napkin. "Besides, if Mark and I ever have a daughter, I don't think I'd name her after me."

Sarah laughed, gave her sister-in-law's hand a quick squeeze, then scanned the cake. "I see my kids' handiwork."

Corrie picked up the spoon again and began smoothing icing. She didn't look up when Sarah asked, "Do you wish you were there?"

Corrie was proud to hear her own voice steady and calm. "Where?"

"Don't give me that. You know what I'm talking about."

"You mean the reunion?" Corrie asked, studiously smoothing icing.

"You've been awfully quiet today," Sarah answered. "I just wondered if you're okay."

Corrie didn't look up. She was making a bigger mess with each stroke.

Finally, she straightened and smiled. "I'm having a good time, really. To tell you the truth, it was kind of a relief not going."

"You keep saying that, but I'm not buying it." Sarah shook her head. "It's your ten-year reunion. All your friends are there. I know you hate missing it, and I don't blame you."

"Well, maybe it would have been fun. But I couldn't miss your folks' fortieth anniversary." She stood back to look at her icing work. "Besides, Bryn is going, and she'll fill me in on all the dirt.

"I think that's enough damage for one day." She put the knife in the sink and wiped her fingers on a towel. "Besides, I know Mark would rather be here. He didn't want to miss this. And he'd have hated the reunion, making small talk with a bunch of people he doesn't know."

"Well, you went to his," Sarah said. "He could have returned the favor."

"It's okay, Sarah. Honestly, I think you're more worried about it than I am.

"We'd better get back in there. They should be done with presents soon." She headed for the door, then stopped. "Don't worry about it, okay? I really would rather be here with all of you."

Corrie pushed open the door, put on her best smile, and walked back into the living room.

"Who's ready for cake?"

That night, long after the rest of the household had gone to bed, Corrie stood on the balcony outside her bedroom. She stared at the black water of the lake below, sipping a cup of herbal tea. Usually, she loved coming to the cabin. Well . . . it was a cabin by her in-laws' definition. It was much bigger than the house Corrie had grown up in.

Most times, she loved it here. She enjoyed the lake and the boat. She was a demon on water skis. And Grace and Tom were easier here. It was the only place she ever saw Tom really relax. Mostly she welcomed a weekend at the lake. She and Mark had spent their honeymoon here, after all. It was a very romantic place.

But tonight she was not enjoying the stars, the quiet, or the light breeze off the water. She stood in the dark, in her robe, staring into space. She wondered briefly if she could sneak downstairs and find a cigarette in Grace's purse, then dismissed the idea. She'd been smoke-free for nearly five years now; she and Bryn had fought that fight together and finally won. But sometimes she thought she'd sell her soul for one good drag of nicotine.

She wondered what was happening back in town, on campus. She wondered if Daniel was there.

Probably not. He wouldn't come back from . . . wherever he is, just for a reunion. She smiled ruefully. *He'd think it was a huge waste of money.*

She shook her head, willing herself into the present.

Just as well to be here with the family.

Corrie swirled the tea in her cup, nearly spilling it onto her silk robe. She was lying to herself and she knew it, but it was too late to do anything about it. She'd missed the chance to see him again, to finally face down the past and be done with it. And she was angry with herself for not going . . . and angry with Mark, too. And she was angry with herself for being angry with Mark. Because Mark, after all, had told her she should go to the reunion.

"You go ahead," he'd said. "Mom and Dad will understand. We can take them out for dinner next week. You go and see your friends."

But Corrie had smiled and said no, it didn't really matter. She would just as soon not go to the reunion.

Mark hadn't pressed her about it. She knew he was glad she hadn't gone.

People always told her how lucky she was to have Mark. What a terrific guy, was the general opinion. And Corrie always agreed. Yes, indeed, she was lucky. Mark was everything anyone could want. He was good-looking, smart, funny; and on top of all that, he was wealthy, a successful architect in a thriving firm. In the beginning she'd been amazed he was interested in her at all. He'd always seemed so remote—Sarah's handsome older brother, so popular, so completely out of her league.

Corrie and Sarah had been inseparable since grade school, and Corrie had spent a lot of time at the Philips' house—mostly because for a long time she was afraid to take Sarah to her house. Corrie's family lived in a little frame house near the university. But it wasn't the house Corrie didn't want her friend to see. It was the state inside the house . . . and then there was her mother.

Patrice was known in polite company as "the neighborhood character." Sometimes the neighbors called her other things—like a drunk or a loon. She was officially too young to have been a hippie, but that didn't slow her down in her quest for nirvana. She breezed through life drinking gin and tonics, oblivious to the neighbors' curious stares and whispered comments, naming her children after whatever held her interest at the time. Maya Chimala, Corrie's younger sister, had been born during Patrice's period of fascination with the Mayan culture. Her brother, Gawyn Caerleon, arrived while Patrice was researching the legend of King Arthur. And Corrie had the misfortune to be born during Patrice's adventures with Indian cooking. Corrie had changed her name to Corrie Ann officially when she married Mark, much to Patrice's dismay.

In addition to drinking and occasionally painting, Patrice collected things. She was not a collector of specific items, like stamps or coins or even Tupperware. No, she was a collector of everything. She couldn't bear to part with things—old cards and letters, books and magazines, bottles, bags, knickknacks, paper clips, anything—and she was forever accumulating more. The house was filled to bursting with stacks of books and papers, every shelf and counter and closet filled. The little yard was cluttered with what Patrice grandly called "garden sculptures." Stone geese, glass balls, pink flamingoes, even an old bathtub Patrice had painted yellow, intending to use it as a planter. Of course, she'd never actually planted anything in the tub, but it still sat in the yard, collecting rainwater and breeding mosquitoes.

Her children had long since given up trying to persuade Patrice to throw anything away. They simply lived with the mess and told themselves it was part of their mother's peculiar charm. But Corrie had never wanted to bring her friends to the house. She couldn't stand the thought of her mother greeting them at the door, tipsy in her red kimono, waving an incense burner in the air and calling delightedly, "Just see, Coriander Bliss, what I found today in the Hendersons' trash."

Of course, Sarah had finally come to Corrie's house. One day while Corrie was out, she simply dropped by. Corrie arrived home to find Sarah sitting on the couch, between a huge pile of *Rolling Stone* magazines and a stack of Tarot cards, drinking tea.

And Sarah had loved the books, the figurines, the lawn art, and especially Patrice.

"Your mom is great," she'd said to Corrie. "She's so much fun. I wish my family was more like yours."

Corrie didn't tell Sarah about the times she had to drag Patrice up the stairs to bed after she'd passed out on the couch. Or the times Patrice spent the grocery money on gin and rum and bourbon. Or the time she had to take a bus to the county lock-up to bail her mother out of jail after she'd been picked up for driving drunk.

For a long time, Corrie never told anyone about her family. She worked hard to rein in her mother's drinking and to shield Maya and Caerl from Patrice's thoughtlessness. In all the years she and Sarah had been friends, it was only after Corrie and Mark had married—after Patrice disrupted the wedding reception, falling drunk into a fountain, exposing her panties and laughing hysterically—that Corrie finally confided in her childhood friend. Mark knew, of course, and Bryn. And Daniel knew.

Two weeks after she first met Daniel in the college cafeteria, Corrie sat in the waiting room of the neighborhood food pantry, voucher in hand. It was a trip she'd made countless times through the years, but one she still hated. As a child, she had trailed along after her mother, studiously avoiding eye contact with the other people there. Once Corrie turned sixteen and got her driver's license, Patrice had simply stopped going, relying on Corrie to keep the pantry filled.

"Coriander Matthews?"

She rose from the bench, looked up, and saw Daniel standing before her.

"Oh, hey," he said when he recognized her. "Are you here to volunteer? You need to check in at the office upstairs."

"Uh, no. That is, I . . ." Her voice trailed away. Her cheeks burned.

"Oh," he said, his voice gentle. "I'm sorry, I didn't mean to . . ."

"It's okay," she said, not looking at him. "My mom needs some things."

"Sure," he said. "That's okay." He waited, but she didn't reply. "So, do you have your voucher?"

She wanted to turn and run. Instead, she handed him the slip of yellow paper, her family's key to meals for the next two weeks.

Daniel read the slip and made a note in the file he carried. "Looks good," he said.

She nodded and reached for a bag.

"It really is okay, you know." His voice was soft.

She forced a small smile. "Can you please not mention this to anyone at school?"

"Sure," he said. "No problem."

He followed her as she walked the familiar aisles, choosing canned vegetables and beans, spaghetti and sauce, macaroni and cheese, tuna, and soups, the foods of her childhood.

"We have fresh bread today," Daniel said, pointing her toward a table.

Corrie nodded and added a loaf to her basket.

"And . . . uh, do you need any . . . personal items?"

Oh, God, why are you here? She fervently wished one of the regular volunteers had pulled her name, even the nasty old lady with the limp, anyone but this boy she couldn't look in the eye.

"My sister is twelve," she whispered.

He pointed her toward the table with tampons, then waited for her by the back door.

"Thank you," she said, her eyes fixed firmly on the ground.

"No problem."

She stepped past him into the brilliant sunshine of a September day, felt him watch her as she walked, spine straight, to her mother's ten-year-old Buick. She put her bags on the floor of the car and drove away, never looking back.

Two days later, he knocked on her door in the dorm. "Hey," he said, smiling at her. "Do you want to get a Coke?"

Bryn's eyebrows rose as she grinned at Corrie.

"Oh," Corrie stammered. "I can't, really. I've got so much homework." She waved her hand at the stack of papers on her desk.

"I thought you were finished," Bryn said.

Corrie shot her a dark look.

"Just a Coke," Daniel said. "Half an hour."

Corrie sighed. "Oh, all right."

She followed him to the coffee shop, wishing she could simply sink into the earth.

"I wanted to say I'm sorry if I embarrassed you the other day. There's no shame in needing help sometimes. Lots of people are having a hard time these days. You know that, right?" Daniel smiled at her.

They sat on the grass with their drinks.

Corrie sighed. "It's just embarrassing," she said. "My dad died when I was twelve and since then my mom . . . well, she doesn't cope very well."

"Does she work?"

She sighed again. "She paints," she said. "And sometimes someone feels sorry for her and buys one of her paintings. But other than that, no, she doesn't work. Mostly she drinks."

She sat a moment in mortified silence. She had never told anyone about her mother's drinking. Her high school counselor had known, and a few of the neighbors. But she had always tried so hard to pretend that her mother was just like anyone else's, a normal mom.

"I shouldn't have said that. Can you please forget I said that?"

"Don't be embarrassed," Daniel said. He touched her arm softly. "Alcoholism is a disease, you know. It's not a sin."

"I guess."

They sat in silence for a minute.

"So, what about your family?" Corrie asked, mostly to fill the silence.

"It's just my mom and me," Daniel said. "My dad bailed before I was born."

"I'm sorry."

"It's okay." He shrugged. "My mom's a lawyer, a public defender in Atlanta."

"Wow, that's pretty cool."

He shrugged again. "Yeah, she's great."

"So how did a guy from Atlanta end up in Middlebrook, Indiana?"

"Scholarship." He laughed. "How about you? Why did you stay so close to home?"

"My dad taught here before he died. So I'm tuition-free."

"Cool," he said. "What did he teach?"

"History. He loved history, especially East Asian history. He was fascinated by China. He always wanted to go there."

"Maybe someday you'll go for him."

"I doubt it," she said, smiling. "I've never been out of the States. I've never even been on a plane."

"Seriously? You've never been on a plane?"

"Seriously," she said. "It's way too expensive."

"Well, someday you will definitely fly."

"Oh, and you're sure about that?"

"Yeah," he said. "I have a feeling you're going to go lots of places."

She laughed and took a sip of her soda.

"Well, right now, I'm going back to my room. I really do have a lot of homework."

"Okay," he said, standing and offering his hand to help her up.

They walked back to the dorm in silence. At the door he leaned in and kissed her cheek. "Do you want to go to a movie on Friday?"

"Sure."

"Cool. I'll come by at six and we can get dinner first."

And just like that, they were dating. Bryn had teased her endlessly about how quickly she had "taken herself off the market." But Corrie was happy to be with Daniel. He knew about her mother, about her past, and it didn't seem to matter to him. He accepted her just as she was. She, in turn, admired his drive to help others, his idealism, and his seemingly endless energy.

* * *

"What are you doing out here?"

Corrie spun around, finally spilling tea on her robe, to see Mark in the doorway, shifting from one foot to the other. He had forgotten his slippers. She smiled.

"I was just coming in," she lied. "I thought I'd have a cup of chamomile." She walked inside and closed the door behind her. "I couldn't sleep."

Mark slipped his arms around her waist and rubbed his lips against the auburn hair that hung, straight and shining, halfway down her back. "You should've gotten me up," he whispered.

Corrie pulled away from him slightly. "I didn't want to wake you. You know the kids will be up early tomorrow, and I didn't want both of us to be tired and cranky."

She dropped her robe onto a chair and slipped into bed. "I'm really tired now. The tea did it. I think I'll be able to sleep."

She turned her back to him and pulled the covers up to her chin. She felt him lie down next to her, hesitate, then sigh and roll over. After a few minutes, he was snoring softly.

Corrie rolled toward him, propped on her elbow, and watched her husband sleep, moonlight from the window casting shadows on his face. He looked so young when he slept. His cheeks were slightly burned from an afternoon in the sun. He really was so handsome. Why would she waste her time thinking about Daniel? She shook her head and leaned back into her pillow. Daniel and she had been over ten years ago. He had moved on, and so had she. So why was she lying here beside her perfect husband, wondering if her ex had gone to the reunion?

Mark sighed and rolled onto his side. She pulled the blanket over his shoulders and kissed his cheek softly. Probably she should have responded to his kiss before. She hated to disappoint him. But it was too early in the cycle for her to be ovulating. And somehow it seemed wasteful to have sex when there was no chance of getting pregnant, as if it might hurt their chances later in the month. Why couldn't she just get pregnant like everyone else?

She'd watched Mark earlier with his sister, offering his hand to help her out of a chair, carrying Laurel to the bedroom so Sarah didn't have to lift her. On the patio, Corrie saw him rest his hand on Sarah's stomach and grin widely when he felt the baby kick. The man was made to be a father. Only Corrie couldn't make him one.

She chewed her lip, thinking of all the attractive young women at Mark's office—the pretty receptionist, the striking redhead in accounting, the busty blond who'd just made partner. Any one of them could probably give Mark a child, and probably would if she had the chance. She'd seen women watch her husband; she knew how attractive he was.

What if someday he got tired of the endless disappointment? What if he decided that she was damaged goods, that he could have a child with any number of other women? What if, finally, he left?

She thought of all the nights Mark came home late from work, all the trips he took to New York, Chicago, and Miami. Had he traveled this much when they first got married? Didn't he used to come home for dinner every night? Was he pulling away from her, just like she always somehow knew he would?

Dear God, she prayed silently. *Thank you for my husband and my family and my friends. Thank you for my life. Please help me to be a better wife, a better daughter, a better sister and friend. Please help me to accept your will for me. Amen.*

The sun was rising when Corrie finally fell into an uneasy sleep.

❧ 4 ❧

Corrie watched the scenery flash by and held tightly to the door handle. Mark always drove too fast on these hilly, narrow roads, sometimes pulling into the oncoming traffic lane to swerve around someone going slow. Now and then she caught a glimpse of the lake through the trees. Soon they would be on the highway and she would relax.

"Mom really liked the bowl." Mark's voice broke her reverie.

She turned to him and smiled.

"I think your dad even liked it," she answered.

"Of course he did. What's not to like?" Mark leaned over and squeezed her shoulder. "You have great taste, Cor. Dad likes everything you've ever gotten them."

Corrie watched her husband's profile in silence. He was so handsome. Tall and broad-shouldered like his father, with the same easy, commanding air. His light brown hair turned golden in the summer, in sharp contrast to his dark brown eyes. The combination was arresting, and he never failed to turn women's heads when he walked down the street. Corrie thought again about the redhead in accounting.

"What are you looking at?" he asked, catching her stare. "Am I wearing my breakfast?"

"Just admiring the view." She laughed, looking away.

Sometimes it still surprised her that she was married to Mark, that she had the life she'd always wanted as a child—a dream life, her mother called it. A beautiful, big house on the right side of town, money to buy nice things, the respectability she'd so longed for, everything neat and tidy. She sighed, wondering why she couldn't just relax and enjoy it all, why she was always waiting for it to be snatched away.

Mark caressed her shoulder. "Thanks for coming this weekend, babe. I know it meant a lot to Mom and Dad. And to me, too."

Corrie smiled and said nothing for a while. She thought of the reunion she had missed, wondering for the hundredth time if Daniel had been there. Would the attraction still have been strong between them? Would he still want her? Would she still care?

She felt her cheeks grow hot and turned away from Mark to look out the window again. *Why should I care if he was there? What does it matter?* She shook her head angrily. *I'm a happily married woman. I have a great husband, a great life . . .*

She looked again at Mark. He really was beautiful to watch, so boyish and charming.

"How 'bout we go away next weekend?" she asked suddenly. "Just the two of us, someplace romantic?" She held her breath and waited.

Mark looked at her in surprise and studied her face carefully for a moment. Then he smiled. "Are you sure?" he asked.

"Yes, sure," she said. "It'll be fun. Can you get away from work?"

"For a weekend with my wife? I think I can arrange that," he said with a laugh. "Where do you want to go?"

"How about Chicago?" she suggested. "We could take the train up on Friday and stay downtown, maybe see a show."

"Wherever you want," Mark answered. He was pleased; she could tell. He reached over, gathered the hair at the back of her neck, and twisted it around his hand. "I'll make the reservations." He paused, looking at her closely again. "What brought this on?"

"Nothing," she replied, laughing self-consciously. "Can't a girl go away with her handsome husband for a romantic weekend?"

They drove in silence for a while, each wrapped in private thoughts.

They hadn't been away together for over a year, hadn't been silly or romantic or spontaneous. Making a baby had turned into a deadly serious business. When Corrie started hormone treatments, sex became a scheduled activity, ruled by the calendar and her temperature.

It wasn't Mark's fault, she knew. It was hers and hers alone. Every time they made love, she tensed up, wondering if this would finally be the time they conceived, knowing somehow that it wasn't. And always afterward, she cried. No wonder he hardly even approached her anymore.

Corrie watched her husband driving, his hair glinting gold in the sun.

God, he's so handsome, she thought. *We would have made such beautiful babies.*

She felt a catch in her throat as she said, "Why don't we stop for coffee at the next exit?"

5

"All work and no play . . ."

Corrie looked up from her computer to see Bryn, blindingly bright in a neon-pink tank top and lime-green miniskirt. She was wearing long, silver earrings that sparkled beneath her severely short black hair, and clunky brown Birkenstocks that seemed singularly inappropriate. She pushed her trademark dark sunglasses up over her forehead and stared down at Corrie, her dark eyes bloodshot. "Did you forget lunch?"

"Oh, God, Bryn. I'm sorry." Corrie began sliding photos into a folder and stacking pages. "We're putting the fall issue to bed and I just forgot. Things have been like hell in here today." She hung the folder in the photo file and stood, smoothing her gray linen skirt. "I'm ready.

"I'm going to lunch, Kenetha," she called to her assistant on her way out. "I'll be back in an hour. If Gordon calls, do *not* let him off the phone without getting a firm deadline."

"You're such a good worker bee," Bryn said with a laugh, dropping the sunglasses back over her eyes. "What would happen if you took an hour and five minutes? Maybe the magazine would fold."

"Shut up." Corrie elbowed her friend. "Just because you live in Neverland doesn't mean the rest of us don't work for a living."

"I beg your pardon," Bryn objected, raising the glasses slightly off her nose to stare at Corrie accusingly. "I do work. I just don't work on a stultifying, bourgeois, nine-to-five schedule. You, my friend, are simply jealous." Again the glasses dropped.

"You're right." Corrie laughed. "Today, I am."

They left the white limestone building that housed Middlebrook University's alumni magazine, walked across the wooded campus, and turned left onto Kendle Street, the hub of Middlebrook's eateries. It was a bright September day, hot and humid. Occasionally, a man turned to watch the two young women walk past. They made an attractive pair, a study in contrasts.

Corrie wore a fitted suit with gray high heels, her auburn hair coiled around her head in a French braid. She looked every inch a young professional. Bryn, on the other hand, was a bona fide bohemian. She even looked like a gypsy, with her jet-black hair and huge dark eyes. Corrie often wondered if Bryn and she had been switched at birth, if perhaps Bryn was Patrice's real daughter and she, Corrie, somehow belonged to Bryn's fashionable, imminently respectable mother.

Bryn had done what she set out to do all those years ago, although not as profitably as she might have hoped. She was a freelance graphic designer, waiting tables when money got tight. She was not married but had an on-again, off-again relationship with an adjunct professor at the university. They had met, in fact, when Bryn was a student in his junior economics class, which had caused a minor scandal in the dorm. After graduation, Bryn had settled in Middlebrook to be near Paul, and for ten years they had been arguing and making up. Currently, they were sharing Paul's apartment. But they had tried that before, and it never seemed to work out.

Corrie and Bryn walked the four blocks to the restaurant in near silence, enjoying the sun on their backs. As they sat down in a corner booth, however, Bryn blurted out, "I can't stand it. Aren't you even going to ask?"

Corrie didn't pretend ignorance. They'd been friends a long time. Bryn knew her too well. She looked down at the table, arranged her silverware, smoothed her skirt. "Are you going to tell me?"

"Not until you ask."

"Witch!" Corrie shook her head and laughed. "Okay, was he there?"

"Who?" Bryn asked, removing her dark glasses to stare in wide-eyed innocence.

Corrie didn't laugh this time, only stared back at her friend.

"Oh, all right," Bryn sighed. She laid her glasses on the table. "He was there. He asked about you."

Corrie sat quietly, not looking at Bryn. She felt her cheeks redden, felt hot and awkward. She picked up the napkin in front of her, disarranging the silverware, and began tearing the paper into small pieces. What should she ask next? What could she?

"Can I take your order?" The waitress hovered over their table, pad in hand.

"Umm, Caesar salad, please," Corrie mumbled. "And a glass of your house blush."

Bryn looked up, surprised, then smiled and looked back down at her menu. "I'll have a falafel," she said. She paused. "And a large glass of milk."

"Milk?" Corrie asked, grinning, glad of a diversion.

"What?" Bryn replied, reddening. "Why shouldn't I have a glass of milk now and then?"

"It's just so healthy, so . . . not you," Corrie said.

"No more than you having wine on a workday. Which brings us back to the subject," Bryn responded. "Do you want to know what he said? What he wore? How he looked?"

Corrie nodded. She looked up, cleared her throat, and said clearly, "Tell me."

"He looks pretty much the same, maybe better groomed. He definitely has a better haircut, although I suppose that could've been just for the reunion." Bryn was in her element now, dishing.

"He came late, spent a lot of time hanging out by the door, just looking around. He always was antisocial. Finally, he sort of sauntered over to me, real casually, you know? And he asked how I was doing, what I had been up to. He never was good at small talk. Fits him like a bad suit." She paused and eyed Corrie carefully. "I never did understand the attraction."

"You wouldn't." Corrie smiled. "What did he say then?"

"Well." Bryn leaned across the table. "He asked if I had seen you around. I told him we were still friends, had lunch most days. Then he said, like he didn't already know, 'Oh, so she still lives in town?' "

Bryn laughed. "Like he didn't know you live here. Bob talks to him all the time. Anyway, I told him, yes, you did. So he asked if you were coming to the reunion, and I told him you were out of town for the weekend. I didn't say why. Was that okay?"

Corrie nodded silently.

Bryn continued. "So he hung around a little while longer, maybe half an hour, making chitchat. He's in Los Angeles now, working for a social services agency in Pasadena. I said I didn't realize Pasadena needed social services, since it had the Rose Bowl, and he got on his soapbox just like always, started telling me about gangs and drugs and homelessness. He never could take a joke. Anyway, he's still trying to save the world. But at least he wore a suit. So that's something, I guess."

Bryn paused, then added, "He's just as charming as ever. Anyway, he said he'd be staying at Bob's for a couple days, and if I saw you, would I tell you that."

Bryn paused and studied Corrie's face. "Are you going to call him?"

The waitress arrived with their drinks. Corrie waited until she had left, then took a sip of her wine, grateful for the pause it allowed.

"I don't know. Maybe. Who else was there?"

Bryn returned home from lunch exhausted. She climbed the stairs to the third-floor apartment she shared with Paul, counting each step, amazed at how hard it was to make her foot reach each one. Usually she had infinite energy. Now she felt drained . . . and nauseated.

Her drowsiness faded as a wave of nausea swept over her. She bounded up the last four steps and fumbled with the key in the door. Running down the hall and into the bathroom, she promptly threw up her lunch.

"Shit," she said out loud to no one. *"Shit."*

She sat down on the bathroom floor and held her head in her hands, moaning. "Why, God? Why me? Why not Corrie? She really *wants* a baby. Shit."

After a few minutes she stood, steadying herself on the sink, and walked into the bedroom. She stepped out of her shoes and dropped onto the bed, not bothering to undress or pull back the covers. Her head was spinning.

What would she tell Paul? He didn't want a baby. He'd never wanted a baby. He didn't even want a wife.

Bryn had known for almost a week, but she hadn't yet thought of a way to break the news to Paul.

At first she'd thought she wouldn't tell him at all. Just get an abortion and be done with it. She'd even called a clinic in Chicago to make an appointment, an appointment that was now just eighteen days away.

He doesn't need to know, she said to herself. *It'll just upset him. It's not like he'd be any help anyway.*

She rolled onto her back and stared at a crack in the ceiling, slowly put her hand on her stomach, and began rubbing it softly.

"Stop it," she said out loud. She sat up on the side of the bed. From here she could see down the hall to the kitchen table, where the computer screen beckoned with a half-finished job. She started to rise, felt her head begin to throb and a new wave of nausea, sat down again, and flopped back on the bed.

Think about something else, she commanded herself. She forced her mind back over the past few days, to the reunion, to Corrie and Daniel, to lunch. She wondered, for the hundredth time, what it was that Corrie saw in Daniel. *He's such a self-absorbed jerk,* Bryn thought. *Nothing to recommend him.* He wasn't well built or even good-looking, with that pale skin and red mop of hair. He was judgmental and had a caustic sense of humor. In college, he had challenged Corrie about everything—her clothes, her friends, her choice of major—always pushing her to justify her choices.

"I didn't say it wasn't a good idea." Bryn could hear his voice now, after Corrie joined a gym. "I just want you to think about your choices. Because every 'yes' is a 'no' to something else."

It was exhausting talking to Daniel. He was self-assured and pushy and just . . . exhausting.

Of course, Bryn had not been a huge fan of Mark's in the beginning, either, and she'd given her friend hell when Corrie decided to marry him. Bryn thought Mark was a little too self-confident, too full of himself.

"I know he's good-looking and rich," she had laughed, "but other than that, what's he got to recommend him?"

Over the years, however, she had come to appreciate that Mark was a good guy—boring maybe and definitely a workaholic, but basically a good guy. And he did love Corrie and was good to her. Bryn could forgive his blandness for that.

Bryn rolled onto her stomach again, trying to ignore the persistent nausea. *Why she even gives a damn about Daniel being in town is beyond me. For Christ's sake, the guy left her ten years ago.*

She closed her eyes, willing herself to focus on Corrie and Daniel, on anything but her stomach. Corrie was nervous at lunch, no doubt about that. Bryn knew her habits well, and when she started shredding paper, it was a sure sign.

Lunch. *Milk?* Bryn shook her head. *Why did I order milk?*

The nausea was too much, and she ran to the bathroom to throw up again.

6

Corrie paced the living room floor, staring at the cell phone in her hand. She had purposely worked late to avoid this. That way, she thought, she'd get home after Mark did. But he was tied up at the office again, preparing a report that had to be done by tomorrow. And here she was, pacing.

To make matters worse, tomorrow he was flying to New York again.

"Damn it," Corrie had exploded. "Why does it have to be now?"

"Don't worry," Mark said, laughing. "I'll be home on Thursday. We'll still have our weekend in Chicago."

But she was worried. She didn't want him gone, not this week.

The phone rang, startling her out of her reverie. She stood, hesitating. On the third ring, she answered.

"Hello? . . . Oh, hi, Sarah. No, I'm up. . . . Just reading manuscripts," she lied, glancing at the stack she'd brought home from the office sitting untouched on the hall table.

"Are you okay? You're not having labor pains this early, are you?"

But Sarah was not in labor, just wanting to share the latest tales of Ian and Laurel. Corrie talked with her for a while, then resumed pacing.

Would he call? Should she call? Was it too late to call now? She looked at the clock—9:30, not too late. She stared at the phone for a long minute, then shoved it into the pocket of her sweater. What would she say? "Hi, Daniel. What have you been up to for the last ten years? Miss me?"

"I don't think so," she said aloud. "If he wants to talk to me, he knows where I am."

She walked into the kitchen, poured a second glass of cabernet, and sat down at the table with a manuscript. "The Bridges of Brown County." She smiled wryly, shaking her head. *Oh well, points for trying,* she thought, laying the article aside.

She sat for a moment, staring vacantly at the blue and white stripes of the wallpaper. Maybe she ought to repaper the kitchen. Mark really didn't care much for the blue and white, after all. But Corrie loved it. It was clean and crisp and happy. She loved her kitchen.

She stood suddenly, smoothed her skirt, and pulled the phone from her pocket. Before she could talk herself out of it, she dialed Bob's number.

"Hello."

It was Bob's voice and it calmed her immediately.

"Hi, Bob. It's Corrie."

"Hey, stranger. We missed you at the reunion."

"Yeah, I was doing the good daughter-in-law thing. Did you have fun?"

"It was okay. A little depressing, maybe."

Corrie could imagine how depressing it had been, explaining over and over why Wendy wasn't there with him.

"I'll bet," she said softly. "How're you doing?"

"I'm okay," Bob replied. "I'll have the kids this weekend. That'll help."

Bob and Wendy had two boys, seven and five. Since Wendy left, the kids had been living with her and her new boyfriend in an old duplex on the outskirts of town.

"You got big plans?" Corrie asked.

"Nope, just gonna hang out here," he answered. "I figure they get enough excitement with Wendy. I'm going the stability route."

"Have you seen a lawyer yet?" Corrie asked.

"No," he answered slowly. "I know I should. I just keep thinking she'll come to her senses and come home. How long can she stay with that jerk?"

"I don't know, Bob. But you need to think about what you're going to do if she doesn't come back. You need to see a lawyer."

"I know, I know. I will. If nothing else, I've got to make sure I don't lose the boys."

Corrie paused, feeling guilty. She loved Bob and she felt awful for him. His life had pretty much been turned upside down in the last couple months, and she hadn't called often or been much help. Too busy, was her excuse—too lazy, more likely. And now she was calling . . . to talk to Daniel? What kind of friend was she?

She decided she wouldn't even ask about Daniel. As it turned out, she didn't have to.

"Hey," Bob said, "enough about that. Did you know Daniel is here? Well, not here right now. He's out with Jeff Arvin tonight. But he's staying with me until Saturday."

"Yeah, Bryn mentioned that," Corrie mumbled.

"Why don't you and Bryn come over tomorrow night?" Bob suggested. "We could cook dinner together, like the old days . . . Mark, too," he added.

"Mark will be in New York tomorrow," she answered. "And I really can't. I've got so much to do at work this week. We're behind deadline and the issue is a mess. I'm sorry, I just can't."

"Come on, Corrie. I know Daniel wants to see you. Can't you come just for a little while? If not for dinner, then come for a drink later."

"Let me call you tomorrow, Bob, after I see what my schedule looks like. Okay?"

"Sure," he said. "You let me know, and Bryn, too. Hey, speaking of Bryn, is she okay? We were supposed to have lunch on Thursday, and she never showed."

"You know Bryn," Corrie said. "She's not the most reliable person in the world."

"I know," said Bob, "but she didn't even call. And she didn't seem like herself Saturday night, either."

"What do you mean?" Corrie asked.

"I don't know, just not herself. Kind of bitchy. And she looked bad—pale and tired and . . . just not like herself. I just wondered if she's all right."

"Well, I had lunch with her today and she seemed fine. No more bitchy than usual." Corrie laughed. "She was giving me all the dirt."

"I don't even want to know," Bob said.

"I'm sure you don't. You're too nice," Corrie replied.

"So you think she's okay?" Bob asked.

"Yeah, I think she's okay."

"Well, I'll call and ask her to come tomorrow, too. Try to be here, okay? I don't want to be the only buffer between her and Daniel."

"Hey, that's a pretty picture," Corrie said. "All right, I'll try to come after work."

She hung up and smiled. Bob was such a good guy. She wondered, not for the first time, why he had married Wendy, after she'd cheated on him before they were even married. And why Wendy would leave him. And what she saw in the loser she was living with now. She shook her head, frowning slightly. *Life can be so screwed up.*

She was glad to have talked to Bob. Glad Daniel hadn't been there, after all. *Now all I have to do is think of a reason to miss dinner tomorrow, and by the weekend, life will be back to normal.*

She heard Mark's car pull into the driveway. She walked back into the kitchen to see what they had in the fridge. He never ate supper when he worked late, and he would be hungry.

❧ 7 ❧

At four o'clock the next afternoon, Corrie called and left a message on Bob's answering machine. She was so sorry, but she was going to have to beg off. They had missed the deadline on the fall issue, and she was going to have to stay and finish it up. Then she left the office and drove to the mall. She spent the next three hours wandering from store to store, halfheartedly looking at baby clothes for Sarah's shower. At a quarter till nine, she bought an ice cream cone for dinner and headed home, exhausted but pleased with herself for making it through the day and avoiding dinner at Bob's.

She'd nearly finished the ice cream when she pulled into her driveway and jerked to a stop, dropping the last of the cone into her lap. There in her spot was a jeep she recognized as Bob's. Leaning against it was the driver. Corrie would recognize that shock of red hair anywhere. Daniel looked up as she pulled in next to him, then he smiled at her.

He walked over to open her car door, as she frantically scrubbed ice cream from her lap with a napkin.

"Hey, you," he said, taking her hand and pulling her from the car.

Corrie stood before him, not looking up, still concentrating on her skirt.

"I spilled ice cream," she said lamely.

"They have soft serve at your office?" he asked softly.

She looked up at him finally and saw his blue eyes smiling at her. She couldn't help smiling back.

"I didn't think I wanted to spend the evening with you and Bryn," she said. "I didn't know if I wanted to see you."

"So you left poor Bob to referee?" he teased her. "I'm sure he spent the whole dinner thanking you for that."

"Why, was Bryn on a bender?"

"Let's just say Bryn was her usual charming self." He leaned forward to look her squarely in the face. "Maybe I was just grumpy because you stood me up."

Corrie leaned against her car, away from his gaze. She looked away, then stared back at his face. "Maybe I thought it would be easier not to see you."

"Well, I wanted to see you. I came all this way, and I didn't want to leave without seeing you."

They stood a moment, then Corrie laughed softly. "I'm glad," she said. "I'm glad you came."

He reached out for her, wrapping her in a tight embrace. Her face was pressed against his shoulder; his lips brushed her hair. He held her for a long moment, then released her awkwardly, letting his arms drop to his sides.

"I wanted to see you," he said. "I had to see you. I have something I want to talk to you about."

Direct as ever, Corrie thought. *Daniel always cut right to the chase.*

"Okay," she said, walking up the steps to the front door. "Come on in."

She unlocked the door and set her purse and keys on the small table in the entryway. Daniel stood for a moment, looking around, taking in the huge oak stairway, the high ceilings, the generous proportions of the rooms. Then he spotted the white furniture and gave a low whistle.

"Nice digs," he said, grinning. "No kids, I guess?"

"What do you want to talk about, Daniel?" she asked abruptly. She could imagine the disdain he felt for her house, her life.

"How about a cup of coffee, for starters?" he asked.

They walked into the kitchen and Corrie started a pot of decaf, resisting the urge to pour herself a glass of wine. She didn't want her senses dulled right now. She wanted to stay alert. She'd been drinking a lot of wine in the last few weeks.

They sat at the kitchen table with their cups.

"This is a nice room," Daniel said, by way of making amends. "Feels homey."

Corrie smiled, accepting his apology. "It's my favorite room in the house," she said, "except for the cupola. I'll have to show you that; you'll like it, too."

"It's a nice house, Corrie. It fits you—all neat and respectable and beautiful."

"Careful," she warned, smiling again, "you might offend me."

It had been a sore point between them, all those years ago. Corrie had longed for stability, respectability, a gracious home—everything Daniel didn't want.

She looked across the table at him, sitting in her beautiful kitchen with its stainless steel appliances and marble countertops. She wondered what he thought of her choices.

"What was it you wanted to talk to me about?" she asked again, more quietly this time.

"Bryn said you work for the alumni magazine?" Daniel said.

"I'm the editor," she said, proudly.

"Then you make the decisions about what goes in?" he asked.

"Yes," she answered. "I have a lot of freedom that way. Of course, I have to report to the university board. I can't include just anything."

"Do you ever profile alumni?"

"Almost every issue," she said. "Haven't you ever seen *The Current?*"

"I don't get it," he answered. "I haven't kept up to date with the university."

"Too busy saving the world, Daniel? How noble." Corrie felt

herself getting edgy. *Damn it,* she said to herself. *Calm down.* Daniel could always push her buttons so easily.

"I'm sorry, Corrie. Look, I didn't come here to insult you or your magazine, or your house or your life."

"Could've fooled me," she answered. "Why did you come?"

"Actually, to ask you to help me with something."

He put down his coffee cup and leaned across the table.

"I'm working for a community center in Pasadena, and it's about to go under. We've lost our funding from the state, and our federal grant just fell through, and we're about to lose our building."

He stood up and began pacing the room.

"The damned Republicans get into office, and everything I've worked for in the last eight years is about to go up in smoke."

He stopped pacing and looked at her. "I was hoping you could profile me in your magazine—you know, a worthy graduate doing something notable? And you could put in the article how the center is going to close without help, and give the address for people to send money. Maybe the college will even do a matching grant."

"I don't know if I can do that, Daniel."

"Why not?" he asked. "You're the editor, aren't you? And most MU grads have so much money, they could make a real difference."

"It's not that simple," Corrie answered carefully. "I'd have to run it by the board. We have a policy about soliciting funds through the magazine, even for good causes."

"But listen, Corrie, this isn't just a good cause. This is a place that touches people's lives, real people—kids. Not just causes."

"And we've just put the fall issue to bed," Corrie continued, forcing her voice to stay flat. "The next issue won't come out until December, and that one is already planned."

"Can't you unplan it?" he asked. "You're the editor, right? You can just unplan it."

"Daniel, you don't understand. It's not that simple. We've signed contracts with writers who are counting on us to print their stuff. We've got photos and layout started. We have a format we follow. I can't just scrap it all because you want me to."

"I'm not asking you to change the whole magazine," he said.

"Just find room for one more article." He smiled across the table at her. His eyes were still so blue.

"About you?" she asked.

"Not about me," he said, "about the center. It's such a great place, Corrie. We serve so many kids. Without the center, I don't know what will happen to a lot of them. It's a pretty rough neighborhood, and we've been making a real impact on the community. You could come see it for yourself, if you want. Then you'd understand why I'm asking. Can't you just think about it?"

Corrie sat back in her chair and closed her eyes. What if she moved the alumni profile she'd planned to the next issue? No, she couldn't do that. She shook her head.

"Look, Daniel," she said quietly. "I don't know if I can help you or not. But I'll check it out. At the earliest, it would be the spring issue."

"By then the center will be gone," he said softly.

"I'm sorry," she answered, "it's the best I can do."

He rose and put his cup in the sink.

"Just think about it, okay? I know I don't have any right to ask you for help, and if it was just me, I wouldn't. But the kids we serve, they need it so much. And it would be something new for you, something important to write about, something you could make a real difference with."

She shook her head again, felt the color rise in her cheeks. "The magazine does cover important things," she said. "If you read it, you'd know."

"I'm sorry." Daniel smiled at her. "I didn't mean it the way it sounded."

"Yeah," Corrie said, "you did."

They stood awkwardly for a moment, the silence heavy between them.

"I'll go," he said finally. "Thanks for at least hearing me."

She followed him to the door, where he paused. Then he leaned forward to kiss her cheek. "It really is good to see you."

"You too," she whispered.

She closed the door behind him, leaned against it, and cried, just as she had the day ten years earlier when he'd left. It was September 14, 2001—three days after the terror attacks in New York and Washington. They'd been living together since graduation in a tiny basement apartment, Corrie working for the university's news bureau, Daniel tending bar at a place on Kendle.

For three days, they'd sat glued to the television, watching the terrible footage from the Twin Towers, the Pentagon, the field in Pennsylvania. Finally, Daniel said he couldn't take it anymore. He couldn't just stay in Middlebrook and tend bar. He needed to be there, in New York. He needed to help.

He'd begged Corrie to go with him. "Think of how much you can do there, how much we can help."

But Corrie couldn't leave Middlebrook. "My family is here. My mom needs me. And Maya . . ."

"Maya is sixteen," Daniel said. "In a couple years she'll leave for college. There's nothing forcing you to stay, Corrie. You have a choice. Come with me."

In the end, he had gone and Corrie had stayed, spending the next two weeks curled up in the bed they'd shared, crying, wishing she'd had the courage to go, wishing he'd loved her enough to stay.

8

Bryn leaned back on the couch, watching through the door to the kitchen as Bob washed dishes. She smiled, looking around the living room. Worn, overstuffed chairs, nicked and scratched end tables, a small truck under the coffee table. It was comfortable and homey—just like Bob. She picked up a framed photo from the end table and studied it, a family portrait taken last year. Bob and Wendy and two chubby-faced little boys, all smiling for the camera. Bryn's eyes darted from the photo to the man in the kitchen. *His hair is turning gray so fast,* she thought. *I didn't realize it till now. He'll be completely gray soon.*

She shook her head, studying the picture again. Wendy's smile was bright, and a mass of dark red ringlets circled her freckled face like a mane. Her left hand rested on Bob's shoulder, a small diamond sparkling on the third finger.

What is wrong with her? Bryn wondered. *Why would she leave someone like Bob? And for such a loser.*

Bryn had met Wendy's new boyfriend only once, and that had been enough. She knew the type—a middle-aged, beer-bellied, chain-smoking good ole boy with nicotine-stained teeth. The kind who measured the year by hunting and fishing seasons.

She looked again at Bob, wiping the counters now. Short, solid, kind, dear Bob. She laid the picture facedown on the table.

Stupid witch, she said to herself. *Stupid, selfish witch.*

"Are you sure I can't help?" she asked.

"I'm finished now," he answered, laughing. "Your timing, as always, is impeccable."

Bob walked into the room, carrying a tall glass. "You sure you don't want a drink?" He stood over her, waving the glass.

"No thanks." She smiled, shaking her head. "What is that, anyway?"

"Rum and coke," he answered, dropping into a chair. "I've developed quite a taste for them lately."

"Be careful." Bryn eyed him cautiously. "That can be habit-forming."

"I know." Bob put the drink down on a coaster. "I usually just have one at night. So I can sleep."

"Is it hard?" Bryn asked softly.

"Yeah, it's hard."

They sat in silence for a few minutes, each wrapped in thought. Finally, Bob leaned over and turned on the stereo. The opening notes of "Angel" floated through the air.

"God, I haven't heard that in a while."

"I took Wendy to a Sarah McLachlan concert on our first date," Bob said quietly.

Bryn leaned over and turned the music off. "Stop that!" she commanded. "Just stop it."

Bob simply looked at her.

"Okay," Bryn said quietly. "Look, she's gone. She left, and she's not coming back. You can't make her come back. I don't know why she left, and I think she's a fool. We all do. But she's gone, and you have to deal with it."

"I know," Bob said. "But I keep thinking maybe . . ."

"She's not coming back this time, Bob. And even if she did, you couldn't take her back again. Not this time. My God, she took your kids! She took your kids to live with that hill jack. How could you even want her back?"

"When I married her I said for better or worse, in sickness and in health. I keep thinking, maybe she's sick. You know? And she'll get better, and then she'll come back."

Bryn shook her head. She was feeling queasy again.

"It's his fault," Bob suddenly exploded, rising. He walked around the room, carrying his drink. "It's that bastard's fault. He took advantage of her."

"Listen, Bob, I could buy that if this was the first time. But this is the third time. She's not a child. She made a choice—an active choice."

But he wasn't listening.

"You know how she met him, right? He was going to give Micah guitar lessons. Instead, he ends up sleeping with Wendy. What kind of predator takes advantage of someone like that?"

"He's a prick," Bryn agreed softly, battling a wave of nausea. "That's why you've got to get a lawyer, so that prick doesn't end up raising your kids."

"Are you okay?" he asked suddenly, stopping directly in front of her. "You look like hell."

"Thanks so much," she smiled weakly.

"I mean it, Bryn. You just don't look like yourself."

Bryn sat silently, running her hand through her short-cropped hair. She felt her lip begin to quiver. *Oh no,* she thought. *Don't cry. Stop it!* She felt a tear slide down her cheek.

Before she could stop she heard herself say it out loud. "I'm pregnant."

"Oh my God, Bryn. That's great!" Bob dropped to one knee beside the couch. "That's great! Are you having a lot of morning sickness? Is that what's wrong?"

"Yes, I'm sick. No, it's not great." Bryn felt the tears welling in her eyes now, let them spill over and run down her face. "I don't want to be pregnant. Paul doesn't know. He doesn't want a baby. I can't have a baby!"

Bryn was sobbing now, her face buried in the couch.

"It's not fair," she cried. "Why didn't this happen for Corrie? She *wants* a baby, she wants one so much."

Bob sat on the floor by the couch, rubbing her back softly.

"Shhh," he said. "Stop with that. It's not your fault Corrie can't have a baby. She'll be happy for you. You just worry about taking care of yourself right now. I remember when Wendy was pregnant with Micah—"

"Stop it! I'm not happy about this, okay? You don't understand. Paul doesn't want a baby. He's never wanted a baby. And me? God, can't you just see me, a mother?" She buried her face again. "This just isn't fair."

"You're right, life isn't fair," Bob said quietly. "But yes, Bryn, I can see you as a mother. Maybe not a traditional, cookies-and-milk mom, but any kid of yours will have a free-spirited, unconventional, loving mom." He cupped her chin in his hands and looked directly into her eyes. "You can do this."

Bryn looked up at him and tried to smile. "You're such a sweet man. But you just don't know . . . you don't understand. Paul doesn't want a baby."

"What about you? Do you want a baby?"

"I don't know," she sighed, shaking her head and pulling away from him. "I didn't think so. But now that I'm pregnant, I keep thinking . . . I don't know, maybe. I mean, I'm thirty-two. Maybe this is the only chance I'll get."

She stopped and shook her head again, grimacing. "I can't even believe I said that. Don't pay any attention to me. I think I'm losing my mind. I can't have a baby, and that's that."

"You haven't told Paul yet?"

"No," she said firmly, "and I'm not going to. It would just make him mad."

Bob took her face in his hands again and looked into Bryn's eyes.

"You've got to tell him," he said firmly. "You can't do anything until you tell him. It's his child, too, and he has a right to know. Besides, maybe he'll surprise you. Maybe once he gets used to the idea, he'll be happy about it. Wendy didn't think she wanted kids, but once she got pregnant, she was thrilled."

"Yeah, so thrilled she left," Bryn snapped, then, seeing Bob's wounded expression, she immediately regretted her words.

"I'm sorry, Bob. Oh God, I'm sorry. Don't pay any attention to me. I just need to learn to shut up."

"It's okay," he said. "I'm okay. But you've got to tell him. You know that, don't you? You've got to."

Bryn sighed, nodded. "I know," she said softly. "I just don't want to."

An hour later she stood fumbling with her key. She could hear the television blaring inside the apartment. Paul was home. She turned the key, set her shoulders in determination, and opened the door.

"Paul? I'm home."

He sat on the couch, watching the news and eating peanut butter on crackers. He looked up at her with a vacant smile, then turned back to the television. The smell of pot hung heavily in the room. Bryn winced at the smoke, willing her stomach to stay calm. *Oh well,* she thought, *now is obviously not the time to tell him.*

She dropped her purse onto the table in the kitchen and plopped down beside him on the couch. "Any messages?" she asked.

"Huh? Oh . . . no," he replied, his eyes never straying from the screen. "Hey, did you ever notice how long this guy's nose is? Man, it must be a mile long." He stared transfixed at the newscaster, who was reporting on a bomb threat at the Miami airport.

"How much did you smoke?" she asked, looking into the ashtray.

"Just one joint. Geez, don't start," he whined. "I just had one little joint to unwind. Don't get all bent out of shape."

"I didn't say anything," Bryn said soothingly. "Just asking."

"I've got another one, if you want to join me." Paul nodded toward a wooden box on the shelf. "It's pretty good stuff. . . . Might make you feel sexy." He leaned over and nuzzled her neck.

Bryn pulled away. "You need a shave," she snapped.

"So I'll shave," he said with a shrug. He smiled and reached his hand out to touch her breast, then slipped it beneath her shirt. "Come on, baby. It's been a while. Why don't you smoke a joint and loosen up a little?"

He took her nipple between his fingers. "I'll make it worth your while," he whispered hoarsely.

Bryn rose abruptly. "I'm tired," she said. "And I have a lot of work to do."

"What's wrong with you?" Paul asked. "You're always tired these days."

"Maybe I'm just getting old," Bryn said, shrugging her shoulders.

Maybe I'm just growing up, she thought. *God, how could I even think this man would be ready for fatherhood?*

Paul stood up, wobbled slightly. "Head rush," he said, smiling.

He walked over to Bryn, put his arms around her, slid his hands under her shirt again. "You're not getting old, baby. You're still my sleek sex kitten. Now come on, let me warm you up."

He took her hand and pulled her toward the bedroom.

Bryn allowed herself to be pulled along. Pot usually made Paul horny. She knew if they didn't have sex, there would be a fight. And she was just too tired to fight tonight.

Paul fell back onto the bed, pulling her on top of him, his hands clutching at her breasts. She looked down at his red-streaked eyes gazing up at her blearily and shook her head. He lifted her shirt over her head and raised his lips to her breast. She sucked in her breath sharply as she felt his teeth nip at the swollen, tender nipple. It hurt. Now he fumbled with her belt. She pushed his hand aside and unbuckled the belt, but he had already reached his hand down to shove her skirt up around her waist. She sighed and stood, letting the skirt slip to the floor, and waited.

Paul sat up and pulled her panties down to her ankles, then reached out to tickle the fur between her legs.

"There's my little kitten," he murmured, pulling her back down onto the bed. He rolled over on top of her, burying his face between her breasts, his hand still between her legs.

Bryn closed her eyes tightly. She felt sick and puffy and tired. She felt like glass. She wrapped her hand around his head, playing absently with the hair at the nape of his neck. *Just don't get sick,* she told herself.

"What's wrong, baby?" he asked, raising his head to stare at her face. "You're so stiff."

"I'm just kind of tense, I guess."

"Well," he said, rolling onto his back, "let's just make this easy, then."

He walked into the living room and returned with a joint. "Come on, Bryn. Loosen up and let's have some fun."

A wave of nausea rolled through her and she bolted from the bed. She slammed the bathroom door behind her and knelt before the toilet.

"Bryn?" Paul's voice was muffled. "You okay?"

"No," she called back. "I'm sick."

She threw up the little she'd eaten at dinner, then leaned back against the wall, feeling tears well up in her eyes. When her stomach had finally settled, she rose cautiously and walked back to the bedroom, where Paul lay on the bed, snoring loudly.

She sighed and pulled a blanket from the bed to sleep on the couch.

❧ *9* ❧

Corrie sat at her desk, her head between her hands, staring blankly at the pages laid out before her. The winter issue was always so crowded. Christmas articles, alumni news, items put off from earlier issues that she wanted to run this year. And there were so many alumni pieces this time. She shook her head. *Concentrate,* she said to herself sharply. *Just concentrate on this.*

Her mind would not obey. Even during Mass earlier that morning, her mind had wandered. Usually, early Mass grounded her. The candles, the incense, the rosary, they calmed her like nothing else, but not today.

Like I can unplan an issue, just because he asks me to. Of course, his work is always the most important thing in the world, and mine is just . . . fluff.

She looked at the tentative layout before her. A piece on a student trip to Bethlehem. An opinion piece on religious displays on government property. A profile of a retired alum who worked as a department store Santa, complete with photos of the old guy with kids on his knees. The usual short blurbs about faculty publications and alumni awards. Class notes. Reunion news. Corrie was holding a page for the class photo from her reunion. She hadn't gotten the file from the photographer yet. She'd asked for an extra copy of the photo to keep.

Yesterday, she'd been pleased with the way the issue was shaping up. Today, it looked like crap.

Fluff, she said silently. *Fluff and mistletoe.*

She put out a good magazine. The administration loved it. *The Current* consistently brought in contributions to the alumni fund. She did a good job.

So Daniel comes to town and it's all just fluff? Some things never change.

She stood abruptly, knocking pages onto the floor.

"Kenetha," she called. "Can you bring in the winter folder?"

Her assistant walked in, carrying a green folder bulging with papers and photos. She took one look at Corrie's face and said, "Don't even say it. Don't even tell me you're making changes. I *am* taking a vacation this month. I *am* going to Tampa with Jared. I am *not* missing another vacation."

Corrie laughed. "Just a little change," she said soothingly. "Just one little change."

Kenetha sighed, dropped the folder onto Corrie's desk, and lowered herself into a chair. "That's what you always say."

"This time I mean it. We're just going to change the alumni profile."

"You're not using the old guy playing Santa? That's such a nice piece. And you already paid the writer *and* the photographer."

"I know, I know." Corrie nodded, sitting on the edge of the desk. "But it just feels too fluffy. We need a harder-edged piece to balance all the saccharine in this issue."

"It's the Christmas issue, Corrie. People want saccharine."

"Yeah, and we'll have plenty of it. But let's give them some meat, too."

Kenetha sat back in the chair, resigned. She knew the look on Corrie's face, and she knew it was pointless to argue. "Okay, what are we doing instead?" she asked.

"I want to profile a guy I know. He graduated the same year I did, and he runs a community center in California that's about to lose its funding."

"There's a cheery Christmas story," Kenetha grumbled.

"Well, it could be if our readers decide to do something to help."

Kenetha simply stared at her in disbelief for a moment, then shook her head slowly. "If you're going to ask for money, you'd better talk to the board first. You know how they feel about fundraising in the magazine."

"Hell, Kenetha. We ask for money in every single issue for the alumni association. This is a worthy cause."

"Honey, they're *all* worthy causes. You know that. What's so special about this one?"

Corrie didn't answer. Kenetha looked at her closely, then smiled.

"Or is it the man that's special?"

"He's just an old friend, and it's a good cause," Corrie said firmly. "Besides, it's a good story—especially for Christmas. You know, the Scrooges in Washington taking away the kids' community center. Give our readers a chance to play Santa themselves instead of just reading about one."

"And who is going to write this article on such short notice?" Kenetha asked, noting Corrie's reddening cheeks and bright eyes.

"I'm going to do it," Corrie said quietly. "I'll fly to Los Angeles next week, spend a couple days, shoot some pictures, and be home before the weekend."

Kenetha rose and walked to the door. "Have you told Mark yet?" she asked.

"No, but he won't mind. Why should he? He's in New York this week. He travels all the time."

"But he's not visiting old girlfriends," Kenetha said tartly as she walked away. "Is he?"

Corrie shook her head as she picked up the phone and dialed the travel agency.

Kenetha has a vivid imagination, she thought. *This is going to be a good article, that's all, a chance to write about something important.*

"Hey, you." Bob stood in Bryn's doorway looking slightly rumpled in chinos and a corduroy jacket. He always looked slightly rumpled. He smiled. "How are you feeling this morning?"

Bryn turned and walked back into the apartment, leaving the door open for him to follow. She was wearing Paul's blue terry bathrobe over nothing. She felt like death warmed over.

"Sorry, I haven't gotten dressed yet," she said, waving him toward the couch as she stumbled to the bedroom to change.

She reemerged a few minutes later wearing shorts and a wrinkled T-shirt. "You want coffee?" she asked, heading for the kitchen.

"Sure, okay," he answered, following her.

She began making a pot of coffee. Bob sat at the table, watching her expectantly.

"So?" he finally asked. "Did you tell him?"

"No, and I'm not going to."

Bryn turned to face him, her pale face staring bleakly beneath a fringe of dark bangs.

"This isn't your problem, Bob, it's mine. Okay? I appreciate your concern, but it's my problem and I'll deal with it."

Bob rose and walked to the counter. He put his hands on her shoulders and said, "Hey, I'm just concerned about you. I want to help."

"Well, you can't," she snapped, turning away. "I'll handle it myself."

As she poured the water into the coffeemaker, she felt her stomach lurch. "Damn! I'll be glad to be done with the morning sickness," she said, turning toward the bathroom.

Bob sat listening as she threw up in the toilet. He watched the coffeepot filling, noted the dishes piled in the sink, the ashtrays filled with cigarette butts, the mini-blinds coated with a film of dust.

He filled the sink with soapy water and began washing dishes. By the time Bryn returned, shaky and paler than ever, he had cleared the sink, emptied the ashtrays, and was wiping down the blinds.

"What are you doing?"

"Just picking up a little. You know, you should ask Paul not to smoke in the apartment. It's not good for you or the baby."

"Stop it, Bob. I'm not having this baby. I told you last night, I can't." She grabbed the dishrag from him. "And I don't need you to clean my damn house!"

He stood watching as she poured two cups of coffee, added cream and sugar to one, and handed it to him, keeping the black brew for herself. Then he followed her silently into the living room. She flopped down onto the couch and stared darkly at him. He sat down and sipped his coffee, waiting. He knew Bryn, knew if he waited she would calm down and talk to him, knew better than to be offended by her outburst.

They sat in silence for a few minutes, drinking coffee. Finally, Bryn breathed a long, shuddering sigh and set her cup down.

"Okay, look," she said, leaning forward, "I cannot have a baby. Not with Paul. He's just not father material. He doesn't like kids and he doesn't want them. He'd be a terrible dad. Hell, he's still a kid himself."

"He's forty-six," Bob said quietly.

"I know that, but he still thinks he's twenty. Christ, he spends almost every night sitting here getting stoned. He's still teaching as an adjunct after all these years. The school is never going to offer him a tenure-track position, and he knows it. But still he stays. He has no savings, no long-term plans, no goals or ambitions. Everything we own is in this apartment," she said, waving her hand at the room. "What the hell kind of life could we offer a kid? Besides," she added, "I'd be a lousy mom. I can't even leave Paul and take care of myself. How would I take care of a kid?"

"Why don't you leave him?"

"What would I do? I'm thirty-two and I've never worked a full-time job. I don't think I could even get a full-time job at this point. Who'd hire me? And I can't afford a decent place on my own." Bryn took a pack of cigarettes from the end table, pulled one from the pack, and began tapping it with her fingernail.

"You're not smoking again, are you?"

"No," she sighed, returning the cigarette to the pack. "It took too long to quit last time. But, God, I wish I could have one now."

Bryn stood and began pacing around the small living room. She looked like a caged animal, Bob thought. Taut, wired, and ready to spring. He waited again, silently.

"I know I should leave," she said at last. "I know he's not going to change. He's not going to grow up. I know that." She sighed. "It used to be so much fun, you know? He was so charming and fun. He seemed so *free*. But it's not free, really, it's just irresponsible."

She picked up the cigarettes again, held the pack for a moment, then crushed it slowly in her hand.

"I could stay another ten years and nothing would change. He wouldn't change. I wouldn't change. Nothing would change."

"Then leave." Bob leaned forward. "Leave him and have this baby. You don't need him. You can do it on your own—lots of women do. And you have so many friends to help you."

Bob rose and took Bryn's hand. "Corrie will help you, and Kenetha and Sarah. She knows all the good babysitters. And I'll be there for you, too."

Bryn stared at him in silence.

"You'll be a good mom, Bryn. There's no one with more love to give than you. I know it will be hard. Of course it will be hard. Even with two parents and a steady income, parenting is hard. But, God, it's so worth it. You can't even know. When you hold that baby in your arms, and he's just looking up at you, trusting you, and you're his whole world—or hers. God, it will just blow you away."

Bryn let the tears spill down her cheeks. She didn't even bother wiping them away. "You make it sound so easy," she said. "You make it sound so good."

"I didn't say it would be easy," he said, stroking her cheek. "But you won't be alone."

Bryn pulled away, wiping her hand across her face and sniffling. "God, can't you just see my mother's face? 'No, Mom, I'm not finally marrying Paul. But I am leaving him. Oh, and by the way, I'm having a baby.' She'd croak." She began pacing again. "She'd finally disown me for good."

"Until she saw her grandchild. You'd be amazed at the difference a baby makes."

"You think?" She stopped pacing and stood in the middle of the room, staring toward the window. Then, abruptly, she turned to the kitchen. "I need more coffee, and then I've got to get to work. Aren't you supposed to be at work now?" she asked.

"I'm running a group session at ten. But I've still got some time."

"Well, I don't," she said, smiling slightly. "I've got a deadline to meet."

She walked him to the door. "Thanks for coming, Bob. You're a sweetheart."

"Don't worry, Bryn. It will be all right."

"Sure, I know."

She closed the door behind him, then went to the bedroom and began pulling her clothes from the dresser drawers.

Corrie looked up from the email she was reading to see Bryn standing in the doorway of her office, suitcases in hand.

"Hi," she said. "Where are you off to?"

"Can I crash at your place for a few days?"

"You and Paul fighting again?"

"No, I'm leaving him."

Corrie smiled as Bryn dropped the suitcases and sat down.

"I mean it this time. It's really done."

"Okay, sure, whatever. If you're finally leaving him, then I'm glad. But I'll reserve judgment for a few weeks."

"Witch." Bryn laughed.

Corrie smiled again. Then her brow furrowed. "But about staying at my house . . . it's okay with me. But I won't be there next week. So it'll just be you and Mark."

"Where are you going?"

"I'm going to L.A. for a story," Corrie said, straining to keep her voice flat.

"Kind of a sudden trip, isn't it? You didn't mention it the other day."

"What are you, my mother?"

"No, but you hate to travel. Usually, you bitch and moan for weeks ahead of time. Now all of a sudden you're going to L.A., and you never even mentioned it?"

"It just came up."

"You're not going to visit a certain community center in Pasadena, are you?" Bryn asked, watching Corrie's face closely.

"How did you know?"

"He was talking about it at dinner last night, about you doing a story in the magazine. I told him you wouldn't. Apparently, I was wrong."

"It's a good story," Corrie said quietly.

"I can't believe you! He comes into town, crooks his finger, and you go running off to Los Angeles to write about his project. God, Corrie, what is wrong with you?"

Corrie's cheeks reddened and her mouth set into a hard line. She sat silently for a moment, staring at Bryn. When she spoke, her voice was so soft Bryn had to lean forward to hear her.

"You're one to talk. Jesus, Bryn, since when have you started handing out advice? I'm going because this will be a good story for the magazine, a strong story, an important story. And if it does some good for some kids there, all the better."

Bryn smiled. "An important story, huh? Now where have I heard that before?"

"Okay," Corrie said, smiling. "He still pushes my buttons. But he's doing so much to help people, and all I do is this magazine. I need to do something for someone, and this is a good opportunity."

"And are you planning to stay with Daniel in L.A.?"

"No!" Corrie looked up, aghast. "Of course not. I'm staying at the Pasadena Hilton. I've already made the reservation."

"Does Mark know?"

"Not yet. He's in New York till tomorrow. I'll tell him when he gets home. He won't mind."

Bryn grinned, then looked down at her suitcases. Her smile faded.

"Well, hell," she said. "Where am I gonna stay then?"

"You can still stay at the house," Corrie suggested.

"I don't think so. I can't see rooming with Mark while you're out of town." She leaned forward and giggled. "People might talk, you know."

"That could be fun." Corrie smiled. "How many people would

tell me about it when I got back, do you think? Or maybe call me in California? We could start some very fine rumors."

Bryn shook her head ruefully. "No, I'm afraid I've started too many of those just on my own." She stared at the floor, thinking, *And I definitely could start a few more right about now.*

"What about staying with Sarah and Kevin?" Corrie asked.

"No." Bryn shook her head again. "They've got two kids, and Sarah's pregnant. They don't need a houseguest."

Suddenly, Bryn's face brightened and she stood, picked up her suitcases, and walked to the door.

"Where are you going?" Corrie asked.

"To Bob's," Bryn said. "Daniel is leaving tomorrow. I figure we can stand each other for one night. Then he'll be gone, and I can room with Bob for a while."

"I don't know, Bryn. Do you suppose that will upset Wendy?" Corrie's brow wrinkled in worry.

"That's the plan." Bryn grinned. "I hope it upsets her big-time."

"Bryn, you're wicked." Corrie smiled. "Still, I'm not sure it's a good idea, right in the middle of their divorce mess. And his kids will be coming and going. Are you sure you want to do that?"

"Sure, why not? I like kids," Bryn said, raising her chin slightly. "I happen to be very good with kids."

"Okay," Corrie said doubtfully. "But do me a favor. Don't mention to Daniel that I'm planning to come to Los Angeles, all right? I want to just show up at the center next week, and I don't want him to have the time to arrange anything."

"You mean to stage anything?"

Corrie smiled wryly. "Yeah, that's what I mean. Daniel is a good, bleeding-heart liberal. And if he thought it'd make people send money, I wouldn't put it past him to stage some stupid stunt. Anyway, don't tell him. Okay?"

"Sure," Bryn called over her shoulder as she left. "Whatever."

Corrie stared at the door for a long minute after her friend had left.

Now what is she up to?

Then she shook her head and smiled. She would never understand Bryn.

❧ 10 ❧

Bob arrived home after work to find Bryn and Daniel eyeing each other warily across the living room. Bryn's bags were piled in one corner, and she was curled up on the couch, her face pale, her eyes huge and dark, her mouth set in a tight line.

"Hey," Bob said softly, bending down to kiss her forehead. "What gives?"

"I've left Paul," she answered, staring up at him defiantly.

Bob smiled and rubbed her shoulders, then looked up at Daniel, who was pretending to read the newspaper.

"How 'bout you? What did you do today?"

"Well." Daniel folded the paper and laid it on the coffee table. "I was going to head down to the Boys Club and talk with the agency director. I hear they've expanded their program in the last couple years, and I'd like to ask him about his funding. But"—he nodded toward Bryn—"I decided I'd better hang out here, make sure the silverware didn't disappear while you were at work."

"Jerk," Bryn said, smiling weakly.

Bob laughed as he headed for the kitchen. "Well, let's see what we've got to eat in here."

Bryn groaned softly and laid her head down on the arm of the couch, closing her eyes. Daniel followed Bob into the kitchen. As soon as the door closed behind him, he whispered, "What's wrong with Bryn? She looks like hell. I was afraid to leave her alone. Do you think she's going through detox or something?"

Bob's back was to him, so Daniel couldn't see his smile as he rummaged through the refrigerator. "She's just upset over leaving Paul. But it's the best thing she could do for herself right now. We talked about it last night, and I told her she's nuts to stay with him."

"I never did like that guy." Daniel grimaced. "Always spouting his supply-side crap and hitting on all the girls. What a prick."

"Yeah," Bob agreed, pulling leftovers from the previous night's dinner from the fridge. "But Bryn's invested years in the relationship, and I don't think she knows what she wants to do, or can do, without him."

"So does she think she's going to stay here with you?"

"I guess so." Bob smiled again. "It's okay with me."

"Are you sure, man? What about Wendy? What'll she say?"

Bob put a casserole dish in the microwave. He didn't answer Daniel as he set the timer and hit the start button. Finally, he turned and smiled ruefully. "I wish I could say I thought she would care. But she won't. She won't even give a damn. And honestly, I hate being alone. So, if Bryn wants to stay for a while, until she gets her life sorted out, it's fine by me."

He opened the door to the living room and looked at her small form, huddled on the sofa. She looked twelve years old.

"Hey, Bryn. Dinner's on in about ten minutes."

She looked up and shook her head slightly, but he just smiled in return.

"No arguments. You need to eat."

Bob walked over and sat on the sofa beside her. "You're not just taking care of you now," he said softly. "You've got another life in your care."

"I can't eat anything," she mumbled. "I'll just throw it back up."

"Just some bread or crackers then," he urged. "You'll feel better if your stomach's not completely empty. After dinner I'll go to the drugstore and get you some vitamin B—is it six or twelve? I'll ask the pharmacist. Wendy took that while she was pregnant, and it helped with the nausea."

Bryn looked up, suddenly alarmed. "You didn't tell *him,* did you?"

"No," Bob reassured her, "of course not. Don't worry. You don't have to tell anyone until you're ready. I'll just tell him I'm picking up some cough syrup for Cody, which I need to do anyway, since the kids will be here this weekend. Will that be okay for you?"

"Sure." Bryn dropped her head back onto the couch. "I like kids." She smiled weakly again. "But where am I gonna sleep?"

"We'll put you in the guest room." Bob rose. "Daniel's been in there, but I'll move him into Micah's room for tonight. The guest room is kind of apart from the rest of the bedrooms, so it'll be the quietest."

"Thanks, Bob. You're so good."

"That's me." He grinned. "Old Saint Bob." He laughed as he walked to the kitchen. "Old Saint Bob's gonna have a drink."

Bryn smiled as she let her eyelids drop. *What a love. What an absolute love.* And she wondered again what was wrong with Wendy.

Fifteen minutes later, the three of them were seated at the kitchen table. Bob and Daniel were making good headway with the leftover lasagna, but Bryn could only push hers around on the plate with her fork. Her stomach churned. She nibbled at some crackers Bob had found in the cupboard and sipped water.

"So how come you're not staying with Corrie?" Daniel asked abruptly.

Damn him, Bryn thought. *When will he ever learn social niceties, like telling little white lies and refraining from embarrassing questions?*

She took another sip of water, her mind scrambling for an answer. Then she set the glass down slowly, deliberately, and smiled.

"Oh, you know, it's Bryn and Mark's anniversary next week. And she's got all kinds of romantic things planned. We went shopping last week so she could get some new lingerie . . . stuff I *never* figured she'd wear. Wow! I don't think they need me hanging out, in their way. Those two have a hard time keeping their hands off each other anyway, let alone on anniversaries."

She smiled sweetly and wide-eyed at Daniel, and was delighted to see a faint blush spread across his cheeks. He didn't answer right away, took a drink of wine, and finally mumbled, "I'm glad she's happy."

I'll bet you are, Bryn thought. *I'll just bet you are.*

She finished her crackers and water in silence, watching Daniel intently, wondering anew what it was that Corrie had seen in him—apparently still saw in him.

I hope to God she knows what she's doing. If she gets involved with Daniel again, it'll kill her.

Bryn remembered vividly the scenes of ten years before, when Daniel left Middlebrook. In the month before graduation, Corrie had spent weeks looking for just the right apartment for the two of them. She'd gone directly from student to employee status at the college, walking into a plum position at the news bureau.

Daniel, on the other hand, had floundered. He'd moved from the dorm into Corrie's newly rented apartment and spent his days moping at the bookstore or the library, researching job opportunities and drinking coffee. Nights he tended bar.

Bryn smiled, remembering that first apartment of Corrie's. What a dump it had been, and she'd been so proud of it. Bryn had gone with her to garage sales and thrift shops, and they'd dragged home mismatched chairs and a threadbare couch. Corrie made curtains from old sheets, and they'd painted and scrubbed and scoured until the little rooms didn't look half bad. Even in those digs, Corrie had created an orderly and pretty little haven.

Bryn remembered how upscale her own apartment had seemed in those days. It was the same one she'd shared off and on with Paul in the ten years since. *What a dump,* she sighed to herself. She smiled at the irony. Corrie now had a big, expensive, decorator-perfect house in the suburbs. And Bryn had nothing.

Still, in those days Bryn had felt like the world was hers for the asking. She had an exciting, taboo relationship with an older man; she was bright and talented and ambitious. She'd had it all. And Corrie's world was on the verge of imploding.

Bryn could still see her, huddled on the floor of that tiny apartment, weeping after Daniel left. Bryn had actually worried that Corrie might do something rash and hurt herself.

But, of course, she didn't. No, Corrie stayed in the dingy little apartment and worked her way from assistant to head of the news bureau, and then to assistant editor of the alumni magazine. After a couple years, she started dating Mark, and then they got married. And when she moved out of the apartment, Bryn had taken possession of it. That had been during one of her "out" times with Paul.

It had taken Corrie almost two years to get over the grief after Daniel left. Bryn had never understood why she loved Daniel so, but she never doubted Corrie's commitment to him. She'd been like the walking dead for months. She wouldn't date, or even think about dating anyone else. Once, eight months after Daniel left, Bryn asked Corrie why she didn't just go to New York and be with him, since she was so miserable without him. And Corrie had cried again and admitted that she didn't even know where Daniel was. The bastard hadn't written to her, not even once.

She's got her life together now. Bryn stared angrily at Daniel, sitting across from her calmly eating lasagna. *And you'd better not mess that up, you jerk!*

11

"Why do you have to go next week?"

Mark was folding shirts into the suitcase for their weekend in Chicago.

"Because I need to get the story done for the winter issue. We're already going to be late. I can't put it off and make us later."

Corrie stood at the door of the closet, surveying dresses.

"Which one should I take?" she asked, holding up two for his appraisal.

"The green," he said, without hesitating. "That one looks great on you."

She smiled and hung the blue dress back in the closet.

"I guess I don't understand why you have to do this story for the winter issue," he said, turning back to the suitcase. "Why not just run it in the spring?"

Corrie sat down on the bed beside the suitcase. "Because this center is about to lose its funding," she explained. "By spring it might be gone."

"Isn't there someone out there who can write it?" Mark frowned slightly. "What about the guy who runs the center? Why can't he just write about it himself?"

Corrie sighed. "Because I don't know if he can write. Besides"—

she smiled and tugged at his tie—"you travel all the time. Why can't I go someplace?"

He kissed her forehead. "It's just bad timing, that's all. Sarah's shower is coming up. She'll be upset if you're not there."

"I'll be back before the shower."

She leaned over the suitcase and smoothed the shirts lying neatly inside, each one paired with a matching tie. Mark was an impeccable dresser. Not like Daniel. She felt her cheeks redden, remembering the flannel shirts Daniel always wore. She'd slept with one for a year after he left. Maybe this trip was a bad idea.

"Besides," Mark continued, "you have a nice winter issue already. Why do you want to do an article on this place anyway? There are plenty of charity cases a lot closer to home. I bet Bob could take you to several right here in town."

"I know," she said, "but it's good to have stories that aren't all local, you know? And this center is run by one of our alums, and it's really touching people's lives. I think our readers will be interested. That's all."

"So who's the alum who runs it?" Mark asked. "Do you know him?"

Corrie had wondered how she would answer the question. She'd even thought of lying, making up a name. But Mark always read the magazine. And anyway, she couldn't lie to him.

"His name is Daniel," she said, her eyes fixed on the suitcase. "Daniel Chapman."

Neither of them spoke for a long minute. Corrie kept smoothing his shirts, running her palms over and over the soft fabric.

"Daniel Chapman?" Mark's voice was soft when he finally spoke. "The same Daniel Chapman you lived with after you graduated?"

Corrie nodded, finally raising her head to look at her husband.

"Oh," he said. "Oh."

"It's just a story, Mark." She stood, her hands reaching for his. "Just a good story for the magazine. That's all."

"When did you see him?" His eyes searched her face.

"A couple days ago," she said, still holding his hands. "He came here, to the house, after the reunion, to ask me to do the story."

"He was here?" His eyes never left hers.

She nodded. "We had coffee, and he told me about the center and asked if I'd write a story about it."

"Why didn't you tell me?"

She stood quietly for a minute, never letting go of his hands. She'd rehearsed telling him, played it out in her mind several times. Now, however, she couldn't get the words out.

"Corrie?" He leaned down till his eyes were level with hers. "Why didn't you tell me?"

"I thought you might not like it." She finally forced out the words. "I thought you might think . . ."

"What?" he asked. "What would I think? That you were going to run away with him? God, Corrie, I wouldn't have thought anything if you'd told me. I would've been glad you had a chance to see him, maybe to get some closure. If you'd told me, it would've been all right."

He dropped her hands and walked to the window, running his hand through his hair the way he did when he was agitated.

"But you didn't tell me," he said, his voice low and angry. "Why?"

He turned to face her. "Because you found out you still have feelings for him?"

"No, Mark, that's not—"

"Is that why you're going to L.A.? To see if you can rekindle the old feelings?"

"No!" Corrie's voice was louder than she'd expected. "No," she repeated more softly. "I'm going to L.A. because it's a good story, and I think our readers will be interested in it, and because it might make a positive impact on some children's lives. I want to do this story." She was pleading now. "I want to write something that's important, Mark. I'm tired of writing fluff!"

"Fluff? Since when is *The Current* fluff? You've never been unhappy with it before. Is that what Daniel thinks of it?"

Her cheeks were red now. She could feel the heat in them.

"So this *Daniel,* this guy who dumped you, who broke your heart, who never even wrote you a goddamned letter, breezes into town, meets you in my house . . . in *our* house, and you have to fly off to goddamned L.A. to write about his little charity project?"

"Mark, stop it. Please, just sit down and listen to me, okay? It's not like that, and you know it. At least you should know it.

"I love you. You're my husband, and I love you. And this story, this trip, has nothing to do with the fact that Daniel is an old boyfriend."

"An old boyfriend? Come on, Corrie, he's more than an old boyfriend. You almost married this guy. It took you years to get over him. You told me he's the only other man you ever loved. And now you're flying to L.A. to see him? What am I supposed to think of that?"

"You're supposed to believe in me," she said, her voice shaking. "You're supposed to believe in us, and think that . . . and *know* that I am going out there to write a story about a project that's in trouble and is worth supporting. You're supposed to trust me, Mark. Why aren't you doing that?"

"Why didn't you tell me?" His voice was flat.

"I'm sorry," she whispered.

He walked out of the bedroom, slamming the door behind him.

Corrie sat down on the bed and cried.

∼ 12 ∼

Bryn pulled the sheets over her head, trying to block the sunlight streaming through the window onto her pillow. *Damn,* she thought. *If I'm going to stay here, I have to get some blinds for that window.*

What time was it? The room had no clock. Judging from the light, it was mid-morning. Bob must have let her sleep in. She smiled and snuggled farther under the sheet. *Work can wait a little while.*

Moments later, however, she was jolted from her nest by what sounded like a riot. She grabbed her robe and went to see what the commotion was about.

"Hey," she called as she entered the front room. "What's all the . . ."

Bob was on the floor, wrestling with two small, shrieking boys. Their laughter stopped abruptly when they caught sight of Bryn.

"Oh." Bryn stood uncertainly, clutching her short robe around herself.

"Bob?"

Bryn turned to see Wendy standing in the doorway to the kitchen, holding a coffee cup. Wendy stared from Bryn to Bob, her eyes narrowed, her jaw set. Bryn could see the mug shaking in her hand.

"Hi, Wendy," she said brightly. She turned to Bob and said, "I'm going to get dressed."

She smiled as she walked back to the guest room. *Let the witch think what she wants!*

"Hey, guys," Bob said to the boys who were still clinging to him on the floor. "Why don't you take your stuff to your rooms, and I'll make some pancakes."

He smiled, watching them drag their backpacks behind them to their rooms.

"What the hell is Bryn doing here?" Wendy's voice, sharp and angry, carried down the hall to the room where Bryn was looking through her suitcase for something to wear. Bryn smiled again.

She heard Bob's voice, low and cajoling, but she couldn't make out his words. A few minutes later, she heard the front door slam. She buttoned her blouse and went to the kitchen, where Bob was pulling things from the fridge.

"So, that went well." She laughed and sat at the breakfast bar.

"No, Bryn. That did not go well." Bob's voice was low and angry. He turned to stare at her.

"How could you do that?" he asked, slamming a carton of milk onto the counter.

"What?" Bryn asked, shrugging her shoulders. "I just said hello. Besides, it's not like we're having an affair. I mean, where does *she* get off being mad at you? She's the one shacking up with Grizzly Adams."

Bob shook his head. "I'm not talking about Wendy. I'm talking about the boys. How do you think they felt, seeing you here in your robe?"

Bryn's smile faded. "Oh," she said, "I didn't . . . I guess I didn't think about that."

She leaned against the breakfast bar, resting her head in her hands. "God, Bob . . . I'm sorry. I didn't even think about the boys. Should I go talk to them . . . explain?"

"No, I'll handle it." His voice was softer now. "I'll tell them the truth—that you're staying as a guest for a while. But, Bryn, if you're going to be a mom, you have to start thinking about things like that. Because, no matter what's going on in your own life, your kids have to come first."

"I really am sorry. And . . . and, I'll do better. I promise." Her voice grew stronger. "I *will* do better. I'll be the perfect houseguest, and I'll be really nice to Micah and Cody. And, if you want . . . I'll even apologize to Wendy."

Bob smiled. "Okay, let's not expect any miracles. I'll handle Wendy. You just concentrate on learning to think like a . . . Hey, guys! You remember Bryn, don't you? She's going to be staying with us for a little while, in the guest room. She's looking for a new apartment."

"Hi, guys." Bryn smiled at them uncertainly. They stared back at her.

"Are you going to live with us like Luke does with Mommy?" Cody, the five-year-old, asked, never taking his eyes from Bryn's face.

"Oh no, honey. I'm not going to live here. I'm just staying in your guest room until I find a new apartment."

"Did you bring your computer?"

Bryn smiled, remembering the last time she'd visited Bob and Wendy before their split. She'd brought her laptop, and Cody had been fascinated with what she could do with pictures in Photoshop.

"I did." She nodded. "Maybe after breakfast, we can play with some pictures."

"Cool!" Cody grinned at her.

Micah said nothing.

"Micah, you set the table. Cody, why don't you show Bryn how we make shape-cakes?"

Cody dragged a chair from the dining room into the kitchen, shoving it next to the stove.

"Look!" He grinned over his shoulder at Bryn. "Daddy bought these shapers. And when you put the pancake batter in them, the pancakes get shapes."

Bryn watched as Bob and Cody poured batter and flipped pancakes. She poured apple juice and carried glasses to the table, passing Micah on the way. The seven-year-old never looked at her, keeping his eyes firmly on the ground.

As they sat down to a platter of pancakes shaped like cars and trucks, Bryn felt her stomach lurch. *Damn! When will this morning sickness end?*

"Hey, guys," she said, trying to smile. "Will you excuse me? I have to . . ." Her voice trailed off as she backed away from the table.

"Go on," Bob said. "It's okay."

Bryn ran for the bathroom, slammed the door shut, and heaved. *So much for a nice, homey breakfast with the kids,* she thought, leaning against the toilet. *They probably think I'm a nut job.*

When she returned to the table, Bob was sitting alone, pushing bites of pancake around a puddle of syrup. Cartoons blared from the television in the front room. Breakfast, apparently, was over.

Later, Bryn sat at the table with Cody, manipulating images on her laptop. The five-year-old stared at the screen, grinning as Bryn turned the face blue with green highlights.

"Hey, Micah, look!"

Micah was sitting on the floor, putting together a Lego set with his dad.

"What?" he said, not raising his eyes.

"Bryn made Luke all blue."

Micah rose to look at the laptop screen. He smiled. "He looks better blue."

Bryn smiled over the kids' heads at Bob, who was trying to suppress a grin.

"Now do this one." Cody handed Bryn another photo.

She took the photo without looking at it and fed it into the portable scanner, then pulled the image into the program.

She stared at the image in silence for a moment, until Cody jabbed her with his elbow. "Make it purple!"

"Um, Bob? You might want to see this picture."

Bob rose to look at the computer screen, but Micah was there before him, standing between his father and the image.

"You weren't supposed to bring that!" he yelled at Cody.

Bob reached over Micah's head to take the laptop from Bryn. He stared at the image for a long minute, then closed the program.

"When was that taken?" he asked, looking from Micah to Cody.

"It was just a joke," Micah said. "Cody wasn't supposed to have it."

Cody's cheeks reddened under Micah's gaze.

"Okay, come here." Bob sat on the floor and pulled both boys down beside him.

"Look, I'm not mad," he said gently. "I just want to know when the picture was taken . . . and why."

"Mommy said not to tell you," Cody said.

Bryn stared at Bob. His face was ashen.

"Well, this time, Cody, just this one time, I'm going to ask you to do something Mommy said not to. I need you to tell me about the picture."

Cody sat in silence, staring at the floor.

Finally, Micah spoke.

"Last weekend Mommy and Luke had some people over for a party. And Jeremy brought some special cigarettes that made people act funny."

"Who is Jeremy?" Bob's voice was soft, but Bryn could hear the effort it took him to keep it that way.

"He's a friend of Luke's," Cody said.

"And he was blowing smoke in Ginger's face. That's our dog at Mommy's," he said, turning to Bryn.

Bob sat, waiting. He didn't want to push the boys too hard. Bryn chewed at her fingernail. She wanted to scream.

"So Luke took a picture of him doing it."

"Did he blow smoke in your face, too?" Bob asked, watching the boys carefully.

"He blew some at Cody," Micah said, staring at the ground. "Mommy told him not to, but he did anyway."

"Are you . . . okay?" Bob's voice shook.

"I'm okay, Daddy. I felt kind of funny, but Mommy made me go to bed and then when I woke up, I was okay."

"Are you mad at Mommy?" Cody asked. " 'Cause Mommy said you'd be mad if you knew."

"Well, Mommy and I need to talk about it. I don't like it when she asks you to keep secrets from me. But I'm not mad at *you* . . . at either of you. Okay? You guys didn't do anything wrong."

"Dad?" Micah's voice was small. "Can we throw the picture away?"

Bryn pulled the photo from the scanner and handed it to Bob.

"I'll take care of it," he said, carrying the picture to the kitchen. "Don't worry about it."

"You want to do a different picture?" Bryn asked, holding her hand out to Cody. "I've got some animal shots in here somewhere."

Cody returned to the couch and soon was engrossed in green zebras and orange chimps. After a few minutes, Micah rose and came to lean in next to his brother.

"Do you have any alligators?" he asked, looking up at Bryn for the first time all day.

"I think so," she said, searching through the thumbnail sketches on the screen before her. "What color do you want to make it?"

"So, what are you going to do?" Bryn asked, after Bob had tucked the boys into bed.

"I'm going to call a lawyer on Monday, and I'm going to make sure my sons are never in that house again." His voice was quiet and firm.

"Good!" Bryn said. "That's good. You need to get them out of there. God! What was she thinking?"

"Wendy doesn't think," Bob said. "She just does whatever it is that she wants to do, and the hell with everybody else."

Bryn watched him quietly for a while. "That's good, Bob. It's good that you finally see her for what she is. Now maybe you can do what you need to do to take care of yourself and the boys. And, Bob?"

"Yeah?"

"I will be here every step of the way to help. Okay? You said you'll be here to help me with this." She patted her stomach lightly. "And I promise that I'll be here to help you with that." She pointed to the image flickering on the laptop, an image of a small boy standing beside a big mutt, surrounded by a haze of smoke blown by a stoned-looking man, grinning at the camera, a rubber hose twisted tightly around his arm.

"Thanks, Bryn." Bob smiled faintly. "That's a deal."

∽ 13 ∽

Corrie gripped the armrest of her seat as the plane lifted from the runway. She hated flying. Fingering her rosary, she glanced around at her fellow travelers, smiling at the young mother across the aisle nursing a baby.

It had been a terrible weekend. The trip to Chicago had been scrapped. Mark had barely spoken to her since Friday.

She felt guilty for making him so unhappy, but she'd remained steadfast in her plans for the California trip.

"I'll be home on Thursday," she'd said before Mark left for work that morning.

He'd said nothing.

"I'll call you tonight."

"Okay." Mark had straightened his tie and picked up his briefcase, not looking at Corrie, standing in the kitchen in her nightgown.

"Honey?"

Finally, he'd turned to look at her.

"I love you." She'd tried to smile at him.

"I'll talk to you later," he'd said, turning toward the door.

Then he'd left.

Now, feeling the familiar stomach lurch that came with flight,

Corrie wished she'd never committed to this trip, that she hadn't seen Daniel, that he'd never come back to town.

Sighing, she released her death grip on the armrest and leaned back into her seat. She bought a glass of wine from the flight attendant, opened a magazine, and tried not to think about Mark, about how angry he was with her, how hurt.

Why couldn't he just trust her? Corrie had never given her husband a reason to worry before. Why did he have to overreact so badly now?

Because I lied to him, she admitted silently. *Why didn't I just tell him when I saw Daniel in the first place?*

She'd make it up to him next week. When she got home from Pasadena, she'd plan another weekend getaway. Maybe at the lake house . . . he'd like that. She'd go down on Friday morning and set it up, then pick him up at the office after work and drive him down.

I'll make curry. He loves that. And cheesecake and wine. Maybe take some massage oil. I'll get a new chemise.

I'll make it up to him.

She smiled, thinking of how surprised Mark would be. He'd forgive her then for not telling him about Daniel, for taking this trip.

This trip . . . She wished now that she'd called ahead to arrange for a car. She'd thought about taking a cab from the airport, but that would leave her stranded at the hotel. You had to have a car to get around in L.A. She cringed at the thought of driving on the freeways. She'd only been to Los Angeles once before, and then Mark had done the driving.

Giving up the pretense of reading her magazine, Corrie let her mind wander back to her final year of college, when she was engaged to Daniel. They'd planned so many things, starting with a trip to the Philippines, where Daniel's uncle worked on a UN medical project. Daniel had filled out all the paperwork for their visas, when his uncle abruptly died of a stroke. With his death, their Philippines plans got scuttled.

Corrie was quietly relieved at the change. She thought she would have followed Daniel anywhere . . . even to the Philippines. But what she really wanted was to settle in Middlebrook, get a job, get married, and start a family. She hoped Daniel would learn to love the idea. But, of course, he hadn't.

Bryn had asked her once why she didn't try to find Daniel, why she didn't follow him to New York, when she'd been willing to follow him to a third-world country. And Corrie couldn't tell her the reason, the secret she'd held in the weeks after he'd left—that she was pregnant. Pregnant with Daniel's child. She hadn't told him before he left. She'd known for a couple weeks, but she'd been waiting for the right time.

And then September 11 happened and Daniel left. And he never looked back, never called or wrote, never even let her know where he'd settled.

Corrie wondered sometimes if he would have stayed had he known about the baby. What would their life have been like if he'd stayed, if she'd had the baby? But she couldn't bring herself to search for him, tell him he was going to be a father, trap him in a life he didn't want.

So she'd quietly made arrangements with a clinic in Chicago. Three weeks after Daniel left, the baby was gone. And Corrie spent the next two years mourning the loss of her love, her child, and her innocence. She'd never gotten over the guilt. She went on with her life, married Mark, even tried to get pregnant. But she always knew the reason they couldn't have a child was because of the abortion. She had killed her first child. God would not give her another one. That was her penance, the price she would pay for her sin.

When she and Mark married, Corrie had converted to Catholicism, confessing her sin to the kind priest who baptized her.

He advised her to tell Mark, told her that God loved her, and explained what she must do to be forgiven. But Corrie knew she would not be forgiven, could never be forgiven. She knew her inability to have children was her just punishment.

She never told Mark.

She came to love the church, though, the sacred rituals, the holy feeling that came with communion. Growing up, her mother had taken them to a Baptist church sporadically, but Corrie never really felt part of it. Instead, she always felt like Patrice was putting on a show, trying to prove to the community that she was a good mother. At home, however, there were no prayers, no talk about faith.

In the years since her marriage, Corrie had found a home in their local parish. She went to Mass every Sunday, sitting with Sarah when Mark was traveling. She often went to early morning Mass before work, especially when she felt troubled about something. She belonged to the women's group at Holy Spirit and helped with bake sales and food drives. She even went to confession on occasion, although she felt out of place in the confessional, as though the abortion had ruined her chances for redemption.

She stared out the window of the plane, wishing she could atone for that sin. Finally, she crossed herself, closed her eyes, and began softly, "Hail Mary, full of grace, the Lord is with thee."

Corrie nudged the rental car into traffic, chewing her lip till it hurt. She'd never seen so many cars, all vying for space on the six lanes of freeway. The cell phone in her purse rang shrilly, but she couldn't dig it out in time. She checked the caller ID—Sarah. She hoped her sister-in-law wasn't in early labor. More likely, she was calling to fret again about Corrie's trip.

"It's not a good idea," she'd insisted the night before. "Mark is really mad."

"I know." Corrie had sighed. "But I've already made the reservations. Besides, it's only a few days."

Sarah hadn't pushed it, but Corrie knew she was upset.

At last, her exit appeared and she pulled off the freeway with a sigh of relief.

After settling into the hotel, she checked the phone book for the community center's address, then got online for driving directions. She took a shower and put on a business suit, scrutinizing herself in the mirror. Too formal. She changed into a skirt and blouse with sandals. Better.

She applied her lipstick, smudged it, washed her face, and tried again.

Finally, she deemed herself presentable, picked up her notebook, recorder, and camera, and walked to the door. She paused with her hand on the doorknob. What was she doing here? She should turn right back around and head for home, back to Mark and Sarah and Bryn. Back to the December issue and a Santa Claus feature.

She shook her head, straightened her shoulders, and steeled herself for another driving adventure.

The North Pasadena Community Center was a small building of faded yellow stucco with iron bars on the windows. The playground was a blur of running children. At the other end of the building, a group of teenagers played basketball. Corrie pulled her camera from its case and shot a few photos before walking to the door, welcoming the blast of cool air inside after the heat of the California sun.

"I'd like to see Daniel Chapman," she said to the young woman at the reception desk.

"You and everyone else," the woman said, not looking up from the magazine in her lap.

"Excuse me," Corrie said more firmly. "Is Mr. Chapman in?"

The woman raised her head and met Corrie's eyes, then smiled at Corrie's stare. Beneath a shock of bright pink, blunt-cut hair, the receptionist's eyes were a startling hue of brilliant aquamarine, completely at odds with her Asian coloring and features. Her nose, eyebrows, and cheek all bore metal studs. Around her neck she wore a black leather, studded dog collar.

"So, is Mr. Chapman in?" Corrie asked, trying not to stare.

"Yeah, he's in. Jaden!" The woman yelled down the hallway. A young man's head poked out from a doorway.

"Where's Dan?"

"Upstairs, I think."

"Well, go get him. Tell him . . ." She turned back to Corrie. "What's your name?"

"Corrie Philips."

The young woman smiled, then yelled down the hall again. "Tell him Corrie Philips is here to see him."

The young man strode down the hall and disappeared, leaving Corrie alone with the pink-haired, aquamarine-eyed Asian woman.

"I'm Capri," the woman said. "And I know who you are."

Corrie's eyes widened, but she said nothing.

"Daniel's great love, from, where is it? Some university in Indiana, right? You came to do the story. He said you would."

"Coriander Bliss!"

Corrie turned to see Daniel pounding down the hall toward her. He wore gym shorts and a ragged T-shirt. His red hair was plastered to his head with sweat, but he was grinning widely. She couldn't help but smile back.

"I knew you'd come!"

Daniel pulled her into a fierce hug, then spun her through the lobby. "I knew I could count on you!"

Corrie struggled as her feet lifted from the ground. This was definitely not the professional greeting she had planned.

"Daniel, put me down!"

He lowered her to the ground and dropped his arms abruptly.

"Sorry," he said. But his grin showed no remorse.

Daniel walked beside Corrie, talking fast. Corrie smiled. He always talked fast when he was excited.

"We serve a mostly Hispanic population. A lot of our kids are in the States illegally, but some were born here. Their parents are almost all illegal. We've had to work hard to gain their trust. INS shows up on a regular basis, but Capri usually handles that."

Corrie took notes and snapped pictures of kids playing games, being tutored, shooting hoops. In one room, a group of pregnant girls practiced diapering dolls. In another, preschoolers played a frenetic game of Simon Says.

"Tomorrow, I'll set you up to meet with our board of directors," Daniel said as they walked. "And then you can tour the transition apartments. We have ten units, with three bedrooms each. Kids who are aging out of foster care rent the apartments. The first year they pay a hundred dollars a month, the second year two hundred, the third year three hundred. After that, we hope they're ready to move out on their own. We've had a couple dozen kids go through them already, and most are independent now.

"Hey," he added, "you should talk to Capri about the apartments. She's one of our graduates. Maybe you could come to dinner tonight, and she can tell you about her experience."

"I don't know, Daniel." Corrie wasn't sure she wanted to have dinner with Daniel and the pierced young woman. "I probably should go back to the hotel and write up my notes."

"Come on." He tugged at her arm. "I'll cook."

Corrie stared at him and grinned. "You'll cook? Since when do you cook?"

"I've been on my own for ten years, Coriander Bliss. I'll have you know that I'm a great cook. I make a mean vegan stir-fry."

"Are you a vegetarian?" Corrie remembered Daniel's love of bacon from their time together.

"Hell, no." Daniel declared. "I still love bacon . . . and a good steak. But Capri's a vegan."

Corrie wondered how often Daniel cooked for his receptionist. Maybe every night?

"Capri and I are roommates," Daniel said suddenly, as if reading her thoughts.

"Ah," Corrie said, her cheeks reddening. *Of course he's involved with her. What did I expect? That he's been waiting for me all these years?*

"Just roommates," Daniel continued, seeing her red cheeks. "We used to be involved, sort of, but Capri has a lot of issues—trust issues. She got dumped in foster care when she was nine and then bounced around from home to home. I don't think she'll ever be able to commit to anyone.

"Anyway, she splits the rent with me and we cook together sometimes. Otherwise, she does her thing and I do mine."

Corrie nodded, not raising her eyes from the sidewalk. What did it matter whether Daniel was involved with Capri, or with anyone? And why did he feel like he had to explain himself to her?

"Hey, freak girl," Daniel said as they entered the front lobby.

"Fuck you," Capri replied cheerfully.

"What are you up to tonight?"

"Going to the Voodoo Lounge with Mia."

"Skip it," Daniel said. "Stay home and have dinner with Corrie and me. She wants to interview you for her story."

"Daniel . . ." Corrie started to interrupt. She hadn't agreed to dinner.

"Yeah?" Capri smiled. "I guess that'd be okay. I've never been interviewed before."

"Good, that's settled." Daniel glanced from Capri to Corrie. "So, do you have a car here? You can just follow me back to the apartment. It's kind of hard to tell you how to get there."

So Corrie found herself back in her rental car, following Daniel through a maze of back streets toward La Cañada. She hadn't agreed to dinner, but she couldn't refuse once Capri agreed to be interviewed. She pulled out her cell phone as she drove and dialed Sarah's number.

"Hi. How are you?" Sarah's voice was a welcome return to the familiar.

"Okay, I guess. I just finished touring the center. It's pretty amazing."

"How was it, seeing Daniel again?"

"Okay," Corrie said, cradling the phone to her ear with her shoulder as she turned a corner, trying to keep up with the blue VW Bug ahead of her. "It was nice, actually. He's living with a woman named Capri. She works at the center, too."

There was a pause. Then Sarah asked cautiously, "Did you meet her?"

"Yes," Corrie said, proud to hear that her voice was calm. "She's really interesting . . . Asian, with lots of piercings and a couple tattoos. And she's got the weirdest color eyes I've ever seen.

"Anyway, how are you?" Corrie asked. "I'm sorry I missed your call earlier."

"I'm fine, just sitting around waiting. The doctor says eight more weeks, and I am *so* ready." Sarah's voice sounded tired.

"Well, at least wait till I get home!" Corrie laughed. "I want to be there when my namesake makes her appearance."

"When are you coming home?"

"Thursday morning," Corrie said. "I have a nine o'clock flight."

"Have you talked to Mark?"

"Not yet," Corrie replied. "I'll call him later tonight. I'm going to an interview right now."

"Well, don't forget to call him. He's really not happy with this trip, Corrie."

"I know." Corrie sighed. "But he'll be all right. I'll call him later. I have to go now, Sarah. I'm just getting onto the freeway."

In reality, she was pulling into a driveway behind Daniel.

"Okay, be careful. And Corrie?"

"Yeah?"

"Be good!"

"I will." Corrie laughed as she hung up the phone.

The Spanish-style stucco apartment building climbed up the side of a hill, each unit stacked above and slightly behind the one below. Corrie parked her car in the lot at the base of the hill and followed Daniel up a long flight of stairs to the top unit.

"This is nice," she said as she stepped inside. The building was old, with ceramic tile floors and arched doorways. The south-facing wall was entirely windows, opening onto a patio, built on the roof of the apartment below. The afternoon sun shone bright through the windows, creating a golden glow.

"Yeah, it is," Daniel agreed, watching Corrie. "I've been here for seven years now. Do you want to see the rest of it?"

They walked from the front room to the tiny kitchen, which was filled with electronic gadgets.

"Capri's," Daniel explained, grinning. "She loves to buy cooking gadgets, but she never cooks."

He opened a door to a small bedroom. A single bed graced the corner, strewn with women's clothes. A vanity was littered with jewelry, makeup, and hair products. A black bra hung from a corner of the mirror.

"She's a slob," Daniel said. "But at least she keeps the mess confined to her room."

After Capri's room was a short hall with a small bathroom. The counter there was also strewn with makeup and skin-care products. "Mostly confined to her room," Daniel corrected himself, laughing.

He opened the door at the end of the hallway, and Corrie stepped into the second bedroom. Antique oak furniture filled the room, at the center of which stood a huge, four-poster bed, the covers neatly drawn. Several paintings hung on the walls. Corrie stopped beneath one and touched it with one finger.

"This is really nice," she said softly, admiring the brushstrokes, the subtle play of colors and texture.

"Isn't it?" Daniel stood just behind her. Corrie could feel his warmth. "All of these were painted by one of our graduates. His name is Darrel, and he was a foster kid. When he showed up at the center, he was eighteen, just kicked out of his last foster home. He didn't have his diploma, no job . . . just a whole lot of attitude.

"So we got him into one of the apartments, and he started working on his GED. One day he showed me his drawings, and I was just blown away. They were so good. So I gave him a job at the center, teaching art classes to the younger kids. And after he got his GED, we found him a grant so he could go to art school.

"He's pretty successful now. Sells his work at a couple galleries in North Hollywood. But he still teaches twice a week at the center."

"Wow." Corrie walked toward another painting. "You must be really proud."

"Of what?" Daniel asked. "I didn't teach him to paint."

"No, but you gave him his first job, found him a place to live, helped him get into school."

She turned to smile at him. "No wonder you're so passionate about the center. You wanted to make a difference, and you're doing it."

"You have to meet Darrel!" Daniel said. "Maybe he can come by the center tomorrow."

"That would be great." She smiled at him again, then let her eyes wander around the room, until they finally rested on the bed.

"Um, so . . . can I see the patio?" She walked out of the bedroom abruptly.

Stopping in the kitchen, Daniel poured her a glass of cabernet.

"You still drink it red?" he asked as he handed her the glass.

She nodded, pleased that he'd remembered.

The view from the patio was stunning. They stood gazing at the late afternoon sun, just dipping behind the Southern California hills.

"This is really beautiful," Corrie said softly. *And it could have been mine.*

Stop it! Don't think like that.

She resolutely avoided looking at Daniel, standing beside her.

"Yeah, it'd be perfect if not for the noise. You can't live anywhere in the L.A. Basin and be far from the freeway."

The sound of rush-hour traffic hummed in the background.

"Still, it's a hell of a lot nicer than my first place."

"Where was that?" Corrie asked, dropping into a lawn chair.

"When I first came out, I rented a place in South Central L.A. It was a dump, but it was cheap. I got a job working at a men's shelter. God, that was a nightmare . . . right in the middle of gang turf. We had guys get shot at least once a week. Most of them were addicts, the rest were predators. It was hell on earth, even for me. And I only had to work there. I can't imagine what it was like for the guys who lived there."

"How did you end up in L.A.? I thought you went to New York."

"I was there for a year, but man, I just couldn't handle the city. Too big, too cold, too depressing, even for me. So, I figured people needed help in warm places, too. And I bought a bus ticket and came. Didn't know anyone out here at first. Just worked and slept."

He turned to look at Corrie, her auburn hair shining copper in the setting sun.

"That's why I never called, you know."

She didn't answer, just stared at the sky, turning orange now.

"I couldn't ask you to live like that."

He sat in silence for a minute and then poured more wine into Corrie's glass.

"Anyway, I'd been out here for about a year and was working in the shelter when this gangbanger comes in looking for a guy who shot his brother. He found me instead. I tried to talk to him, but he wasn't in a talking mood."

Daniel smiled at Corrie's face, now turned toward him, her eyes wide.

"He shot me," he said quietly.

"My God, Daniel! I didn't know. Why didn't you . . . why didn't you call me? I never even knew."

"I thought about it," Daniel continued. "I wanted to. But what was I going to say? 'Hey, Corrie, I know I walked out on you two years ago and never called you or even wrote. But now I'm shot and I want you.' I couldn't do that."

"Were you hurt bad?"

"I got hit in the side. I turned away just as he shot. The bullet went straight through without hitting anything major. I got lucky."

"I wish you'd called. I hate to think about you all by yourself in the hospital."

"My mom was there."

"She must have been hysterical."

"Actually, she was pretty good about it." Daniel smiled, shifted in his chair, and sipped his wine. "She wanted me to come home, of course. But she knew I wouldn't. She knows I need to be doing this."

"I always liked your mom." Corrie smiled, remembering the red-haired woman so passionately devoted to human rights.

"She liked you, too. She wanted me to call you."

They sat in silence for a minute.

"Anyway," Daniel said, "I decided I really didn't like working with adults. Most of the guys at the shelter were beyond helping. I wanted to get to kids before they were lost. So I hooked up with a guy who was working at a community center in Van Nuys, and we applied for a grant to start the center here.

"Nick had all the right contacts. His family is wealthy . . . he knew how to work the system. So we got a start-up grant and found a building, and that's how we opened the center."

"Is Nick still around?" Corrie didn't remember anyone named Nick at the center.

"He got married a couple years ago and decided he needed to make a real living wage. He's working for the state now, doing something with computers. But he still comes by. Last year he got us a bunch of computers from some office that was upgrading."

"And now you're doing what you always wanted to do." Corrie smiled at him, leaning back in her chair. "You must be really proud."

Daniel leaned forward, setting his glass on a small table.

"I'm not proud of the way I treated you," he said softly.

"It's okay," Corrie said, not looking at him. "I got over it."

"Looks like you did," he said. "I'm glad you're happy, Coriander."

"No one calls me that anymore, Daniel. I changed it to Corrie Ann when I got married."

"I'm sorry you did that." Daniel looked away from her.

"Hey!"

A woman's voice chimed from the door. Corrie turned to see Capri, holding a large shopping bag.

"I got fresh veggies at the park," she said. "Let's get cooking. I'm starved!"

≈ 14 ≈

"How was the meeting with the lawyer?" Bryn was laying dishes on the table when Bob came home.

"He thinks I've got a good case for sole custody."

"So what do you do next?"

"Well, I paid him a retainer and he's putting together the papers. Where are the boys?"

Bryn smiled. "They're asleep, actually. I think I wore them out today."

Bob grinned at her. "See? You can totally do the mom thing."

Bryn walked to the kitchen to stir spaghetti sauce.

"Thanks for watching them today. I'll have to work out some kind of day care, I guess."

"It's no problem. I had fun."

Bryn pushed her bangs, sticky from the steam rising from the spaghetti, from her forehead.

"Wendy called three times today. I didn't pick up the first two, but Micah answered the third time."

"Oh God," Bob sighed. "I told her not to call."

"Well, he talked to her for a minute, and then he said she wanted to talk to you. So I got on the phone and told her you were at work, and if she wants to talk to you in the future, she'll have to do it through your lawyer. . . . I hope that was okay."

Bob nodded. "I probably should call her tonight."

"No, you shouldn't!" Bryn turned from the stove to face him. "You said everything you needed to yesterday. She made her own bed. Let her lie in it!"

"Daddy?" Cody stood in the doorway, rubbing sleep from his eyes.

"Hey, buddy." Bob scooped the child into a hug. "How was your day?"

"We had fun." Cody smiled, relaxing into his father's arms. "Bryn took us to the zoo, and we had a picnic. And she let us watch *Power Rangers* and made popcorn."

"Cool." Bob smiled at Bryn over Cody's head. "Sounds like a great day."

"When is Mommy coming?"

Bryn saw Bob's back stiffen, then relax. "Not for a while, Cody. You and Micah are going to stay here with me. Micah has to start school next week, and then you'll go back to preschool. Won't that be fun?"

"But isn't Mommy coming back?"

Bob sat down on the kitchen floor and pulled Cody into his lap.

"Mommy is going to stay where she is, Cody. She's going to live with Luke. And you and Micah are going to live here with me. But you'll still see Mommy on the weekends sometimes, okay?"

"But my Game Boy is at her house." Cody stared up at Bob, his eyes round and unblinking.

"I'll get your Game Boy, buddy. Don't worry about it. I'll get all your stuff back, so you can have it here."

"Okay. . . . What's for dinner?"

"Bryn made spaghetti." Bob smiled and ruffled his son's hair.

"With meatballs?"

Cody looked up at Bryn expectantly.

"Absolutely with meatballs!" Bryn smiled. "Do you want to taste the sauce?"

Bob went to wake Micah, while Cody stirred the spaghetti sauce. As they sat down to supper, Cody grinned at Micah.

"Daddy said we're going to live here now."

Micah looked from his brother to Bob, his face blank.

"What do you think about that, Micah?" Bob asked.

The seven-year-old shrugged his shoulders. "Whatever," he said, twirling spaghetti on his fork.

"And he's gonna get my Game Boy and all our other stuff, and bring it home," Cody continued.

Still Micah said nothing.

"Will Bryn live with us, too?" Cody turned to Bob.

"No, Cody," Bob said. "I told you, Bryn is just staying for a little while. Just until she finds a new apartment."

"But who will take care of us after Bryn leaves?"

"I'll work that out." Bob buttered a roll. "Besides, you guys start school next week."

"But who will pick me up from preschool?" Cody's brow furrowed.

"We'll work it out," Bob said.

"So I'm going to my old school?" Micah spoke softly.

"Yep, you'll be back with all your friends at your school."

"Mommy said I was going to a new school."

"Well, if you stayed at Mommy's, you would be at a new school." Bob spoke slowly, measuring his words carefully. "But I thought you'd rather go to your old school, where your friends are."

Micah chewed on his roll for a minute. "Okay. I didn't want to go to a new school."

Bob smiled as he caught Bryn's eye.

"Is Mommy coming home?" Micah's voice was very quiet.

The question hung in the air for a long moment, before Bob finally leaned forward to cup Micah's chin.

"No, buddy. Mommy isn't coming home. Mommy is going to live with Luke. And you and me and Cody are going to live here. Just us guys."

Micah said nothing, returning to his roll.

"Daddy?" he finally asked, staring down at his plate.

"What?"

"I wish things were like before, when Mommy lived here with us."

"I know. But it's going to be okay. You'll see . . . it'll be okay."

Bob sat with the phone cradled in his hand, staring into space.

"You don't have to call her." Bryn sat on the sofa, watching him. "You don't owe her anything."

"I have to." Bob sighed. "I can't leave things the way they are."

Bryn leaned forward, watching his face. "You said everything you needed to say yesterday."

The scene the night before had been ugly. Bryn had taken the boys for ice cream, so they wouldn't be home when Wendy arrived. Bob had confronted his wife with the photo, telling her that she could not take the boys. Wendy had screamed, then cried, and finally left, slamming the door behind her, the threat of an ugly custody battle hanging in the air.

"Just let your lawyer . . ." Bryn began.

They both jumped at the sudden banging on the door.

"Bob? Open the damned door!" Wendy's voice was shrill.

"Damn!" Bob rose, slamming the phone down.

"You want me to stay?" Bryn rose.

Bob shook his head as he walked to the door. "I'll handle it."

Bryn went to her room, but left the door open.

Bob opened the door and stared down at his wife, the mother of his children. Wendy's curls were wild, her cheeks flushed, her hands clenched tightly together. She pushed past him into the living room.

"Where are the boys?" she yelled. "I'm taking them home. Micah? Cody?"

"Shut up, Wendy." Bob grabbed her arm, pulling her back out the door onto the porch.

Bryn walked softly down the hall and stood just out of sight in the dining room.

"I want my kids, damn it!" Wendy was screaming now. "Where are my kids?"

"The boys are in bed . . . they're asleep. Keep your voice down, or you'll wake them up."

"I want to wake them up! I'm taking them home!"

Bryn cautiously peered into the living room, clutching her cell phone. She'd call the police if she had to.

"Listen to me, Wendy. You are *not* taking the boys. They are never going back to that house. Not as long as Luke is there."

"You can't keep them away from me, Bob. I'm their mother, for God's sake."

"And you put them in a dangerous situation. God, Wendy! What were you thinking?"

"It was fun, Bob. Just fun. Something you don't know a god-damned thing about."

"Well, your fun just cost you your kids." Bob's voice rose. "You aren't fit to be their mother. And I'm not going to let you put them in a situation like that again."

"Oh, and yours is so much better? Hell, you're living with Bryn. She's not fit to take care of a dog!"

"Leave Bryn out of this." Bob's voice shook with anger. "She has nothing to do with it. And even if she did, she would never put the boys in danger like you did."

"Damn it, Bob. I want my kids and I want them now!"

Bryn ducked back into the hallway as the front door opened.

"No!" Bob's voice rang through the house.

Behind her, Bryn heard a bedroom door creak open. She turned to see Micah standing, pale and shaking, in the hall behind her.

"Shhhh," she whispered, crouching to pull Micah into her arms. "Let's go back to bed. It's going to be okay."

Bryn crooned over and over, "It's going to be okay," as she steered the child back to his room, closing the door behind them. The din from the living room continued.

"You are not taking the boys, Wendy. If you try, I'll call the police."

"I'm their mother! You can't keep them away from me."

"Listen, Wendy." Bob's voice was low and steely. "The boys are staying with me. I've already got a lawyer. I showed him the picture. And he assured me I will get custody."

There was a long silence.

"You showed that picture to your lawyer? You bastard!"

"And I'll take it to Child Protective Services, if I have to. And then you will never see the boys again."

"You can't do that!" Wendy's voice rose to a wail. "You can't do that to me."

"I can and I will. And then I'll send a copy to your parents."

"You son of a bitch! You wouldn't."

"Yes, Wendy, I would. I will . . . unless you give up custody. I want sole custody. You can have visitation . . . but not if Luke is there. I will not allow my sons to be in the same house as him ever again."

Bryn sat on Micah's bed, holding his shaking frame, whispering, "It's going to be okay." She hoped against hope the yelling wouldn't wake Cody, too.

"You can't do that! I'll get a lawyer. I'll take you to court."

"You can try, Wendy. But you won't win. I promise you, you won't win."

Wendy collapsed onto the couch, crying.

"How can you do this to me?"

Bob stared down at her. They'd been married for ten years, shared a bed, made love, fought, had two children. He fought the urge to wrap his arms around her, tell her he still loved her, give in. Instead, he said quietly, "I'm doing what I have to do to take care of my sons.

"I think you should go."

Wendy stared up at him, tears coursing down her red cheeks.

"I won't let you do this."

"Just go, Wendy."

A moment later, Bryn heard the front door slam. In an instant, Micah broke free from her embrace and ran down the hallway to the front room.

"Daddy?"

Bob turned slowly to face his son.

"It's okay, Micah," he echoed Bryn. "It's going to be okay."

❧ 15 ❧

"Let's eat on the patio." Capri carried dishes from the kitchen. Corrie was on her second glass of wine, watching Daniel stir-fry broccoli, water chestnuts, bean sprouts, and tofu in a sauce he'd made from scratch. It smelled of ginger and basil.

They sat on the patio, brightly lit with strings of tiny white lights.

"This is really good," Corrie said, pushing the last of her dinner around her plate.

"Don't sound so surprised," Capri said. "Daniel's a great cook."

"That's just because you buy me all those gadgets." Daniel smiled at Capri.

Corrie watched them closely. They seemed comfortable together, almost like a brother and sister.

"Well, you're going to lose all those gadgets when Mia and I get married."

"Never gonna happen." Daniel grinned. "You'll never get within ten feet of an altar."

"Fuck you," Capri said, laughing. "Just for that, you can't come to the wedding."

She turned to Corrie and smiled. "Mia and I are driving up to

San Francisco next month to get married. She knows a judge there who does gay weddings."

"But I thought . . ." Corrie stopped herself.

"Me and Daniel? Yeah, we were together for a while. But you know, I decided against the whole guy thing. Women are so much . . . easier.

"Besides," she added, rising to collect Corrie's plate, "Mia and I wear the same size."

Capri took the dishes into the kitchen, leaving Corrie staring behind her.

"She's gay?"

"Actually," Daniel said, "she's bi. Capri is always looking for something she'll never find. A mother, a father . . . who knows."

"No fathers, thank you." Capri had returned, carrying a bottle of dark beer. "Fathers are completely unnecessary. My dear old dad beat the crap out of my mom on a regular basis," she said to Corrie. "And after Mom left, he beat the crap out of me."

Corrie pulled out her recorder. "Do you mind if I tape?"

"Is this the interview?"

Corrie nodded. "If that's all right with you."

"Sure." Capri took a drink from her beer and leaned back in her chair. "Shoot."

"You said your mother left. . . . How old were you?"

"Seven. I guess she'd had enough of my father. She was really young when they got married. Dad was stationed in Korea when they met. She was only eighteen. She was nineteen when she had me.

"She used to sing me songs in Korean." Capri smiled, remembering. "And she told me stories about her family. I never met them."

She sighed and took another drink. "Anyway, I guess it got so bad she had to leave. One day I came home from school . . . I was in second grade, I think . . . and she was gone.

"My dad went ballistic. He threw away all her things, tore up all her pictures. I kept one, though. I put it under my mattress. I still have it. Do you want to see?"

Capri ran inside and returned with a faded photo of a young woman holding a baby.

"She was beautiful," Corrie said softly.

"Yeah . . . so, she left. And after that, my dad spent his days drinking and his nights getting in fights with the neighbors and hitting me. When I was nine, DCF came and took me. I was glad, at first. My dad scared the shit out of me. I was glad to get away from him.

"So, I got put in this foster home with three other foster kids. The dad worked all the time and the mom screamed at us a lot. But no one hit us.

"I stayed there a couple years, and then they got divorced and I got moved to another home. That one was nice. The mom there was really sweet. She baked cookies and stuff . . . just like a real mom. I liked her."

Capri stopped for a minute, staring into the dark.

"But, after a couple years, they moved me again. And then again. I ended up in seven houses by the time I was eighteen. Then . . ." She made a chopping movement with her hand. "I got the ax. No one pays for you after you turn eighteen.

"That's when I met Daniel. My caseworker sent me to the center, to see if they could help me get an apartment. I shared an apartment with two other girls till I moved in here. That was three years ago.

"But now"—she turned to grin again at Daniel—"I'm moving on. And poor Danny will be all by himself."

"I'll believe it when I see it," he said. "Tell Corrie about your career plans."

"I've been taking evening classes at Pasadena Community College," Capri said. "I'll have my associate degree by Christmas. Then I'm going to apply to UCLA. Daniel thinks I'll get some scholarships. I want to get my degree in counseling. I figure with my background I'd be a good counselor for other foster kids. Daniel says he'll hire me when I'm done."

"That's great," Corrie said, smiling. "I think you'd be a great counselor."

"So," Capri said, rising to strike a dramatic pose. "You want photos? I am very photogenic."

"Probably not here," Corrie said. "I think I'll leave out the bit about you living with Daniel."

Capri laughed. "Okay, whitewash it if you have to. Just get us some money for the center."

"I'll bring the camera tomorrow, and we'll get a picture of you at the center."

"Great!" Capri leaned over to kiss the top of Daniel's head.

"Okay, Dad," she said, laughing. "I've done my part. Now I'm off to the Voodoo. . . . Mia's waiting."

With that she was gone, leaving Corrie and Daniel on the patio.

"She's great," Corrie said. "I can't believe she's so . . . sane after everything she's been through."

"Well, she puts on a good front, anyway," Daniel said. "But don't let her fool you. She pretends to be all grown up, but inside she's still a scared little kid."

"Did she ever try to find her mother?"

"Yeah, but she never did. For all we know, her mom could be back in Korea."

"That's so sad."

"The world is full of sad stories, Corrie. Don't you know that?"

Corrie didn't answer. Of course she knew there was sadness in the world, even in her own perfect, little world. Why did Daniel always make her feel inadequate?

"Come on," he said, rising abruptly. "Help me with the dishes."

They stood side by side at the sink. Daniel washed while Corrie dried.

"I can't believe you don't have a dishwasher."

"Don't need one." Daniel smiled, handing her a plate. "Usually, it's just me. It'd take me a month to dirty up enough dishes to fill a dishwasher."

"Do you think Capri will really move out?"

"I don't know. I never thought she would, but once she starts college, she just might fly the coop."

"And then you'll be alone again." Corrie swiped a towel across the counter. "Will you be lonely?"

Daniel watched her, saying nothing.

She stopped to look at him. "Won't you?"

"Yeah," he said finally. "If Capri leaves, I'll probably be lonely. Hell, I'm lonely now."

He watched her carefully.

"What about you?" he asked. "Are you lonely?"

Corrie hung the towel on the refrigerator door and turned away.

"No," she said, her voice sharp. "Of course I'm not lonely. I have Mark."

"Tell me about him."

They walked back out to the patio, Daniel carrying the wine. He poured her another glass.

Careful, she thought. *You don't want to get drunk.*

"Mark is wonderful," she said, not looking at him. "He's an architect. He's done some lovely buildings. Right now he's working on an apartment building in New York."

"How did you guys meet?" Daniel relaxed in his chair.

"Actually, I've known him since I was a kid. He's Sarah's brother. You remember Sarah?"

"Yeah, I remember her."

"Mark is her big brother, so I already knew him some. But we didn't really get to know each other until a couple years after you . . . after graduation."

She took a sip of wine.

"I was on a blind date," she said, smiling into her glass. "I let Bryn fix me up with a guy from the university, a friend of Paul's. We were at Brennan's having dinner and I saw Mark at the bar. He was there with a client. And when the client left, he came over to our table and just . . . sat down.

"If you asked him, he'd tell you that he could see I was bored and he rescued me. But really, Mark just does stuff like that. He saw me, thought I was cute, and barged in on my date. Just sat down and waited the other guy out."

"That's kind of presumptuous," Daniel said.

"That's Mark."

Corrie smiled again. "He sees what he wants and he goes for it. And honestly, it felt good to be wanted like that."

"Is he good to you?"

Corrie smiled, swirling the wine in her glass.

"Yes, he's very good to me." She laughed. "He even likes my mom."

"Why wouldn't he?" Daniel asked. "Your mom is great. I loved your mom."

"I know, but Mark is . . . he came from a wealthy family, you know? His parents are so . . . proper. I wasn't sure what he'd think of mine."

"Well, if he didn't love your mom, I'd say there was something seriously wrong with him."

"Mark is good," Corrie said softly. "He's very good to me."

"How come you don't have kids?"

Corrie felt herself tense. *Damn, he is just as direct as ever.*

She sat quietly for a minute, then said, "Oh, I don't know. The time just never seemed right."

"That's a load of crap." Daniel's voice was flat. "You always wanted kids, Corrie. What happened?"

She sipped her wine before answering.

"Apparently, I can't have them."

"Oh, Coriander. I'm sorry. You were meant to be a mom."

"Well," she said, trying to smile. "I guess God doesn't think so."

He stared at her. "Since when do you believe in God?"

"I converted to Catholicism when I married Mark," she said. "He's not particularly religious, but it was important to his parents. I never thought about faith before that, but I like going to church. It's very . . . calming."

"Well, I don't believe that God doesn't want you to have kids. You'd be a great mother."

She didn't answer.

"Why don't you adopt? There are lots of kids out there who need good homes."

He leaned toward her, looking her full in the face. "Seriously, Corrie, I could put you in touch with an agency here. We work with several good ones. There are so many babies who need—"

"Thank you, Daniel. But I will handle my life by myself."

"Sorry," he said, smiling at her. "I slipped into social worker mode. I'm a big believer in adoption. I've even thought about adopting myself."

Corrie stared at him in disbelief.

"You?" She laughed. "I can't see that."

"I know, back in college I said I didn't want kids. But I'm thirty-three now. I've got a good job, or at least I will if your article raises some money for the center. I'm tired of living alone. . . . I think I'd be a good dad."

Corrie shook her head. The wine was making her feel fuzzy. This could not possibly be the same man she'd known in college.

"I'm sorry," Daniel said. "I didn't mean to upset you."

"It's okay," she said. "The baby thing is just . . . hard."

"Is it you, or is it him?"

"Damn it, Daniel! That is none of your business."

He didn't reply.

She sighed. "It's me," she said finally. "I'm sure it's me."

"Did the doctor tell you that?"

"The doctors never could tell for sure what it was. Just that it wasn't happening."

"I'm really sorry."

Daniel stood and walked to the railing of the patio.

"There are a lot of things I'm sorry about, Corrie. The biggest thing, though, is that I'm sorry I left you the way I did."

Corrie didn't reply.

"I still don't know why I did what I did, running off that way. I felt . . . I don't know, I guess I felt like if I stayed, I'd never leave. Never leave Middlebrook, never leave the Midwest, never get to do anything . . . important."

"You don't have to explain anything, Daniel."

"Yes, I really do," he said, turning to face her. "Because I hurt you. I was a real bastard, and I'm sorry."

"It's okay," she said softly, rising to stand beside him, leaning against the railing. "I'm okay."

"Yeah," he said, looking away. "You're okay. . . . But I'm not."

Corrie watched his face, wished she could reach over to brush the red hair away from his collar.

"I thought I could save the world, you know? I thought it was my calling, that I could change the world."

"You are helping people. Look at what you've done for Capri, and for that artist, and for all the kids at the center. You've had a huge impact on their lives."

"Maybe," he said, turning to look at her. "But for the one person I loved more than anything, the only difference I made was to hurt her . . . to hurt you.

"And now—" He turned away again. "Now you are happily married. You have the nice house you always wanted, the nice husband, the nice life. And all I can think of is, I still want you.

"How selfish is that?" he said. "Now that you're finally happy, all I want to do is grab you and hold you and never let you go."

Corrie stood absolutely still. She heard the hum of traffic from the freeway below, felt a warm breeze on her skin. She closed her eyes and leaned against the railing, her mind spinning dizzily.

Then she felt Daniel's arms around her, let herself be pulled to him. His lips found hers, softly at first, then harder, more insistent. She leaned into his body, his familiar smell enveloping her. She tilted her head, opened her lips, and kissed him. She felt electric, as if the past ten years had slipped away and she was twenty-two again, in the arms of her lover.

His hands were in her hair, pulling her face closer. She ran her hands down his arms, felt him shudder. God, she felt alive.

An image of Mark appeared in her mind, standing on the balcony of the lake house in his bare feet, smiling at her. What the hell was she doing?

Abruptly, she pulled away from Daniel, ran her hand across her eyes, and shook her head furiously.

Daniel stared at her, his face flushed. She turned and ran from the patio, into the living room, grabbed her purse, and fled the apartment. Running down the stairs, she heard him pounding behind her.

"Corrie! Coriander, wait!"

She didn't stop. Fumbling for her keys, she fought the urge to turn and run back to him. Safely in the car, she gunned the engine and backed out of the lot, looking in the rearview mirror to see him come to a stop in the street behind her. His feet were bare.

"Corrie!"

His voice trailed away behind her.

She drove a block, turned the corner, and stopped the car. She was sobbing now, great heaving gulps. She made no attempt to stop, letting the tears stream down her face and drop onto the steering wheel. What was wrong with her? How could she behave like that? What would Mark think if he ever found out? Oh God, what had she done?

Finally, she sniffled to a calm and realized she had no idea how to get back to the hotel. She'd followed Daniel through this maze of streets and she didn't know how to get back. She sat a few minutes, willing herself not to scream, then pulled her cell phone from her purse and the scrap of paper he'd given her earlier with his phone number.

He picked up on the first ring.

"Corrie?"

"I don't know how to get back to my hotel," she said, trying hard to keep her voice steady.

"Corrie, please . . . just come back. I promise I won't kiss you again. Just come back."

"I can't."

"Please, Corrie. I promise—"

"Damn it, Daniel! I can't. I can't go through this again. You left us before and . . . I can't! Please, just tell me how to get to the freeway. I can take it from there."

She wrote down the directions he gave, then hung up. The phone began ringing as she pulled away from the curb, but she didn't answer.

When she got to the hotel, she took a long, hot shower, as if she could wash away the day, the dinner, the kiss. She picked up her cell phone, started to dial Mark's number, then stopped. It was after nine in Pasadena, after midnight at home. She couldn't call now and wake him up.

Setting the phone aside, she closed her eyes and crossed herself.

Dear God, please forgive me. I'm so sorry! I don't know why I kissed him, but I won't ever do it again. I promise, God. I promise I'll be a good wife. Please give me strength. Please bless my marriage. Please . . .

She lay back on the bed, her arm over her eyes, and thought of Mark. He'd be asleep by now, alone in their bed. She would make it up to him. As soon as she got home, she'd try harder to be happy, to be a good wife, to love him more.

16

The cell phone woke Bryn from an uneasy sleep. She looked at the caller ID . . . Paul again. He'd called several times the day before, but she hadn't picked up.

Oh well, I can't avoid him forever.

Leaning back in bed, she flipped open the phone.

"Hello?"

"Hey, baby. Where are you? I've been going out of my mind."

"It's over, Paul. I've moved out."

"Look, baby, whatever I did, I'm sorry."

"You didn't do anything." Bryn ran her hand across her eyes. Her stomach churned.

"Then why'd you leave? Come on, Bryn. The bed is lonely without you."

"I'm not coming back."

"Look, you always say that, and you always come back. So why don't you spare us both the big scene and just come home now?"

Bryn closed her eyes, willing her stomach to calm down.

"I'm pregnant, Paul."

The words slipped out before she could stop them.

Bryn waited, listening to the quiet on the other end of the phone.

"Well," Paul finally sputtered. "Well . . . don't worry about it. We can fix that. I know a good clinic in Indianapolis. . . ."

"I'm not ending this pregnancy, Paul."

"What?"

"I said, I'm not having an abortion. I'm having this baby."

Silence again.

"Listen, I'm not asking for anything from you," Bryn said. "I'm having this baby, and I don't expect you to have any part of it."

"Well, shit, Bryn . . . You can't just drop something like this on me and . . . what do you want me to do?"

"Nothing." Bryn sighed. "Just leave me alone."

She snapped the phone closed and sat up. *Damn morning sickness!*

She heard the phone ringing as she ran for the bathroom.

Bob poured her a cup of tea as she sat holding her head in her hands.

"Well, at least he knows. That's good."

He handed her the tea, smiling as she moaned at the smell.

"Go on, drink it. And eat some crackers. It'll help."

He watched her sip at the tea and nibble a saltine.

"What did he say?"

Bryn raised dark eyes to look at him. "He told me he knew a good clinic where I could get an abortion."

Bob shook his head and sighed. "Maybe he just needs some time to get used to the idea. He wasn't expecting it."

"Whatever. I don't care. I told him I don't expect him to be part of it."

"What if he changes his mind? What if he wants to be part of it?"

Bryn shook her head and reached for another cracker. "He won't.

"I guess I'd better start looking for an apartment," she said, wiping crumbs from the table into her hand.

"There's no rush, Bryn. You can stay as long as you want."

"You're sweet," she said. "But you have the boys now. It'll be easier on everyone if I'm not here."

"Well, don't worry about it today," he said. "Just take it easy.

And maybe . . . maybe you could watch the boys for me again today? I'm going to call Sarah to get some names of sitters, but I have to go to work this morning."

"Sure," she said, smiling. "You go ahead. We'll have fun."

Bryn's phone rang again after Bob left for work. She turned it off without looking at the caller ID.

❧ 17 ❧

Corrie sat watching the sunrise. She hadn't slept more than a couple hours, watching the numbers on the clock click steadily by.

I should go home, she thought. *This morning . . . now. I should just go home. What am I doing here?*

The ring of her cell phone startled her. She checked the number, her sister's.

"Hey, Maya," she answered. "What's up?"

"Hey, sis! What's up with you? I called the house last night and Mark said you're in L.A. How come you didn't call me? I could've come down for the day."

Maya was in graduate school in San Francisco.

"Oh," Corrie stammered, "I'm sorry. It was a last-minute trip, a story for the magazine. I'm only going to be here a couple days."

"When are you heading home?"

"Thursday, in the morning."

"How about if I come down there tomorrow? I can get an early flight into Burbank. We can at least have lunch."

Corrie sat a moment, pulling her thoughts together. She hadn't seen her little sister since Christmas.

"Corrie?" Maya's voice rang through the phone.

"Oh, Maya, I don't know. I'm doing this story . . ."

"About Daniel, yeah, I know. Mark told me."

"What did he say?" Corrie clutched the phone tightly.

"That Daniel came into town for your class reunion, and now you've flown off to write a story about him. He didn't sound very happy."

"He's not." Corrie sighed.

"So?" Maya asked.

"So, I'm writing the story."

"And . . . ?"

"And nothing," Corrie said firmly.

"Okay, then make time to have lunch with me tomorrow. There's a regular flight that gets into Burbank at ten. Can you pick me up, or should I get a cab?"

Corrie smiled. Maya was a force of nature.

"I'll pick you up," she said.

She wrote down the flight information, then rose, took a shower, got dressed, and drove to the community center. She had a story to write, and she damned well wouldn't let Daniel interfere with that—not after she'd come all the way to California. It was eight o'clock . . . eleven at home. Too late to call Mark. He'd be at work by now.

"Hello, Miss Bliss." Capri smiled when Corrie walked in. Corrie stood, startled. Capri's hair was lavender today.

"I'm ready for my close up," Capri told her with a laugh.

"I think I liked the pink better."

"Oh, you'll get used to it. Daniel's upstairs. I'll get him."

Capri padded down the hallway, her blue paisley skirt hanging low on her hips beneath a short-cropped T-shirt.

Wait till the alums get a look at her. Corrie smiled at the thought.

She heard Daniel before she saw him.

"Hey, I'm glad you came back. I thought you might not."

"I have a story to write," she said, fiddling with her camera to avoid his eyes.

"I'm sorry about last night," he said softly, reaching for her arm.

"It's okay." She shrugged away from him. "Let's just do this."

"Corrie . . ."

"So, is the artist here today? What was his name? I'd like to interview him."

Daniel sighed. "Darrel, yeah, he's here. Come on, I'll take you to his class."

Corrie spent the morning talking to Darrel, then to several pregnant teenagers who were learning how to care for newborns. She ended the morning in the nursery, snapping photos of toddlers climbing, crawling, and swaying on unsteady legs as they laughed and played. A tiny girl with dark curls and coal-black eyes clung to Corrie's leg as she sat in a rocker.

"Oh, you are just too precious," Corrie cooed, reaching down to raise the baby onto her lap. "Look at these curls."

"That looks good on you."

Corrie turned to see Daniel smiling at her from the doorway. She smiled back, then set the little girl down on the rug and rose.

"I think I have everything I need here," she said. "Except a picture of Capri."

"Let's do that now. Then I'll take you to lunch and we can go meet the board . . . or at least part of it. I couldn't get all of them here on such short notice."

In the lobby, Corrie shot several photos of Capri. She wasn't sure if any of them would be appropriate for the magazine, though. The younger woman posed as if she was on a photo shoot for *Vogue*.

Finally, Daniel laughed. "Okay, that's good. Let's get some lunch."

Corrie stood uncertainly. "Are you coming?" she said finally to Capri.

"Oh," Capri said, turning to Daniel. "I don't know. Am I coming, boss?"

"Do," Corrie said firmly. "I'll buy."

They walked to a nearby falafel shop. Corrie smiled at the reaction Capri inevitably drew from passersby. *Bryn would love her!*

"When are you going back?" Capri asked over her sandwich.

"Thursday morning."

"Why don't you stay a while?"

"I've got to get back to the office. We're putting the December issue together, and I want to make sure this story gets in."

"Well, tonight you should definitely come clubbing with me."

Capri nodded, her lavender head bobbing up and down.

"Come on, it'll be fun. You can meet Mia. Her ex is playing in a great club in Westwood."

"I don't know." Corrie smiled. "I've never been . . . clubbing."

"Then you have to come! Daniel will go, too, so it won't be just girls."

She smiled at Daniel. "Sometimes it's good to have a penis along . . . keeps the other penises away."

"Good to know I have some use," Daniel said, laughing.

"So, that's settled." Capri rose, brushing crumbs from her bare belly. "We'll go at eight. The club won't be too crowded that early."

"I don't . . ." Corrie stammered.

"And come by the apartment first," Capri continued. "I'll find something for you to wear."

With that, she left, her hips swaying, a dark tattoo peeking above the waistline of her skirt.

Corrie sat with Daniel, shredding a paper napkin.

"Don't worry," he said, reaching over to take the paper from her hands.

She pulled her hands away from his.

"I'm not worried."

"Yes, you are," he countered. "You always tear up napkins when you're worried."

She smiled ruefully. He remembered so much.

"And you don't need to worry," he continued. "I promise I will be a perfect gentleman tonight."

He leaned forward. "Seriously, Corrie, I'm sorry about last night. It won't happen again."

Corrie nodded. "You're right," she said firmly. "It won't happen again. It shouldn't have happened at all. I am a married woman, Daniel. Last night I had too much wine and . . . and I got caught up in old memories. It will not happen again."

He raised his hands as if in surrender. "Point taken," he said.

She rose from the table and turned away from him. *By God, it would not happen again!*

After a long, somewhat dull meeting with several board members of the community center, Corrie was glad to be back outside in the hot California sunshine. At least she'd gotten a few good quotes for the story.

She smiled at Daniel, walking briskly ahead of her, then slowing to let her catch up. Daniel was always in such a hurry.

"Did you get everything you need?" he asked.

She nodded, then said, "And I was very impressed."

"At what? My board? They're a good bunch of people, but I wouldn't call them impressive."

"At you," she said, laughing. "God, Daniel . . . you hate meetings. You always hated meetings. And you sat there so . . . so professional. Very impressive."

He laughed with her. "I still hate meetings. But I have to do them for the center. Sometimes it feels like that's all I do . . . meet with the board, meet with donors, meet with parents. All I really want to do is be with the kids."

Corrie smiled. "You might actually be a good father, Daniel. I never would have guessed that."

"There are a lot things you wouldn't have guessed." He smiled at her teasingly.

"Such as?"

"Oh, that's for you to find out on your own."

They walked in silence the rest of the way to the center.

"So," Daniel said when they reached the building, "do you want to follow me again?"

"I don't think so, Daniel." Corrie shook her head. "I think I'd better not go tonight. Maya is coming in tomorrow morning, and I have to pick her up at the airport."

"Come on! You have to go. Capri has her heart set on it. If you don't come, I'll never hear the end of it. And I promise it'll be an early night. I'm too old to stay out late."

* * *

So once again, Corrie found herself following the blue VW Bug through the side streets toward Daniel's apartment. She looked at her watch. Six o'clock here . . . nine o'clock at home. Tuesday night . . . Mark would be at home. She reached for her cell phone and began dialing, then flipped the phone closed, chewing her lip. What would she say to him? *Hi, honey, I'm following my ex-lover back to his apartment, where he kissed me last night. Oh, and by the way, tonight we're going clubbing with his bisexual roommate.*

She would call him in the morning, first thing. She'd set the alarm for four, so she could get him before he left for work. Maybe she'd even move her flight up to tomorrow afternoon. She'd get home tomorrow night and surprise him. She'd make it up to him. She'd be the perfect wife from now on.

"Okay, I've got a bunch of choices." Capri pulled Corrie into her small bedroom, where an assortment of skirts, pants, and tops lay on the bed. "Try this set first."

She shoved a tiny miniskirt and halter top into Corrie's hands. Corrie stared at them, aghast.

"I can't wear that!"

"Sure you can . . . they'll fit you."

"Capri, I am way too old. . . ."

Capri sighed and took the clothes from Corrie. "Okay, then, these."

She handed Corrie a pair of fawn-colored pants that laced up the sides and another tiny top.

"Don't argue, just try them!"

Corrie sucked in her stomach as she pulled the pants on, then turned to stare at her reflection in the mirror. She looked . . . different. Definitely younger. The plunging neckline of the lace T-shirt showed off her cleavage. She looked like she belonged in L.A.

"Okay, that's good." Capri tilted her head, examining Corrie. "But it needs something."

She rummaged through a pile of things at the bottom of her closet.

"Here." She held up one spiked high-heel slingback. "Damn, where's the other one?"

Corrie slid her foot into the shoe, smiling at the rhinestones that sparkled up at her.

"And here!" Capri emerged from the closet, triumphantly holding the other shoe aloft.

"Now," she said, as Corrie teetered unsteadily on the heels. "You need some ornaments."

Corrie sat at the vanity as Capri sorted through a pile of jewelry. The young woman settled on a leather cord necklace with a large turquoise pendant, dangling silver-and-turquoise earrings, a bangle bracelet, and a silver ankle bracelet.

"Okay," Capri said finally. "Now for some face paint."

"Oh no," Corrie said. "I don't think . . ."

But Capri was already tilting Corrie's head back and brushing a dusty rose bronzer on her face.

Fifteen minutes after entering Capri's room, Corrie emerged looking wholly unlike herself. Her cheeks were rouged, her eyes sparkled under black-mascara lashes, her lips shone a brilliant coral, and her hair had been fluffed and sprayed into a mass of curls. She wasn't sure if she felt like a femme fatale or a fool.

Daniel's eyes answered her question. They widened as he took in her slim legs, her flat, bare stomach, the turquoise pendant dangling between her breasts.

"Whoa," he said softly. "You look . . . amazing."

She smiled, then toddled forward. "I feel ridiculous," she said. "I can't even walk in these shoes."

"You'll take them off at the club," Capri promised behind her. "They're just for entrance effect. . . . God, Daniel! You are not wearing that! I am not walking into the Coyote with you dressed like that. Go put on something decent, for God's sake."

Daniel obediently changed into dark pants and a shirt Capri deemed barely adequate, and they walked toward his tiny car.

"I'm not riding in that!" Capri shook her head. She turned toward the red Saturn Corrie had rented. "We'll take Corrie's."

There was no arguing with Capri. Corrie simply handed Daniel the keys to her car.

❧ 18 ❧

The Coyote Club was dark and loud. Corrie followed Capri through the crowd of beautiful people, feeling completely out of place and grateful for Daniel's steadying hand on her back. They found a small table near the stage and Capri headed for the bar. Daniel's eyes never left Corrie. She felt them on her no matter which way she looked.

"You really do look amazing," Daniel shouted above the noise.

"I feel like an adult chaperoning the prom." Corrie laughed. "I feel ancient!"

Capri returned with drinks and another young woman in tow.

"This is Mia," she said, "the love of my life!"

She turned toward the spiked-haired blond she held by the hand and planted a long, wet kiss on her lips. Corrie shook her hand and smiled. And then the two young women were gone, off toward the dance floor, leaving Corrie and Daniel alone at the table.

Corrie sipped at the drink Capri had set before her. "God!" she sputtered. "What is that?"

Daniel took a sip and smiled. "Vodka tonic," he said. "Capri's drug of choice. Do you want me to get you something else?"

"No." Corrie tried to smile. "It's fine."

They sat in silence, watching Capri writhe with her girlfriend to the throbbing beat of the music. It was too loud to talk, too crowded, too hot, too . . . hip. Corrie rubbed her temples, which were beginning to ache.

"Come on." Daniel stood, holding his hand out to her.

She stared at him, then laughed. "God, no! I am *not* going to dance!"

Daniel grinned down at her. "I wasn't asking you to. Let's go."

"What about Capri?"

"She'll go home with Mia," he said. "Come on . . . before my eardrums burst."

He steered her back toward the door, waving at Capri as they left.

She followed him to the car, feeling disoriented and slightly disconcerted.

"So, all that prep for five minutes?" she asked as he started the car.

"Isn't five minutes enough?"

"Yes," she admitted. "I guess it is."

Daniel turned the car west on the Santa Monica Freeway.

"Where are we going?" Corrie asked, staring at the palm trees flashing by.

"To the beach."

"The beach? I can't go to the beach like this."

"Why?"

"Daniel, I can barely stand in these shoes on solid ground. I certainly can't do it on the beach."

"So leave them in the car," he said, reaching up to open the car's sunroof.

"I think I'd better just head back to the hotel," she said. "I have an early—"

"You're meeting Maya, I know. But you can't come all the way to California and not see the ocean."

They parked the car and walked out on the pier. Behind them, the lights of the city spread out for miles. Ahead, the ocean churned, dark and choppy.

"Feels like it's going to rain," Corrie said, wishing she'd brought a jacket. The air was chilly by the water.

"Good, we need it."

Corrie leaned against the railing, staring at the dark expanse of water.

"I love the ocean," Daniel said. "It's so . . . limitless. You feel like you could just get in a boat and go anywhere, you know?"

Corrie shivered. "I think I'll keep my feet on dry land."

"Are you cold? Here, take my jacket." Daniel pulled off his blazer and wrapped it around her shoulders. Corrie breathed in the scent of him, inhaling deeply.

"I'm sorry about last night, Corrie."

"Don't worry about it." She didn't look at him.

"I was a jerk," he said. "You are happily married, and I had no right to kiss you."

They stood in silence, listening to the waves hurl themselves at the shore.

"It just felt like old times, you know? Like when we were in college and everything was right."

Corrie didn't answer. She breathed in the scent from Daniel's jacket, feeling the butterflies in her stomach that had been absent for so many years.

"We'd better go," she said. "I really do have to get back to the hotel."

Sighing, he followed her to the car and drove back to the apartment.

"I'll just change and get going," Corrie said, eyeing the patio where they'd kissed the night before.

"Have a glass of wine first. Just one," he said quickly, before she could respond. "Just one glass of wine for old times' sake. I have a nice pinot noir."

Corrie walked out to the patio while he disappeared into the kitchen. When he returned, he carried a tray with two glasses, a bottle of wine, a loaf of bread, cheese, and strawberries.

"You need to eat something," he said, smiling. "And so do I."

They were eating bread and cheese, sipping wine, and talking idly about college days when Corrie's cell phone rang. She scanned the caller ID. Bryn's apartment. Corrie frowned. *Damn! I thought she left him for good this time.*

"Hey, Bryn, what's up?"

"Corrie? It's Paul."

"Paul? Oh . . . uh, hi."

"Where's Bryn?"

"I'm sorry, Paul. But she doesn't want to see you."

"Look, she might not want to see me, but she damned well *needs* to see me. God, Corrie, I'm going out of my mind. I need to make sure she's okay."

"She's okay, Paul."

"Then where is she staying? I called your house and Mark said you're out of town. So where the hell is Bryn?"

"Paul, I am not going to tell you where she is. She doesn't want to see you."

"I just need to talk to her. I need to make sure she's all right."

Corrie sighed. "She's fine, I promise. She's staying with a friend."

"What friend?"

"I'm hanging up now, Paul."

She flipped the phone closed, leaned back, and sighed.

"So I guess Bryn is finally leaving old Paul for good," Daniel said. "It's about time."

Corrie nodded. "He's no good for her. He never has been."

"Maybe she and Bob will hook up?"

Corrie laughed. "I don't think so. Bryn is *not* the homebody type." She shook her head. "I don't see Bryn settling down anytime soon."

"Not like you," Daniel said. "You are nicely settled down."

"Yes," she said with a slight smile. "I suppose I am."

He filled her glass again. "And are you happy?"

"I guess so." She sipped the wine, felt the smooth, easy buzz of good red wine.

"You guess so? Don't you know so?"

She stood, carrying her glass to the railing, and looked out at the lights of the San Gabriel Valley sparkling below. "I'm happy enough."

"And how much is that . . . happy enough?"

Corrie didn't answer. How much was happy enough?

"You deserve more than that, Corrie. You deserve fireworks and champagne and . . . and bliss."

"That's not real," she replied sadly. "Fireworks and bliss don't last forever."

"Why not?" he asked, rising to stand beside her. "Why can't bliss last forever? You and I kept it going for four years. . . . Why couldn't it last forever?"

"Because you left." Corrie's voice was flat.

"And I'll never forgive myself for that. I'll pay for it forever." His voice was tired.

Corrie turned to him, reached out to touch his face.

"You'll never know," she said softly.

He looked at her, his eyes narrowed.

"Corrie, last night on the phone, you said I left you . . . but you didn't say 'me,' you said 'us.' "

Corrie shook her head, turning away.

"Why did you say that?"

Corrie felt her legs begin to tremble so hard she had to clutch the rail for support. The tears she'd fought all day spilled over, trickling down her face. *God! I can't do this. I have to get out of here.*

She turned to go, but Daniel had her by the arm. "Corrie?" His voice was soft.

"I was pregnant when you left."

She let the tears come, leaning heavily against him, sobbing into his chest.

"I was pregnant . . . and you left."

"Oh my God, I didn't know. Oh, Corrie-Andy, I didn't know."

At the sound of the name—the name only Daniel called her— Corrie gave up all pretense of holding it together.

"You left me . . . you left me alone, and I was pregnant, and I didn't know what to do." She smacked at him, pulling away, hitting at his stomach, his arms, finally connecting with his jaw. "You bastard! You left us both!"

"Shhhhh," Daniel whispered, pulling her tight to him. "Shhhhh.

Oh, Corrie-Andy, I'm so sorry. I'm so sorry." He whispered it over and over again until her sobs quieted.

"What happened?" he asked finally.

"I had an abortion," Corrie hissed. "I killed the baby."

She pulled away from him and began pacing. "I killed our baby, and now I can't have any more. I can't have any more because I killed our baby."

"Did the doctor say that?"

She shook her head, her curls now hanging limply around her face. "But I know that's why. God is punishing me."

"Bullshit!"

The word exploded in the air, startling them both.

"I mean it, Corrie. That's bullshit! Millions of women have abortions every year and then have other babies. If there is a God—and that's a big *if* in my book—but if there is, I can't believe he'd punish you like that. You . . . God, Corrie! You always do the right thing. You always take care of everybody. What kind of God would be that cruel?

"Look." He pulled her close again. "I don't know why you can't get pregnant, but I promise you—I *promise* you—it's not because you had an abortion. I mean, that wasn't even your fault, honey. That was *my* fault. I'm the one who left. I'm the one who walked out. If you have to blame someone, blame me."

He held her while she cried, wiping her tears on his sleeve until it was a sodden mess. Finally, he began kissing her cheek, her forehead, her nose. She raised her face to his, and he kissed her mouth. All of the longing, all of the pain, all of the hurt she'd been feeling swept away in the force of that kiss. She pushed herself closer to him, eager for his taste, his smell, his hands. His kisses were hard, bruising. His hands were hot where they touched her. He took her breath away.

He led her inside, to the back bedroom, and slowly undressed her, kissing each bit of newly exposed skin.

Afterward, they lay together quietly, Corrie resting her head on his chest. She couldn't remember the last time she'd felt so relaxed and complete.

Daniel traced his finger along the scar on her leg.

"How's your mom?" he asked softly.

"The same." Corrie turned away from him, her cheeks reddening.

"I'm sorry." He pulled her shoulder until she faced him.

"Stay," Daniel whispered.

"What?"

"Stay," he repeated. "Stay here . . . with me."

He pulled her tight against him. "Seriously, Corrie, you should stay. Capri's moving out. We could be together, like before. I've got contacts at some of the local papers. I could help you get a job . . . a real job.

"Think about it! You could work for a real newspaper and write about things that matter. Maybe you could do a story now and then about the center. . . . Oh, and you could do grant writing for the center. We could really use you."

Corrie pulled away from him. "I can't stay, Daniel. I shouldn't even be here now."

"Just think about it. You could move in here. I've got the rent covered. We'd be happy. . . . Maybe we could adopt a baby."

Corrie lay in silence. What would it be like, living with Daniel again? Sharing this apartment, eating together every night on the patio, working for a newspaper. She let her mind drift over the possibilities.

"Just think about it," Daniel repeated. Then, abruptly, he said, "I've got to take a leak."

He went to the bathroom, leaving Corrie alone in the four-poster, her thoughts scattered, her body sated.

The phone by the bed rang.

"Daniel?"

But he didn't hear her.

Finally, the answering machine picked up and Corrie was startled into the present by a woman's voice, soft and purring.

"Hey, lover, it's me. Just wondering what time you're picking me up on Friday. God, I can't believe we have the whole weekend! I've got some lovely new toys. Oh, we're going to have fun. Call me."

The machine clicked. Corrie looked up to see Daniel standing in the doorway to the bedroom.

"It's not what you think," he said.

"It's not?" Corrie sat up in bed, clutching the sheet to her chest.

"I mean, it is but it's not. She's not, we're not . . . she's married. We just have fun together sometimes." Daniel sat down on the edge of the bed, his voice pleading.

"So . . . you have a habit of sleeping with married women."

Corrie was out of bed now, pounding down the hall to collect her clothes from Capri's room.

Daniel followed.

"Corrie, it's not like that. You're not like that." He grabbed at her arm, but she pulled away.

"Apparently, I am like that!" Her voice rose, and she felt a sob catch in her throat.

"Corrie!"

She slammed the door to Capri's room in his face and began pulling on her own clothes. Daniel banged on the door, but thankfully, he didn't open it.

Once dressed, Corrie grabbed her shoes and purse, opening the door to find Daniel blocking her way.

"Let me go!" She pushed at him hard, forcing him to step backward.

"Corrie, wait! Can't we talk about it? Can you please just calm down so we can talk?" He reached for her arm, touched her face with his other hand.

Corrie wrenched her arm from his grip and ran for the door. For the second time in two days she was running down the stairs, away from the apartment, away from Daniel. This time, he didn't follow.

≈ 19 ≈

"Hello?" Bryn's voice was groggy.
"Bryn? It's Corrie. Did I wake you up?"
Bryn looked at the clock. It was past midnight.
"No," she said, sitting up in bed and switching on the lamp. "I'm here. What's up? Are you still in L.A.?"
There was a long silence.
"Corrie? Are you okay?"
"No, I'm not okay," Corrie whispered. "I screwed up, Bryn. I screwed up big-time."
Shit! Bryn gripped the phone tightly. She stifled a scream.
"Tell me you didn't sleep with him."
"Oh, God." Corrie's voice shook.
"Corrie, you didn't! Oh my God, tell me you didn't."
Bryn rose and began pacing the floor. "Why? Why would you sleep with Daniel? He abandoned you, for God's sake! He just left you. I was there, Corrie. I remember how bad it was. And you finally have everything you ever wanted. Why would you risk that for the man who left you?"
"I don't know," Corrie sobbed. "It felt so right. It felt like before. I felt . . . whole again."
Bryn sighed deeply, willing herself to stay calm.

"All right, so you screwed up big-time. But it's over, right?"

"Yes!" Corrie's voice was shrill. "God, yes, it's over!"

"What happened?"

Corrie's voice shook. "Apparently I'm not the only married woman he's sleeping with."

"Oh God, honey! Are you sure?"

"I was still in bed, just lying there, and his phone rang. And this woman is talking about their weekend together. And he said, 'It's no big deal. She's married.' Oh my God, Bryn! How could I be so stupid?"

"Okay, look." Bryn forced her voice to stay calm. "You screwed up . . . big-time. But it's over. It's over and done with. And you're going to be all right. You're not the same little girl who fell in love with Daniel in college. You're a grown woman now. You're strong, you have friends, you have a life. And you *will* survive this."

Bryn waited, but Corrie didn't respond.

"Did you hear me, Corrie? You are going to be fine. It's not like back then. You're stronger now. He can't hurt you again. You'll come home and you'll put it behind you. And you will *never* be stupid like that again."

"I have to tell Mark," Corrie whispered.

"Like hell!" Bryn barked. "The last thing, and I mean the *very* last thing, you will do is tell Mark!"

"I have to tell him. He's my husband."

"Yes, Corrie, he is your husband. And he loves you. And the only thing you will do if you tell him is hurt him."

"But . . ."

"But nothing! It's over, it's done. You messed up. But you will *not* mess up your whole life because of one stupid mistake."

Corrie was silent.

"Do you *want* to hurt Mark?"

"No! Of course not."

"Then you keep your mouth shut!" Bryn paced furiously around the little room, her bare feet slapping the wood floor. "Maybe, *maybe* it would make you feel better to tell him. I doubt it, but maybe. But what will it do to Mark?"

"I can't . . . God, Bryn, how can I not tell him?"

"Corrie, what you're going to do is this—you're going to come home, you're going to be extra nice to your husband, you're going to focus on all the good things in your life, and you're going to forget about this whole thing. Forget about Daniel, forget about all of it. You messed up, yes. Honey, we all mess up. But you are *not* going to destroy your entire life because of one mistake. Telling Mark would be an even bigger mistake. It would hurt him. It would wreck your life. It would be a disaster. You know that, right?"

Corrie was silent for a long minute.

"I've never lied to Mark before."

"Okay, so now you will lie to him. You'll lie to him for his own good. Telling him would be the most selfish thing you could do, Corrie. Don't you get that? Just come home and pretend it never happened. Okay?"

"God, Bryn! I feel so bad. I feel like such a bad person."

"You're not a bad person." Bryn's voice softened. "You are a really good person who made a really bad mistake. But that doesn't mean Mark should suffer, right? Feel guilty for a while. Hell, you probably *should* feel guilty. But Mark shouldn't have to deal with it. You know I'm right."

"But how can I just pretend . . . ?"

"You'll pretend because you have to. Just like you used to pretend your mom was like other moms. You'll lie to protect Mark like you lied to protect Maya and Caerl all those years."

"I'm so tired." Corrie's voice was soft. "I'm so tired of lies."

"You're upset and you're confused," Bryn said. "Just come home, honey. Come home and pretend like it never happened. And after a while, it will be just like it never did happen."

They sat in silence for a minute. Bryn sat down on the edge of the bed, battling a wave of nausea. *Geez, and I thought my life was complicated.*

"Are you okay?" she asked again.

"I don't know."

"You will be," Bryn said firmly. "You're stronger than you know. Hell, Corrie, you are the strongest person I know. And at least now you know, you know for sure, that Daniel is not the saint you thought he was. And maybe you can finally just move on and put him behind you."

"Will you pick me up at the airport tomorrow?"

"I thought you weren't coming home till Thursday."

"I changed my flight. I get in tomorrow night at nine. Will you please pick me up?"

"Sure," Bryn said, digging an old receipt out of her purse and searching for a pen. "What airline?"

She wrote the information on the receipt and assured Corrie again that she would be at the airport. Finally, she hung up the phone and flopped back down onto the bed. She was exhausted and wide awake.

How could Corrie sleep with that jerk again? Why the hell did she ever care about him?

She shook her head and pulled on her robe, heading to the kitchen for a glass of water. When she turned on the light in the dining room, she found Bob sitting at the table, a glass in his hand.

"Hey," he said, blinking in the light. "What's up?"

"I need a glass of water," she said. She wouldn't tell him about Corrie.

"Did I hear your phone ring?"

"Yeah." Bryn poured herself a glass of water and sat down at the table. "Corrie called."

"Is she okay?"

"Yeah. She's coming home tomorrow night instead of Thursday."

He raised his eyebrows and she shrugged.

"I think she's just missing Mark. Why are you still up?"

"Can't sleep."

She rose and kissed the top of his head. "Don't stay up too late."

Bryn walked back to her room, closing the door behind her, wondering how everyone's life got screwed up so fast.

"Corrie!" Maya waved at her across the terminal, grinning broadly. "God, it's good to see you!"

Corrie hugged her sister, amazed as she always was at how tall her little sister had gotten. Maya stood four inches above her.

"I'm glad to see you, too." Corrie stepped back to look at Maya. "You get more beautiful every time I see you."

Maya laughed and looped her arm through Corrie's.

"Back atcha," she said. "But seriously, Corrie, you look great. I think Southern California agrees with you."

"I don't know about that," Corrie said. "But either way, it doesn't matter. I'm going home today."

"I thought you were staying till tomorrow."

"I changed my flight. After lunch, I'm heading straight to LAX to catch a two-o'clock flight."

Maya raised her eyebrows, but Corrie just kept walking.

"I saw a Mexican place on the way here," she said. "How does that sound to you?"

"I'm always up for fajitas."

They walked to the car, arm in arm, in companionable silence.

"How's Mom?" Maya asked as Corrie pulled out of the parking lot.

Corrie sighed. "She's okay, I guess. The same."

"Is Caerl still living with her?"

"He moved out last month. I think he's staying with that guy from the plant, Sam."

Maya snorted. "Sam," she spat. "Good lord, what a loser."

"Well, at least it gets Caerl out of Mom's house."

"For now," Maya said. "But you know he'll be back. He always comes back."

"How about you?" Corrie asked. "How's school?"

"It's good. I'm good. . . . I met someone."

Corrie glanced sideways at her, noting Maya's pink cheeks.

"Someone special?"

"Maybe. I don't know yet. His name is Bryan. He's in the same program. He's nice."

"Well, he'd better be nice." Corrie grinned. "Or he'll have to deal with your big sister."

At the restaurant they ordered fajitas and beers and relaxed into a booth.

"So," Maya said, watching Corrie's face. "How were things with Daniel?"

Corrie didn't answer for a minute, then she tried for a smile.

"Daniel's fine," she said. "Still busy trying to save the world."

"Was it weird seeing him after all these years?"

"Yeah," Corrie said. "It was weird."

"Mark sounded pretty unhappy about your trip."

"He was. He is." Corrie picked up a napkin and began shredding it. "I should have told him right away that I had seen Daniel. But I didn't, not until I told him about the trip."

"Why not?"

"I'm not sure. I wasn't going to come and then I decided I was going to come, and then I had to tell Mark. And he thought I was hiding things from him."

"Which you totally were."

Corrie raised her eyes to Maya's. Her little sister was as blunt and direct as she'd always been.

"I guess so."

"And?" Maya waited, never taking her eyes from Corrie's.

"And . . . I slept with Daniel."

Maya's eyes widened, but she said nothing.

"Go ahead," Corrie said, dropping her gaze. "Tell me how badly I've messed up. Tell me what a bad person I am. I already know."

Maya took her hand across the table.

"Yes, you messed up," she said. "But no, you're not a bad person. You loved Daniel. You've always loved Daniel."

Corrie shook her head, staring at the table.

"So what are you going to do now?" Maya asked.

"I'm going home! I'm going home and I'll write the damned story and then I'll never think about Los Angeles or Daniel again."

"Hmmm." Maya sounded unconvinced.

"Seriously," Corrie insisted. "It was a mistake and it's over and I just want to forget about it."

The waiter brought their beers, and Corrie took a long drink.

"I always liked Daniel," Maya said, smiling. "I liked the way you were when you were with him. You were braver with him. You were happier."

Corrie raised her eyebrows.

"Seriously, remember the time he took us to King's Island and talked you into riding the roller coaster? You never would have done that without Daniel, and you loved it!"

Corrie closed her eyes, remembering the rush of adrenaline as the car topped the first hill, how she'd screamed and clutched at Daniel's arm and how, at the end of the ride, she'd felt so proud of herself.

"Or the time we went camping in Brown County, remember that? God, neither of us had ever even been in a tent before. And Daniel taught Caerl to swim. He was really good to Caerl, even when Caerl was being a jerk."

Corrie smiled at the memory.

"When's the last time you went on a roller coaster, Corrie? Or went camping? Or did anything just for fun?"

Maya leaned across the table, holding Corrie's eyes.

"Mark is a good guy; I know that." Maya's voice was gentle. "He's nice and he's safe and he's predictable."

"And he loves me."

"Yes, he loves you. But do you love him, Corrie? I mean really love him right down to your toes? Do you love him the way you loved Daniel?"

"Daniel left." Corrie's voice was flat.

"But you could have gone with him."

Corrie glanced up at her sister, then took another long drink.

"I remember, Corrie, even if you don't. Everyone else may buy into the whole 'poor Corrie' routine, but he asked you to go with him, he begged you to go. You had a choice. And you chose to stay in Middlebrook."

Corrie shook her head again. "You don't understand it all," she began.

"No," Maya agreed. "I don't understand, and I'm sure I don't know all of it. And I'm not judging you, Corrie. I promise I'm not. But I hate it when you get into that victim mode. You do it with Mom and you do it with Bryn and you do it with Mark. The only person who wouldn't let you be that way was Daniel."

Corrie felt her cheeks burning. Damn it, why did Maya always have to be right?

"Are you going to tell Mark?" Maya's voice was soft.

"I don't know," Corrie said. "I think I should. Bryn says I shouldn't. What do you think?"

"I think you have to do what is going to make you happy." Maya took a bite of her fajita and chewed. "God, this is good!"

"What will make me happy is going home and being with my husband." Even to Corrie's ears, her voice sounded shrill.

"Okay," Maya agreed, smiling. "Then that's what you should do."

They ate in silence for a moment. Finally, Corrie touched her sister's hand.

"Isn't that what I should do?" she asked, her voice trembling.

"Corrie, you're a grown woman, and the only person whose happiness you're responsible for is your own. If you want to be with Mark, then go back to Middlebrook and be with Mark. But don't go back there just because you think that's what you should do. That's not fair to anyone, not to Mark and not to you, either."

"I do want to be with Mark," Corrie said. "He's my husband, and I love him."

"Okay," Maya agreed again. "Then go home and be with him."

"Okay." Corrie took another drink of her beer.

"Just don't kid yourself into believing you're going to just forget about sleeping with Daniel."

"I know," Corrie said softly.

And she did.

~ 21 ~

Corrie pulled her bag from the overhead rack and waited for the crowd in the plane to clear out. Rubbing her bloodshot eyes, she stumbled into the terminal, caught sight of Bryn, and burst into tears.

"Okay, okay, shhh," Bryn whispered, wrapping her arms around Corrie's shaking frame. "It's going to be all right. Everything is going to be fine now that you're home."

Corrie sobbed on Bryn's shoulder for several minutes, then sniffled and straightened up.

"I messed up so bad," she said, digging in her purse for a tissue.

"Yep," Bryn agreed. "You did. But it's over now. You're home, you're safe, and you'll just pick up and go on. You'll go on like it never happened."

Corrie stared at her, eyes brimmed with tears.

"How?" she moaned. "How can I act like it didn't happen? It did happen. I slept with Daniel. I cheated on my husband. I broke my wedding vows! Even if Mark never knows, I'll know. I'll always know."

"You need a drink," Bryn said, taking Corrie by the hand and pulling her toward the airport bar.

Corrie allowed herself to be pulled along, blowing her nose again.

"Cabernet," Bryn said to the bartender. "And a seltzer water."

She glanced at Corrie, expecting a comment on her drink choice. But Corrie simply blew her nose again.

"Tell me you're finally over him," she said, putting her hand over Corrie's. "Tell me, please, that you finally see him for what he is."

"He's just Daniel," Corrie said softly. "He wants to save the world, just like always. But . . . but he doesn't seem to care very much about anyone, really. I mean, he cares in theory, just not in real life. Does that make sense?"

"No," Bryn said, putting a twenty-dollar bill on the bar and reaching for her seltzer. "I mean, yes, in a way." She took a sip, wrinkling her nose at the acidic taste. "He talks a good talk about helping people, but really, he just wants to feel like he's a savior.

"Okay, so now you know. I mean, I wish you'd figured it out ten years ago. But at least now you know. He's not a selfless saint. He's just a jerk with a God complex. And you are finally, *finally* over him. Thank God!"

Corrie sipped her wine again.

"I mean, you are over him, right?"

"Yes," she said softly. "I think I finally am really over him."

"Good!" Bryn's voice rose. "That's something to drink to."

"What are you drinking?" Corrie asked.

"Seltzer water." Bryn took another sip.

"Seriously? Why?"

"I'm driving," Bryn said.

Corrie stared at her for a long minute.

"Are you okay?" she finally asked.

"I'm fine," Bryn said. "Just . . ."

"Just what?"

"Just . . . well, I'm a little bit pregnant."

Corrie sat a minute, waiting for the punch line. Finally, she slapped at Bryn's shoulder. "Yeah, right," she said.

Bryn said nothing.

"Bryn?" Corrie's eyes widened. "Seriously? You're pregnant?"

Bryn nodded, watching Corrie's face carefully.

"Oh my God!" Corrie whispered. "Is that why you left Paul?"

Bryn nodded again.

"So . . . so what are you going to do?"

"I'm going to have a baby," Bryn said.

"Wow." Corrie sat back in her chair, staring at her friend. "Just . . . wow."

"I know." Bryn grinned. "Crazy, right?"

"Are you sure?"

"What?"

"Are you sure you're pregnant? I've had times I thought I was . . ."

"Yeah, I'm sure. I'm positive. I took a test. And then I took another one. And then I took another one. I figure three can't all be wrong. Plus, I'm puking my guts out all the time and my boobs hurt like hell. So yeah, I'm sure."

"Does Paul know?"

Bryn nodded. "I wasn't going to tell him, but Bob told me I had to."

"Bob knows?"

Bryn nodded again.

"Oh." Corrie's voice was small.

"I was going to tell you first," Bryn said, reaching for Corrie's hand. "But you've been kind of preoccupied, and then you went to L.A., and now . . . well, now you know."

"I'm sorry," Corrie said, squeezing Bryn's hand. "I should have been here for you."

"It's okay," Bryn said. "I've only known a couple weeks. And now you know. And I'm going to need so much help. I mean, God, Corrie, I . . . I'm really scared." Her voice trailed away.

"You can so do this!" Corrie spoke firmly. "And I will be here every step of the way. And so will Bob. And . . . and Sarah will be, too."

"Thanks," Bryn said, smiling.

"So what did Paul say?"

"He told me he knew a good clinic."

Corrie squeezed her hand. "Did you think about that?"

"I did at first. But, then . . . I don't know. I guess then I realized it's not just a theory. It's a baby. And then I started thinking maybe this is my only chance, you know?"

"I do know," Corrie said softly.

"I'm sorry," Bryn said. "I know you want to get pregnant so much. I keep thinking it should be you."

Corrie's eyes filled again, but she smiled. "Don't worry about it," she said. "I'm happy for you. A baby . . . wow!"

"Yeah, a baby." Bryn's hand rested lightly on her stomach. "I still can't believe it."

"So, you're really done with Paul . . . for good this time?"

Bryn nodded. "I don't want anything from him," she said firmly. "He is definitely not father material."

"Well, good!" Corrie's voice was louder than she'd expected. "Sorry," she said more softly. "I've waited a long time to hear you say that."

"Me too," Bryn said. "I mean, I've waited a long time for you to be over Daniel."

Corrie's shoulders slumped slightly. She sipped her wine.

"So . . ." Bryn raised her glass to Corrie. "Here's to new beginnings . . . for both of us!"

They touched glasses and drank.

"I love you, you know," Bryn said.

"I know. I love you, too."

"And you're going to get through this."

Corrie nodded at her. "And so will you."

They sat in silence for a minute, each wrapped in private thoughts.

"So," Corrie said, "where are you going to live?"

"Oh." Now Bryn's shoulders slumped. "I'm not sure. I mean, it's great at Bob's. But obviously I can't stay there. He's in the middle of a divorce and all.

"Oh!" Bryn sat up straighter. "And speaking of that, you won't believe what Wendy did."

She told Corrie about the picture Cody had brought home.

"Oh my God!" Corrie gasped. "What is wrong with that woman?"

"I don't know," Bryn said. "But at least Bob is finally being proactive. He took the picture to an attorney and he's suing for full custody."

"Good!" Corrie said. "He definitely needs full custody. I mean . . . God, she's just a loon, isn't she?"

"She is," Bryn agreed. "But if Bob is going into a custody battle, I can't be living in his house, right?"

"Yeah," Corrie said. "That probably wouldn't look good. So . . . you can stay with Mark and me."

Bryn shook her head.

"You guys are going to need some time," she said. "You don't need a houseguest right now."

"No," Corrie said. "You can stay with us. You *should* stay with us."

Bryn simply shook her head again.

"No," she said. "I think it's time, finally, for me to start taking care of myself. I mean, I'm thirty-two years old. I'm going to have a baby, for Christ's sake. I need to learn to take care of things for myself."

"Well, the offer stands, always, if you need it."

"I know. Thank you."

"So, Bryn . . ." Corrie hesitated.

"What?"

"Do you have insurance?" Corrie's brow furrowed.

"Actually, I do," Bryn said, smiling. "Thank God I do! Two years ago, when Paul and I were on the outs, I took out a policy. I figured, I was thirty, I probably should have something, just in case."

"Does it cover maternity?"

"Yeah." Bryn grinned. "Maybe I had a premonition or something. But I got a plan with maternity. So I'm set."

"Thank God!"

"Thank Goddess," Bryn said, laughing. "If I had a pregnancy premonition, I'm pretty sure it was from a goddess, right?"

Corrie smiled, then leaned forward and hugged her tightly. "I really am happy for you."

"Thank you."

✨ 22 ✨

Corrie paced the living room, willing herself not to pour a glass of wine. She needed to be clearheaded now, more than ever in her life. It was almost eleven and Mark wasn't home yet, but he surely would be soon.

Bryn is pregnant. She shook her head, fighting tears. *Bryn is pregnant! God, that is just so . . . amazing.*

She thought back to all the nights in college when they had lain in bed talking about their futures. Corrie's plans had always included children. Bryn's had definitely not.

Corrie sighed heavily. If only she'd had a baby, maybe she wouldn't have gone to Los Angeles. Maybe she wouldn't have felt what she did for Daniel. Maybe . . .

She would write the story about the community center and then never think about Daniel again. Never! She would be the perfect wife to Mark. Maybe they could start pursuing an adoption. She would make it work.

When she heard the garage door opening, she went into the bathroom and splashed cold water on her face.

"Corrie?" Mark's voice called from the hall. "Are you home?"

"I'm here," she said, walking into the kitchen.

"I thought you weren't coming until tomorrow."

"I changed my flight," she said, smiling at him. "I missed you."

He simply looked at her for a long minute, then sat down at the breakfast bar.

"So," he said, his voice measured, "how was L.A.?"

"Awful!"

He glanced up at her. "Why?"

"I shouldn't have gone," she said, sitting beside him at the bar. "You were right. I shouldn't have gone. It was a mistake."

He simply sat silently.

"Daniel is not who he used to be. Or maybe he is and I just didn't see him for what he is before. He's got a God complex, you know? I mean, the center is great and they are doing really good stuff. But in the end, it's all about Daniel."

Mark got up and walked to the fridge. "Do you want a glass of wine?"

She nodded, and he poured two glasses.

"Why didn't you tell me when he was here?" His voice was soft.

"I should have," she said. "I know I should have. I don't even know why I didn't except . . . he still pushes my buttons. I mean, he's here for five minutes and I'm questioning every choice I've ever made. I see myself through his eyes and I never measure up. I don't know how he does it or why it still works, but it's done now. All those years I wondered what my life would have been like if he'd stayed, and now I know it wouldn't ever have worked."

Mark said nothing.

"I'm really sorry," Corrie whispered. "I'm sorry I didn't tell you before when he was here. And I'm sorry I worried you. And I'm really sorry I went out there."

"Do you still love him?" His voice was so low she could barely hear him.

"No. I don't."

She covered his hand with hers. "I love you, Mark. I love you and I love our life and I don't ever, ever want to lose that or mess it up."

Mark smiled then, and Corrie felt a rush of tears welling in her eyes.

"I missed you," he said.

"I missed you, too."

He stood and pulled her to her feet, wrapped her in a tight embrace, and kissed her cheek, her nose, her mouth.

"Do you want something to eat?" she asked.

"No," he said, pulling her toward the stairs. "I want you."

For the first time in as long as she could remember, she let herself relax and enjoy her husband. After, they lay curled together, his arm wrapped tight around her.

"I love you," she whispered. But he was already asleep.

She lay awake in the dark, quietly thanking God for Mark, for her home, for her life.

"I promise, God," she whispered, "I promise I'll be a good wife. I'll never mess up again. And I . . . just, thank you. Thank you, God. Thank you."

She fell asleep just before dawn, still curled against Mark's sleeping body.

∾23∾

"Hey, Kenetha!" Corrie called as she walked into the offices of *The Current*.

"Hey! How was California?" Kenetha followed Corrie into her office.

"Eh." Corrie shrugged. "It was okay, I guess."

"Just okay?" Kenetha grinned at her.

"Yeah, just okay." Corrie set a pile of folders on her desk. "I think it will be a good story, anyway."

"You had a bunch of phone calls yesterday." Kenetha pointed to the phone on Corrie's desk, its red light blinking frantically.

Corrie sighed. "I'll listen later. Right now, I'm going to write this article while it's still fresh."

"Okay," Kenetha said. "There's coffee, if you want a cup."

Corrie turned on her computer and opened her email account, which quickly filled with messages. Most of them were from Daniel.

She moved the messages to the trash folder and highlighted them, her finger poised on the delete button.

She sighed again and opened the top email.

Come on, Corrie, you can't just ignore me forever.
Please call me.

She scanned through the rest of Daniel's messages, each more pleading than the one before.

> *I'm so sorry I hurt you. It's the last thing I wanted to do. I love you. I've always loved you. Please come back and let me explain. Or I'll come there. I have to see you.*

She squeezed her eyes closed, willing her stomach to settle. Then she took a deep breath and hit reply.

> *Daniel, please don't email me or call me or try to get in touch. What happened was a mistake, and I don't want to even think about it, let alone talk about it. I let myself get caught up in old feelings that don't have a place in my life anymore. I love my husband. I love my life. What you and I had was over a long time ago. If you ever cared about me at all, please, just let it go.*

She hit send and deleted Daniel's messages. Then she poured herself a cup of coffee and sat down to write. Three hours later, the article was done. She read it over quickly, smiling at the quotes from Capri. Then she emailed the article and related pictures to her designer, deleted the photos from her camera, and leaned back in her chair, surveying her office. Maybe she would paint it again. The cream-colored walls were starting to look a bit dingy.

"Hey, do you want to get lunch?" Kenetha stood in the doorway.

"Sure," Corrie said. "That sounds good."

Normalcy, she thought. *That's exactly what I need now, just normalcy.*

After work, she drove home, congratulating herself on getting through the day without falling apart. She pulled into the driveway and skidded to an abrupt stop. Standing on her front porch, Daniel raised his hand in greeting and walked toward the car. Corrie's stomach lurched.

She parked in the driveway and got out of the car, not looking into his face.

"Hey, you," he said softly.

"What are you doing here?"

"When I didn't hear back from you, I just . . . I needed to come and make sure you're all right."

"I'm fine," she said firmly.

"Corrie-Andy." His voice was pleading. "Just talk to me, okay? I just want to talk."

"Go home, Daniel." She raised her eyes to his, willing her voice to stay flat. "Go back to Los Angeles and leave me alone."

"I can't." He reached for her hand, but she pulled back, edging toward the front door.

"Well, then go to Bob's. Go to New York. Go to hell. I don't care where you go, just go away!"

"You don't mean that," he said, his blue eyes wide. "We still love each other. We belong together. I know I messed up before, but . . . but don't I get a second chance? Don't we deserve a second chance?"

"It was a mistake," Corrie said, staring him steadily in the face. "I messed up. I let myself get caught up in old, unresolved feelings. But we don't belong together, Daniel. We never did, really. We don't get another chance."

"But . . ." He reached for her arm, and she pulled away again.

"I don't love you," she said. "I don't love you and I don't want to be with you. I love my husband. I love Mark."

"If you loved Mark, you wouldn't have made love to me. You couldn't have. I know you, Corrie. I know you better than anyone else ever will. You couldn't make love to me if you didn't still love me. That's not who you are."

Corrie shook her head firmly. "The girl who loved you is gone. She died when you left and she's never coming back."

She stepped onto the porch, fumbled for her key.

"Go back to California and leave me alone."

"Corrie, wait!"

She slid into the house, locking the door behind her. She leaned against the door, willing him to leave.

"Corrie!" He banged on the door. "Please come out and talk to me."

She slumped to the floor, shaking, waiting. After a long time, the banging stopped. Peeking from behind the curtain, she saw Daniel walk to a car parked at the curb, get in, and drive away.

"Please, God," she begged, "please let him go back to California. Please make him leave me alone. Please don't let Mark find out what I did."

The phone in her purse startled her with a shrill ring.

"Hello?"

"Hey, babe!" Mark's confident voice calmed her immediately. "I'm on my way home and I thought I'd stop at the store for some wine. Do we need anything else?"

"No," she said. "All I need is you."

She paced the floor for several minutes. Then she called Bryn.

"Hey, how are you feeling?"

"Ugh!" Bryn's voice was hoarse.

"Sick?"

"Only all the time. How are you?"

"Daniel was here."

"Shit! When? Is he there now?"

"No, I made him leave. He was waiting on the porch when I got home from work."

"What did he say?"

"That he loves me. That we belong together. That we deserve a second chance."

"Bastard!" Bryn spat. "What did you say?"

"I told him that I don't love him. I love Mark. And he needs to go back to L.A."

"Good! Good for you!" Bryn said. "Do you think he's coming here?"

"Probably. He doesn't have a lot of friends in Middlebrook."

"Let him come! I'll send him packing."

"Bryn, don't!" Corrie's voice rose. "Please don't tell him you know."

"Why?"

"Just, please don't. The only thing I want is for him to go back to California. I don't want a lot of drama. I can't handle it. I just want things to be the way they were."

"Shhh," Bryn whispered into the phone. "Someone's at the door. I'll bet it's him."

Corrie waited.

"What should I do?" Bryn asked.

"Let him in, I guess. But please, Bryn, please don't say anything to him about . . . us. Promise!"

"Okay." Bryn sighed. "I promise. But if he starts in about you, I'm going to kill him. I'll call you tomorrow."

Bryn opened the door slightly and peered out. Before she could say a word, Daniel pushed the door open and walked into the house.

"Where's Bob?" he asked, looking around the room.

"Picking the boys up from the sitter," Bryn said. "What are you doing here?"

"I could ask you the same thing." Daniel sat on the couch and crossed his legs. "Why are you still here?"

"I'm staying for a while, not that it's any of your business." Bryn sat across from him, folding her arms over her stomach.

"Do you think that's a good idea?" Daniel asked. "Bob's going through a divorce, you know. It could get ugly. You could make it worse."

"Bob *asked* me to stay. I'm helping with the boys."

Daniel snorted.

"And you haven't answered my question," Bryn spat. "What the hell are *you* doing here?"

Daniel said nothing.

"Fine," Bryn snapped. "But you can't stay here. The boys are living with Bob now, and I'm in the guest room."

Daniel only smirked at her.

Bryn rose and stamped into the kitchen, where she had a beef stew simmering on the stove. *God damn him!*

A few minutes later, the front door opened and bedlam ensued as the boys raced through the house, yelling and laughing.

"Hey, Daniel! What are you doing back in Middlebrook?" Bob's voice carried into the kitchen.

"I have a few things I need to get sorted out." Daniel's voice was soft. Bryn had to strain to hear him.

"Micah! Take your backpack to your room," Bob called.

Bryn stepped from the kitchen and smiled as the little boy ran into the room, skidding to a stop just short of the coffee table. He grinned at Bryn, picked up his bag, and ran back down the hall, sliding in his stocking feet on the wooden floor.

"So." Bob sat down across from Daniel. "Everything okay?"

"Yeah, I just have a few things I need to figure out," Daniel repeated.

"I told him he can't stay here," Bryn said. "No room."

Daniel looked from her to Bob.

"You can sleep on the couch if you want," Bob said.

"Great, thanks!"

Bob turned to Bryn. "How are you feeling today?"

"I was a hell of a lot better before he showed up!" Bryn returned to the kitchen and put a tray of biscuits into the oven. "Dinner will be ready in ten."

"So," she heard Daniel ask, "is she staying permanently?"

"No," Bob said, "just till she finds a place."

"Hey, Bryn!" Cody ran into the kitchen. "Look what I made today!"

Bryn took the picture the child held out to her.

"Cool!" she said, smiling. "Who's that?"

"It's my family," Cody said. "That's me and that's Micah. And that's Mommy and Luke. And that's you and Daddy."

Bryn felt a small catch in her throat.

"That's beautiful, Cody." She swept him into a hug. "That's really just . . . beautiful."

Looking up, she saw Bob standing in the doorway to the kitchen, frowning slightly.

"Look, Daddy!" Cody held the picture up. "That's all of us."

"Good job, buddy." Bob smiled at his son. "Why don't you wash your hands for dinner."

"Are you gonna put it on the fridge?" Cody asked, holding the picture toward Bob.

"Sure," Bob said, taking the paper from him. "Of course I'm putting it on the fridge. We'll put it right here."

Cody ran toward the bathroom as Bob taped the picture to the refrigerator, then stood back to survey it. Bryn watched him carefully.

"I think it's good, how he's adjusting," she said softly.

Bob sighed and ran his hand through his graying hair.

"I hope so," he said. "I hope so."

Daniel didn't talk much at dinner. Bob seemed quiet, too. But the boys kept up a running dialogue about Legos and Halloween costumes and Spider-Man.

After dinner, Bryn retreated to her room while Bob and Daniel cleaned the kitchen and the boys watched a movie. She didn't want to watch Daniel saunter through the house as if he owned it. When the living room quieted and the boys had gone to bed, she opened the door to her room and tiptoed into the hallway, listening carefully.

"So seriously, man, what are you doing back in Middlebrook?"

"Like I said," Daniel replied, "I have a few things—"

"Yeah, you said that," Bob interrupted him. "What things?"

"Just some things. What are you drinking?"

"Rum and Coke," Bob said. "You want one?"

"Sure."

Bryn shifted from one bare foot to the other, peering around the corner to see Daniel in the same place on the couch. Bob returned with another glass and handed it to his friend.

"Thanks." Daniel took a long drink and leaned back.

Bob sat down opposite him, watching.

"So," Bob said eventually, "I know it's none of my business, but those things you need to figure out . . . is one of them Corrie?"

Bryn held her breath.

Finally, Daniel sighed deeply.

"I still love her," he said, his voice soft. "And I think she still loves me, too."

"She's married." Bob's voice was firm. He leaned forward, hands on his knees. "She's married," he repeated.

"I know," Daniel said. "But I think—"

"I don't care what you think!" Bob's voice rose, startling Bryn and Daniel both.

"You had your chance with Corrie ten years ago, and you bailed on her. She's married now, and she's happy!"

"Is she?"

"Yes, Daniel, she is. She's been going through a hard time with the infertility and stuff, but she and Mark are solid."

"I don't think so."

Bob rose and began pacing the living room. Bryn pulled back so he wouldn't see her standing in the hall.

"Look, man, Corrie is married." Bob's voice was soft but steady. "That means something, Daniel. Just because you saw her and it reminded you of the old days, that doesn't mean you get to come back here and mess with her head."

"I'm not trying to mess with her head." Daniel's voice rose. "I love her. I never stopped loving her. And I think she feels the same way."

"I don't think so," Bob said, shaking his head. "She's good with Mark. They're happy."

"But—"

"But nothing!" Bob's voice rose again, shaking now. "Corrie is married. And you need to stay the hell away from her!"

Bryn shrank against the wall. Of course Bob would feel that way, given the situation he faced with Wendy.

"Marriage doesn't have to be a life sentence." Daniel's voice was flat.

Bob said nothing for a long minute. When he spoke again, it was in a voice Bryn had never heard from him before, gravelly and harsh.

"You can stay for the night. But tomorrow, you need to go back to California."

"But I—"

"We go way back, Daniel," Bob continued. "You're my friend. But if you're here to wreck Corrie's marriage, then you'd better find someplace else to stay."

With that, he stalked into the hallway, nearly bumping into Bryn before he saw her. Taking her hand, he dragged her down the hallway into the guest room and closed the door behind them.

"Did they sleep together?" His voice was soft but firm.

Bryn started to lie, to deny it. Then she looked into his eyes and simply nodded.

Bob sank onto the bed and buried his face in his hands.

"Corrie is really sick about it," Bryn whispered, taking one of his hands in hers. "She knows she messed up, and she just wants to forget about it."

"God," Bob groaned. "What a mess."

They sat side by side on the bed, holding hands.

"Try not to hate her, okay?" Bryn said, squeezing his hand.

"I don't hate Corrie. I could never hate Corrie. I'm just really sorry she slept with Daniel."

"Me too," Bryn agreed.

"Has she told Mark?"

"No!"

Bob looked up in surprise.

"I mean, she was going to, but I told her not to."

Bob said nothing.

"She wanted to," Bryn said. "She was going to. But I told her it would only hurt him. And it would wreck their marriage. And . . . and she's not Wendy, Bob. She's not going to leave Mark for Daniel or for anyone. You know Corrie. She always does the right thing. So she messed up, big-time. But she shouldn't wreck her whole life, and Mark's whole life, because of one mistake. Right?"

Bob sighed heavily. "I guess not."

"Don't tell her you know, okay? She'd die if she thought you knew."

Bob rose and kissed the top of Bryn's head.

"When did life get so screwed up?"

"I don't know," she replied. "But it's not all bad."

He simply stared down at her.

"I mean, you've still got the boys, and they're great. And I've got . . ." She patted her stomach and smiled.

Bob smiled back at her then. "Yeah," he said. "It's not all bad."

He kissed her head again and left, closing the door behind him.

⮠ 24 ⮡

Corrie sat at her desk the next morning, a cup of cold coffee before her, wondering if Daniel had, indeed, gone back to California. What if he showed up at the house again? What if Mark was there next time?

"Please, God," she whispered. "Please just let him go away."

A knock on her office door roused her from her thoughts.

"Hey," Kenetha said softly. "You okay?"

"Yeah," Corrie said. "I'm fine."

"Well, there's a guy here who wants to see you. He says you're old friends."

Daniel's face appeared over Kenetha's shoulder.

Corrie's stomach fell.

"What do you want?" she demanded.

Daniel walked into the office and smiled.

"Don't worry," he said. "I'm going back to L.A. today. I just wanted to see you before I left."

Kenetha looked from him to Corrie, eyebrows raised.

"It's okay, Kenetha." Corrie forced a small smile.

Kenetha left, closing the door behind her.

Daniel sat in a chair opposite Corrie and smiled again. "I'm not going to bite, I promise."

Corrie simply sat, waiting.

"I know," Daniel said, leaning forward. "I shouldn't have come. I shouldn't have come to your house."

"No," she said. "You shouldn't have."

"I just had to make sure you're okay."

"I'm fine."

"Are you? Because you don't seem fine."

Corrie sighed. "Okay, I'm not fine. I'm angry with myself and I hate what I did to Mark. I feel like the worst person in the world. And I just want to forget it."

"I don't," Daniel said, smiling again. "I won't ever forget how it felt to have you in my bed again."

"Stop it!" Corrie stood, holding the desk for support. "Just go back to California, Daniel. For God's sake, please just go away."

"I'm going," he said softly. "I have to be at a board meeting tomorrow. We have a potential donor coming. But I won't just forget about you. You know that, right? I won't ever forget, and I won't stop hoping. And I won't stop trying to convince you to come back. We belong together, Corrie. We always have, we always will."

Corrie shook her head, settling back into her chair, gripping the armrests. "No, we don't," she said firmly. "I belong with Mark. I love him. He's my husband. What I felt for you, that's over, Daniel. I didn't know it until now, but I don't love you anymore. All those years, I wondered if I still did. And now I know I don't."

"Look, Corrie. I know you're upset about Jenny, my . . . friend. I wish to hell you hadn't heard that message. I wish to hell I could make you believe that what we have, what you and I have, is totally different. Jenny is just . . . she's a friend and sometimes we sleep together. That's all. But you, God, Corrie—you're you! You're the one I fell in love with all those years ago. You're the one I never stopped thinking about. You're the one I love. It feels like my life has just been on hold, and now I know why. I love you. I want you back."

"Daniel, I'm sorry. I'm sorry you're unhappy, I am. But . . . but I left because I realized I don't belong with you. I never did, really. My life is here. My family, my friends, my husband—my whole world is here. And it's a good life. I like my life. I love my husband.

And I'm sorry. I don't want to hurt you. But I don't love you any-more."

"I don't believe you." He gazed at her, not blinking.

"Well, that's too bad," Corrie said, rising from her chair and walking to the door of the office. "Because it's the truth."

She opened the door and held it, willing him to leave.

Daniel stared at her in silence for a long moment, then rose and walked to the door. He touched Corrie's hair with one finger, be-fore she pulled away.

"I'm not giving up," he said softly. "I love you, Corrie. There's nothing you can do about it."

"Go home, Daniel. Please just go home."

He leaned forward, kissed her cheek, and left.

Corrie sat back down at her desk, leaned her face into her hands, and cried.

The phone rang, and she sniffled to a stop to pick up the re-ceiver.

"Corrie Philips," she said.

"Corrie? It's Paul."

Shit! Just what she didn't need right now.

"What do you want, Paul?"

"I want you to tell me where Bryn is!" Paul's voice shook. "Look, I know she's pregnant. And I know she thinks I can't han-dle it. But I love her. I love her, and I want to do the right thing. Please, Corrie, just tell me where she is."

Corrie hung up the phone and immediately began dialing.

"Hello?"

"Bryn, it's Corrie."

"Hey! I was just going to call you. How are you?"

"Can you do lunch?"

"Um, sure, I guess so."

"Can you meet me at the Reverie in half an hour?"

"Corrie? Are you okay?"

"No," Corrie said softly. "I'm not."

They sat at their usual table. The waiter, noting Corrie's red eyes, laid a small stack of napkins on the table beside her plate.

"What happened?" Bryn leaned across the table and took Corrie's hands.

"He came to the office today. He said he's not giving up, that we belong together. All the stuff he said yesterday."

Corrie reached for a napkin.

"Well, he's not staying at Bob's anymore," Bryn said. "Bob told him he can't."

"Oh my God!" Corrie's face blanched. "Does Bob know?"

"Not that you slept with him." Bryn felt vaguely guilty lying to her friend, but she knew it would only upset Corrie more to know the truth.

"But Daniel told him last night that he still loves you and that he wants you back."

"Oh God," Corrie whispered. "Jesus Christ!"

"It's okay," Bryn said, patting Corrie's hand. "Bob read him the riot act. Told him you were happily married, and that he needed to leave you the hell alone."

"Poor Bob," Corrie murmured. "That's just what he needed."

Bryn nodded. "He was pretty upset. But not with you! Just with Daniel, for being such a prick."

"It's not just Daniel's fault," Corrie said, shredding the napkin into a small pile on the table. "I'm the one who cheated on my husband."

The waiter appeared to take their orders. When he left, Bryn leaned across the table and touched Corrie's cheek, her fingers gentle.

"Yeah, you did. But it's done. Done is done. It's over and it's time to move on."

Corrie said nothing.

"I wonder where he's going to stay?" Bryn asked.

"He's going back to California today."

"Thank God!"

"He has a board meeting with a donor tomorrow. . . ."

"Whatever," Bryn said. "I'm just glad he's going."

"He said he'll be back." Corrie raised teary eyes to Bryn. "What if Mark finds out?"

"He won't! Not unless you tell him. Does Daniel have your cell number?"

Corrie nodded. "I called him to get directions."

"Give me the phone."

Bryn found the number and punched a few buttons.

"There," she said, handing the phone back. "He's blocked. He can't call you on your cell."

"Thanks." Corrie put the phone back into her purse.

The waiter appeared with their drinks, silently pushed the pile of shredded paper into his hand, and left.

"Do you think we come here too often?" Bryn grinned at her friend.

Corrie smiled wanly.

"Paul called me again this morning," she said, reaching for yet another napkin.

"Oh lord," Bryn groaned. "What did he want?"

"He wants to know where you are."

"Screw him!"

Corrie smiled. "I know," she said. "But honestly, he did sound worried. He said he loves you and he wants to do the right thing."

"Paul wouldn't know the right thing if it bit him in the ass."

"You're going to have to talk to him sometime," Corrie said. "It is his baby, too. He's the father, and he has some rights . . . legally, I mean."

Bryn simply shrugged.

"Well," Corrie said, "it's up to you. I just thought you should know he called."

The waiter returned with their plates and they ate in silence.

"What are you up to this afternoon?" Corrie finally asked.

"Actually, I have my first appointment with the ob-gyn."

"Wow!" Corrie smiled. "Who are you seeing?"

"Dr. Reynolds," Bryn said. "Bob recommended her."

"Are you nervous?"

"A little bit." Bryn took a bite of her sandwich and chewed slowly. "I kind of hate the prospect of going alone, you know?"

"Do you want me to go with you?"

"No, that's okay." She smiled at Corrie. "If I'm going to be a single mom, I'm going to have to get used to doing things on my own."

"Well, just remember, you don't have to do everything by yourself." Corrie took her hand. "I'm always here, if you need me."

❦ 25 ❦

Bryn sat on the exam table, smoothing out the paper gown she wore. The room was cheerful, with yellow-and-blue wallpaper and a bright white border. Posters of babies covered the walls. She resisted the urge to don her sunglasses.

"Hello, Bryn." A young woman offered her hand. "I'm Dr. Reynolds."

"Hi," Bryn said, smiling.

"So, we ran your urine sample, and you are pregnant. Congratulations."

Bryn took a deep breath. *Now it's real,* she thought.

"From the date of your last period, it looks like you're about six weeks along," the doctor said. "That puts your due date in the second week of May. Let's call it May twelfth. That's a rough guess, of course. Most babies don't come on their due dates, especially first babies."

"May," Bryn whispered. "That's a good time to be born, right?"

"It's a great time to be born," Dr. Reynolds agreed. "Perfect month for birthday parties."

"Do you know if it's a boy or a girl?" Bryn asked.

"No, we can't tell that until at least sixteen weeks. We'll do an ultrasound at twenty weeks, and that should let us know. Assuming Baby cooperates."

"What does that mean?"

"Well"—the doctor smiled—"sometimes a baby keeps its knees drawn up during the ultrasound. That makes it hard to tell. What we're going to concentrate on now is just having a healthy baby, okay?"

Bryn nodded.

"I'm going to start you on some prenatal vitamins." The doctor wrote a prescription. "I want you to eat a healthy diet, get some exercise every day, get plenty of sleep, and avoid alcohol and tobacco."

"Okay." Bryn nodded again.

"I see you didn't include your husband's information on your form." Dr. Reynolds's brow furrowed.

"I'm not married."

"Ah." She made another mark on the form. "Will the baby's father be involved?"

"No." Bryn shook her head firmly.

"Well then, you're going to need a support system. Pregnancy is not something you want to do all on your own. Do you have family close by?"

Bryn shook her head again. "But I have good friends," she said. "I'll be fine."

The doctor smiled sympathetically.

"All right, I'll see you back here in a month."

Bryn thought about that smile later, as she washed dishes in Bob's kitchen. Clearly, the doctor thought she was going to need help. *Hmph!* she snorted. *She doesn't know me very well.*

The doorbell rang and she set aside the dishrag and, wiping her hands on a towel, walked to the living room and opened the front door.

"Bryn!" Paul held a huge bouquet of daisies, her favorite flowers. Bryn's knees began to shake.

"God, baby, I've been worried sick about you. Are you okay?"

Paul pulled her into a tight embrace. Bryn stood, her arms hanging limp at her sides, and allowed herself to be hugged.

"Hey!" Paul released her and took her face in his hands. "You are okay, aren't you?"

"I'm fine," she said. "Just . . . I'm fine."

"Can I come in?"

Bryn closed the door behind her. "How about we just stay out here?"

"Oh." Paul looked around the porch, strewn with bicycles and sports equipment. "Okay."

He sat down on the old metal glider and patted the seat beside him. Bryn simply stood still.

"So . . . you're sure you're all right? You look kind of pale."

"I'm fine," she repeated.

"Have you been to see the doctor yet?"

She nodded.

"And . . . ?"

"And I'm pregnant."

Paul grinned up at her. "When are you due?"

"In May."

"Wow, that's such a trip. May . . . wow."

"What are you doing here, Paul?"

Paul sat a moment before responding.

"I just wanted to see you, babe. I mean, I know I didn't react the way you wanted me to. But you hit me out of left field. It's a lot to take in."

"I know." She leaned against the porch rail, her hand protective on her stomach.

"But I've been thinking. I mean, I've been thinking a lot. And . . . and I want you to come home. I want us to do this together."

Bryn stared at him, open-mouthed.

"I mean it, baby. We can totally do this."

"You never wanted kids," she said.

"Neither did you," he pointed out. "But now, well, now it's here. And I realized I do want this kid. And I really want you."

He smiled at her, the crooked smile that used to break her heart.

"I don't know, Paul." She finally sat down on the glider beside him. "We've tried it for so long, and it never changes. You never change."

"I can, though. I mean, I never had a reason to before."

"You had me."

That stumped him for a minute.

"I know, I've been a real shit," he said finally. "But I can change. I've already gone to the university and told them if they aren't going to put me on the tenure track, I'm leaving."

"You didn't." Bryn stared at him again.

"I did." He smiled. "I don't know if they'll do it or not. Probably not. But there are other universities. I can get a better job. I'll take care of you and the baby. I promise, Bryn. I can change."

A small corner of her heart thawed as she sat there beside him, wanting to believe him.

"Please, baby. Just come home. Come home and you'll see."

"I don't know," she said softly.

"We'll make the office into a nursery. Or if you want, we'll look for another place with more room. Would you like that?"

He smiled that crooked smile again.

"Maybe," she whispered.

"That's my kitten!" He wrapped his arms tight around her tiny frame, pulling her closer, kissing her cheeks, her nose, her mouth.

"Hey!" Bob's voice rang from the steps. "What's up?"

"Oh, hey, Bob." Paul stood and extended his hand. "I'm just telling Bryn we can find a bigger apartment if she wants."

"You okay?" Bob ignored the offered hand and looked at Bryn, still sitting silently on the glider.

She nodded.

"You sure?"

"Yeah," she said. "I'm fine."

"Okay." Bob walked past Paul and into the house. "Let me know if you need me."

"What's with him?" Paul asked.

"He's just feeling protective, I guess." Bryn watched the door close behind Bob.

"What's he got to protect you from? In fact, why does he think he needs to protect you at all?" Paul's eyebrows raised.

"He's my friend and he worries. That's all."

"If you say so." Paul sat down beside her again.

"So, how about you get your things and come home?"

Bryn sat quietly for a minute, then rose.

"Let me think about it, okay?"

His disappointment was clear.

"Oh . . . fine. Sure, you think about it. Just remember that I'm waiting, babe. Don't take too long, okay?"

She nodded, allowed him to kiss her again, then watched him walk to his old Saab and drive away.

She walked into the house and flopped down on the couch.

"Are you going back?" Bob emerged from the kitchen with two big glasses of iced tea.

"I don't know," she said. "I mean, part of me says, 'No.' In fact, most of me is screaming, 'NO!' "

"And the other part?"

He handed her a glass of tea and sat down beside her.

"Do you want to go back?"

"It's just that I've put so much time into him. And he says he can change. And . . . and it would be so much easier not to do this alone, you know? I mean, a kid needs two parents, right? You said so yourself before."

"It depends on the parents," Bob said. "If Paul can change, if he can be a good dad, then yeah, it would be a hell of a lot easier. But that's a big if. I guess the bigger question is, do you still love him?" He watched her carefully.

Bryn took a long drink of tea and sighed.

"It's weird," she said finally. "An hour ago I would have said no. But now, I don't know. I mean, what if he really can change? He's not all bad, you know. He has some good qualities."

"Yeah?" Bob smiled at her. "Like what?"

"Like, he's funny. And he's really smart. And he doesn't ever judge."

Bryn paused.

"Okay, he's funny and smart and he doesn't judge. But is he responsible? Is he thoughtful? Is he reliable? I'm not attacking him," he added. "I'm just asking."

"I don't know." She sighed again. "I really don't know."

"Well." Bob squeezed her shoulder. "You don't have to make

up your mind right this minute. It's your choice and you're the only one who can make it. And you should take your time making it, okay? Give yourself a few days to think about it."

She smiled at him, leaned forward, and kissed his cheek.

"You really are a good guy, Bob."

"Yeah, old Saint Bob, that's me."

"Would you take Wendy back again?"

"No."

The firmness of his voice surprised her.

"Really?" she said. "I guess I thought . . ."

"A few weeks ago I probably would have said yes. But now it's a whole different ball game."

"I'm glad."

"Well, you're partly responsible, you know."

She stared at him in surprise.

"Having you here has been a good thing, Bryn. You make me see things differently."

She laughed, her cheeks reddening.

"Seriously, you've been a big help with the boys. And you've helped me feel stronger, too. So thank you."

"I should be the one thanking you," she said.

"Well, let's call it even then." He grinned at her.

"If I move back in with Paul, it will make your life less complicated, that's for sure." Bryn took another drink of tea.

"Don't worry about that," Bob said firmly. "You can stay with me and the boys for as long as you want."

"Thanks, Bob. You're a real friend."

"Back atcha," he said. "Now, what should we make for dinner?"

❧ 26 ❧

"Hi, Aunt Corrie!"

Laurel ran into Corrie's outstretched arms.

"Hi, pumpkin! How's my pretty girl?"

Corrie lifted her niece and kissed her cheek.

"I'm mad," the little girl said, grimacing. "Ian ruined my picture."

"Did not!" Ian appeared in the kitchen doorway. "I made it better!"

"Okay, you two. That's enough!" Sarah walked into the living room and took Laurel from Corrie, setting her on the sofa. "I don't want to hear another word about the picture."

She hugged Corrie lightly. "How are you doing?"

"I'm okay," Corrie said, smiling at her sister-in-law. "I'm glad to be home."

"Do you guys want to watch cartoons?" Sarah turned on the television.

Corrie's eyebrows arched. Usually, Sarah didn't let the kids watch television during the day.

"Nick Junior!" Laurel shouted. Ian climbed onto the couch beside his sister.

"Okay, just for a while." Sarah flipped the remote until a cartoon filled the screen.

"Let's have some tea," she said, walking into the kitchen. "I'm beat!"

"You feeling all right?" Corrie asked, following her.

"Yeah, just tired." Sarah poured water into the teakettle and set it on the stove. "Honestly, I love them to pieces, but they're driving me crazy today."

Corrie put her arm around Sarah's shoulders and squeezed.

"You're just tired," she said. "If you want, I can watch the kids while you take a nap."

"That's okay." Sarah smiled at her. "What I really need is some honest-to-God, grown-up conversation."

They sat at the table with their cups.

"So, how was Los Angeles?" Sarah watched Corrie raise her cup, blow on the steam, then set it back down.

"Pretty much awful," Corrie said. "You were right. I shouldn't have gone."

"What happened?"

Corrie stirred her tea, not meeting Sarah's eyes.

"Nothing, really. Daniel is still just Daniel. He still thinks he's going to save the world. And he still knows how to push my buttons."

Sarah said nothing for a minute, then she sighed. "Are you and Mark okay?"

"Yes!" Corrie smiled at her then. "I told him he was right, too. I shouldn't have gone. And I'm sorry I upset him. But I think he's forgiven me."

"Good." Sarah sipped her tea. "I knew he couldn't stay mad at you for long. He said Maya called while you were there. Did you get to see her?"

Corrie nodded. "She's doing well. I think she has a boyfriend."

"Good for her!" Sarah laughed. "When is she coming home?"

"I don't think Maya will ever move back to Indiana," Corrie said firmly. "She seems pretty happy to be far away from the family."

"She might change her mind someday."

Corrie shook her head. "No, I think she really feels like she's escaped. I can't imagine her coming back to Middlebrook."

"Middlebrook's not such a bad place," Sarah said, smiling at her cheerful yellow kitchen.

"I don't think Maya has a lot of happy memories here."

"Well, I'm glad you came back."

Corrie laughed. "Did you think I was going to stay in California?"

"Not really," Sarah said. "I just . . . worried a little."

"I'm sorry I worried you. And I'm really sorry I worried Mark."

"So, how was it, seeing Daniel again?"

Corrie shrugged, feeling her cheeks redden. She wasn't used to keeping things from Sarah.

"Daniel is just Daniel. And it was . . . weird."

"Did you get a good story?"

Corrie nodded. "I think so. It really is an impressive place. I think it's a good story."

"Mama!" Laurel's voice cried from the living room. "Ian pinched me!"

Sarah sighed and heaved herself from the chair. "Some days I wonder why the hell I wanted another one," she said, patting her pregnant stomach as she waddled into the living room.

Corrie smiled, following her into the room, where Laurel was scowling furiously at her brother.

She sat down on the couch between the children, putting an arm around each.

"You go lie down for a little while," she said, winking at Sarah. "I'll stay with them and watch *SpongeBob*."

"You're an angel." Sarah smiled at the three of them. "Just fifteen minutes. Is that all right?"

"Go nap. We're good here."

Forty-five minutes later, Sarah reappeared. "I can't believe I slept so long!"

"You needed it," Corrie said, smiling.

"But I'd better go now," she said, kissing her nephew and niece and hugging Sarah. "I told Bryn I'd stop by on my way home."

She paused in the doorway to watch Sarah pull her small daughter onto her lap, her arm around Ian. She wondered how anyone could ever get tired of those beautiful children.

"You've got to be kidding me!" Corrie stared at Bryn, aghast. "Please tell me you're kidding."

Bryn sighed.

"I know," she said. "It sounds crazy. But he seemed really sincere. And if there's even a chance he can change, don't I owe it to the baby to try and make it work?"

They sat in Bob's living room, surrounded by trucks and Legos. Bob had taken the boys to the park, and Bryn had invited Corrie for coffee.

"But you were so adamant before," Corrie said. "You said you were through with Paul."

"I know. And I meant it. And maybe I still mean it. I just don't know anymore."

"God, Bryn, this is Paul we're talking about. He's had over ten years to get his act together, and he never does. Why would you think he's any different now?"

"Because of the baby," Bryn said. "He really wants to make it work, to be a family."

"And you believe him?"

"I don't know." Bryn sighed again and sipped her coffee. "Part of me says, 'There's no way he can change.' But part of me really wants to believe he can."

Corrie said nothing for a minute, just watching her friend. Finally, she leaned forward to stare into Bryn's face.

"I know you're scared," she said softly. "I can't even imagine how scary it is to be pregnant and on your own. But you can do this, Bryn. If anyone can do it, it's you. You're strong enough to be a single mom. You don't need Paul."

"It's not just that," Bryn said. "It's the baby. What if Paul *can* be a good dad? Doesn't the baby deserve a dad?"

"Well, if Paul can get himself together, then maybe he can be a father to this baby. But, Bryn, that doesn't mean you have to go back to him. I mean, he can see the baby and help with support, but you can still live on your own."

"I know. And maybe that's what I'll do. I just don't know."

"Well, promise me this," Corrie said. "Promise me that you'll wait a while before you do anything. I mean, if he's serious then let him prove it. Let him court you."

Bryn laughed. "Court me? God, Corrie, are we living in the Middle Ages?"

"I'm serious," Corrie said, grinning. "He never had to court you before. You just jumped into bed with him. If he wants you back, make him work for it."

Bryn smiled. "I kind of like that idea."

"Good! Let him court you. Make him take you on real dates, buy you flowers, all the stuff he should have done in the beginning."

"That sounds nice." Bryn sighed yet again. "But where am I going to live while Paul is wooing me?"

"Right here." Bob stood in the doorway, holding two bags of groceries. The boys ran through the living room, headed for the kitchen.

"Hey there!" Corrie smiled at him. "How are you holding up?"

"I'm good," he said. "And I'm serious. Bryn, you stay here as long as you want."

"I can't just live here forever." Bryn rose and took a grocery bag from him.

"No, probably not," Bob agreed. "But you can live here until you decide what you want to do. And I think making Paul woo you is a very good idea." He winked at Corrie. "Make the bastard work for it."

"What's a bastard?" Micah asked from the kitchen.

"Busted!" Bryn hissed.

"Never mind," Bob said, walking into the kitchen. "It's a word I shouldn't have used. Now help me put these things away."

Bryn returned to the living room with the coffeepot. "Want a refill?"

"No," Corrie said, rising. "I'd better get home and start dinner."

"Okay," Bryn said, hugging her. "Thanks for coming. Thanks for listening."

"Anytime," Corrie said. "See you later, Bob."

She drove home, frowning at the traffic. Why would Bryn even think of going back? Why couldn't she see Paul for the self-absorbed jerk he was?

Probably for the same reason I slept with Daniel.

She shook her head. Weren't they both smart, strong, educated women? How could they fall for such jerks?

She pulled into her driveway and smiled. Mums bloomed along the front porch, small explosions of red, yellow, and orange.

I love this house, she thought. *I love my life.*

"Thank you, God," she said. "Thank you for . . . well, for everything."

In the kitchen she turned the music up loud and sang slightly off-key as she made dinner. Then she showered and changed into a pretty green chemise, set the table, poured the wine, and waited for Mark to come home.

⁓ 27 ⁓

"What do you mean, you'll date me?" Paul's voice rose slightly on the phone.

Bryn smiled. "I mean just what I said. You want me back? Show me you mean it. Show me you can be the man I need you to be."

"Come on, baby. You know I'm the man you need."

"I'm not talking about sex, Paul." Bryn's voice was flat. "I mean, I need to see that you can be a grown-up. I need to see that you can be responsible and thoughtful and . . . I need to see if you can be like a real dad."

"I told you, I talked to the university. And we can look at another apartment, if you want."

"I know what you told me," Bryn said. "But I need you to show me."

Bryn smiled, hearing him sigh heavily.

"Okay," he said, "so, what do you want to do?"

"I want you to ask me on a date, a real date. One where you plan something special, not just sitting at home getting stoned and watching TV."

"So, like dinner and a movie?"

"That's a start."

"Okay, so do you want to go to dinner and a movie tonight?"

She smiled again. "I can't tonight. Bob and I are taking the boys to see *Kung Fu Panda*."

"Oh, you and Bob are going out. So, are you dating him, too?" Paul's voice was sharp.

"No, Paul. I'm not dating Bob. He's my friend and he's been very good to me the last few weeks, and we are taking his kids to see a movie. It's not a date."

"Does Bob know that?"

Bryn laughed. "Seriously? Are you seriously asking me that? God, Paul, this is Bob we're talking about. He's married to Wendy, and I'm preggers with your kid. Does that sound terribly romantic to you?" She giggled again.

"Fine," Paul said. "Then what about tomorrow? Are you free for dinner and a movie tomorrow?"

"Actually, I am."

"Okay, then we'll go tomorrow. What time should I pick you up?"

"Well, that pretty much depends on where we're going, doesn't it? Why don't you make the plans and call me back."

There was a long silence on the phone. Bryn smiled and stretched, yawning, on the couch.

"Fine," he said again. "I'll call you back."

"You look pretty pleased with yourself." Bob walked into the room, carrying a book and his glasses.

"It's kind of nice," Bryn agreed.

"Just be careful," he said. "That guy has hurt you way too much in the past. I don't want to see him do it again."

Bryn just smiled. "What are you reading?"

Bob held the book toward her, so she could see the title: *Helping Your Kids Through Your Divorce*. "My attorney recommended it."

"So, have you filed papers?"

"Not yet." Bob sat down in the lounge chair and put on his glasses. "But he's got everything he needs from me. So, he should have them drawn up in the next week."

"Has Wendy got a lawyer?"

He shrugged. "I don't know. I haven't talked to her since the whole thing with the picture."

"Do you think she'll fight you for custody?"

He smiled sadly. "If she does, she'll lose. I gave the picture to my lawyer, and he said it's pretty much a slam dunk for me."

"Good! Because those boys need you. They need to be here."

"I think so, too."

"Do you think it will hurt your chances if I'm staying here?"

Bob shook his head. "I talked to the lawyer about it. It's not against the law to have a houseguest . . . even a pregnant one." He grinned at her.

"Okay," she said. "But if Wendy starts to make a big deal about it, I'll go stay with Corrie."

"Don't worry about it, Bryn. I already told you, you can stay as long as you want. The boys like having you here, and so do I."

28

Bryn paced the living room, checking her appearance every few minutes in the hall mirror.

"Calm down," Bob said. "You'd think this was a blind date."

"It feels like one," Bryn said. "God, I don't even know why I agreed to this."

She jumped when the doorbell rang.

"Six o'clock, on the nose," Bob said.

"I can't believe he's on time," Bryn said. "Paul is always late."

She opened the front door and found Paul holding another huge bouquet of daisies.

"You didn't have to do that," she said, taking the flowers from him. "Give me just a second to put them in water."

He followed her into the living room and smiled at Bob.

"Hey, how you doing?"

"I'm good," Bob said. "Here, Bryn, I'll take the flowers."

Bryn handed the bouquet to him and picked up her sweater.

"I'll see you later," she said.

"Okay, you kids have fun." Bob smiled at her.

"Where are you going?" Cody appeared from the hallway carrying a comic book.

"Bryn is going out for dinner with her friend Paul," Bob said.

Cody stared at Paul suspiciously. "Why?" he asked.

"Because she's hungry," Bob said.

"Why doesn't she just eat with us?" Cody looked from his father to Bryn.

"I thought you might want some time just with your dad," Bryn said.

Cody didn't respond. He took Bob's hand and simply stared at Paul.

"Okay, well, I'll see you later," Bryn said.

Paul held the door for her as Bryn got into the car.

"What's with the kid?" he asked.

"What do you mean?"

"He acted like you were his mom or something."

Bryn smiled. "He's five, and he really misses his mom. That's all."

They drove to Bryn's favorite Italian restaurant. She felt her heart lift. This might actually go well, after all.

They ordered and the waiter brought their drinks—sparkling juice for Bryn, a glass of red wine for Paul.

"So, how are you feeling?" Paul asked.

"Okay," Bryn replied. "I'm sick a lot, but I'm feeling good right now."

"So, what does the doctor say about it?"

"That it's a normal part of pregnancy."

"But can't you do anything about it? Isn't there some kind of pill you can take?"

She shook her head. "It's okay, it's just a pain in the ass."

"Do you know if it's a boy or a girl?" he asked.

She laughed. "Not until at least sixteen weeks, the doctor said."

"What do you want?"

"I don't know," Bryn said, smiling. "Either one would be okay, I guess."

"Yeah," he agreed. "Have you thought of any names?"

She laughed again. "Nope! I'm still getting used to the idea of the baby. I haven't even thought about names."

"Well, if it's a boy, maybe we could call him Will. That was my dad's name."

"I didn't know that was your dad's name." Bryn leaned forward to stare at Paul. "You've never talked about him at all."

"Well, he died when I was a kid, so there's not a lot to talk about."

"Will . . . I guess it's a good name. Not William, just Will."

The waiter brought their salads. Paul drained his glass and asked for another. Bryn raised her eyebrows but said nothing. Talking about his family always made Paul uncomfortable.

"So, if it's a girl, are you going to want to call her Helen?" Bryn asked.

Helen was Paul's mother.

"God, no!" He spat out the words. "I mean . . . no." His voice softened. "I've never really liked that name."

"Okay, then. Maybe Will. Definitely not Helen. Any other ideas?"

"No," he said. "That's all. I just kind of like Will."

The waiter brought his second glass of wine and they set upon their salads.

"So," Paul said after a brief silence, "do you think Bob's wife is going to come home this time?"

"No," Bryn said. "I think this time he wouldn't take her back even if she wanted to come home."

"Seriously?" Paul's eyebrows raised. "So old Bob has finally grown a pair. Good for him."

"It is good for him," Bryn agreed. "Wendy is a selfish, selfish bitch. Bob and the boys are better off without her."

She told Paul about the picture they'd seen of Cody and the dog and the drugs.

"Yeesh," he said when she'd finished the story. "She always was kind of . . . off. I mean, she's a looker, I'll give her that."

He stared into space for a long minute. "I always loved that wild hair."

The waiter brought their entrees, and Paul ordered another glass of wine.

"Well, it made me think about some things," Bryn said when the waiter was gone. "If we do decide to try again, if I do move back in with you, you can't be smoking pot all the time. And you can't smoke at all in the apartment. It's not good for the baby."

"I know," he agreed. "That's why I was thinking we should look for a different place, maybe one with a balcony. So I could just go outside to smoke."

"It would be better for everyone if you just quit," Bryn said quietly.

"One thing at a time, babe. One thing at a time."

He laughed and rolled his eyes. Then he signaled the waiter and asked for a fourth glass of wine.

Bryn sighed to herself and hunkered down in her chair, waiting for the inevitable.

By his seventh glass of merlot, Paul's voice had grown loud and quarrelsome.

"I bet old Bob wants you to stay right where you are, right? I bet he wants you to stay with him for good and take care of his kids . . . and take care of him."

He leered at Bryn. "I see how he looks at you, babe. I see him look."

Bryn sat quietly, cursing herself for agreeing to the date. Cursing Paul for his drinking. Cursing fate that this man was the father of her child.

"Well." Paul rose and steadied himself with his chair. "Let's hit the road."

Silently, she took the keys from him, poured him into the passenger seat of the car, and drove back to his apartment. Then she guided him up the stairs, into the apartment, and onto the bed.

He grinned up at her, his eyes glassy.

"How about a hit?" he asked. "I've got some killer weed. Let me get it. It's right here."

He began digging through the drawer of the bedside stand for his stash.

Bryn walked from the room and out of the building, walked two blocks to the coffee shop, ordered a chai tea latte, and called Bob.

"Hey." His voice was like a balm on her nerves. "What's up?"

"Are the boys still up?" she asked, blinking back tears.

"Yeah, we're just playing with the Wii."

"I'm at the coffee shop on Third and Kirby. Can you come get me?"

"Sure," he said. "Hang tight. We're on our way."

After he put the boys to bed, Bob sat on the couch next to Bryn, his arm across her shoulders.

"It was bad?"

She nodded and leaned her head against his shoulder.

"It started out so well," she said. "We were talking about the baby and names and stuff. And then he started drinking." Her voice trailed away.

"I'm sorry, Bryn. I know you were hoping he could change."

"The sad thing is, I think he's trying. I think he's really trying to change. He brought the flowers, he put some thought into the restaurant, he talked about getting a new place. But . . . but then he started with the wine. And then of course he wanted to get stoned. He's not even close to father material."

She sighed heavily. "I don't know why I thought he could be."

"Hope springs eternal." Bob smiled at the cliché. "All those times you guys asked me why I took Wendy back after she cheated, it's the same thing. I always thought, 'Maybe this time it will be different.' But it never was."

Bryn nodded.

"At least now you know," Bob said. "At least now we both know."

"Bob?"

She looked up at him and smiled.

"What?" he asked.

"If I didn't like you so much I think I'd fall in love with you."

He laughed and kissed her forehead.

"Ditto," he said softly.

∽ 29 ∽

Corrie stood in her bathroom, staring at the stick she'd peed on, watching it turn from white to blue. She compared the color on the stick to the one on the box, then compared it again. Definitely blue . . . definitely pregnant.

She sat on the edge of the bathtub, clutching the stick in her hand.

Pregnant . . . she was pregnant. After all the years, all the waiting, all the heartbreaks, she, Corrie Ann Philips, was with child.

For a long minute, she simply sat with the fact, the undeniable fact, of a new life in her womb. A baby . . . a tiny boy or girl, the child she had always wanted. Tears ran unchecked down her cheeks and she stared again and again at the stick in her hand. Pregnant!

And then, like a wave, panic overtook her. She was pregnant . . . but whose baby was it?

She walked into the bedroom and stared at the calendar. The date of her last period seven weeks before. Her trip to California two weeks after. Her homecoming to Mark.

Oh God! This cannot be happening. After all these years, after all this time . . . I cannot finally be pregnant and not know if the baby is Mark's! Please, God, please . . .

She stopped abruptly. She didn't even know what to ask God for.

Her knees buckled beneath her and she sank to the floor, still clutching the stick. Sitting on the tile floor, she wept until she felt sick. Then she rose unsteadily, walked to the phone, and called Bryn. Five minutes later she was at Bob's, falling into Bryn's arms.

"Oh my God, Corrie! That's great!"

Bryn threw her arms around her friend and hugged her tight.

"I can't believe it! Finally! You're going to have a baby and I'm going to have a baby, and they'll grow up together and be best friends."

"Bryn . . ."

"Seriously, how perfect is this? I can't believe we're both going to have babies!"

"Bryn, wait."

Corrie pulled away from Bryn and took a step back.

"What's wrong?" Bryn asked.

"I don't know . . . I mean, what if the baby is Daniel's?"

"Oh!" Bryn's face fell. "Oh God, honey, I didn't even think of that. Oh . . . do you think it could be?"

She pulled Corrie by the hand to the couch and sat beside her.

"I don't know," Corrie said. "Maybe. The timing is right."

Corrie slumped on the couch, cradling her head in her hands.

"I just don't know," she whispered. "I don't know."

Bryn held her hand while Corrie cried again.

"What am I going to do?" Corrie said, over and over. "What am I going to do?"

Finally, she sniffed and leaned her head against Bryn's shoulder.

"What you're going to do is have a baby," Bryn said firmly. "You're going to have *Mark's* baby, and that's all there is to it."

Corrie raised her head to stare at her friend.

"But what if it's not Mark's baby?" she asked.

"It is," Bryn insisted. "It is Mark's baby. It should be Mark's baby. It has to be Mark's baby. So it *will* be Mark's baby!"

"But . . ."

"Look." Bryn held Corrie's hands tightly. "For all we know, for all anyone knows, this baby is Mark's. No one ever has to know anything else."

"I can't do that!" Corrie cried. "If it's Daniel's, I can't just pass it off as Mark's. I can't!"

"Why not?" Bryn asked. "You guys were talking about adoption. That baby wouldn't have been biologically either of yours. What does it matter, really, who the father is? I mean, the biological father. Mark will be this baby's father. He will love this baby, and he never has to know it might be Daniel's. Seriously, Corrie . . . why does he ever have to know?"

"And what if the baby comes out with red hair and blue eyes?" Corrie said.

"Well, Maya has reddish hair," Bryn reasoned. "And Sarah has blue eyes. So it's there on both sides, right?"

Corrie simply shook her head and cried again.

"I can't do that," she wept. "It's bad enough I cheated on him. I can't pass Daniel's baby off as his. I can't."

"Shhh," Bryn crooned. "You don't have to decide anything right now. It's going to be okay."

"How is it going to be okay?"

Corrie rose and began pacing the living room. It was a beautiful Saturday in October and Bob had taken the boys to the park.

"It will be okay," Bryn insisted. "We'll figure it out."

"How?" Corrie demanded. "I can't tell Mark I'm pregnant if the baby isn't his. I can't do that to him. God, Bryn, he'd be so hurt."

"All right, let's look at the options."

Bryn counted on her fingers. "First, you have the baby and don't ever say a word about Daniel. Everybody's happy. Second, you have the baby and tell Mark it might not be his. And you lose your husband and hurt him and hurt the baby, too. Because God, Corrie, Mark was meant to be a dad! He'll be such a great dad."

"I know," Corrie said softly. "He'd be a wonderful dad. But—"

"But nothing," Bryn continued. "You have two choices. Plan A, everybody's happy. Plan B, nobody's happy."

"There's another choice." Corrie's voice broke.

Bryn sat in silence for a long minute, watching her friend pace.

"Yes," she finally said, very softly. "You could terminate the pregnancy."

Corrie stopped pacing and stared into Bryn's face, then collapsed on the couch again in tears.

"I can't," she cried. "I can't do that again."

Bryn patted her hand, making small hushing noises. Then she paused.

"What do you mean, 'again'?"

Corrie leaned back on the couch and hugged a throw pillow. She was silent for a while, then took a deep breath.

"When Daniel left all those years ago, I was pregnant." Her voice was so low, Bryn had to strain to hear her.

"I couldn't do it," Corrie continued. "I couldn't have the baby on my own. I just couldn't. So I . . ."

"Oh, honey." Bryn's voice was soothing, soft. "Why didn't you tell me? I could have helped. You know I would have done anything for you."

"I know." Corrie covered her face with her hands. "But you were going through your own stuff then. That was the first time you and Paul broke up. And I just . . . I couldn't tell you. I couldn't tell anyone."

"Oh Corrie, I'm so sorry."

Corrie cried again, her hands over her face.

"Was it really awful?" Bryn asked, thinking back a few weeks to when she had considered terminating her pregnancy. She shivered.

Corrie only nodded and cried.

"And I know that's why I couldn't get pregnant," she whispered finally. "God was punishing me. And now . . ."

"Okay, honey, that's just crazy. You know that, right? That is not how the universe works. If everyone who'd done something stupid or wrong couldn't have children, the human race would have ended eons ago."

Corrie shook her head.

"And now it's like God's testing me," she said. "Like he's just waiting to see if I'll kill this baby, too."

Bryn wrapped her arms around Corrie's shaking shoulders. "Hush now," she crooned. "It's going to be fine."

They sat for a while in silence, Corrie crying and Bryn patting her back.

"All right," Bryn said finally. "So you can't terminate the pregnancy. That's good. Because, honey, you were meant to be a mother. You're going to be a great mother.

"So, we're back to Plan A or Plan B. I vote for Plan A. Have the baby. Assume it's Mark's. Let it be Mark's. And forget about Daniel. You and I both know he's not father material. He's got no more dad potential than Paul, for Christ's sake. Mark wants a baby. You want a baby. Have a baby."

Corrie rose and began pacing the floor again.

"How can I do that?" she asked. "How can I just pretend what happened with Daniel didn't happen? What if the baby looks just like him?"

"First, even if the baby looks like him, who's going to know? You will. I will. Nobody else would ever even think about it. Mark's never met Daniel, right? So how would he know if the kid looks like him?"

Corrie drew a deep, shuddering breath. "I would know," she whispered.

"But it won't matter by then," Bryn said. "The baby will be here. And you will love it, and Mark will love it, and it will be your baby. It will be all right."

"But what if . . ."

"Honey, you worry too much."

Corrie stiffened at the expression she'd heard from her mother her entire life.

"Sorry!" Bryn immediately saw the look on her face. "I'm not trying to be like your mom. I'm just saying that right now you are overthinking this. I know it seems like a big deal . . . like a huge deal. But it's not. I mean, it is, but it doesn't have to be. Men have been raising other men's babies for thousands of years. It happens."

"It is a big deal!" Corrie's voice rose. "God, Bryn, I know you're trying to help, but think about this. We're not living in the Stone Age! What about DNA testing? What if someday the child develops something hereditary, something neither Mark nor I carry? How do I explain that?"

Bryn was quiet for a minute.

"Didn't you and Daniel donate blood when you were in school?"

Corrie paused and nodded. "We went every two months."

"Do you remember his blood type?"

"He's an O, the most valuable type."

"What's yours?"

"I'm A."

"Mark's?"

"He's an A, too."

"Well, then you'll be okay." Bryn smiled now.

Corrie simply stared at her.

"Look, what I remember from school is that two As or two Bs can have a baby with type O, because O is a recessive gene. So even if the baby is an O, there's no reason for Mark to believe he's not the father."

Corrie shook her head. "Bryn, it doesn't matter. I can't tell Mark this baby is his if it's not. I just can't do that. It's . . . it's wrong!"

Bryn sat quietly, watching Corrie pace, letting her process her emotions. At last, she said softly, "Well, we know for sure that you are not going to end this pregnancy. Right?"

Corrie paused and nodded, her hand resting on her flat belly, as if protecting the child in her womb from the very thought of termination.

"So, you have to make a choice and you have to make it soon. Either you let Mark believe the baby is his—which it probably is, anyway—or you tell him there's a chance it's Daniel's. Right?"

Corrie nodded again, tears filling her eyes.

"So, let's look at the possibilities. Say the baby is Mark's, and you never mention Daniel to him, then everything is fine, right?"

Corrie nodded again.

"Now say the baby is Mark's, and you tell him about Daniel. What do you think will happen?"

Corrie shook her head. "I don't know," she whispered. "He'd probably leave me."

"And if he leaves you, either you will be left alone to raise this baby or . . . or, God, Corrie, what if he sued for custody? Then you'd lose both Mark and the baby. Could you handle that?"

Corrie sank to the couch and cried, shaking her head.

"Okay," Bryn continued, holding her hand, "now say the baby is Daniel's. And say you don't ever mention it to Mark. Then you two finally have the child you always wanted. Mark will be the baby's father, and you will both be happy. Right?"

Corrie didn't reply.

"Now," Bryn said, "say the baby is Daniel's and you do tell Mark. Do you think he'll stay with you and raise another man's kid?"

"I don't know," Corrie said. "Probably not."

"So either way, if you tell Mark about Daniel, you will end up losing your marriage, your home, and a father for your baby. Does that seem fair?"

"But what if Daniel comes back?" Corrie said, shaking her head. "He's not stupid, Bryn. He knows how to count on a calendar. And he'll know the baby could be his."

"We'll just have to keep him from knowing you're pregnant," Bryn said. "At least until after the baby is born. Then we'll just wait a couple months and tell him, and he'll think it has to be Mark's."

"Oh God," Corrie cried. "This is not my life! It's like I'm living in a soap opera. I can't believe we are even talking about this."

"I know." Bryn hugged her friend tightly. "I know just how you feel. I felt like that a few weeks ago. But you know what? It will be okay. I promise, Corrie. I promise it will all work out."

"You can't promise that."

"Maybe not," Bryn agreed. "Maybe I can't promise that it will be easy. But I will be right here with you. And I think it will be okay."

"Bob would have to lie to Daniel," Corrie said softly. "They're still friends. They talk. How the hell am I supposed to ask him to lie about the baby's birthday? This won't work, Bryn. It can't work."

Bryn drew a deep breath and took Corrie's chin in her hand, looking straight into her eyes.

"Listen," she said firmly, "Bob already knows you slept with Daniel."

"Oh God!" Corrie's eyes widened, her cheeks reddened. "You told him?"

"No," Bryn said. "He figured it out from the way Daniel was talking. But, honey, Bob loves you. He knows you're supposed to be with Mark. And he is really pissed off at Daniel. He won't tell him the truth."

Corrie simply shook her head, which ached now.

"He might be mad at Daniel," she said. "But I don't think he would ever lie about something like this. I mean, this is Bob we're talking about. He *insisted* that you tell Paul about the baby, right? He's a freaking counselor, Bryn. His job is to help people. He won't just be all, 'Oh, sure, we won't tell Daniel that he has a child in the world.' He won't just say, 'Sure, Corrie, lie to your husband about your baby's paternity.' You should know that as well as I do."

"Well," Bryn said firmly, "then we won't tell Bob you're pregnant for a couple more weeks, not until it's past time that Daniel could be the father. If your baby comes a couple weeks early, that's not unusual at all. My doctor told me babies hardly ever come on their due dates."

Corrie leaned her head against the back of the couch and rubbed her eyes.

"You don't have to decide anything right this minute," Bryn said. "Mark won't be home until Tuesday, right? Just give yourself a couple days to think about it. Don't make a decision today. Promise me?"

Corrie nodded slowly. She felt incapable of deciding anything at all just now.

"When will Bob get home?" she asked.

Bryn glanced at the clock. "Soon," she said. "Why don't you splash some cold water on your face?"

Corrie rose. "No," she said. "I'm going home. I don't want him to see me like this. He'll know for sure that something's wrong."

Bryn nodded and hugged Corrie.

"Call me when you get home, okay? You're upset and probably not in the best shape to drive. So call me."

Corrie promised to call and left.

Bryn sat back down on the couch, her hands on her belly.

"Well, baby," she said softly. "I thought you and I were in a mess. But, man, our situation is a breeze compared to Corrie's."

Then she went to the kitchen to make spaghetti for Bob and the boys.

30

On Tuesday, Corrie took the day off from work. After early Mass, she drove home, dusted furniture, mopped the floors, and started dinner in the Crock-Pot. And she cried.

Mark would be home in the afternoon. One way or the other, she would have to tell him she was pregnant. She couldn't put it off. She was already having morning sickness. He'd know something was wrong.

Mark knew her so well.

At least he thinks he does.

She shook her head and swiped her hand across her eyes.

Please, God, give me the strength to do what's right. Please help me.

She had talked to Bryn every day, argued and cried and listened and argued some more. But in the end, she knew what she would do. She'd known from the start. She would tell Mark the truth. She had to.

She was in the kitchen, wiping down the counter for the third time, when she heard the garage door opening.

Please, God . . .

"Hey!" Mark paused in the doorway, grinning at her. "What are you doing home?"

"I took the day off."

He pulled her into a hug. "Are you okay?"

She nodded and tried to smile. "How was your flight?"

"Long, late, and bumpy."

"There's wine in the fridge," she said. "Do you want a glass?"

"Sure," he said. "Let me just dump this stuff in the laundry."

She poured a glass of wine while he emptied his suitcase.

"How's the project coming?" she asked, handing him the wine.

He took a sip before answering.

"It's good," he said. "I think we're going to come in ahead of schedule and maybe even under budget."

"That's great."

They sat at the breakfast bar.

"Don't you want a glass?" Mark asked, raising his glass in her direction.

She shook her head.

"Are you okay?" he asked again. "You look kind of . . . I don't know, pale or something. Are you feeling all right?"

She started to nod, tried to smile again. Then she shook her head.

"I have something to tell you," she said softly.

"Okay, shoot."

She sat quietly for a long minute, tearing a paper napkin on the counter.

"Corrie?" Mark leaned toward her. "What's wrong?"

"I'm pregnant," she whispered.

"What?" He stared at her, open-mouthed. Then he jumped from the bar stool, swept her into his arms, and whirled her around the kitchen.

"Honey, that's great! Oh my God, I can't believe it. We're going to have a baby!"

"Mark," she said, "wait. There's more."

"When are you due? Have you seen the doctor yet? Oh my God, Dr. Ping is going to be so thrilled for us."

He held her tightly to his chest. "I'm so glad, Corrie. God, I'm just so . . . happy!"

She leaned against his chest, felt tears stinging her eyes.

"Have you told anyone else yet?"

He tilted her head to look her in the eyes.

"Just Bryn," she said.

"Bryn . . . how cool is that! You guys are both going to have babies at the same time. Wow." He kissed her forehead. "Just . . . wow. I love you!"

"Mark," she whispered. "There's something you have to know."

He took a step back, still holding her hands.

"What?" he asked. "Is there something wrong with the baby?"

"No," she said. "I mean, I assume there's nothing wrong. I'm only a few weeks pregnant."

"So, what's wrong, honey?"

She released his hands and turned, so she wouldn't have to see his face when she told him, wouldn't see the hurt.

"When I was in Los Angeles, I slept with Daniel."

The words hung in the air like acrid smoke.

"What?" His voice was soft, disbelieving.

"I slept with Daniel," she repeated.

He said nothing. Finally, she turned to look at him. His cheeks were red, his eyes wide.

"It was a mistake," she said. "Stupid and selfish and . . . awful. I don't even know how it happened. It just did. I'm so sorry, Mark. I'm just so sorry. I didn't mean for it to happen. And I hate that it did."

"You slept with Daniel?"

She nodded, dropping her eyes to the floor.

"I'm so sorry," she repeated.

He sat down on the bar stool, leaned his head into his hands, and sat in silence. She touched his shoulder, and he pulled away.

Finally, after what felt like an hour, he raised his head and stared at her.

"So this baby is Daniel's?"

"I don't know," Corrie said. Tears streamed unchecked down her face. "I don't know if it's his or if it's yours."

She could see he was shaking, could feel the anger in his voice.

"You don't know if the baby is mine? Or if it's Daniel's?" He spat out the name.

She only shook her head, her eyes trained on the floor. She didn't see him raise his arm, didn't see the blow coming. He slapped her hard across the face and she stumbled backward against the break-fast bar.

She stared at him in disbelief, waiting for another blow. But he only turned away abruptly, grabbed his keys from the counter, and left, slamming the door behind him. After a minute, she heard the garage door open. She watched through the window as he drove away, tires screeching on the pavement.

She leaned her forehead against the glass pane and wept. Her life, the life she'd so carefully crafted, was over. Mark was gone.

∽ 31 ∽

"I can't believe he hit you!"

Bryn touched the bruise on Corrie's cheekbone softly.

"I deserved it," Corrie said.

"Don't talk like a crazy person, Corrie. No one deserves to get hit!"

Corrie only shook her head.

They sat in Corrie's kitchen. She had taken another day off work. She couldn't go to the office with a bruise on her face. She couldn't face the questions.

"I just wish I knew where he is," she said. "I just want to know he's okay."

"I'm sure he's fine," Bryn said. "He's probably at Sarah's."

"Oh God," Corrie said. "I hope he doesn't tell her. I can't stand for Sarah to know I cheated on her brother."

"Well, it's going to come out," Bryn said. "He's going to have to talk to someone about it, right?"

Corrie sighed, swirling the cold coffee in her mug.

"Did you try texting him?" Bryn asked.

Corrie nodded.

"I've texted, I've called. He won't answer. It just goes directly to voice mail."

"He needs some time to cool off," Bryn said, patting Corrie's hand. "It's a lot for him to take in. But he'll come home and you guys can talk about it and . . . and figure out what to do."

"What is there to figure out? I'm pregnant. I don't know who the father is. Mark hates me, and he's never going to forgive me."

"You don't know that. Give him time. He might come around." Bryn tried hard to sound hopeful.

Corrie shook her head.

"You didn't see him yesterday. He looked at me like he hated me."

"He's mad, honey. Of course he's mad. And he's hurt. But this is Mark. He's a good guy, right? Give him some time and he'll come around."

Corrie didn't reply.

"Okay." Bryn rose, took Corrie's coffee cup, and pulled her up from her chair. "We are *not* going to sit around here feeling sorry for ourselves. We are going to go out and buy something."

Corrie shook her head again.

"No arguments," Bryn insisted. "Go upstairs and get dressed. We are going to the mall and we are going to buy something for your baby. And then I'm buying you lunch."

She pulled Corrie up the stairs and to her bedroom.

"We'll get salads at Maxi's. We'll drink milk. We'll be disgustingly healthy and smug. We'll be two pregnant ladies out on the town."

Corrie pulled on her jeans and a sweater, applied makeup to her bruise, and allowed herself to be dragged to Bryn's car. They drove to the mall, the radio blaring, the windows rolled down.

She followed Bryn into the mall, concentrating simply on putting one foot in front of the other. She felt like she was walking in thick, oozing mud, each step a concerted effort. All the while, Bryn chattered away.

"We're going to babyGap," she announced. "We'll get something unbelievably cute and very expensive for the baby."

She giggled. "Babies, I mean. God, Corrie, we are going to have babies!"

Corrie glanced at her friend. Bryn's cheeks were pink, her eyes bright. She looked happier than Corrie had ever seen her.

"Come on." Bryn nudged her with her elbow. "I know yesterday sucked. And I know today sucks. And tomorrow will probably suck, too. But, Corrie Ann, you are pregnant. And that's kind of a miracle, right? So, just concentrate on that right now. You're going to have a baby!"

They stood at the entrance of the store, staring at the vast array of tiny sleepers and dresses, overalls and booties. Corrie smiled, in spite of herself.

They wandered the aisles, picking up one adorable item after another.

"We can't buy clothes," Corrie said, laying down a lacy lavender dress with regret. "I mean, I'd love to have this, but what if I'm having a boy?"

Bryn laughed. "Okay, let's look at sleepers then. And these, look at these!"

She held up a tiny pair of white booties, each embroidered with the three little kittens and their mittens.

"Bryn," Corrie said, laying her hand on Bryn's. "We probably shouldn't buy anything yet. It's bad luck."

Bryn simply laughed. "Let's look at our situation, shall we? I'm pregnant by a man who is a total loser. You don't even know who your baby daddy is. I think we've had our share of bad luck, don't you?"

She held the booties out for Corrie.

"Let's both get them," she said. "The babies will match."

Corrie took the tiny socks and held them to her cheek. "They're so soft."

They bought the booties. They bought blankets and hooded towels. They bought onesies and sleepers. By the time they left the store, each carried a large bag. Bryn's had a stuffed yellow giraffe sticking out the top.

At Maxi's, they put the bags under the table, glad to be off their feet.

The waiter took their orders and brought their milk.

"Cheers," Bryn said, touching her glass to Corrie's. "Here's to healthy babies."

"What babies?"

They looked up to see Patrice standing by their table.

"Oh, um," Bryn stammered. "Hi, Patrice. How are you doing?"

"I'm fine, Bryn. What are you two doing here? Isn't it a work day?" She looked pointedly at Corrie.

"I took the day off," Corrie mumbled, willing her mother to go away.

"Oh!" Patrice sounded shocked. "Well, good for you! I'm proud of you."

She sat down in the empty chair next to Corrie, kissed her cheek, and reached for a menu.

"What are you having?" she asked, obviously meaning to join them.

"Just salads," Bryn said.

"Well, I think I'm going to get a grilled cheese," Patrice said. "And a cocktail."

She glanced at the milk glasses on the table, then looked from Corrie to Bryn.

"So . . . what babies were you talking about?"

"Mine," Bryn said, grinning. "I'm preggers."

"Oh my," Patrice said. "Congratulations, Bryn! Are you and Paul going to finally make it legal?"

"Nope! I've finally left him for good."

"Well, good for you, I guess."

"Thanks," Bryn said. She winked at Corrie while Patrice gave her order to the waiter.

"So, are you having twins?"

"What? No! I mean, I don't think so. God, I hope not!"

"Well, you said babies," Patrice pointed out. "Plural."

"Oh," Bryn stammered. "I just meant babies in general."

Corrie stared at the table, reached for her napkin, then stopped and put her hands in her lap.

"So, you're going to be a single mom," Patrice said. "That's a hard row to plow. Lord knows I never expected to have to raise three kids on my own, but I did it. Sometimes I don't know how, but I did it."

You drank your way through it, Corrie thought, her mouth set in a tight line.

"Well, it's a lot easier now, I suppose," Patrice continued. "So many single moms now, not like when I was raising Corrie."

The waiter brought Patrice's gin and tonic, and she drank half of it in one swallow.

"What are you doing today?" Corrie asked, watching her mother swig the drink.

"I just got my hair cut," Patrice said. "Do you like it?"

Corrie nodded. It didn't look any different from her usual style.

"Excuse me," Bryn said, rising. "I'm going to the little girls' room."

Patrice watched her walk away, then turned to Corrie.

"So, kiddo," she said. "Are you okay?"

"I'm fine, Mom."

"Are you? Because you look like hell."

"Well, thanks."

"I mean, you look like you don't feel well. And is that a bruise?" She touched Corrie's cheek.

"I slipped in the shower," Corrie said.

Patrice gazed at her steadily. "Are you upset because Bryn is pregnant?"

"No." Corrie shook her head. "I'm happy for her. Really," she insisted, as her mother gazed at her. "I'm happy."

"Your time will come," Patrice said. "You'll get your baby someday."

Corrie nodded, not meeting her mother's eyes.

The waiter brought their food and Patrice ordered a second drink. Corrie sighed.

"I was going to call you," Patrice said. "I need your help."

Bryn rejoined them.

"What's up?" Corrie asked.

"It's Caerl," Patrice said. "He's in a little trouble."

Corrie sighed again and glanced at Bryn, who rolled her eyes.

"What's he done now?" she asked.

"Well, it's not his fault," Patrice began. "He was just in the wrong place at the wrong time."

"Whatever, Mom." Corrie took a drink of her milk. "Just tell me what happened."

"He was at a bar with some friends, and someone started a fight. You know how boys are." Patrice finished off her drink and smiled at the waiter, as he handed her another.

"Caerl didn't start it, but he got dragged into it. He was just trying to help his friend, you know. Anyway, the police came and the whole lot of them got arrested."

Corrie closed her eyes, her head beginning to throb.

"He's been charged with assault, and he's in lockup. And I need three thousand dollars to post bail for him. I'll pay you back," she said. "Once he goes to court, I'll get the money back and I'll pay you back every penny."

"When are you going to stop bailing him out, Mom?" Corrie's voice shook. "He's never going to learn until he has to finally pay for the stuff he does."

"He's my son," Patrice said, her voice flat. "If you had children, you'd understand."

Bryn's eyes widened, her cheeks flushed red.

Corrie sighed and pulled out her checkbook.

"Thanks, honey." Patrice kissed her cheek. "I'll pay you back. And Caerl has a lead on a new job. You just wait; he'll be okay. You'll see."

They finished lunch in awkward silence. Driving home, Bryn reached over and took Corrie's hand.

"When are you going to tell her?"

Corrie shook her head. "I don't know. Maybe never?"

Bryn laughed. "You don't suppose she'll notice when you start gaining weight?"

"She's going to have a cow," Corrie said. "Actually, she's going to be so angry with me for taking away her cash cow."

"How many times have you bailed Caerl out?"

"This is the fourth."

"Has she ever paid you back?"

"No."

Now Bryn shook her head. "I'm sorry, hon. My mother's no picnic, but she's a saint compared to yours."

"Have you told your mom yet?" Corrie asked.

"I'm going up tomorrow." Bryn set her shoulders as if preparing for battle. "Bob keeps telling me that once the baby comes, Mom will be fine. He says a baby makes everything okay. I hope to God he's right."

❦ 32 ❦

Corrie slept fitfully that night, waking at every small noise, but Mark did not come home.

She woke early, feeling groggy and disoriented. She had to go back to work today. The winter issue was in production.

She trudged down to the kitchen and stopped short in the doorway. Mark sat at the breakfast bar, a cup of coffee in his hand. He didn't look at her.

"Are you okay?" she asked.

He nodded.

"Where have you been?"

"I stayed with my folks," he said, staring at the coffee cup.

"Do they know?"

He nodded.

"Oh God," she said. "I'm sorry."

He shrugged.

She poured a cup of coffee and sat beside him at the counter.

"Do you hate me?" she asked.

"I don't know how I feel right now," he said.

"I'm so sorry," she repeated.

"I know."

He stood and put his cup in the sink.

"I'm going to stay with Mom and Dad for now, until I can find an apartment. You can stay here. It's really always been your house, anyway."

She stared at him in silence for a minute.

"You're moving out?"

He nodded. "I can't stay here. I need some time and space to think about things."

"I'll sleep in the guest room, and you can have the bedroom," she said, her voice catching. "Please don't leave."

He shook his head. Finally, he looked at her.

"I'm sorry I hit you," he said softly. "I can't believe I did that."

"It's okay."

"No, it's not okay. It's not okay at all. That's why I can't stay. I'm too angry right now. I need to just be by myself."

Corrie stood, willing herself not to cry.

"Please stay," she whispered. "We can work this out if we try."

He shook his head again.

"I don't know how," he said. "Especially if this baby is . . . isn't mine."

"It will be yours." Corrie was begging now. "If you want it, this baby will be yours."

"Damn it!" Mark slammed his fist on the counter. "You can't just pretend like it will be fine, Corrie."

Tears welled in her eyes.

"Look," he said. "I'm sorry, but I can't stay. Not now. I need some time. I just came by to get some things."

"Okay." Her voice was small.

Mark got his suitcase from the laundry room, where he'd left it. Then he went upstairs, closing their bedroom door behind him.

Corrie sat at the kitchen table, her head cradled in her hands, tears dripping from her face.

Fifteen minutes later, Mark reappeared, lugging his suitcase and a garment bag.

"I'll talk to you later," he said.

"When?"

"I don't know, Corrie. Just later."

He left, closing the door behind him.

Corrie sat for a long time, crying until her head ached. Finally, she got up, took a shower, dressed, and went to work.

～❦ 33 ❦～

Bryn chewed her lip as she pulled into the sweeping driveway of her parents' house, the house she'd grown up in. Funny that she never called it home.

Her mother had sounded surprised when she called. Bryn hadn't been to visit in nearly a year. But Keri had said to come; she would change her plans so she could be here.

"Here goes nothing," Bryn said as she got out of the car.

She rang the doorbell and, after a minute, her mother answered. She hugged Bryn lightly and led her into the living room.

"Hi, sweetheart. How are you? It's been such a long time."

"I know," Bryn said. "I'm sorry. I've just been really busy."

"I know, sometimes life intervenes. I'm just glad you're here. Sit down. Do you want some coffee?"

"No, thanks."

Bryn perched on the edge of an ornate wing chair.

"So, what brings you home today?" Keri asked.

"Well, actually, I have some news." Bryn sat opposite her mother and tried to smile.

"Don't tell me you and Paul are finally getting married? Oh honey, it's about time!"

"No, Mom. Actually, I, um . . . well, I've left Paul."

"Oh." Keri raised her eyebrows. "Are you all right?"

"Yes," Bryn said. "Actually, I'm better than all right. I'm pregnant!"

Keri's eyes widened. "You're what?"

"I'm pregnant. I'm going to have a baby."

"Is it Paul's?"

"God, Mom! Of course it's Paul's."

"But then . . . why are you leaving him?"

Bryn sighed. "Because Paul is not father material. He's never going to grow up and be a responsible adult. He's never going to change, and I can't just keep waiting on him to."

"But, Bryn, how are you going to take care of a baby all on your own?"

"Well, I have good friends. And lots of women do it."

"But you hardly make enough money to take care of yourself! Babies are expensive, honey. Paul may not be perfect, but at least he makes a decent salary."

"Look, all Paul does is sit around the apartment smoking pot and watching television. I don't want my baby to grow up around that."

"Paul uses drugs?"

"Not drugs, Mom. Just pot. But it's all he does."

"Does he know you're pregnant?"

"Yes. He suggested I get an abortion."

"He didn't!"

"Yeah, he did."

"Well, good riddance then!"

Bryn nodded.

"But, honey, how are you going to make it on your own?"

"I have a good client base now, Mom. I make enough to live on."

"Maybe you should move back home. You can have your old room, and I could make the guest room into a nursery."

"No, Mom. I'm not moving in with you and Dad."

"Why not?"

"Because I have a life." Bryn stood and took her mother's hands. "Look, I appreciate it, I really do. But my life is in Middlebrook."

"You can work from anywhere."

"Not just my work, Mom. My friends are there, my whole support system is there. Besides, I'm thirty-two years old. I'm perfectly capable of supporting myself and this baby."

"I think I need a drink."

Bryn followed her into the kitchen, where Keri poured herself a glass of chardonnay.

"I'd offer you a glass, but you can't drink if you're pregnant."

"That's okay. I'll have a glass of orange juice."

Keri poured the juice and they sat at the kitchen table.

"So," Keri said, "when are you due?"

"May twelfth."

"Well, we'll have a shower in April. Will that be okay? Just a few friends and family. Maybe we'll do it at the club."

"Sure, Mom." Bryn smiled. This was going better than she had imagined it would.

"Bryn?" Keri set her glass on the table. "If you've left Paul, where are you living?"

"I've been staying with Bob Carter. Do you remember him?"

"Isn't he married to that awful woman with the red hair, the loud one?"

"Yeah, but he and Wendy are separated now. She left him for another guy."

"Good lord! Don't they have children?"

"Two boys," Bryn said. "Bob is going for full custody."

"So you are living with Bob while he's going through a divorce and custody battle? Do you think that's a good idea?"

"I'm not living with Bob. I'm just staying in his guest room until I find a place of my own."

Keri shook her head. "I don't understand your generation at all. When we got married, we married for life, for better or worse. You all don't even bother getting married. And when you do, it seems like it's a temporary arrangement."

Bryn took a drink of juice. She had no answers for her mother.

"Well, it's a different world, I suppose." Keri rose and rinsed her glass in the sink.

"So, you're going to look for an apartment in Middlebrook?"

Bryn nodded.

"How much do they rent for down there?"

"Well, Paul's is a two-bedroom and we were paying just over six hundred a month."

"Can you swing that on your own?"

"I think so."

"Well, if you need help, you ask. Do you hear me? Don't be too proud to ask. Your father and I are always here if you need us."

"Thanks, Mom."

Bryn rose and hugged her mother.

"A grandbaby," Keri said, smiling. "I'm going to be a grandma."

"Yes, you are."

"My baby is going to be a mommy."

Bryn smiled.

"Well, let's go get some lunch," Keri said. "And then let's do some serious shopping. I haven't been baby shopping in years. Oh, this is going to be fun!"

Bryn arrived home that evening just before dinner.

"Hey!" Bob grinned at her from the front porch. "How did it go?"

"Actually, it was great! I can't believe how well she took it."

"Good!" he said. "It looks like she bought out a store or two."

Bryn dropped the four large bags she carried on the ground.

"I think this kid has enough clothes to last till kindergarten," she said. "And you should see what's in my trunk. She bought a car seat and a baby swing and a porta-crib. I think she may actually have gone insane."

Bob laughed and hugged her.

"I'm glad it went well," he said. "I told you, a baby makes everything right with the world."

He picked up the bags and carried them into the house, Bryn following.

"Where are the boys?" she asked. The house was strangely quiet.

"They're having a night out with Wendy's parents. Carla called today and asked if they could see them."

"Is that okay?" Bryn asked. "I mean, they won't take the boys back to Wendy, will they?"

"No. They don't see Wendy at all anymore. They're pretty much appalled at what she's doing."

"I don't blame them," Bryn said. "It's pretty appalling."

"So, I guess it's just the two of us for dinner. There's some left-over stew in the fridge."

"Sounds good. Let me just change into my sweats, okay? I'm ready to relax."

Bryn carried the bags of baby clothes to her room. When she reappeared, in gray sweatpants and a red shirt, she carried a tiny sleeper. "Isn't this just the cutest thing you ever saw?"

Bob smiled. "Pretty cute."

"Hey," Bryn said, plopping down on the couch. "Do you mind if we ask Corrie to eat with us?"

"Sure," Bob said. "Is Mark out of town again?"

Bryn took a deep breath.

"No," she said. "He's in town. He's just not at home."

Bob raised his eyebrows.

"Corrie told him about what happened with Daniel."

"Oh lord," he said. "I bet that went over well."

"And that's not all," Bryn continued. "Bob, Corrie is pregnant."

Bob's eyes widened.

"Oh my God," he said. "Is the baby Daniel's?"

"She doesn't know for sure."

Bob leaned his head against the wall. "What a mess," he said.

"Yeah," Bryn agreed.

"Does Mark know she's pregnant?"

Bryn nodded.

"And he's left her?"

She nodded again.

Bob sat down heavily in the recliner and shook his head.

"I can't believe this," he said. "Corrie's so . . . she's just so good, you know? She never breaks the rules. She always does the right thing. And now, it just doesn't seem fair."

"I know," Bryn said. "She's torn up about it."

"I'll bet. Does she know that I know about Daniel?"

Bryn nodded.

"Well, you call her and tell her to come for dinner. We'll do what we can to cheer her up."

Bryn rose and kissed the top of his head.

"You really are the dearest man."

He grinned at her.

"You call, and I'll start heating up the stew."

∞34∞

Corrie arrived bearing a large bunch of chrysanthemums and a loaf of sourdough bread.

"Hey," Bob said, wrapping her in a hug. "You all right?"

She leaned against his chest for a minute.

"No," she said. "Not really."

"You will be," he said. "It's going to be okay."

"Hi!" Bryn called from the kitchen. "Wait till you see all the stuff my mom bought for the baby."

She walked into the dining room carrying a large pot of hot stew.

"You told her?" Corrie asked.

"Yep." Bryn nodded, setting the pot on the table.

"How did it go?"

"So well! I can't even believe how well it went."

"Bryn, that's great. I'm so glad."

"I know! It was almost like, 'Who are you, and what have you done with my mother?' "

Corrie laughed. "I always liked your mom. I know you didn't, but I always did."

"She's okay," Bryn said. "She's mellowed a lot in the last few years."

"Maybe you have, too," Bob said.

"Maybe."

They sat at the table and Bob raised his glass.

"A toast," he said. "To good friends."

"God knows what we'd do without them," Bryn said.

They touched glasses.

"Thanks for having me tonight," Corrie said. "I really hate being home right now."

"You should stay the night," Bryn said. "We'll have a slumber party!"

Corrie smiled and shook her head. "I have to work in the morning. And I think Wendy might just die of a heart attack if yet another woman moves in with Bob."

"Serves her right," Bryn said.

"I filed the divorce papers today," Bob said quietly.

"I'm so sorry." Corrie put her hand over his. "I know that must be so hard."

"Thanks," he said. "I just want to get it over with and move on."

"Well, we are quite the trio, aren't we?" Bryn said. "Two pregnant ladies with no husbands, and a husband with no wife."

Bob grinned ruefully. "If you had told me a year ago that we would be here today, I wouldn't have believed you at all."

"I feel like I'm living someone else's life," Corrie said. "Like I'm in a soap opera or something."

They sat in silence for a moment.

"Well," Bryn said finally, "it could be worse."

Corrie raised her eyebrows.

"How could it be worse?" she asked.

"We could be back in Biology 101."

They all laughed.

"God, I hated that class," Bob said. "Jenkins was such a bad teacher."

"I know," Bryn agreed. "That's why I had to copy from you."

"I only got through that class because Daniel tutored me every single day," Corrie said.

Immediately, she regretted the words. They sat in awkward silence for a long minute. Corrie's cheeks reddened.

"Does he know about the baby?" Bob asked.

She shook her head.

"Are you going to tell him?"

"I don't know," she said. "Right now, all I can think about is Mark. He came to the house this morning and packed up a bunch of his stuff. He's getting an apartment."

Bryn reached over to squeeze Corrie's hand.

"He just needs some time to sort things out," Bob said. "But Mark loves you. He'll come back."

"I don't know," Corrie said. "If this baby is Daniel's, I don't know if Mark can ever get past that."

"How soon can you find out?" Bryn asked.

"I'm not sure. I looked online, and I think they can't do testing until at least ten weeks," Corrie said.

"Have you been to the doctor yet?" Bob asked.

Corrie shook her head. "I can't bring myself to go into Dr. Ping's office and tell him, 'Hey, I'm finally pregnant. But oh, by the way, Mark might not be the father.' "

"You should see Dr. Reynolds," Bryn said. "She's really nice."

"Maybe," Corrie said.

"Actually," Bob said, "you probably should see your own doctor. He's got all your history. And I'm sure you're not the only patient he's ever seen who wasn't sure about her baby's paternity."

"God!" Corrie said. "I can't believe I'm in this position. This isn't me. I don't cheat on my husband and get pregnant with someone else's baby. This is not how it's supposed to be."

She dropped her head into her hands and felt the tears sting her eyes.

Bryn rose and wrapped her arms around her friend.

"It will all work out," she crooned. "I know it doesn't seem like it now, but it really will be okay."

Corrie leaned into her and cried. "How is it going to be okay? How will it ever be okay?"

"Because, Corrie, you're going to be a mommy."

"I'm going to be a single mom. That's not what I wanted."

"Coriander Bliss!"

Bryn's raised voice startled Corrie into looking up.

"For as long as I've known you, you've wanted a baby. Even when we were freshmen, you'd stop to play peek-a-boo with kids at the mall. You were meant to be a mother. And now you're going to be one. After all this time, it's kind of a freaking miracle. And no, it's not how you imagined it. That's life, honey. It never turns out just how you planned it. Sometimes you just have to go with the flow."

Corrie wiped her eyes and stared at Bryn.

"Do you think this is how I planned my life?" Bryn continued. "I was supposed to be a world-famous artist by now, and I don't even have a place to call my own. I'm thirty-two years old, and I don't even have my own apartment."

"You're braver than I am," Corrie said softly.

"That's bullshit and you know it. You are brave enough and strong enough to get through this. Your perfect little world has been shaken. And oh well, life happens. But you're going to have a baby, and you're going to love the baby, and you're going to make a good life for you and the baby. Because you are Coriander Bliss Philips. You survived your rotten childhood, and you can survive this."

Corrie sat silently staring at her friend. At last, she smiled weakly.

"I love you," she said.

"I know," Bryn said. "I'm just a lovable person."

Bob laughed then, and they all relaxed in their chairs.

"Now seriously," Bryn said. "You have to come look at the stuff my mom bought today. I am going to have the best-dressed kid Middlebrook has ever seen!"

"Congratulations!" Dr. Ping smiled as he entered the exam room. "You are officially pregnant!"

Corrie managed a small smile.

"Are you all right?" Dr. Ping asked. "I thought you'd be over the moon."

"I'm just . . . well, to be honest, I'm not sure the baby is Mark's."

The words hung in the air between then. Dr. Ping said nothing for a long minute.

"Oh," he said finally. "Oh."

"I made a really stupid mistake." Corrie's cheeks were the color of bricks. "Just once, but . . . but now I don't know who the father is."

She buried her face in her hands and let the tears come.

"Does Mark know?" Dr. Ping's voice was gentle.

"Yes, I told him."

"I'm very sorry, Corrie. I know how much you've wanted a baby. And I can't imagine how painful this must be for you and Mark."

"Thank you," she whispered.

"Are you going to continue with the pregnancy?"

"Oh yes," she said. "I want this baby!"

"Well, good then. I know it's not the way you wanted things to work out, but sometimes life just throws us a curveball."

"Doctor, how soon can we find out if the baby is Mark's?"

"Well, that depends." Dr. Ping sat down across from Corrie. "We can do an amniocentesis after the fourteenth week. That's where we use a long, thin needle through your abdomen to draw out a little bit of amniotic fluid.

"Or, we can do chorionic villus sampling at about eleven weeks. In that case, we use a long, thin tube through the vagina to gather a bit of tissue from the wall of the uterus."

"Okay," Corrie said firmly. "Let's do the one at eleven weeks."

"Corrie, I have to tell you there are risks involved with either of the procedures. With either, there is a small chance of miscarriage."

"How small?" Corrie wrapped her arms around her stomach, as if to shield the baby inside.

"With amnio, about one in four hundred. With CVS, it's one in one hundred. The only really risk-free method is to wait until the baby is born, draw blood, and do the test then."

Corrie shook her head. "I can't wait that long. Mark is in hell, I'm in hell. We need to know."

"All right." The doctor made a note on his chart. "Then let's decide which procedure is your best option. Because the risk is significantly lower, I'd recommend an amniocentesis. It's only three weeks longer to wait, and it's statistically safer for you and the baby."

"So, fourteen weeks?"

"Can you wait that long?"

Corrie took a deep breath and nodded.

"Okay, I'll go ahead and schedule you for mid-December. It's an out-patient procedure. We'll do it here in the office. In the meantime, I'm writing you a prescription for prenatal vitamins. I want you to get lots of rest, eat healthy meals, and try hard not to worry too much. Okay?"

"So, when do you think I'm due?" Corrie asked.

"We'll call it June tenth. How does that sound?"

"Good," she said. "That sounds very good."

The doctor took her hands and spoke firmly. "You are going to need as much support as you can get. Have you told your mother yet?"

She shook her head.

"I hope you'll do that right away. And get some good friends around you. And . . . and just take care of yourself, Corrie. Will you do that?"

"Yes, Dr. Ping," she said. "I will."

Corrie turned her phone on as she left the doctor's office. She had a voice mail.

She stopped in the lobby to listen.

"Hey." Mark's voice was low. She sat down in the nearest chair, her knees shaking.

"I just wanted to let you know that Sarah had the baby last night, a girl. They named her Grace. They're both fine. I just thought you'd want to know."

Corrie gripped the phone tightly and listened to the message again.

They'd named the baby Grace. That would please Mark's mother. Of course, they couldn't very well have named her Corrie. Not after what she'd done.

She sat for a few minutes. Should she go see Sarah? Would Sarah even want to see her?

Finally, she stood, put her phone in her purse, and walked from the medical office building to the hospital next door.

"I'm here to see Sarah Burton," she said to the woman at the reception desk. "She had a baby last night."

The woman checked her computer and smiled. "She's in room 248, in the east wing."

Corrie stopped at the gift shop and bought a bunch of pink balloons and a small pink lamb. When she knocked on the open door of room 248, Sarah's husband raised his head.

"Oh," he stammered. "Um, hi, Corrie."

"Hi, Kevin." Corrie smiled. "Congratulations."

"Thanks," he said. In his lap he cradled a tiny, pink-blanketed bundle.

"Sarah's in the bathroom," he said, nodding toward the closed door.

Corrie walked to his side and gazed at the baby asleep in his arms.

"She's beautiful."

"Yeah," he agreed. "She is, isn't she?"

"Corrie?" Sarah stood in the doorway, her hand on her belly.

"Hi," Corrie said. "I hope it's okay I came."

"Sure." Sarah walked to the bed and lowered herself slowly onto it. "It's fine. I'm glad you came."

"Here." Kevin laid the baby in Sarah's arms. "I think I'm going to get a cup of coffee. Do you want anything?"

"No," Sarah said. "I'm good."

"Okay then." Kevin edged toward the door. "I'll be back in a little while."

An awkward silence ensued. Finally, Corrie said, "She's really beautiful, Sarah. She looks so much like Laurel."

"She does, doesn't she? You should see the two of them together. Here . . ." She lifted her phone from the nightstand and did a quick search. "Look." She held the phone up so Corrie could see a picture of three-year-old Laurel holding tiny Grace in her lap.

"Oh my God," Corrie breathed. "That's precious."

She touched the top of the baby's head with her finger, felt the fine fuzz of blond hair. Tears stung her eyes.

"Are you okay?" Sarah asked.

Corrie nodded. "Just . . . just happy for you."

"Mark told me what happened," Sarah said.

"I'm so sorry," Corrie whispered. "I'm so damned sorry."

"I know." Sarah reached for her sister-in-law's hand. "I'm sorry, too."

"Thank you." Corrie squeezed her hand.

"I mean, I'm really mad at you," Sarah continued, holding Corrie's hand tight. "I don't understand how you could cheat on Mark. But you are still my friend, my oldest friend. And no matter what, you'll always be my sister."

Tears brimmed in Corrie's eyes and a lump filled her throat. She didn't deserve Sarah's friendship. "I love you," she finally managed to say.

"I love you, too." Sarah shifted in the bed. "Do you want to hold her?"

"Can I?" Corrie reached for the baby, kissed her head, breathed in the intoxicating aroma of spit-up and baby shampoo.

"How's my granddaughter?"

Corrie's mother-in-law stopped in the doorway when she saw Corrie.

"Oh," she said. "I'm sorry. I didn't realize you had . . . company."

"Hi, Grace." Corrie's voice was small.

"Hello." Grace looked at her coldly. Corrie's stomach lurched.

"I was just going," she stammered, handing the baby back to Sarah. "I'll call you soon." She kissed Sarah's cheek and walked quickly past Grace, still standing in the doorway.

"The nerve!" Grace's voice followed her down the hall.

❧ 36 ❧

When she got home, Corrie sat down at the computer to write an email to Mark. Ignoring her in-box, she wrote:

Dear Mark,

I just wanted to say thank you for calling me about Sarah. I know you are hurt and angry. I know I messed up. I wish I could take it all back. I wish there was some way I could make it up to you, or prove to you how sorry I am. I love you so much.

I had my first appointment today with Dr. Ping. He confirmed the pregnancy and set up an appointment on Dec. 14 for me to have an amniocentesis. That will tell us for sure whether or not you are the father. I am praying so hard that you are.

I wish you would come home. I miss you so much. I hate sleeping in the bed without you. I hate not having you here in the morning. I just hate you not being here.

Please call me if you want to talk. I won't keep trying to call you. I know you need some time and

space to work things out. Please just don't forget that
I love you.
   Always yours,
   Corrie

She hit the send button and closed her eyes, willing her stomach to settle. Finally, she sighed and looked at the long list of messages in her in-box. Most of them were from Daniel. She read the most recent:

   Dear Corrie,
   I'm trying hard to be good and not harass you.
   But I wish you would just email me and let me know
   you're okay. I haven't heard from you since I came
   back, and I'm starting to worry.
   I love you,
   D

Corrie sighed heavily and began reading through the older messages. He loved her. He knew she loved him. He didn't want to mess up her life, but he really wanted to give them another chance. On and on they went. Eventually, she rose and threw the nearest book across the room.

"Damn you, Daniel!" she yelled. "Damn you! Why can't you just leave me alone?"

Her phone rang, startling her into silence. She looked at the caller ID and sighed before answering.

"Hi, Mom. What's up?"

"What's going on with you and Mark?" Patrice's voice demanded.

"What do you mean?"

Oh God, Corrie thought, *she knows already*.

"I ran into Grace at the mall this morning, and she walked right past me. She didn't even say hello. And when I called after her, she just kept walking and didn't turn around. Are you and Mark all right?"

"No, Mom. We're not all right."

"What happened?"

"Mark left me."

"What! Why? What did you do?" Patrice demanded.

Corrie sat down at the kitchen table, willing her voice to stay calm.

"I slept with Daniel while I was in California."

"Oh, Corrie, no! Why would you do that?"

"It just happened. I messed up big-time."

"And you told Mark about it? What were you thinking?"

Corrie sighed heavily. "I'm pregnant, Mom."

That silenced Patrice for an instant.

"Is the baby Daniel's?"

"I don't know. Maybe."

"Good lord, Coriander Bliss, how could you be so stupid?"

"I don't know." Corrie's voice shook.

"I mean it, how could you be so stupid? You have a perfect life—a nice house, lots of money, a husband who adores you. Why would you throw that away for a man who dumped you years ago?"

Corrie didn't reply.

After a minute, Patrice said in a calmer voice, "Okay, you messed things up. Now what are you going to do to fix them?"

"I don't know," Corrie said. "I went to the doctor today and he's set up an amniocentesis for me in December. That will tell us who the father is."

"I cannot believe you told Mark about Daniel. Why would you do something like that?"

"Because he's my husband, Mom. I love him and I couldn't just lie about him being the father."

"I cannot believe I raised such a selfish child!" Patrice's voice rose again. "What do you think you're going to do when he divorces you? Who will support you? Don't even think about moving back in here. I did my job. I raised you kids. It's your turn to take care of me now."

Corrie's hand shook and she bit her lip so hard she tasted blood.

"Don't worry," she spat. "I would never move back in with you, not if my life depended on it."

She ended the call and sat staring at her beautiful kitchen, the granite countertops, stainless steel appliances, cheery tile backsplash. Her mother was right about one thing. She'd had the perfect life. And now she'd lost it.

She rose unsteadily, walked to the bedroom, and flopped down on the bed. Then she cried until she had to run to the bathroom to throw up.

"Oh God, honey, I'm so sorry."

Bryn sat on the edge of the bed, holding Corrie's hand.

"Are you okay?"

Corrie nodded. Her eyes were puffy and red.

"I knew she would be upset," she said. "But God! She's my mother. She's supposed to be on my side, you know?"

Bryn hesitated briefly, then said, "She hasn't really been a mother to you for a long time, Corrie. Maybe it's time, finally, to let it go. Just take care of yourself and the baby now. Let Patrice figure things out for herself."

"I guess so." Corrie sighed. "I just wish—"

"I know, it's the same thing you always wish. That she was a normal mom. But she's not. And you have got to start standing up for yourself. And not just for you, for your baby. All this drama can't be good for the baby."

Corrie nodded. "You're right."

"Come on," Bryn said, pulling Corrie up from the bed. "Let's make something to eat. I'm really hungry."

"Ugh," Corrie said. "I'm not."

"Have you eaten anything today?"

Corrie stopped to think about it. "I had half a bagel this morning."

Bryn shook her head. "You have to start taking better care of yourself. You're eating for two now."

They made chicken salad sandwiches and ate them with grapes on the back porch, watching the autumn sun sink below the horizon.

"So are you sure you want to do the amnio?" Bryn asked.

"I have to," Corrie said. "I can't wait nine months to know. I think I'd go crazy."

"I'll go with you."

"You don't have to." Corrie smiled at her friend.

"You can't go by yourself," Bryn said firmly.

"Thanks."

"Have you told Daniel yet?"

Corrie shook her head.

"Have you heard from him?"

"I've had about a million emails from him."

"You probably should answer him," Bryn said. "I know, it sounds weird coming from me; we both know he's not my favorite person in the world. But if you just keep ignoring him, he might end up on your doorstep again. You don't want that, do you?"

"No!" Corrie shook her head. "I just don't want to deal with Daniel right now. If he is the father, I'll let him know in December. Right now, I'm just concentrating on the positive. I keep thinking if I pray hard enough, the baby will be Mark's."

Bryn smiled and shook her head.

"I know it's silly," Corrie said. "But that's what is keeping me sane right now."

"Hey, whatever works." Bryn rose and took Corrie's plate. "Let's go get some ice cream."

Corrie laughed, and Bryn said, "Hey, as long as I'm not throwing up I might as well be eating, right?"

"I guess so."

They put their dishes in the sink and found their shoes.

The doorbell rang.

Bryn's eyes widened. "Do you think it's Mark?"

"I don't think so," Corrie said. "He just came in last time."

She walked into the living room and opened the front door. Her father-in-law stood on the porch, his hands in his pockets.

"Oh, Tom," Corrie said. "I wasn't . . . Is everything all right?"

"Can I come in?" His voice was low.

"Sure."

He stopped when he saw Bryn. "I'm sorry. I didn't realize you had company."

"It's okay," Corrie said. "Bryn was just leaving."

"You call me if you need me," Bryn whispered in her ear as she hugged Corrie.

Corrie closed the door behind her.

"Do you want a drink?" she asked.

"That would be good," Tom said.

He followed her into the kitchen and sat at the table.

"So . . . what's up?" Corrie asked, handing him a glass of wine.

"I'm just so sorry about you and Mark," he said. "I know Grace was unpleasant when you saw her at the hospital, and I wanted to apologize for that."

Corrie sank into a chair across from him.

"You don't have anything to apologize for," she said. "I'm the one who should be apologizing. I'm so sorry . . ."

Tom held up his hand.

"Listen," he said, "just let me say what I came here to say."

"Okay." She sat back in her chair and waited. After a long pause, Tom spoke.

"I was unfaithful to Grace once, a long time ago. It was a terrible mistake, and I've never stopped regretting it."

Corrie stared at her father-in-law.

"The point is that sometimes these things . . . happen. But that doesn't have to mean the end of the marriage. Grace finally forgave me, and we've had forty wonderful years together."

He paused and sipped his wine.

"I think that's part of why she's so angry with you," he said. "It brings back old hurts."

"Does Mark know?" Corrie whispered.

Tom nodded. "I told him a couple nights ago. I thought he needed to hear it, to see that you can work through it if you try."

"Thank you." Corrie's voice shook. "Really, thank you. I can't imagine how hard it was to tell him."

"He's my son." Tom smiled at her. "I want him to be happy. And I know he loves you."

"But if the baby isn't his . . ." Corrie's voice trailed away.

"That will be hard," Tom said. "But again, if you want to make it work, you'll find a way. That's what I told him, and that's what I'm telling you."

They sat silently for a minute, then Tom rose and put his glass on the counter.

"I won't keep you," he said. "I just want you to know that Grace and I both love you. And we are both praying that you and Mark can work things out."

He hugged her as she cried into his chest.

"Thank you, Tom. You have no idea how much that means to me."

"Oh, but I do," he said, smiling down at her. "That's why I'm here."

He kissed the top of her head and left.

Corrie folded her legs beneath her on the couch, wondering at the conversation she'd just had.

Maybe if Tom could forgive her, Mark could, too. Maybe they could work things out, after all.

Please, God, let that be true.

She sat in silence for a while, then picked up the phone and dialed Maya's number. Her mother might not be on her side, but her little sister damned well would be.

～37～

Corrie sat in Father Carmichael's office, fingering her rosary. "What's troubling you today, Corrie?" The priest smiled at her encouragingly.

Corrie bit her lip. Finally, her voice trembling, she spoke.

"I'm pregnant, Father."

"Corrie, that's wonderful!" Father Carmichael grinned widely. "I know how much you and Mark have wanted a baby."

"Um, well . . ." Corrie stammered. "The thing is . . . I slept with another man, Father. When I was in California last month, I slept with the man I was involved with before Mark."

She paused, her cheeks burning.

"Oh," the priest said softly. "Oh."

A long pause ensued. At last, he spoke again. "Does Mark know?"

Corrie nodded, not meeting his eyes.

"He's left me."

"I see."

"I'm so sorry, Father. I wish so much it didn't happen. I know I've sinned, and it's unforgivable." Corrie squeezed her eyes shut, trying to block the tears.

"A sin, yes," the priest said quietly. "But not unforgivable."

Corrie raised her eyes to meet his.

"We all make mistakes, Corrie. God knows we are human and that we all make mistakes. The mystery of God, the mystery of God's grace, is that he loves us in spite of our mistakes."

"I don't see how he could possibly love me, after what I've done."

They sat in silence for a moment. When Father Carmichael spoke again, his voice was soft but firm.

"Corrie, God loves you because you are his child. Consider the child you're carrying now. Do you love your baby?"

Corrie folded her arms across her stomach and nodded. "More than anything," she whispered.

"Then think how much more God loves you. God's love surpasses our understanding. Your child is human. Someday he or she will make mistakes and disappoint you. That doesn't mean you'll stop loving him or her."

Corrie thought about that for a while. Finally, she raised her head to look at the priest. "Thank you, Father."

She paused again, longer this time. When she spoke once more, her voice faltered.

"I think I have to leave Holy Spirit," she said. "This is Mark's church, his family's church. I don't want to make it hard for him to be here. He's going to need you more than ever."

"The church is big enough for everyone, Corrie."

Corrie shook her head. "I think it would be best if I found a new parish."

Father Carmichael smiled sadly.

"St. Luke's is a wonderful parish," he said. "They even have a Parents Without Partners group meeting there on Tuesday nights. It might be a good fit for you."

Corrie nodded, tears filling her eyes.

"I'll miss you, Father. I'll miss Holy Spirit."

"We'll be here, Corrie. We'll always be here, if you want to come back."

38

Corrie sat in the waiting room at her doctor's office, shaking from head to toe. Beside her, Bryn sat looking through a parenting magazine. Her hand rested on her belly, which was just beginning to show a tiny bulge.

"I don't know if I can do this," Corrie said.

"You can," Bryn assured her, laying aside the magazine. "You need to know so you can get on with things."

Outside, the December sky was gray and cold. Corrie felt as if she'd been sleepwalking for the last few weeks, waiting to find out if she and Mark could pick up the pieces of their marriage. They'd met for coffee twice, both times awkward and painful.

Please, God, please let this baby be Mark's. It had become her mantra, one she repeated hundreds of times each day. Soon she would know the truth.

"Corrie Philips?" The nurse holding a clipboard called her name.

Corrie and Bryn both rose. The nurse smiled.

"How are you?" she asked.

"I'll be better once this is over with," Corrie said. "Is it okay if my friend comes in with me?"

"Sure," the nurse said.

Bryn waited outside the exam room while Corrie undressed and donned a hospital gown.

"You can come in," Corrie called. She felt horribly exposed sitting on the exam table, clutching the faded blue gown around her.

"You're going to be okay," Bryn said firmly, taking her hand. "In a few minutes, it will be over and done with. And next week, you'll know."

"I know," Corrie said. "But what if . . ."

"No what ifs right now," Bryn said. "Right now, we're going to see your baby."

The nurse came in and took Corrie's blood pressure and temperature. Then Dr. Ping arrived. He smiled at Corrie and patted her hand.

"Are you ready?"

"I guess so."

"Okay, I'm going to give you local anesthesia," he said. "Just a small prick."

Corrie squeezed her eyes shut as the doctor squeezed cold jelly onto her belly. Then she heard the whoosh-whoosh of the ultrasound.

"There's your baby."

She opened her eyes and stared at the monitor. Beside her, Bryn drew in a quick breath and squeezed her hand.

"See, there's the head and that's the heart. And feet and hands." The doctor pointed to the monitor. Corrie couldn't stop staring at the image on the screen. The baby moved slightly, and she felt tears sting her eyes.

"Now," said Dr. Ping, "I'm going to insert the needle just here." He pointed to a place a bit removed from the baby. "I want you to hold very still."

Corrie closed her eyes again, praying as hard as she had ever prayed. *Please, God, please! Let the baby be Mark's. And please, please,* please *let the baby be okay.*

After only a minute, it was over. Dr. Ping took the tube with the amniotic fluid, sealed it, and attached a label. "I'll be back in a few minutes," he said. "You just lie still."

"Did it hurt?" Bryn asked, using tissues to wipe the jelly from Corrie's stomach.

"No," Corrie said. "Just the first shot."

"Do you feel okay?"

Corrie nodded, chewing on her lip. *Please, God. Please . . .*

Bryn drove Corrie home and made her lie on the couch.

"I'm going to make some soup," she said. "You just lie there and be good."

Corrie smiled at her friend.

"Thank you," she whispered. "I'm glad you came with me."

"Me too."

The phone rang in the kitchen, and Corrie heard Bryn answer.

"Oh, hi, Mark. Yes, she's all right. She's on the couch. She's supposed to take it easy for the rest of the day."

Corrie listened intently.

"Do you want to talk to her?"

Corrie started to rise, felt a tiny cramp, and leaned back onto the cushion.

"Okay," Bryn said, "I'll tell her. Sure thing."

"That was Mark." Bryn walked into the room carrying a glass of milk. "He just wanted to make sure you were okay."

"He didn't want to talk to me?" Corrie's voice wavered.

"He said he was on his way into a meeting."

Corrie's eyes filled.

"At least he called," Bryn said. "At least he cares enough to worry about you."

Corrie nodded.

"Now drink your milk." Bryn put the glass on the coffee table.

"Bryn?"

Bryn stopped in the doorway to the kitchen and turned. "Yeah?"

"Have you heard from Paul at all?"

"Not since that last call after our date. I told him to stay the hell away from me, and I guess he took it seriously."

"Do you miss him?"

Bryn leaned against the door frame, her hand on her stomach.

"Sometimes," she admitted. "I mean, I did tell him not to call. But I guess I thought he would anyway.

"Oh well." She straightened her shoulders. "I knew from the start he wasn't father material, right?"

"We're quite a pair, aren't we?" Corrie said, willing herself not to cry.

Bryn walked back to the couch, sat down, and hugged her tightly.

"We're going to be just fine, you and me," she said. "We have each other, we have Bob, we have our babies. We're going to be okay."

"I love you," Corrie whispered.

"I love you back."

A week later, Corrie and Bryn sat in Dr. Ping's office, holding hands, waiting. After what felt like an eternity, the doctor walked in, carrying some papers.

"How are you?" he asked, smiling at Corrie.

"I'm okay." Her voice was small.

"Well, you have a healthy baby," he said.

Corrie said nothing. She simply stared at him, clutching Bryn's hand.

"I'm sorry, Corrie," Dr. Ping said gently. "The baby is not Mark's."

Corrie crumpled in her chair. "Oh God. Oh my God."

Bryn wrapped an arm around her shoulder and squeezed.

"I'm very sorry," the doctor repeated. "I know this isn't how you wanted things."

He waited a long minute while Corrie cried, shaking hard.

"But, Corrie," he said finally, taking her hand. "You have a beautiful, healthy baby."

"I know," she said, trying to smile. "I'm so glad it's healthy."

"Do you want to know if it's a boy or girl?"

Corrie raised her head. Beside her, Bryn was nodding.

"Yes," Corrie said.

"It's a girl." Dr. Ping smiled at her. "A healthy baby girl. You have a daughter."

She sat a moment, letting it sink in. A daughter. Not Mark's daughter. Daniel's daughter.

No, she thought then, *my daughter. This baby is mine.*

"Everything looks good," Dr. Ping said. "The baby is developing normally. No chromosomal defects. It all looks good."

"Thank you, Dr. Ping."

"Are you all right?" He smiled at her again.

"I guess so." She tried to sound confident.

"I'll see you in two weeks for your regular appointment. In the meantime, take care of yourself. I mean it, Corrie. I want you to eat and sleep and exercise and try not to worry too much. Just concentrate on having a healthy baby."

❧ 39 ❧

The doorbell rang and Corrie rose slowly, laying aside the magazine she had been pretending to read.

Oh God, please help me. And please, God, help Mark!

She opened the door and Mark smiled at her tentatively.

"Are you okay?" he asked.

She nodded.

"And the baby?"

"The baby is fine."

"Good," he said, sitting down in the recliner.

She stared at him for a minute, steeling herself. *Please, God . . .*

"The baby isn't yours," she whispered.

"Oh." His voice was so soft she barely heard it.

"I'm sorry, Mark. I'm so sorry! I wanted it to be yours so much. I hate that she's not yours."

He sat still, staring at the floor. "Me too," he said at last.

"Are you all right?" she asked.

He shook his head. "No, I'm not all right."

They sat a minute, neither of them speaking.

"Okay," he said finally. "Well, at least now we know. At least now we can move on."

"What do you mean, move on?" She watched him, her stomach churning.

"I mean, move on. There's nothing holding us together now." He rose and began pacing the floor.

"Look, I've put off getting an apartment because I thought if the baby was mine, maybe we could work it out."

"We can still work it out!" Corrie's voice shook.

"No." He shook his head. "I've thought about it a lot, Corrie. And I can't do it. I can't raise Daniel's kid and just pretend it's mine, pretend that it's okay."

"But, Mark . . ."

"I'm sorry." His voice was gentle. "I'm not trying to punish you or hurt you. I just can't do it."

Corrie sank back into the couch. She felt like she might throw up.

"You can keep the house," he said. "I'll make a list of stuff I want to take. We can work this out without a bunch of lawyers."

She stared at him in disbelief.

"You want a divorce?"

"I don't *want* a divorce," he said. "I need a divorce. I can't do this, Corrie. I'm sorry, but I just can't."

"But your dad said . . ."

"I know what my dad said!" Mark's voice rose. "He told me about his affair, what he did to my mom. But at least he didn't get some other woman pregnant! He didn't ask my mother to raise his bastard child!"

Corrie felt the words like a slap across the face. She lowered her head and let her tears fall unchecked.

"I'm sorry," Mark said. "This is exactly what I didn't want to do. I don't want to yell and fight. I don't want to hurt you, and I know you don't want to hurt me. I just want it over and done with."

He walked to the front door and paused.

"I'm filing for divorce," he said. "I hope we can do this without a bunch of fighting."

He looked at her for a long minute, then sighed heavily and left, closing the door behind him.

Corrie lay back on the couch and cried, her arms wrapped around her stomach.

Mark was gone and he wasn't coming back. Her life was over.

And then she felt something she'd never felt before. A tiny fluttering in her stomach, as if a moth had been let loose inside her. She sat up, her hands on her belly, waiting intently. And felt it again.

Could it be? Again, a small flutter.

Through her tears she smiled and then she laughed. It was life, her baby moving inside her, her tiny daughter making her presence known. It felt just the way Bryn had described it a couple weeks earlier, like a tiny butterfly fluttering in her womb.

She rose, her hand still on her stomach, and reached for the phone. She started to dial Sarah's number, then stopped. She hadn't seen Sarah since Grace was born. Now that she'd joined St. Luke's, she didn't even run into her old friend at church anymore.

She bit her lip, gripping the phone tightly. This was a moment she'd dreamed of for so long, one that had always included Sarah. Now . . . she shook her head. Sarah was Mark's sister. He would need her now more than ever. She had no right to intrude on that.

She sat a moment, hand still on her belly, and then she called Maya.

❧ 40 ❧

Corrie took a deep breath and dialed. After only one ring, she heard Daniel's voice.

"Daniel Chapman."

"Daniel, it's Corrie."

"Corrie! God, I'm so glad to hear from you. How are you?"

"I'm fine," she said softly. "Is this a good time to talk?"

"Hang on just a minute. I want to close the door.

"Okay, we're good. God, Corrie, I've been going out of my mind missing you. I mean, I've been good. I haven't called even once. I really have been trying. But you can't believe how much I've missed you!"

"Daniel, I have something I need to tell you." Corrie's voice shook slightly.

"Okay." He sounded apprehensive.

"I'm pregnant."

There was a long pause.

"Oh," he said finally. "That's . . . that's great, Corrie. Congratulations. I know how much you've wanted this."

"The baby is yours."

Corrie sat, waiting for his response, chewing her fingernail.

"Oh," he said again. "Oh God, Corrie. Are you sure? Does your husband know?"

"Yes, I'm sure," she said. "I had a DNA test done. It's your baby. And Mark knows. In fact, he's filing for divorce."

"Oh, Corrie-Andy, I'm sorry. I mean, I'm not sorry the baby is mine. I just . . . I'm sorry you're going through so much. Are you okay?"

"No, I'm not okay. I'm a mess."

"I'm coming out there."

"No!" Her voice rose. "Please don't come, Daniel. Not right now. Let me just get through the holidays and then . . . and then we'll talk."

"Corrie, you just told me you're having my baby. Our baby! I am *not* going to wait until after the holidays. I need to see you now. We have so much to decide."

"Please, Daniel. Please don't come now. I can't handle any more. I just have to get through Christmas. Then we'll talk. Please?" Her voice quavered.

"Corrie, I don't want to make things worse for you." Daniel's voice was soft now, reassuring. "I promise I don't. But I need to see you. We have to talk about this, about the future. I'm not trying to make it hard for you, but I'm this baby's father. It's not just your baby."

"It's a girl," she said so quietly he had to strain to hear her.

"Oh wow," he breathed. "A girl. We're going to have a daughter. Corrie, that's just freaking amazing!"

She allowed herself a small smile. "It is kind of amazing."

"I'm booking a flight for tomorrow," he said. "No arguments. And no pressure. We don't have to decide everything right now. But I really need to see you, Corrie. We need to see each other."

She sighed. "All right," she said. "But I don't think you'd better plan on staying at Bob's."

"Does he know?"

"Yes," she said. "He and Bryn and my mother . . . everybody knows."

"Everybody but me, apparently. Why didn't you tell me before?"

"I was waiting until I had the test. If the baby had been Mark's, well, it would be a whole different story."

"I'll bet," he said. "Okay, I'm going to book a flight and I'll let you know when I'm getting in. And don't worry, I won't bother Bob. I'm sure he's pretty pissed off at me right now. I'll just get a hotel."

She didn't reply.

"Corrie?" His voice was tentative. "It's going to be all right. I promise it will."

"I hope so," she said. "Good-bye, Daniel."

The next afternoon, Corrie left work early. When she pulled into her driveway, Daniel was already there, leaning against a rental car. He grinned at her as he opened her door. Then, before she could stop it, he swooped her into an embrace, lifting her feet from the ground.

"God," he said, kissing her forehead. "I am so glad to see you!"

"Stop it, Daniel! Put me down."

He set her back on the ground and she pulled away from him.

"Sorry," he said, still smiling. "I really am glad to see you."

Corrie retrieved her purse and briefcase from the car.

"Come inside," she said. "I don't need the whole neighborhood watching us."

He followed her into the house and waited while she put away her things.

"Are you okay?" he asked, eyeing her anxiously. "Do you feel all right?"

"I'm fine," she said. "I'm pregnant, not sick."

"I can't believe you're pregnant." Daniel's blue eyes sparkled. "I can't believe we're going to have a daughter."

"Do you want coffee?" Corrie walked into the kitchen. He followed.

"You can't have coffee, can you? Isn't caffeine bad for the baby?"

She sighed and let herself smile just a bit. At least someone was worrying over her.

"I can make decaf," she said.

"Decaf sounds good."

Daniel took a seat at the breakfast bar in the spot Mark usually occupied.

"Let's sit at the table," Corrie said. She measured coffee into the pot and poured in water.

They sat across from each other, Daniel staring at Corrie, Corrie staring at the wall above Daniel's head.

"So, when is the baby due?"

"June," she said.

"June," he repeated. "That's good. Summer birthdays are more fun."

She shook her head.

"It's going to be all right, Corrie."

She smiled at him. "Just because you keep saying it doesn't make it so."

"It's true, Corrie. It will be all right. I know this isn't what you planned. And I can't imagine how hard it is for you right now. And I can't believe your jerk of a husband just left you high and dry."

"Don't talk about him like that!"

Corrie rose and walked to the counter.

"None of this is Mark's fault. He didn't cheat on me. He didn't conceive a child with another woman. All he's ever done is loved me. And you don't get to pass any kind of judgment on him."

"Okay." He raised his hands above his head. "I won't talk about it. I just don't understand how he could leave, just like that."

Corrie said nothing as she poured two mugs of coffee, then added cream to hers.

"If we are going to talk," she said as she set a mug down before him, "then here are the ground rules. First, Mark is off-limits. I mean it," she said as he opened his mouth. "Not another word about my husband, or we're done."

"Sure," he said. "All right."

"Second," she continued and then paused. "Okay, there is no second. Just the one rule."

"Got it," he said.

"So . . ." She took a sip of coffee and wrinkled her nose.

"What's wrong?" he asked.

"It needs sugar," she said, reaching for the sugar bowl.

His eyebrows raised. "You always drank your coffee black."

"I know." She spooned sugar into her cup. "But ever since I've been pregnant, all my tastes have changed."

He smiled at her.

"So, let's talk," he said. "Let's talk about you and the baby and us."

"There is no us, Daniel. There's you and there's me and there's the baby. But there is no us."

He reached across the table and took her hand.

"There can be, though," he said, staring into her eyes. "It can be us, you and me and our daughter."

She simply shook her head.

"Come to Los Angeles," he said. "Seriously, Corrie, move in with me. We can make a life together."

"You and me and Capri?"

"Capri is moving out," he said. "She and Mia are getting a place together. In fact, she's going to meet Mia's parents at Christmas."

"That's nice," Corrie said. "I hope it works out for her."

"So," he said, "we can turn her room into a nursery. She's even offered to paint it before she moves out. She's excited about the baby."

"You told her?"

"Yeah," he said. "It's not a secret, right? I mean, you've already told everybody."

"I just didn't know you told her."

"She's happy for us. And she said to tell you thank you for sending the magazines. She was really happy with the article."

"Good."

They sat a minute, and Daniel said again, "Come to California."

"I can't," she said, smiling at him. "My whole life is here. I can't just leave my job and everything."

"Why not? Look." Daniel rose and began pacing the kitchen floor. "What's here for you, anyway? Just your soon-to-be ex-husband and his family and all your mutual friends."

"There's my mom," Corrie started, then stopped.

"Does she know about the baby?"

She nodded.

"So what does she think?"

"That I'm a terrible daughter."

Daniel stopped and stared at her. "You can't be serious. We're talking about Patrice, right? She can't be passing judgment on you because you had an affair."

"A fling," Corrie corrected him. "And no, she's not mad about that. She's mad about the divorce."

Daniel sat down and looked at her.

Corrie sighed. "Mark and I have been pretty much supporting her since I married him. She's mad because her gravy train is leaving the station."

"I'm sorry, Corrie," Daniel said. "That's rough. But it's all the more reason to come to L.A. You can always get another job."

"I happen to love my job," she said. "And I love this town. All my friends are here. It's home.

"Besides, I'm not even divorced from Mark. I keep hoping that maybe he'll change his mind and come home. I love him."

Daniel said nothing for a minute. Finally, he leaned forward across the table and stared at her.

"I know you love him," he said. "But you loved me first. And you're having my baby."

Corrie stared down at her coffee cup.

"I loved you a long time ago," she said softly. "I was a different person then. A lot has changed since college. I moved on."

"Then why did you sleep with me?"

She leaned her face into her hands. "It was a mistake," she whispered. "It should never have happened."

"But it did happen, and you're pregnant. And whether you like it or not, Corrie, I am this baby's father. Doesn't that count for anything?"

Corrie rose and carried her coffee cup to the sink.

"Of course it counts," she said, her back turned to him. "But it doesn't change the way I feel."

She turned to look at him.

"I don't love you, Daniel. I did a long time ago, but we were kids then. Yes, the baby is yours. And we'll have to figure out how to make that work. I don't want to keep you away from her, if you want to be in her life. But I am not moving to California. I am not moving in with you."

"So you're planning on raising this baby on your own?"

She nodded.

"I have a good job. I have a good support system. I have great insurance. I will be okay. We will be okay."

"A baby needs a father." His voice was grim.

"A baby needs people to love her, and this baby will have that in spades."

Daniel rose and took her hands.

"I know you aren't ready to think about it now, but promise me you won't rule it out altogether," he said. "Just promise me that."

She shook her head.

"I'm really tired," she said.

"Okay, I'll go. But I'm not going back to L.A. until we've talked again."

She nodded and walked with him to the front door, allowed herself to be pulled into a hug.

"I love you, Corrie-Andy," he whispered.

"Good night," she said, pulling away from him.

She locked the door behind him and sat on the couch to cry.

❧ 41 ❧

The next morning, Daniel was at the door bearing bagels with cream cheese.

"I have to go to work," Corrie protested.

"Take the day off," he said.

"I can't."

"Come on, Corrie. I'm only here today. I have to go back to L.A. tomorrow for a Christmas program the kids are putting on. And we have a lot of stuff to talk about."

She sighed.

"All right. Let me call the office."

Daniel made coffee while Corrie called Kenetha. By the time she walked into the kitchen, he had set the table and was pouring orange juice.

"I'm really not much of a breakfast person," she said.

"You need to eat. Breakfast is the most important meal of the day. I can scramble some eggs."

"No, just a bagel."

"You need some protein," he said. "It's good for the baby. You just sit down and I'll make breakfast."

She smiled. It felt nice having someone take care of her.

Daniel rummaged through the refrigerator, pulling out an onion, a green pepper, eggs, and cheese.

"When did you get to be so domesticated?" Corrie asked.

"I've been taking care of myself for a long time," he said to her. "The first couple years in L.A., I pretty much lived on fast food. It got old. So, I learned how to cook."

She watched him move about her kitchen as if he were at home, chopping vegetables, toasting bagels, scrambling eggs. The Daniel she'd known in college never cooked.

"There you go." He set a plate before her.

"Thank you. It looks good."

Daniel sat down across from her with his own plate. They had just taken a first bite, when they heard a knock at the back door.

"Who could that be?" Corrie said, rising. "It's eight o'clock in the morning."

She opened the door to find Mark standing on the back steps.

"I hope it's okay," he said. "I need to pick up a couple things before . . ."

His voice trailed away as his eyes locked on Daniel, sitting at the kitchen table. He looked from Daniel to Corrie and back again.

"I didn't know you had company," he said, his cheeks reddening.

"It's okay," Corrie said. She could feel her own cheeks burning. "Um, Mark, this is Daniel. Daniel, this is my husband, Mark."

Daniel rose and extended his hand. "Nice to meet you, Mark."

Mark simply stared at him, ignoring the outstretched hand.

"I'll come back another time," he said, turning away.

"Mark!" Corrie followed him into the yard. "Wait, please. Let me just explain. . . ."

"You don't need to explain anything, Corrie." His voice was cold. "It's all pretty clear."

"No, it's not! Mark, please wait."

But he only got into his car, not looking back. She watched him drive away and felt tears stinging her eyes.

"I'm really sorry."

Daniel stood behind her, his hands on her shoulders.

She pulled away from him and walked back into the house, Daniel trailing behind her.

She splashed cold water on her face in the bathroom, willing her stomach to settle down. Finally, she came back to the kitchen, where Daniel was eating a bagel.

"I can't do this," she said, sinking into her chair.

"Do what?"

"This . . . any of it. This is not my life."

He said nothing.

"That was my husband," she said, her voice shaking. "We are sitting here eating breakfast in the house that *he* bought. God, he probably thinks you spent the night!"

"He's the one who left," Daniel said softly.

"Because I cheated on him!" Corrie's voice rose. "And now he comes over to find me sitting here with the man I cheated with. God, I'm such an awful, awful person."

She buried her head in her hands and began crying again.

Daniel sat quietly for a minute, then rose and walked around the table to wrap his arms around her.

"You are not an awful person. You are the farthest thing in the world from that. You are kind and wonderful and amazing. And you are human."

She leaned into him and sniffled to a stop.

"The eggs are cold," he said. "So eat your bagel and you'll feel better."

She managed a few bites before giving up. Her stomach was in knots.

"Okay," Daniel said, taking the plates to the sink and rinsing them. "Let's go for a walk."

"It's cold outside," Corrie protested.

"So put on a coat. Come on, it'll do you some good."

They bundled up and walked through the neighborhood.

"Pretty ritzy," Daniel said as they passed one beautiful house after another.

"It's a good neighborhood," Corrie said.

"Are you going to stay here after the divorce?"

"I don't know," she said. "I'm not sure I can swing the mortgage on my own. Besides, it feels really empty without Mark there."

"The offer stands, you know. You could come to California."

"I can't, Daniel."

"You can't, or you won't?"

"Both, actually."

"So if you're here and I'm there, how are we going to do this parenting thing?"

She sighed. "I don't know. I mean, it will be hard to be involved in her life when you're so far away."

They walked in silence for a minute.

"You could move back here," she said.

He shook his head. "I can't leave the center. There's still too much to do there."

"How's the funding?" she asked.

"We got some checks after the article came out. Thanks," he said. "But the big news is that we have a potential new donor, a big-time donor. He's coming to the Christmas program tomorrow."

"I hope it works out."

"I think it will. He seems pretty excited about the work we're doing."

"It really is cold," Corrie said, shivering.

"It feels good," Daniel said, smiling. "One of the only things I miss about Indiana is winter."

"Ugh," she said. "I could live without it."

"Come to L.A. and you can."

She just smiled and shook her head.

"I'm ready to go back," she said. "I'm freezing."

He laughed. "Let's go make some cocoa."

They sat in the living room with steaming mugs.

"This is nice," Daniel said.

Corrie felt a tiny flutter inside. "Oh," she said. "The baby is moving."

"Seriously? You can feel it moving?" Daniel put his hand on her stomach. "I don't feel anything."

"It's too early," she said. "Mostly it just feels like a butterfly in my stomach."

"Have you thought about names?"

She nodded. "I really like Emmaline. Emmaline Marie. What do you think?"

"It's pretty. I like it. God, I can't believe we're having a baby!"

She smiled. "Kind of an unorthodox family."

"But still a family," he said. "I'll just have to rack up a lot of frequent-flier miles, I guess."

"When she's old enough, she can come visit you."

He sighed. "It's not the same as being in her life all the time. I really wish you would come to L.A."

She said nothing.

"Come back with me for Christmas," he said suddenly. "I'll buy your ticket. Just come out and spend Christmas with me."

She shook her head. "I can't. I can't take time off work. And I already told Bryn and Bob I'd come to their house."

"Is she still living with him?"

Corrie nodded. "It seems to work for them both."

"Has he filed for divorce yet?"

"Yes, it should be final in January."

"What about the kids?"

"They're staying with Bob. Wendy can have them every other weekend, but only at her parents' house. As long as she's living with Luke, she can't have them at her house."

He raised his eyebrows.

"She made some very stupid choices," Corrie said.

"She must have," he agreed. "Well, good for Bob. Now he can move on. Maybe he'll meet someone else . . . if Bryn ever moves out of his house!"

"She will. I think after the holidays she's going to start looking for a place."

"It's about time."

Corrie laughed. "Actually, they seem almost like an old married couple these days. She's pregnant, too, you know."

"Bryn? Bryn is pregnant? Who's the father?"

"Paul, but they've broken up for good this time."

"So, is she expecting Bob to be her baby's daddy?"

"No, she's not. They're just really good friends. I think her being there has been good for both of them."

"If you say so."

They spent the rest of the morning talking about the baby. Corrie made grilled cheese sandwiches and tomato soup for lunch, and in the afternoon they went to the mall. Daniel bought a car seat for the baby and Corrie bought half a dozen tiny dresses.

"This feels right," Daniel said as they walked through the parking lot toward the car. "Just like a regular couple planning for their baby."

"It does feel nice," she agreed. "But we're not a couple. You know that, right?"

"I know you keep telling me so."

"Because it's true."

He took her to her favorite restaurant for dinner, then walked her to the door of her house.

"You sure you won't come for Christmas?" he asked.

"I can't," she said.

They stood on the porch for a long, awkward minute.

"I'm really tired," she said.

"I know. You should get some rest."

He hugged her and kissed her forehead.

"I'll call you when I get home," he said. "And we'll figure out when I'm coming again."

"Okay." She unlocked the front door and turned to him.

"Daniel, thank you for today."

"You're welcome, Corrie-Andy. It was fun."

She went inside, turned on the television, and fell asleep on the couch.

❧ 42 ❧

Bryn awoke on Christmas morning to a light tapping on her bedroom door.

"Bryn?" Cody's voice was soft.

"What do you need, Cody?" Bryn looked at the clock. Seven a.m.

"Are you awake?"

"I am now."

"Are you getting up?"

"I guess so."

"Good! Daddy says we can't open our presents until you get up."

"Daddy also told you not to wake her up!" Bob's voice startled her.

"But, Daddy, she's already awake."

"Sorry, Bryn," Bob called through the door.

"It's okay," she called back. "I'll be out in a minute."

She yawned, stretched, and reached for her robe.

The living room was strewn with brightly wrapped packages. The lights on the tree sparkled. Micah and Cody sat on the floor, picking up packages and shaking them.

"Merry Christmas," Bryn said, smiling.

"Merry Christmas, Bryn! Look at all the stuff Santa brought!" Cody's eyes shone.

"Here." Bob handed her a mug of hot coffee. "Sorry about the early wakeup call."

"It's fine," she said, beaming back at him. "It's Christmas!"

"Can we start now, Daddy?" Micah was holding a long box wrapped in festive red-and-white paper.

"Yeah." Bob smiled at his sons. "Have at it."

The next half hour was pure bedlam, filled with torn paper, scattered bows, and cries of delight.

"Thanks, Bryn!" Cody had just unwrapped a huge Transformer. "Look, Micah, it's Optimus Prime!"

"Cool," Micah said, not looking up from the package he was opening. Bryn watched him intently, as a huge smile spread across his face. He pulled a pair of binoculars from the box.

"Whoo!" he breathed. "How did you know?"

He raised his eyes to Bryn, who grinned down at him.

"An elf told me," she said.

"Thanks, Bryn!" Micah ran to the couch, every trace of his seven-year-old coolness erased, and threw his arms around her.

"You're welcome." Bryn felt tears sting her eyes. She looked over Micah's head to where Bob sat, gazing at them, his own eyes shining with tears.

"Okay," Bob said, rising. "Why don't you guys pick up the paper and bows, and I'll start breakfast."

Bryn followed him into the kitchen.

"That was fun," she said, refilling her coffee cup.

"Yeah," he said softly. "I was kind of worried about this, their first Christmas without Wendy. But they seem okay."

"Yes, they do. You're a great dad, Bob."

He turned and smiled at her. "And next year, you'll have a baby of your own for Christmas."

"It's still hard to believe," she said, patting her belly.

"Thanks, Bryn," he said, taking her hands. "You made this morning a whole lot easier."

"Back at you," she said, kissing his cheek.

The doorbell rang.

"That's got to be Corrie," Bryn said. "I'll go."

She walked into the living room just as Cody opened the front door.

"Mommy!" He threw his arms around his mother, grinning broadly.

"Hey, baby!" Wendy knelt down and wrapped Cody in a tight embrace. "Merry Christmas!"

"Wendy?" Bob stood in the living room, staring at his not-quite-ex-wife.

"Merry Christmas, Bob." She smiled up at him. "I hope it's okay. I just had to come see them."

"I wish you had called first. But . . . sure, it's okay. Come on in. I was just making breakfast."

"Micah?" Wendy turned to look at her older son, standing just behind his father, watching her.

"Hi," he said softly.

"Don't I get a hug?" Wendy asked, opening her arms.

Micah walked toward her slowly and allowed himself to be hugged.

"Where's Luke?" he asked.

"Oh, Luke is out of the picture," Wendy said, smiling at him. "We broke up. So . . . now maybe we can spend more time together."

Bob met Bryn's eyes across the room. She raised her eyebrows and he shrugged.

"Bryn." Wendy's voice was sharp. "I didn't even see you there." She eyed Bryn with obvious distaste, her eyes traveling from Bryn's tousled hair to her short robe.

"Hi, Wendy," Bryn said, feeling suddenly very exposed. "Merry Christmas."

"So." Wendy turned away from her and said to Bob, "Are we making Christmas pancakes? Because I brought real maple syrup!"

She followed him into the kitchen, the boys right behind them. Bryn wrapped her robe more tightly around herself and sighed. She was surprised at how deflated she felt.

Get it together, Bryn. It's not like they're your family.

She went to her room to pull on some jeans and a sweater. By the time she came back to the living room, the boys were setting the table. In the kitchen, she could hear Wendy laughing. Her stomach tightened.

"What can I do to help?" she asked, walking into the kitchen.

"We've got it covered," Wendy said, not turning from the stove, where she was flipping pancakes.

Bob smiled at Bryn. "Why don't you just sit down and relax?"

So Bryn sat at the table, watching the family settle swiftly into an old routine. She was grateful when the doorbell rang again.

"I'll get it." She opened the door and wrapped her arms around Corrie.

"Thank God you're here," she whispered.

"Are you okay?" Corrie pulled back to look at her.

"Yeah," Bryn said, forcing a smile. "Wendy is here."

Corrie stared at her. "Did Bob invite her?"

Bryn shook her head. "She just showed up."

"Great." Corrie grimaced. "That's just what we all need."

She followed Bryn into the house and set a covered dish on the table.

"That smells great!" Bob kissed Corrie's cheek.

"It's a hash brown casserole. Thank you for having me."

"I'm glad you're here," he said, taking her coat. "Do you want some coffee?"

"Hi, Corrie." Wendy smiled at her. "So, we're quite a crew today. Where's Mark?"

Corrie's cheeks reddened. "He's not coming," she said softly. "We've separated."

"I'm sorry." Wendy turned back to the stove. "That seems to be going around."

Bryn rolled her eyes at Corrie. Bob just shook his head.

They sat down to a table loaded with pancakes, bacon, pecan rolls, and Corrie's hash brown casserole. Wendy regally claimed her regular place at the table, smiling sweetly at Bob.

"I brought maple syrup," Wendy said, pouring some on Cody's pancakes.

Cody grinned at his mother. "Are you coming home now, Mommy?"

"Well, I don't know, honey." Wendy smiled back at him. "That depends on Daddy."

Bryn choked on her orange juice. Corrie stared firmly at her plate.

Micah rose from the table. "Can I be excused?" He sprinted toward the bathroom.

"Wendy." Bob spoke quietly. "Now is not the time."

"I was just answering his question," she said, smiling at Bob.

"Is she coming home, Daddy?" Cody looked from his mother to his father.

"No, Cody." Bob put his hand over Cody's. "Mommy doesn't live here anymore."

"But she broke up with Luke," Cody said. "So now she can come home."

"It's not that easy," Bob said, measuring his words carefully. "Mommy and I will talk about it later. Right now, let's just enjoy our pancakes, okay?"

"Anyone need more coffee?" Bryn rose and walked into the kitchen, chewing the inside of her cheek to keep from screaming.

Micah returned to the table, studiously avoiding his mother's eyes.

"Are you okay, honey?" Wendy asked.

"Yeah."

"Well, eat your pancakes," she said.

They ate in uncomfortable silence. Finally, Wendy said, "Corrie, I just love that casserole. I'm going to have to get that recipe."

"Sure," Corrie said. "I'll email it to you."

"So, here's a question," Wendy said. "Since you and Mark are separated, why doesn't Bryn just move in with you?"

"Wendy!" Bob stood, dropping his napkin to the table. "Can I talk to you outside?"

Wendy raised her eyebrows. "What's wrong? It's a simple question. I mean, they lived together before; it seems like the perfect solution to Bryn's housing problem."

Bryn rose and carried her plate to the kitchen. Corrie followed, carrying her own plate.

Then they heard Micah. "Bryn can stay with us if she wants to!" he yelled. "You left. You don't get to say who can stay with us!"

Micah ran to his bedroom.

"Daddy?" Cody's small voice brought tears to Bryn's eyes. "Why is everybody mad?"

"It's okay, buddy. We're all just a little bit stressed. But it's all good. Why don't you show Mommy your new Transformer."

Bob walked into the kitchen, carrying more plates.

"God, I'm so sorry," he said, wrapping Bryn in a hug. "You know I don't think that way, right?"

She nodded, leaning into his chest.

"I need to talk to Micah," he said. "Are you all right?"

"I'm fine." Bryn smiled at him. "Go help Micah."

Bryn and Corrie rinsed dishes and began loading the dishwasher.

"What the hell is wrong with her?" Bryn hissed. "Showing up here unannounced and ruining Christmas for everyone."

Corrie laid her hand on Bryn's shoulder.

"It sounds like she wants to come back," she said quietly.

"Over my dead body," Bryn said.

"My, Bryn, that's a pretty thought."

They turned to see Wendy standing in the doorway, holding her coffee cup.

She walked to the counter, leaned against it, and smiled at Bryn.

"This is *my* family," she said, staring directly into Bryn's eyes. "Go get your own."

Bryn brushed past her and walked swiftly down the hall, toward her room.

Corrie stood staring at Wendy for a long minute. Finally, she couldn't stop herself.

"You have a lot of nerve! My God, Wendy, you left! You left Bob for another man! What is this, the third time? You walked out on him and on your sons. And now you just breeze in, like nothing happened? What is wrong with you?"

She stopped, shaking, when she saw Bob in the doorway.

"I need to go," she said. She walked past Bob and headed toward Bryn's room.

"Bryn?" she called at the door. "Can I come in?"

She opened the door and found Bryn sitting on the bed, staring at the floor.

"Are you okay?" Corrie sat down beside her.

"Yeah," Bryn said. "She's right, though. They're not my family."

Corrie put her arm around Bryn's shoulders. "But they are your friends. And they love you. And so do I."

Bryn smiled. "I love you, too."

"So, how about we get out of here, at least until Wendy leaves?"

"Where should we go?"

"My house." Corrie stood and held her hand out to Bryn. "Come on, let's go."

They walked into the living room to find Bob sitting alone.

"Where are the boys?" Bryn asked.

"Micah's in his room. He's pretty upset. Cody went with Wendy to see her parents."

She sat on the couch beside him and took his hand.

"I'm so sorry, Bob," she said softly.

"It's not your fault." He sighed and leaned back against the couch.

"Are you sure it's all right for her to have Cody?" Corrie sat down opposite them.

"Yeah," he said. "He'll be okay with her parents."

They sat quietly for a minute. Then Bob rose and walked to the kitchen. He returned a minute later, carrying a glass.

"Kind of early in the day for that, isn't it?" Bryn said.

"It's been a hell of a day," Bob said, sitting back down on the couch. "I'd offer you one, but neither of you can drink."

"I'd take a cup of hot chocolate," Corrie said, rising. "Bryn, do you want some?"

"Sure," Bryn said.

Corrie walked into the kitchen. Bryn touched Bob's hand. "Are you okay?"

"Yeah," he said. Then, "No, not really."

"I'm sorry," she repeated. "I don't understand Wendy, I really don't. How can she say the stuff she does and just expect everything to be fine?"

"She's like a child," he said. "It's magical thinking."

"But you're not buying it again, are you?"

"No, this time I'm not buying it. This time, it really is over."

Bryn squeezed his hand. "You and the boys are going to be fine, you know."

"I know. I mean, I know I'll be okay. I'm really worried about Micah."

"He's pretty mad." Bryn glanced at the doorway to Micah's room. "But maybe that's a good thing. I mean, his mom is a loon. And he knows it. So yeah, he's mad. But maybe that's a good first step toward . . . I don't know, toward dealing with it."

"Maybe." Bob sighed. "I just hate that he's so hurt."

"At least he's got one good parent." Bryn smiled at him. "He's got you. He'll be okay."

"Thanks, Bryn. You really are a godsend. Thank you for being here, especially today."

She leaned her head against his shoulder. "Well, you all are my family, in a way. Besides, where else would I be?"

✧43✧

Corrie paced her living room that evening, watching the snow fall outside. By morning, everything would be blanketed. She'd spent most of the day with Bob and Bryn, but finally she had to come home. Home, to her beautiful but oh-so-empty house. She hadn't even decorated for Christmas this year.

She dropped into a chair and tucked her legs underneath her. Last year, she and Mark had hosted his family for Christmas dinner. This year, they would all be gathered at Sarah's house, cooing over the baby, playing cards, and just being a family. She loved Christmas with Mark's family. Everyone got along; no one got drunk or mean. It was all very different from the way her childhood Christmases had been.

She remembered the year after her father died, how her mother had told her that she would not have any presents. There wasn't enough money, she'd said, and the little bit she had she was going to use to get Caerl and Maya each a gift, since they were still so young.

Of course, Patrice had enough money for gin. That day was the first time Corrie had to help her mother up the stairs and into bed. Then she'd made scrambled eggs and toast for her little brother and sister and read them stories until they fell asleep.

She had not seen or spoken to her mother since the day she told Patrice about the pregnancy. She thought about calling sometimes, but she never did.

She sighed and resumed pacing, her cell phone in her hand. Should she call Mark? Would he talk to her? Would he even answer the phone? She'd been debating with herself all day. She wanted to hear his voice, that was all. Just to hear him. She wanted to explain that Daniel had only been there to talk about the baby, that he had not spent the night with her, that they were not lovers. She wanted him to tell her that it would be okay, that he loved her. She wanted her husband back.

Finally, she punched in his number, her fingers trembling. After the third ring, she heard his voice.

"Hello?"

"Mark, hi. It's me, it's Corrie."

"Oh." Nothing more. Just, "Oh."

"I hope I'm not interrupting a card game," she said. "I assume you've already had dinner."

"Yeah, we've eaten." He paused, then asked, "What do you want, Corrie? Are you all right?"

"I just wanted to hear your voice," she said. "I miss you so much, especially today."

He said nothing.

"And I wanted to tell you that when you came the other day and Daniel was here, he wasn't staying here, in the house. He stayed at a hotel. We just needed to talk about the baby."

"Whatever." His voice was flat. "What you do and who you do it with is none of my business anymore."

She drew a quick breath, hurting so much she couldn't speak.

"I'm sorry, Corrie," Mark said after a minute. "I don't want to fight, and I don't want to hurt you. I just can't do this right now."

"Okay," she whispered.

The line went dead.

She sank into the couch and cried, letting the waves of sadness wash over her.

"I'm alone," she said out loud. The words echoed through the room. "I'm really alone."

And then the baby moved.

She was not, in fact, alone.

She sat up and wiped away the tears, put her hands on her belly. "Thank you, baby," she said. "Thank you."

She walked upstairs and into the nursery, where she had sat and cried so many times. She touched the crib, the changing table, the dresser. She picked up a stuffed rabbit and cradled it in her arms.

"We're going to move, baby," she said suddenly. "We are going to find a new house to live in."

She sat down in the rocking chair, still holding the rabbit.

"This house is just too sad," she said. "I don't want you to live in a house that's so sad."

She sat for a long time, rocking the stuffed rabbit, staring out the window at the snow. Finally, she went to bed, taking the rabbit with her.

∽44∾

On New Year's Eve, Corrie and Bryn made pizzas while Bob and the boys built an elaborate structure with Legos. Then they ate in front of the television, watching *Elf*. Cody lay with his head in Bob's lap. Micah sprawled on the floor, occasionally adding a new brick to the Legos building.

The phone rang at eight o'clock.

"Hello, Wendy," Bob said. "What's up? Sure, you can talk to them."

He handed the phone to Cody.

"Hi, Mommy! It's a new year almost. Did you know that?"

He wandered into the dining room, chattering about the movie and the Legos.

Then, "Yeah, she's here."

Bryn's spine stiffened.

"Hey, buddy." Bob reached for the phone. "Let's give Micah a turn to talk."

Cody told his mother good-bye and handed the phone to Bob.

"I don't want to talk to her," Micah said loudly, refusing to take the phone from Bob.

"Okay," Bob said soothingly. "You don't have to if you don't want to."

He took the phone into his bedroom and closed the door. A few minutes later, he returned.

"Everything all right?" Bryn asked.

"Yeah," he said. "She wants to take the boys to a movie tomorrow."

"I don't want to go with her," Micah said firmly. "I'm supposed to go to Matt's tomorrow."

"Why don't you want to go with us?" Cody asked.

"It's okay," Bob said again. "If you don't want to go, you don't have to go."

"But why don't you want to go?" Cody asked again.

"Because she's a bad mom! She left us because she wanted to be with Luke."

"Shhh." Bob sat beside Micah on the floor and wrapped his arms around the little boy. "She's not a bad mom. At least, she's not trying to be a bad mom. She just . . . sometimes your mom makes mistakes. But she does love you. You know that, right?"

"If she loved us, she wouldn't have left." Micah's voice was firm.

"But she wants to come back," Cody said. "So that means she does love us, doesn't it, Daddy?"

Bob switched off the television and sighed, pulling both of his sons onto his lap.

"Okay, look," he said. "Your mother does love you. She loves you both very much. I think she just doesn't love me very much. She didn't want to leave you. Remember, she took you with her at first, until I told her she couldn't anymore. Not while she was with Luke, anyway."

"She's a whore!" Micah spat the word out.

"Micah! Don't you ever say that about your mother! Where did you even hear that word?"

"Dillon told me," he said. "He said that's what Mommy is, because she was sleeping in Luke's bed and they're not married."

Corrie rose. "I'm going to make some cocoa," she said.

"I'll help," Bryn agreed, following her into the kitchen.

In the living room, they could hear Bob talking softly to the boys.

"First, that is a very bad word. It's not a word I want you to use, ever. Do you understand me?"

"Yes, Daddy."

"Second, your mom has made some bad decisions, but she is not a bad person. She loves you and she will always be your mom."

"What's a whore?" Cody asked.

"It's something we'll talk about when you are older," Bob said. "Right now I just want to make sure you guys know that your mom loves you very much."

"Can she move back in with us?" Cody's voice was small.

"No, Cody. She is not going to move back in with us. Mommy and Daddy are getting divorced. But you will still see her, and she will always be your mother."

"Are you going to marry Bryn?" Cody asked.

Bob laughed. "No, buddy, I'm not going to marry Bryn. She's my friend, but she's not going to stay here forever. You know that, right?"

"Why not?"

"Because she's going to get a house of her own."

In the kitchen Corrie watched Bryn closely.

"You okay?" she asked quietly.

Bryn nodded.

"Who wants cocoa?" she called, carrying a tray of mugs into the living room.

They watched the rest of the movie and Bob put the boys to bed, Micah complaining vigorously that he should be allowed to stay up until midnight.

"Whew," Bob said, flopping down on the couch after he'd turned out the lights in the boys' rooms. "What a night."

"I think you handled it really well," Corrie said.

He just shook his head. "I can't believe he called her a whore!"

They all started laughing then, softly at first, then more loudly.

"You should have seen your face!" Bryn sputtered.

"And then Cody asking, 'What's a whore?'" Corrie said. "Priceless."

"Who knew I would ever have to tell my seven-year-old that his mom isn't a whore." Bob shook his head again.

"Maybe you should take Micah to see a counselor," Corrie said. "It might be good for him to vent a little."

"Maybe," Bob agreed. "I still can't believe this is my life. You know what I mean? I had a life with a woman I loved and we had two beautiful kids, and now she's gone. Just like that. And I'm a single dad. It's not what I expected, you know?"

"Yeah," Corrie said. "I'm right there with you. I had a wonderful marriage, and now I'm going to be a single mom. Of course, your situation is not your fault. Wendy's the one who left. Me, I brought this all on myself."

"Stop it!" Bryn stood and put her hands on her hips. "We are not going to spend New Year's Eve throwing ourselves a pity party. We are young, we are healthy, we have jobs, you have two great kids." She nodded at Bob. "And you and I are both going to have babies this spring!" She smiled at Corrie.

"You're right," Bob said. "No more sob stories."

Corrie smiled at them both. They really did seem like an old married couple.

"I think I'm going to head home," she said, rising.

"But it's only nine o'clock," Bryn protested. "You're not staying till midnight?"

"No." Corrie put her coat on. "I'm really tired, and my feet are sore, and I just want to go to bed."

"Okay." Bryn hugged her friend. "Drive carefully. It's amateur night, you know."

Corrie looked at her quizzically.

"You know, the night the amateur drinkers are out in force."

Corrie laughed. "I'll be careful."

"Thanks for coming," Bob said.

"Thanks for having me."

When she'd gone, Bob and Bryn settled on the couch.

"Do you want to watch a movie?" he asked.

"Okay, but first I'm going to make some popcorn."

"You just had half a pizza!"

"Hey, I am eating for two."

"Yeah, you and Orson Welles."

She swatted his head as she walked into the kitchen.

～45～

On New Year's Day, Bryn was reading a magazine on the couch when the door opened and Wendy walked in.

"Are you always here?" Wendy asked, glaring at her.

"Do you ever knock?" Bryn spat back.

"Hey." Bob emerged from the hallway. "Cody's just getting his jacket."

"You sure you don't want to join us?" Wendy smiled at Bob, tilting her head slightly. "It will be more fun if we go as a family."

"No," Bob said. "I've got stuff to do."

"More important stuff than spending time with your kids?"

Bryn stared down at the magazine intently, wishing she were anywhere else.

Bob's voice was low and angry. "Wendy, I am not playing this game with you. You want to see Cody and he wants to see you. Let's just leave it at that."

"What about Micah?"

"I told you last night, he already had plans today."

"And you just let him go, even though you knew I wanted him today?"

"He didn't want to go with you." Bob's voice shook slightly. "I don't think you have any idea what he's going through, how mad he is that you left."

"I'm sure you've just been filling his head with poison." Wendy was shouting now.

"Daddy?"

They turned to see Cody standing in the dining room.

"It's okay, buddy." Bob scooped him into a hug. "Mommy's here to take you to lunch and see a movie."

Cody looked anxiously from one parent to the other. Wendy smiled at him.

"Come on, baby," she said, stretching out her hand. "Let's go see a movie."

Cody walked to his mother and took her hand.

"I'll have him back by five," Wendy said, and they left.

"God! She is such a witch!" Bryn's voice shook. "How can she stand there and make you out to be the bad guy? I don't know how you can stand it."

Bob shook his head and sat down. "I feel kind of sorry for her, actually."

Bryn stared open-mouthed.

"I do," Bob insisted. "She's lost her kids. She's lost her home. She left everything because of a dirtbag, and now she's lost him, too."

"Well, I don't feel sorry for her at all. She's the one who left. And she doesn't even see what she does to the boys."

"Yeah, she's not the greatest mother in the world."

He smiled ruefully at Bryn. "I'm sorry you got stuck in the middle today."

She shrugged. "I could have gotten up and walked out, I guess. But I didn't want to leave you alone with her."

He laughed. "She's a spoiled, selfish child, but she's not dangerous. She's just Wendy."

"I didn't mean she was going to kill you or anything. I just . . . I want you to know I'm on your side. Always."

"Thanks, Bryn. That means a lot to me."

He rose and ran his hand through his hair. "What are you going to do today?"

"You're looking at it." Bryn raised the magazine. "It's too cold to go out."

"Do you want to help me with something?"

"Sure." She laid the magazine on the table. "What are we doing?"

"I need to go through a bunch of stuff in the attic, pull out Wendy's stuff and box it up for her. I've been meaning to do it for a long time, but I just keep putting it off."

"Okay, let's do it." Bryn put on her tennis shoes. "It'll be easier if you have company."

They walked up the stairs and Bob unlocked the attic door.

"Wow!" Bryn drew a quick breath. "This is an awesome space! I can't believe you don't use it for anything. The light is incredible."

"We always talked about doing a playroom up here, but we never got around to it.

"You seriously should do something with it. This room is amazing."

He smiled. "It's amazingly dusty, that's for sure."

They began at one end of the room, opening boxes and making piles—one of things to stay and one of things to go. And a separate pile for things Bob wasn't sure about.

"God, look at these." Bob held a photo album out to her. "Look how young we were."

"And how goofy." Bryn laughed at the picture of Bob and Wendy, Corrie and Daniel, and she and a boy whose name she couldn't remember, all sitting on top of a cannon in the town square.

They carried the album to the window and flipped pages.

"There's Paul. Look how young he was! God, he was just a little older then than we are now. I thought he was so grown-up and sophisticated. Turns out he's the least grown-up adult I know."

"I love this one of Corrie and you." Bob smiled at the picture. "You look like you're about to break into song."

He turned the page and stopped.

"My dad took this one the day Wendy and I got engaged," he said softly.

"You look happy," Bryn said, looking down at the picture of

Bob with his arm around Wendy's waist, both of them smiling at the camera.

"I was," he said. "I thought the best part of my life was about to begin."

He stared at the picture for a long minute before closing the album.

"Okay, I guess this stays." He put the album in a pile.

"Do you still love her?" Bryn didn't mean to ask the question, but it slipped out before she could stop herself.

"In a way, I guess." Bob sat down on the floor next to the "keep" pile. "I mean, she was the first girl I ever loved, the first girl I ever slept with. She was my wife for almost ten years, and she's the mother of my children. I can't just erase all that."

"She's the first girl you slept with?"

"First and only."

"Seriously? You've never had sex with anyone but Wendy?"

"I know, pretty sad, right? But we were all of seventeen when we started dating and then we got married."

"I think it's sweet."

He just laughed.

"Oh, wow," Bryn said, opening a box. "Look at all the records! There must be a hundred here."

"Those were my dad's," Bob said, grinning. "Wait right there."

He walked to the other end of the room and opened a cabinet.

"Here!" He sounded triumphant.

"A record player? Seriously, you have a record player? Does it work?"

"I think so." He carried the turntable to an electrical outlet and plugged it in.

"What do you want to hear?"

"Oh, we have to play some disco! I mean, it's a record player."

Bryn handed him an album by the Bee Gees, and watched while he placed the needle on the vinyl. The record popped and crackled for a second, and then the pulse of "Stayin' Alive" filled the attic.

"Oh, hell yeah!" Bryn was on her feet in a moment, dancing to the music and singing along. Bob watched her, grinning widely.

"Come on!" She grabbed his hand. "Dance!"

And so they danced until they were out of breath. And then they danced some more. And then the pace changed and they were listening to "How Deep Is Your Love?"

"Uh oh," Bryn teased. "A slow one. Are you going to slow dance with me?"

He hesitated just a second, then took her in his arms and began swaying with her to the music.

Bryn leaned into his chest, her arms draped around his neck. She was surprised at how nice it felt just to be held. She'd forgotten the thrill of dancing with someone new, even if the someone new wasn't completely new.

They moved around the attic, Bob humming along with the music. Neither spoke.

When the song was over, neither of them let go. They stood close together, arms around each other, for a long minute. Finally, Bryn took a step back and looked up at him.

"Thanks," she said. "That was fun."

He leaned forward and kissed her then, not a friendly, just-pals kind of kiss. A real, open-mouthed, heated kiss. And for just an instant, she kissed him back.

Then she pulled away abruptly.

"No," she said.

"I'm sorry," he mumbled. "I shouldn't have done that."

He turned from her, his cheeks reddening.

She took his hand and made him turn around.

"It's not that I don't want you to kiss me," she said.

"Then what?"

"You're still married to Wendy. You said just a while ago that you still love her. You're in a bad place right now. I can't be your rebound."

"That's not what I was thinking."

"I know." She smiled at him. "You would never do that on purpose. But trust me on this, I would be a rebound. And I just can't do that right now."

He walked to the window and said nothing for a minute. Then, he turned back to face her.

"I don't think that's it, Bryn. I mean, I know it might seem that way. But having you here the last few months, it's been great."

"For me, too." She sat down on a box. "It's been a lifesaver for me. But you're married, Bob. More than that, you're still in love with your wife."

He sat down on the floor by her feet.

"I know," he said softly. "But this feels so . . . right. You and me, we just work."

Bryn watched him, her heart pounding hard.

"If you still feel that way after the divorce—and I don't mean right after the divorce, I mean after a while—then we'll think about it."

"I'm sorry," he said.

"It's really okay. I'm in a weird place, too. I mean, I'm pregnant and facing raising a child alone. Part of me wants to grab hold of you and hang on for dear life. But I can't."

"Why not?" He looked up at her. "Seriously, why not?"

"Okay," she said steadily. "You're the counselor. You should know this. We're both going through hard transitions. How many rebound relationships survive?"

"I guess," he conceded.

They sat for a minute, then Bryn rose and dusted off her jeans.

"I think we've made a dent here," she said, nodding to the piles on the floor. "I'm ready for a shower."

She left him in the attic, still sitting on the floor.

↭ 46 ↭

"So you're not going to stay in the house?"

Bryn stood at the counter in Bob's kitchen, making scrambled eggs. The boys were at school and Bob at work.

"No," Corrie said. "I mean, I love the house. But it's *our* house, Mark's and mine. I can't stay in it without him. It's just too sad."

Bryn nodded, putting bread into the toaster.

"Plus, I'm not sure if I can afford it on my own."

"I wondered about that," Bryn said. "I mean, it's a great house. But you could find something nice for a lot less."

She scooped eggs onto plates, buttered toast, and set the plates on the table.

"Thanks," Corrie said. "This looks good."

"I'm glad your appetite is back." Bryn laughed. "Mine is back with a vengeance. I feel like I'm hungry all the time. Pretty soon, I'm going to look like a beached whale." She patted her stomach.

"You're hardly even showing," Corrie said. "Besides, you're supposed to eat well when you're pregnant."

"Well, so are you, so eat up."

They ate in companionable silence.

"I was thinking," Corrie said, not looking up. "Maybe we could get a house together."

"Oh." Bryn sounded surprised.

"Only if you want to," Corrie said. "I mean, if you want to get your own place, that's fine. Or maybe you'll just stay here. . . ." Her voice trailed away.

"No, I can't just stay here," Bryn said. "I've been putting it off for months now and Bob's been great. He's been so great. But I do need to find a place."

"So what do you think?" Corrie asked. "We could look for a house to rent together. Something with four bedrooms, maybe near the park. Between the two of us, we could afford something nice."

"Maybe," Bryn said.

"We don't have to," Corrie said. "I understand if you don't want to."

"It's not that! I mean, I've actually thought about it, us living together. It would be fun, and we wouldn't have to do it all on our own. But . . . what if you and Mark get back together? Or, what if you decide to go to Los Angeles with Daniel? Or . . . I don't know, what if you just decide you don't like living with me? Then where would we be?"

Corrie smiled at her friend.

"I know I like living with you," she said. "We did it for four years in college."

"That was a long time ago," Bryn said. "We were kids. We didn't have kids. I just don't want to do anything that would ruin our friendship."

"Nothing will ever ruin our friendship, Bryn! You are my best friend in the world. I love you. Yeah, it might take some getting used to. But I think we could make it work, if we tried."

"And if Mark decides he wants to make it work?"

Corrie shook her head. "That's not going to happen. He's filed for divorce. He's made it pretty clear that he can't forgive me and he won't raise Daniel's baby."

"And what about Daniel?"

Corrie smiled ruefully. "Daniel is in California, and he's going to stay in California. I don't want to live with him or even see him, really. If I could, I'd forget about him completely."

"Well, you do whatever works for you," Bryn said firmly. "You take care of you and your baby, and let Daniel take care of himself."

They washed the breakfast dishes.

"I should probably go to work," Corrie said. "I've been out of the office so much in the last few weeks, I think Kenetha is ready to quit."

"Have you told her yet?"

Corrie shook her head. "I've been waiting until I had the test results, and then Christmas came and I just put it off."

"She'll be so excited for you."

"I hope so. I hope she doesn't freak out."

Bryn laughed. "I don't think so. This is Kenetha we're talking about. She's not going to judge."

Corrie hugged her tightly. "Thanks, Bryn. I don't know what I'd do without you."

She picked up her purse and briefcase.

"Corrie?"

Bryn smiled at her.

"This weekend, let's look at houses."

"Okay!"

Two days later, newspaper in hand, they drove through the quiet park neighborhood of Middlebrook. The park was blanketed lightly in snow.

"There it is." Bryn pointed to a small, yellow, craftsman-style house facing the park, sporting a FOR RENT sign in the tiny front yard.

Corrie parked on the street and they got out of the car.

"It's cute," Bryn said. "And it's got a great view."

Corrie nodded. "It is cute. But it looks kind of small."

They knocked on the front door, which opened immediately, revealing a large, matronly looking woman.

"Mrs. Winston?" Corrie said. "I'm Corrie Philips. We spoke on the phone."

"Yes, come in." The woman stepped aside so Corrie and Bryn could enter the house. "It's cold out there today!"

The living room was small but cheery, with a stone fireplace and a cozy window seat.

"This is the living room," Mrs. Winston said. "And through there is the dining room and behind that the kitchen. Then you've got two bedrooms down the hall and two more upstairs."

They wandered through the house, opening closets and flushing the toilets. It was much smaller than Corrie's house, but it felt homey.

Later, they sat in the car out front, talking.

"It's awfully small," Corrie said again.

"But it has four bedrooms," Bryn said. "You can have the two downstairs, and I can take the upstairs. Or you can have upstairs, if you'd rather."

"Do you like it?"

"I love it!" Bryn's face shone. "It's cute, it's cozy, and the park is right here!" She waved her hand toward the park. "It's by far the nicest one we've seen. It's not far from campus, and it's not far from Bob's. It's perfect!"

Corrie smiled. "Okay, I'm glad you like it. But you know I can't move on it until I talk to Mark about the house. We'll have to put it on the market. I can't afford that mortgage and this rent at the same time."

Bryn's face fell.

"Maybe I can," Corrie said. "If Mark keeps paying half the mortgage on the house, maybe I can do both. I'll talk to him about it. Are you okay?" She eyed Bryn's face. "Last month you seemed perfectly content to stay at Bob's, and now it seems like you're in such a rush to leave."

"He kissed me." Bryn didn't look at Corrie as she spoke. "A couple weeks ago, we were packing up some of Wendy's stuff in the attic, and we found some old records, so we played them. And we danced. And then . . . he kissed me."

Corrie stared at her for a minute. "Oh my God," she said. "Did you kiss him back?"

Bryn nodded. "I did at first. It's been so long since I've kissed anyone but Paul, and it felt really nice. But then I stopped. And I told him we couldn't do that."

"Why not?" Corrie asked. "You're single. He's about to be single. You obviously care about each other."

"He's not single yet. And he still loves Wendy. He told me so."

"Ah," Corrie said. "That does make things complicated."

"I can't be his rebound," Bryn said. "I just couldn't take that."

"You care about him, don't you?" Corrie asked. "Not just like a friend. You have feelings for him."

Bryn hesitated, her cheeks red. "Maybe," she said. "I don't know."

"Well, either way, it's time for you to move out." Corrie hugged her friend. "I'll talk to Mark and get the money stuff figured out, and let's take this house."

"Thanks." Bryn smiled at her. "That sounds really good."

Two weeks later, they were ready to move in. Corrie hired a mover to pack and move her things. Bryn packed a single suitcase. The baby things her mother had bought were already in the car.

"You know you don't have to go." Bob sat on the bed in Bryn's room, watching her pack.

"I know," she said. "You've been so great, Bob. I can't tell you how much I appreciate your letting me stay for so long."

"Is it because of the kiss?" He watched her carefully. "Because I promise that won't happen again."

"No," she said, closing the suitcase. "I just . . . look, being here has been great, almost like we've been playing house. But now, it's time for us, for me, to get on with the real world. I need my own place. And you need some time to figure out what's next for you."

He sighed.

"I'm only going a few blocks," she said, smiling at him. "And you guys are coming for dinner tonight, right?"

"I know," he said. "I'm being selfish. I'm just going to miss you. And so are the boys."

"You guys will be fine. I'm sure they're ready to have their house back."

"I think they're going to miss you."

"Well, I'm only a few blocks away." She picked up the suitcase and surveyed the room that had been her home since September.

"I really do appreciate everything you've done for me."

Bob rose and wrapped his arms around her. "It's been fun."

"Okay." Bryn stepped away from him. "So we'll see you guys tonight at six for pizza and unpacking."

She walked to the front door and hesitated for just an instant. Then she dropped her key on the entry table and left.

❦ 47 ❧

"My God, Corrie! How is all this stuff going to fit?" Bryn stood in the doorway of the bungalow, staring at the furniture crowding the living room and spilling onto the porch. Boxes sat stacked against the walls. Framed pictures leaned precariously against the door.

"I know." Corrie smiled at her from the dining room. "I brought too much."

Bryn shoved her way into the living room and dropped her suitcase onto the floor.

"Well, some of it is going upstairs, right? That will give us some more room."

Corrie sat down on a large box.

"Actually, the stuff that's going upstairs is already there."

"Okay, that's everything." A man walked down the stairs, carrying empty boxes.

"Thank you," said Corrie, rising. She reached into her purse and pulled out some cash.

"Do you want us to move anything around down here?" The man looked from Bryn's pregnant belly to Corrie's and smiled.

"Um, no. I think we'll be okay." Corrie handed him the money. "We have some friends coming later to help."

"Well, don't try to move that by yourselves." The man pointed to a huge sideboard in the center of the room.

"We won't, I promise."

Another man appeared from upstairs, carrying more boxes.

"The beds are set up," he said. "So at least you'll have some-place to sleep tonight."

The movers left, carrying still more empty boxes as they went.

"Why didn't you let them put everything where you want it?" Bryn asked, staring forlornly at the moving van as it pulled away.

"I don't know where I want anything."

Corrie waved her arm at the room. "Where do you think every-thing should go?"

"You're asking me?" Bryn laughed. "You're the one with the designer show house."

"Designer being the key." Corrie slumped onto a box. "I had a designer tell me where to put everything before. I don't have a clue about design."

"Okay then." Bryn set her shoulders and stared around the room. "Let's start with the couch over here."

They shoved furniture around the living room until they had a small seating area facing the fireplace, then sat on the couch sur-veying their progress.

"That would look nice over the mantle." Bryn pointed to a large Degas print.

"Mark got me that for Christmas the first year we were mar-ried." Corrie smiled at the memory. "We'd just gone to the museum in Chicago and I fell in love with that painting, so he got me a print."

They sat quietly for a minute, each wrapped in thought.

"Okay, enough." Bryn stood and pulled Corrie up by her hand. "Let's start on the dining room."

By the time Bob arrived with the boys, the house was beginning to resemble a home.

"Pizza's here!" he called.

"Oh thank God!" Bryn appeared from the kitchen, towel in hand. "We're starving!"

"This is nice," Bob said, looking around the room. "Where's the rest of this stuff going to go?"

"I have no idea," Bryn said. "That won't fit anywhere." She pointed at the sideboard. "And the rest . . ." She plopped down on the couch and threw her hands in the air.

"The rest you'll find room for or get rid of. Meantime, let's eat." Bob set the pizzas on the dining room table.

"Micah, do you have the sodas?"

Micah stood with Cody in the living room, staring solemnly at them.

"Is this where you're going to live now?" he asked, looking at Bryn.

"Yep," she said. "What do you think?"

"Why aren't you gonna live with us anymore?" Cody asked.

"I told you, honey. It's time for me to get a place of my own, a place for me and my baby."

Micah walked into the dining room and set two large bottles of soda on the table.

"You know you don't have to go," he said, staring at Bryn earnestly. "My mom can't make you move out."

Bryn knelt down and put her arms around the boy. "I know, Micah. It's not because of your mom. It's just . . . time. I loved staying with you guys. But we always knew it wasn't forever, right?"

He said nothing, just leaned into her and buried his face in her neck.

Then Bryn felt another small pair of arms around her as Cody joined the embrace. Tears stung her eyes.

"Hey, guys," Bob said. "You'll still see Bryn all the time. You know that, right?"

"That's what you said about Mommy." Cody's voice was muffled against Bryn's shoulder.

"Hey!" Corrie came down the stairs, carrying a broom and dustpan. "When did you guys get here?"

"Just now," Bob said, grinning at her. "Looks like you two have been busy."

"Yeah, but we've got a lot to do."

"The first thing we need to do is eat!" Bryn stood, gently untangling herself from the boys.

"That sounds like a very good idea. I'll find some paper plates." Corrie disappeared into the kitchen.

"I'll get cups." Bryn followed her.

"Are you okay?" Corrie whispered.

Bryn nodded. "I didn't know it would be so hard to leave them," she said.

Corrie squeezed her hand. "It's for the best."

"I know."

After dinner, Corrie and the boys sat on the kitchen floor, unwrapping dishes and pans and cutlery and putting them into neat piles.

"So, give me the grand tour." Bob smiled at Bryn. "Where are you and the baby going to sleep?"

"We're upstairs," she said, leading him toward the steps.

"Here's mine." She opened a door and waved him into a pretty room, wallpapered in yellow with white curtains. "The furniture is all Corrie's, from her guest room. I've never had such nice stuff."

"It's nice." Bob walked around the room. "I like the quilt."

"That's Corrie's, too."

"Well, at least you don't have to go out and buy everything at once."

"And this is for the baby!" She opened a second door.

The room was pale blue, again with white curtains. The port-a-crib and swing sat in boxes on the floor, beside a huge bag of baby clothes.

"Are you leaving it blue?" Bob asked.

"I think so. I like the color really well."

"What if you're having a girl?"

"Then she'll like blue!"

Bob laughed.

"If you need a crib, I've still got the one the boys used. It's in pretty good shape."

"Thanks," she said, smiling. "My mom said she wants to buy one, and a changing table. She really has gone mad over this grandma thing."

"That's good," he said. "This is nice, a nice room for a baby."

They walked back downstairs.

"Okay, so you've seen all this." Bryn waved around the living room. "And here's Corrie's room."

Bob gazed at the heavy cherry furniture and smiled. "It's definitely Corrie."

"And this is for Emmaline." Bryn opened a door and flipped on the light, then stopped and stared at the empty room.

"Corrie? Where's all your baby stuff?"

Corrie walked into the room and smiled. "I'm getting new."

"But you had the whole nursery," Bryn said. "And you loved it."

Corrie shook her head. "I got that with Mark, for our baby. I don't want it anymore."

Bob took her hand and squeezed it.

"You're going to be okay," he said. "So, here's to new beginnings . . . for all of us."

Bryn raised her eyebrows and cocked her head. "You all right?"

"Yeah," he said. "My lawyer called today. The judge signed the papers. I am officially divorced."

"I'm sorry." Corrie squeezed his hand now.

"I'm fine, actually." Bob smiled at her. "I've been ready for a while. I'm just glad it's finally over."

"And you have full custody?" Bryn asked, watching him carefully.

"Yeah." Bob ran his hand through his hair. "Wendy's parents wrote supporting statements for me, and I had the picture of Cody and that asshole blowing pot at him. The judge agreed I'd be the better parent. Wendy gets them every other weekend."

"Thank God!" Bryn let out a sigh of relief.

"Yeah," Bob repeated. "I'm really glad it went my way."

"Do the boys know?" Corrie asked, looking back toward the kitchen where the two little boys still sat making piles.

"I told them this afternoon."

"Are they okay?"

"Honestly, I think they're more upset about Bryn moving out than they are about the divorce."

Bryn stiffened, tears stinging her eyes again.

"Sorry," Bob said abruptly. "I didn't mean to guilt you like that."

"They'll be fine," Corrie said. "They have you, and you're the best dad in the world."

"Thanks." Bob smiled at her, then glanced toward Bryn, who was still staring at the floor.

"It's getting late," he said, shifting from one foot to the other. "I'd probably better get the boys home and to bed. They have school tomorrow."

When they finally got to bed after midnight, Bryn lay wide awake in her new yellow room, the pretty quilt drawn up to her chin.

This was the right choice, she told herself. *I couldn't just stay there forever, pretending they were mine. This is a good thing.*

She rolled onto her side, willing herself to go to sleep. After a long while, she gave up the pretense and went down to the kitchen for a glass of water.

"Hey." Corrie stood in front of the refrigerator holding a gallon of milk. "I'm making warm milk. Do you want some?"

Bryn nodded.

They drank their milk in the living room, talking about college and babies and where to put the sideboard. At three, Corrie trudged off to bed. Bryn lay on the couch staring at the ceiling until she finally fell asleep, just before four.

❧ 48 ❧

On a snowy day in February, Corrie pulled into the driveway of the house she'd shared with Mark. The FOR SALE sign was now topped with a bright red bar, proclaiming, SOLD!

She sat in her car for a few minutes, then got out and pulled her key from her purse. The back door creaked open, the way it always had. The kitchen was clean and bare. The blue and white stripes she loved so much brought tears to her eyes.

"Hey," Mark called from the front of the house. "Is that you?"

"It's me." Corrie set her purse on the breakfast bar and walked slowly into the living room, where Mark leaned against the mantle.

"How are you?" he asked, staring at her slightly rounded belly.

"I'm good."

They stood awkwardly for a moment, then he said, "There are a few things upstairs I thought you might want."

She nodded and followed him up the stairs, stopping at the top to stare into the nursery, still decorated in Beatrix Potter. She squeezed her eyes tight, willing herself not to cry.

"Here," Mark called from the bedroom they'd shared.

She walked into the nearly empty room and concentrated hard on not crying.

"I think this was your dad's, right?" Mark pointed to a globe on a stand in the corner of the room.

"Yeah," she said softly. She put her hand on the globe and set it spinning, just the way her father had done when she was small. He would spin the world and let her stop it with her finger, then tell her all about the place her finger had landed.

"And there are a few things in the closet I wasn't sure about."

She sorted through clothes, putting some into a bag and piling the rest on the floor.

"Goodwill is coming tomorrow," Mark said. "You can just leave what you don't want there."

In the guest room, she pulled a few books from the pile on the floor and dropped them into the bag, too.

"Are you sure you don't want anything from the nursery?" Mark stopped in front of the room and looked around. "I know you loved this stuff."

Corrie walked past him, shaking her head, blinking back tears.

"Okay," he said, following her down the stairs. "Well, somebody will love it."

In the kitchen, Corrie added three cookbooks to her bag.

"I guess that's it," she said. She pulled the house key from her key chain and set it on the counter.

"I guess so." Mark stood in the middle of the room, staring at the floor.

"Are you going to look for a house?" Corrie asked, unwilling to leave just yet.

"No, I'm okay in the apartment. I don't need all this space."

They stood quietly, then Mark asked, "How do you like your new place?"

"It's okay." Corrie shrugged. "We're having a hard time trying to find space for everything. Are you sure you don't want the sideboard?"

He smiled and shook his head. "I've got nowhere to put it. Maybe you should call Goodwill, too."

"Maybe."

Corrie looked around the kitchen one more time, then picked up her bag.

"I guess that's it," she said again.

She walked to the back door.

"Corrie?" Mark's voice was soft, hesitant.

She turned to look at him.

"Take care of yourself, okay?" He didn't meet her eyes.

"I will. You too."

She carried the bag of clothes and books to the car, then returned for the globe. Mark watched as she closed the trunk and got in the car. He was still watching when she pulled away.

"Was it pretty gruesome?" Bryn took the bag from Corrie in front of their house.

"Yeah, it was."

"Well, at least it's over."

Corrie nodded, pulling the globe from the trunk.

"Where are you going to put that?" Bryn eyed the globe with suspicion. There was not a single square inch of space available in the living room.

"In the baby's room," Corrie said, smiling at the globe. "A little bit of her grandpa."

She carried the globe into the empty nursery, now painted a pale mint green.

"There," she said, standing the globe in the corner. "Now she has something in her room."

Bryn put her hand on Corrie's shoulder and squeezed.

"You know, Bob said I could use his crib. I'm sure he'd let you use it."

"No," Corrie said. "I mean, that's sweet. But I really am going to buy something."

"Well, you have a while."

The doorbell jarred them both.

"Who could that be?" Bryn walked into the living room and peeked out the front door.

"Oh hell," she breathed.

"Who is it?" Corrie walked into the room.

"Paul." Bryn backed away from the door, shaking her head.

"Do you want me to tell him you're not here?"

Bryn stood a moment, then sighed again.

"No," she said. "I guess I'll talk to him."

"Well, I'm right here if you need me. I'll be in the kitchen. Just yell."

"Thanks."

Bryn opened the front door and stared at Paul.

"Hey," he said, smiling. "How are you?"

"I'm okay," she said, not stepping aside from the door.

"Can I come in?"

After a long pause, she stepped backward so he could enter the house.

"This is nice," he said, looking around the room. "Like a real house."

"What do you want, Paul?"

He took off his coat and draped it over the wing chair, then settled onto the couch.

"I thought we should probably talk," he said.

She sat across from him in the rocking chair and waited.

"Is Corrie here?" he asked, looking around.

"She's in the kitchen."

"Oh . . . okay." He sat a moment, then said, "Here's the deal. I didn't get tenure at the university. But I've got a job offer from the University of Kentucky. It's in Lexington, just a couple hours away."

"Oh," she said. "Well, good. I mean good for you. I'm glad you've got a job."

"And I think you should come with me." Paul leaned forward, his hands on his knees.

"It's a good job," he said. "Tenure-track. I think I could do well there. And it's better money. And . . . and I think you should come with me."

He sat back, waiting for her response.

Bryn simply watched him.

"Come on, Bryn. I want you to come with me. We can start over—you, me, and the baby. I'll get us a house with a yard and a studio for you. We can be a family. Don't you want that?"

Still she said nothing.

"Are you seeing someone else?" he asked finally.

"No," she said.

He relaxed a bit and smiled. "So, you're alone. I'm alone. We don't need to be alone, baby. We can be together. Don't you want the baby to have a father?"

"Not if that father is a pot-smoking drunk." Her voice was flat.

"Okay, fair enough." He leaned forward again. "I've stopped smoking weed."

Her eyes widened.

"I mean it. I haven't had anything for over a month. I gave my whole stash to Larry."

"Okay," she said.

"And I've cut back on the drinking. Way back. Like just a beer, maybe two, on the weekend. And I'm trying to quit smoking. That one's a killer, but I'm trying."

She sat back, letting that sink in.

"I really am trying, Bryn. I want to be a father to this baby. I want to be with you. I want us to get married, the whole nine yards."

She shook her head. It was too much to believe.

"I know you have to think about it. I know you probably don't believe me. Can we just see each other? Just like . . . date, like we were going to before? Can we just give it a try?"

"When are you going to Lexington?"

"In August, when my lease is up."

She said nothing.

"So, that gives us a while to work things out," he continued. "That's, like, six months. You'll see, I can do this. I can be a family guy."

She shook her head again.

"Don't say no." Paul rose and reached for his coat. "Just think about it, will you? Just think about how good it will be for us to raise this baby together."

He crossed the room and kissed the top of her head.

"Call me, okay?"

She nodded, not rising as he left.

"Are you all right?" Corrie stood by the chair, her hand on Bryn's shoulder.

"Yeah."

"You don't sound sure about that."

Corrie sat down where Paul had been moments before, watching Bryn carefully.

"He sounded sincere," Corrie said, sighing. "I mean, I know he's been a jerk before, but he did sound sincere."

Bryn shook her head. "He always sounds sincere when he wants something," she said. "But he never follows through."

"What if he does this time?"

Bryn didn't answer.

"Do you want some tea?" Corrie asked.

"What I want is a whiskey sour!"

Corrie stared at her.

"Don't worry," Bryn said. "I didn't say I was going to have one."

Corrie smiled at her. "So, tea?"

"Yes."

They sat at the table in the dining room with mint tea.

"What are you going to do?" Corrie asked.

"I don't know." Bryn set her cup on the table and rested her head in her hands.

"I mean, what if he can do it?" she asked, not looking at Corrie. "If he really can grow up and be a dad, am I just crazy to let him go?"

Corrie didn't answer. After a long minute, she asked, "Do you still love him?"

Bryn shook her head. "I don't know. I mean, I think I don't. I know I don't. And then he shows up and does that 'I can be different' routine, and I start wondering. Maybe I do love him. Is that crazy?"

"Love is always crazy," Corrie said, smiling.

"Do you think I should give him another chance?"

Corrie shook her head. "I don't know. I think you have to do what you want to do."

They sat in silence.

"I think what you really want is to go back to Bob's," Corrie said softly.

Bryn stared at her, then rose, carrying her cup to the kitchen.

"That's not going to happen," she said.

"I didn't say it would," Corrie replied. "I just said I think that's what you really want."

Bryn walked to the front room and pulled on her parka.

"I'm going for a walk," she announced.

Corrie watched her cross the street into the park. Then she called Bob.

❧ 49 ❧

"So, what's up?" Bob smiled when he opened the front door.

"Are the boys here?" Corrie looked past him into the living room.

"They're with Wendy this weekend. Are you okay?"

She smiled as she took off her coat. "I'm fine. It's Bryn I'm worried about."

"What's up with Bryn?"

"Paul came over today."

"Great." Bob sat down on the couch. "Is she upset?"

"I think so. I don't know. He's got a tenure-track position at the University of Kentucky. He wants Bryn to go with him."

"She's not seriously considering it, is she?" He stared at her, eyes wide.

"I don't know. I can't tell."

Bob sighed heavily. "I guess she still loves him, then."

"I don't know that, either." Corrie paused, then plunged ahead. "She told me what happened, that you kissed her."

Bob shook his head. "I know, it was a mistake."

"Maybe," Corrie agreed. "But I watch you guys together and, honestly, Bob, you just seem to fit. It's like you're an old married couple. And I know she loves the boys and I know she misses them . . . and you."

Bob stared at her again.

"She made it pretty clear she didn't want me," he said softly.

"Because she thinks you're still hung up on Wendy," Corrie said.

Bob rose and began pacing the living room.

"How do you feel about her?" Corrie asked.

"Who, Wendy?"

"No, Bryn. How do you feel about Bryn?"

Bob stopped pacing and stood for a minute, staring out the window.

"I don't know," he said finally. "I mean, I love Bryn. She's my friend. She has been for a long time. And having her here was great, really great. She's fun and she's smart and she's great with the boys."

"And?"

"And . . . she's beautiful and annoying and sexy and frustrating and wonderful. And she's probably still in love with Paul. And even if I wanted to, I can't go after her. Not now. I just got divorced. It's too soon. She thinks she'd just be my transition relationship."

"Do you think that?"

He sighed heavily. "I don't know, Corrie. But I am not going to do anything to ruin our friendship. And I don't want to start a relationship with Bryn and then lose her. I couldn't take that. And neither could the boys."

"Okay," Corrie said softly. "I just had to find out."

"I hope to God she doesn't go back to Paul!" Bob's voice exploded into the room.

"Me too," Corrie agreed. "Me too."

When Corrie got home, Bryn was in the kitchen making brownies, music blaring from the computer.

"Hey," she said, looking up from the bowl. "Where have you been?"

"I went in to the office," Corrie lied. "I had to pick up a file." She patted her bag.

"You work too much." Bryn poured batter into the pan.

"So, are you okay?"

"Yeah," Bryn said.

"Are you mad at me?"

"No." She put the brownies in the oven. "I mean, I was pissed at first, but I know you just want me to be happy."

She turned to face Corrie.

"You're wrong about Bob," she said. "I'm not pining for him, wishing I could go back. He's a friend, and that's that."

"Okay," Corrie said. "And what about Paul?"

"Paul is a jerk," Bryn said firmly. "He can't change. He'll never change. I'm glad he's going to Lexington. Out of sight, out of mind."

"Okay," Corrie said again. "Well, good for you."

Bryn hugged her tightly, then said, "Don't worry, Mom. I'm a big girl. I can take care of myself."

~~50~~

Bryn stood in the dark hallway the next day, key in hand, staring at the door of the apartment she had shared with Paul for so many years. He'd be in a faculty meeting today. Every Monday afternoon for all the years she'd known him, faculty meetings had been the bane of his existence.

She felt foolish even being here. Of course he hadn't changed. He couldn't change.

Still, if there was a chance . . . She'd just slip in and look around. She knew where he kept his pot, his clips, his bong. She'd check the fridge and cabinets for liquor. At least then she'd know for sure.

She took a deep breath and unlocked the door.

"Hey, babe!" A voice came from the living room. "I thought you had a meeting today."

Bryn stepped into the kitchen and looked into the living room. A young blond woman—not a day over twenty-five, if that—sat on the couch in an oversized jersey and panties, painting her toenails.

Her smile froze when she saw Bryn.

"Who are you?" She rose, holding the polish brush in front of her like a weapon.

"I'm Bryn."

The woman's face remained blank.

"I'm Paul's ex."

The young woman relaxed a bit. "What are you doing here?"

"I . . ." Bryn paused. What the hell was she doing here, anyway?

"I just came to drop off my key."

She removed the apartment key from her ring and handed it to the young woman.

"Okay." The blond took the key. "I'll give it to him."

Bryn turned to leave, then turned back.

"This is his baby, you know." She opened her coat to pat her belly.

The girl simply stared at her.

"Take my advice, get out while you can."

Bryn closed the door behind her and walked to her car, feeling lighter than she had in a long time.

"Oh my God!" Corrie took Bryn's hands. "Are you okay?"

"Actually, yes." Bryn smiled. "I'm fine. I mean, you'd think I'd be angry or sad or something. But mostly I'm just relieved."

"I cannot believe him! I cannot believe he would come over here and beg you to move to Kentucky with him and promise you he's changed, and he's got a girl living with him. What an unbelievable ego!"

"Yeah," Bryn agreed. "Paul has enough 'self-esteem' for an entire city."

"So, you're really fine?"

"Yes, I really am. I knew he was who he was. I just had to make sure. I should have trusted my instincts. I feel kind of stupid for even half believing him, but I had to see for myself."

"And now you know."

"And now I know."

Someone knocked on the door, hard.

"I'll go." Bryn rose and opened the door. Bob stepped into the house without a word and took her hand.

"Okay, I know I shouldn't have kissed you. It was stupid and selfish and . . . stupid. And I know I only just got divorced. And I know you think I still love Wendy. But you're wrong. I mean, I do still care about her. She's the mother of my kids, and she'll always be part of my life. But I'm not in love with her anymore. I'm through with that chapter, and I'm ready to get on with my life."

Corrie rose and tiptoed into the kitchen.

"Bob . . ." Bryn began.

"No, wait," Bob interrupted her. "Hear me out. Just sit down and listen for a minute."

Bryn walked back to the couch and sat down, keeping her eyes on Bob as he paced back and forth before the fireplace.

"Look, Bryn," he said. "I don't know how you feel about me. I mean, we've been friends forever, and maybe that's all you want to be. And that's okay. I mean, it's not really okay, but it is. I mean . . . God, I'm making a mess of this."

He dropped down beside her on the couch.

"What I'm trying to say is that I care about you. I really care about you. As a friend, but not just as a friend. As . . . I don't know, but more than a friend. I miss you. I hate that you left and I hate that I miss you so much and I hate that I'm probably freaking you out right now and you'll never want to see me again. But I won't just stand by and watch you go back to that jerk! You're too good for him. You've always been too good for him. And . . ." His voice trailed away and he stared at her, smiling at him.

"And I'm not going back to Paul," she said softly. "I'm never going back to Paul."

"Oh. Well . . . good, then. I mean, I'm glad."

He rose. "Then I should probably go. Right? I mean, you probably were doing something and I just barged in and . . ."

"Bob, sit down." Bryn took his hand and pulled him back down to the couch. She took a deep breath and said, "You are so great."

"Okay," he said, turning away. "I get it. We're friends and that's all you want. And that's fine, really."

"Are you going to let me finish?" She held onto his hand.

He sighed and sat back, looking away from her.

"You really are so great," she said again. "And yes, we've been friends forever. And yes, it's scary to think about screwing up that friendship. And yes, it freaks me out to think about being in a relationship with you. But . . ."

He turned to look at her finally.

"But what?"

"But I really care about you, too. As a friend and as more than a friend. I do worry that you're not over Wendy. And my situation is a mess. And the timing is all wrong. And it's probably a huge mistake to even think about it. But . . . I miss you, too. I miss you so much. And I miss Micah and Cody and Saturday morning pancakes and Friday night movies. I miss them. I miss feeling like I'm part of a family. But mostly, I miss you."

He grinned at her then. "Are we crazy?"

"Probably," she said.

"Are you scared?"

"Definitely."

"Me too."

They sat for a minute, holding hands and watching each other. Then Bob leaned forward, tilted her chin up, and kissed her.

Bryn felt her breath catch in her chest. She leaned into him and savored his smell, his taste, his touch.

Then the baby kicked.

"Wow!" She sat up straight, her eyes wide.

"What's wrong?" He watched her closely. "Is it too much? I'm sorry. We can take things slow if you want."

"No!" She laughed and guided his hand to her stomach. "Do you feel it?"

He paused, focusing intently on her hand on his. Then he laughed.

"The baby kicked! You've felt it before, right?" He left his hand on her stomach.

"Yeah, but never a real kick like that."

"So maybe it's a sign." Bob kissed her forehead. "Maybe the baby is giving us a blessing."

"Or maybe Baby doesn't like what I had for lunch."

They both laughed then.

"So, what do we do now?" Bryn asked softly, leaning against his shoulder.

"Now . . . I don't know. Maybe we go on a date?"

She laughed. "That sounds nice. Maybe we can take the boys to see *Alvin and the Chipmunks*."

"Or maybe," he said, kissing her cheek, "we can go out like real grown-ups and see a movie with real people in it. And have dinner someplace besides Pizza Hut."

"That sounds lovely."

"Friday night?"

"Don't you have the boys then?"

"I can find a sitter."

"Okay," she said, smiling. "Friday night."

❦ 51 ❦

"Are you and Bob going out on Valentine's Day?" Corrie poured coffee into a mug and handed it to Bryn.

"I think so," Bryn said. "We're going to try that new Thai restaurant on Fourth Street."

"That sounds nice." Corrie poured a second cup of coffee and sat down at the table.

"What are you going to do that night?" Bryn watched as Corrie sipped her coffee.

"Nothing, I guess."

"I'm sorry, hon. You can go to dinner with us."

"That would be *very* romantic." Corrie laughed. "I'm fine. I'll be fine."

"I know it's going to be a hard day."

Corrie nodded. February 14 was her wedding anniversary. Every year, Mark had planned a special evening for Valentine's Day. Last year they had flown to Bermuda for the whole week.

"I can watch the boys while you go out," she said.

"I think they're going to Wendy's parents'," Bryn said. "But I'll ask Bob."

They drank their coffee in silence. Then Bryn said, "We don't have to go out that night. We can stay in and cook something together."

"No," Corrie said, smiling. "It's your first Valentine's Day as a couple; you should do something special."

Bryn protested several times over the next couple days, but on Monday evening she stood before the mirror in her room, surveying herself in the glass.

"You look nice," Corrie said.

"I look like a stuffed sausage."

"I think it's time you broke down and bought some maternity clothes."

"Ugh!" Bryn grimaced. "That's romantic."

"You're pregnant, honey. And you're beautiful. Bob thinks so. I think so. Anyone who sees you will think so."

"Hmmm." Bryn simply stared at her reflection, trying to smooth the fabric stretched tight across her belly.

"Screw it," she finally said, pulling the dress over her head. "I'll wear pants."

The doorbell rang and Corrie went to answer it. On the porch, Bob stood clutching two bouquets of roses.

"Happy Valentine's Day," he said, handing the bouquet of yellow roses to Corrie.

"Oh, you didn't have to do that." Corrie held the bouquet to her face and breathed in deeply. "They're beautiful, Bob. Thank you."

"Are you sure you don't want to come with us?" Bob asked.

"No," Corrie said. "I'm just going to kick back and watch a movie."

"Hey!" Bryn appeared at the top of the stairs wearing jeans and a black tunic.

"Hey, you!" Bob smiled and held out the bunch of red roses. "Happy Valentine's Day!"

Bryn kissed him, then handed the bouquet to Corrie.

"I'll take care of these," Corrie said. "You guys go have fun."

After Bob and Bryn left, Corrie filled two vases with water and began arranging the roses. She placed one vase on the dining room table and the other on the coffee table in the living room. Then she sat on the couch and let the tears come. She and Mark had been married seven years today. They should be together, celebrating. Instead, she didn't even know where he was.

After a while, she rose and walked into the kitchen. She poured herself a bowl of cereal and a glass of orange juice. "Happy Valentine's Day, baby," she whispered, patting her stomach.

She turned on the television and watched a generic movie until she fell asleep.

At eleven, Corrie was startled awake by the front door. Bryn came in, closing the door softly behind her.

"Hey," Corrie said. "How was dinner?"

"I didn't think you'd be up." Bryn sat down on the recliner. "It was good."

"Where's Bob?"

"The boys have school tomorrow."

Corrie yawned and stretched and sat up, rubbing sleep from her eyes.

"How was the restaurant?"

"It was good," Bryn repeated, not meeting her eyes.

"Are you all right?" Corrie asked, watching her carefully.

"Yeah," Bryn said. "I'm fine."

"What's wrong?"

Corrie leaned forward to catch Bryn's eyes.

Bryn hesitated for a minute, then said softly, "We saw Mark at the restaurant."

"Oh." Corrie sat back, waiting.

"He was there with a woman from his office, a redhead," Bryn continued. "Her name is Paige."

"Paige?" Corrie nodded slowly. "Paige Chapin. I remember her. She's only been with the company a couple years."

"I wasn't sure if I should tell you," Bryn said. "Bob said I shouldn't, but I thought you'd want to know."

Corrie nodded again. "Paige," she repeated softly. "Mark took Paige Chapin out for Valentine's Day."

294 • *Sherri Wood Emmons*

She let the notion sink in for a long minute.

"Our anniversary," she said then. "He took someone out on our anniversary."

"I'm sorry, Corrie." Bryn wrung her hands together.

"Did you talk to him?"

"We said hello," Bryn said. "And he introduced us to his . . . to her."

"I almost called him earlier," Corrie said. "I just wanted to hear his voice. I'm glad I didn't."

She lay back on the couch, her arm across her eyes.

"Are you okay?" Bryn came to sit on the edge of the couch, her hand on Corrie's arm.

"I'm okay," Corrie said. "I mean, I don't know. . . . Why shouldn't he be out with someone on Valentine's Day? We're getting divorced. I cheated on him. He is obviously moving on."

"I'm really sorry," Bryn whispered.

"I'm going to bed now." Corrie sat up and gave her friend a brief hug. "I'm just really tired."

"Are you sure you don't want to talk?"

Corrie just shook her head. "I'll see you in the morning."

Bryn watched her walk to her room and shut the door behind her.

"Damn you, Mark!" she hissed.

She sat a minute, wondering if she should knock on Corrie's door. Then her eyes fell on the roses on the coffee table and, beside them, Corrie's cell phone.

Bryn took a deep breath, then picked up the phone and carried it upstairs.

She dialed with shaking fingers, praying that he'd be home.

"Hello?"

"Daniel? It's Bryn," she said softly. "Listen, I know Corrie told you not to come out, but I think it might be a good thing for you to come anyway."

❧ 52 ❧

The following Saturday, Bryn and Corrie sat in the living room drinking coffee when the doorbell rang.

"Bob?" Corrie asked, looking at Bryn.

"I don't think so," Bryn said. "He's taking the boys roller skating today."

Corrie rose and walked to the door, pulling her robe closed around her. When she opened the door, she stood absolutely still.

"Daniel?"

"Hey, gorgeous!" Daniel swooped her into a hug, lifting her off her feet.

"What are you doing here?" Corrie pulled away from him.

"I came to see my favorite girls. Are you going to let me in?"

Corrie stepped back so that he could enter the house.

"Hey, Bryn," he said, grinning at her. "You're looking huge."

"Screw you!" Bryn snapped, but she smiled at him.

"You, on the other hand, are positively beautiful." Daniel kissed Corrie's forehead. "Pregnancy obviously agrees with you."

He looked around the tiny living room, crowded with furniture.

"Nice place," he said.

"We're still trying to figure out where everything goes," Bryn said.

"Maybe some of it needs to go to Goodwill?" Daniel laughed. "But it's a nice house. And how great to have the park right across the street."

Corrie still stood in the doorway, watching him in silence.

"Why did you come?" she finally asked.

"To see you, to see how you're doing, to see how the baby is doing. I know you said not to, but this is my daughter, too, Corrie. I wanted to see you, to make sure you're taking care of yourself."

"Do you want some coffee?" Bryn rose and walked into the kitchen. "Black, right?"

"Thanks," he called after her.

He turned to look at Corrie. "Aren't you even going to say hello?"

She smiled at him. "Hello."

"I brought something for you." Daniel reached into the bag he was carrying and produced a big heart-shaped box of chocolates. "Happy belated Valentine's Day," he said, holding the box toward her.

Corrie felt tears sting her eyes.

"Thank you," she whispered, taking the box.

"I brought something for the baby, too!" He pulled another box from the bag, this one gift-wrapped in pink-and-white paper. "Are we still calling her Emmaline?"

Corrie nodded, sinking down onto the couch.

Daniel laid the box in her lap. "Open it," he commanded.

She unwrapped the present and opened the box. Inside she found a tiny pink L.A. Dodgers jersey and an equally tiny Dodgers baseball cap.

"I thought about the Lakers," he said, "but I figure this is Pacers' country, so I went with the Dodgers."

She lifted the small jersey and laid it across her stomach.

"It's so tiny," she said. "And cute . . . really cute."

"Well, it's her first Valentine's Day," he said. "I couldn't just let that pass by without doing something."

"How long are you in town?"

"Till Tuesday," he said. "I fly back Tuesday afternoon."

"Where are you staying?"

"At Bob's," he said, smiling. "I guess he's finally forgiven me for messing up your life so bad."

"No, he hasn't!" Bryn appeared from the kitchen carrying a mug of coffee. "He just can't ever say no."

"So you guys are dating now?" Daniel took the cup from her.

"Yeah."

"Be good to him," he said.

Bryn just shook her head.

"I'm going to get dressed," she said. "And then go to the store."

"I thought we were going to get haircuts this morning." Corrie watched Bryn walk up the stairs.

"We can do that another day," Bryn said.

Corrie sat a moment, looking from Bryn's back to Daniel's face.

"She knew you were coming, didn't she?"

Daniel's eyes widened. "No, of course she didn't. Not unless Bob told her."

She stared at him intently for a long minute, then seemed to relax.

"When did you get in?" she asked.

"Just this morning," he said. "I wanted to see you. I've really been missing you."

"You shouldn't have come. I asked you not to come."

"I know," he said. "But like I said, Corrie, this is my baby, too. I want to be part of her life, even if you won't let me be part of yours."

She sighed and leaned back against the couch. "Well, I'm glad to see you," she admitted.

He grinned at her and sipped his coffee.

"So, what should we do today?"

"I don't know," she said.

"How about we buy stuff for the nursery?"

Her eyes widened in suspicion again.

"How do you know I need anything for the nursery?"

"Bob said he'd offered you his stuff, since you didn't bring anything from your old house."

Corrie shook her head. "Sometimes I think we all know each other too well."

"Maybe," he agreed. "But I still think we should buy a crib today. And whatever else you think this baby needs."

She smiled at him. "Deal."

Bob came with the boys that evening after their roller skating adventure. He and Daniel assembled the new crib and changing table in the nursery while Corrie and Bryn made stuffed peppers and salad. The boys ran from room to room, supervising.

"Hey!" Daniel called from the bedroom. "We're done. Come see it."

Corrie walked into the pale green bedroom, now sporting a white crib and changing table, with a matching chest of drawers. White curtains hung in the window and a pink-and-white rug covered the floor. In the corner, her father's globe stood beside the closet door.

"It's beautiful," she breathed.

"It really is," Bryn agreed.

"Whose room is this?" Cody stood in the doorway.

"This is for my baby," Corrie said, smiling at him.

"When did you get a baby?"

"I haven't gotten her yet," Corrie said. "She'll come in June."

"How can you get a baby if you're not married?"

Corrie's cheeks flushed red.

"It's okay, buddy." Bob lifted Cody onto his shoulders. "There are all kinds of families in the world. Like our family isn't how it used to be, but we're still a family, right?"

Cody nodded thoughtfully.

"But you used to be married to Mommy," he said. "When you got me and Micah."

"Yes, that's true," Bob agreed. "But remember, we talked about this. Sometimes people who aren't married yet want to be parents. Like Bryn, remember?"

Cody stuck his fingers in his mouth and thought about it for a long minute.

"When are we eating?" he asked.

Corrie's shoulders relaxed and she smiled at him. "In just a few minutes," she said. "Why don't you go wash your hands?"

"Sorry about that." Bob touched her shoulder.

"It's okay," she said, shrugging. "I'm sure he's not the only one I'll have to answer about that."

Bob and Bryn followed the boys from the room, leaving Corrie and Daniel alone.

"Marry me," he said softly. "Marry me and come to L.A. and you won't have to do this alone."

She shook her head.

"The nursery is really beautiful," she said. "Thank you."

Then she walked back to the kitchen to toss the salad.

The next morning, Daniel was back bearing bagels and cream cheese.

"What are you all dressed up for?" he asked, staring at Corrie's plum-colored dress with matching pumps.

"Church," she said.

"Since when do you go to church?"

He put the bagels on the kitchen counter and poured himself some coffee.

"Since I got engaged to Mark," she said.

"You don't go to the same church he does, do you?"

She shook her head. "I go to St. Luke's now. Mark still belongs to Holy Spirit."

"Skip it today."

She shook her head.

"Come on, I'm only in town until Tuesday. You can go to church any Sunday. Skip it and I'll make you breakfast."

"You can make breakfast for Bryn."

"As delightful as that sounds, I didn't come to make breakfast for Bryn. I came to spend time with you."

"Well, I am going to church." She snapped her purse closed and pulled on a coat.

"Fine," he sighed. "I'll go with you."

She stopped and stared at him. "You don't go to church."

"How do you know?" He grinned at her. "Maybe I go to church every week. Or maybe I go to a Hindu temple."

She stood a minute, just watching him. "I'd really rather you didn't come."

He feigned a hurt expression. "Well, that's really . . . Christian of you! Denying me the opportunity to find God and get myself saved."

She cocked her head. "And this is exactly why I'd rather you didn't come. You don't take faith seriously, Daniel, but I do. I go to church to pray and have some quiet time to think and listen for God. I don't want to have to sit and worry about you doing something stupid."

"I'll be good," he said, pulling his jacket back on. "I mean it. I promise I'll be good."

Corrie sighed and shook her head.

"God help us both," she whispered.

True to his word, Daniel did behave in church. He knelt when she knelt and rose when she rose. He sang hymns, sharing a hymnal with her. He bowed his head during prayers. He even got up to receive communion, before Corrie pulled him back down and explained that he needed to stay put.

After the service, Corrie stopped to speak with several people, including the priest.

"How are you, Father?" she asked, shaking his hand.

"Just fine, Corrie. How are you?"

"I'm fine."

"Who is this?" Father Martin smiled at Daniel.

"This is my friend Daniel. He's visiting from California."

Corrie paused, tense, waiting for Daniel to make a flippant remark about being her baby daddy, but he only shook the priest's hand and said how much he had enjoyed the service.

In the car, Corrie finally allowed herself to relax. She sighed deeply.

"You really do take it seriously, don't you?" Daniel was watching her thoughtfully.

"I told you I do."

"I guess I just never pictured you as a church lady," he said. "No, I'm not making fun of you!" He held up one hand to stop her reproach. "I'm not making fun. I'm impressed, actually."

She glanced at him briefly, waiting for the punch line. Daniel simply smiled.

"Seriously, Corrie," he said, "I'm glad you have a community. I may not believe in God, but I do believe in community. That's what I'm trying to build at the center. So many people are just so alone these days, especially in a city like Los Angeles. That's why so many kids get drawn into gangs; they're looking for family, for community. So, if you've found a community in the church, that's a good thing. I'm happy for you."

"Thanks," she said. "I'm still getting settled in at St. Luke's. I've only been coming for the last couple months. Holy Spirit is my home . . . was my home."

"I'm sorry," he said softly. "I really did screw up your life, didn't I?"

"Well, you had company," she said, smiling ruefully. "It takes two to tango."

"Yeah, but I think you'd have come home unscathed if I hadn't pushed you so hard."

She shook her head, feeling her eyes burn.

"I'm starving," she said, turning onto her street. "How 'bout you make me that breakfast?"

So Daniel made an omelet while Corrie toasted bagels. They sat together quietly for a while.

"You really are a good cook," she said, finishing her eggs.

"Don't sound so surprised," he said. "I told you, I've been on my own a long time. I had to learn to cook, because I got sick of fast food."

"I want to have the baby baptized." She said it quickly, relieved to put the idea on the table.

"I figured," he said, laying aside his napkin.

"And?" She watched him, twisting her own napkin into a knot.

"And, okay," he said.

"Really? You don't have a problem with that?"

"I told you, Corrie, I believe in community. If you have a good community to raise our daughter in, then I'm glad of it."

She let that sink in a minute.

"Of course, I'll tell her my beliefs, too," he said. "I mean, I'm not going to beat her over the head with agnosticism, but I do want her to know both sides."

"That's okay."

"So here's a question for you," he said. "Why the Catholic church? Why not a church that lets women be leaders?"

"Well, at first I joined because that's what Mark wanted. It didn't really matter too much to me either way; it just made things easier with his family. But I like it. I've really come to love it, actually.

"I love the ritual and the ceremony. It's special, kind of sacred. I don't agree with everything the church says, of course. But I feel at home there. Does that make sense?"

"I guess so," he said. "I mean, it's not for me. But whatever works for you is okay."

"Have you told your mom about the baby?" Corrie asked.

"Yeah. She's pretty excited." He smiled at her. "She wants to come visit after the baby is born. I hope that's okay."

"It's fine," she said. "I always liked your mom. She's great."

"She liked you, too. I think she's really hoping we'll get back together now."

Corrie just smiled and shook her head.

"Why not?" he continued. "Why are you so dead set against us being together?"

She leaned her elbows on the table and cupped her chin.

"I just don't see it," she said softly. "You live in California. I live here. Neither of us wants to move."

"But," he began.

"And," she plowed ahead, "I don't think getting married just because you're having a baby is a good idea. We both know that doesn't work. Marriage is hard enough, but when you're only getting married because you're pregnant, you're doomed from the start."

"If you'll remember, I wanted you to come to L.A. a long time before I knew you were pregnant."

"It's no good, Daniel." She took his hands and looked directly into his face. "You are wonderful, and if you want to be in the baby's life, then I'm happy about that. But this, you and me . . . it's not going to happen."

"But why?"

"Because every time I look at you I see the end of my marriage. I see my mistakes and my stupid, selfish behavior, and I see the hurt on Mark's face when I told him I was pregnant and the baby wasn't his. Every time I look at you I see loss."

He sat quietly for a minute. Then he squeezed her hands.

"Maybe that will change," he said. "Maybe once the baby is born, you'll look at her and see that she is not a mistake, that we are not a mistake. Maybe then you'll be able to look at me and see a man who loves you and wants you and would do anything for you."

She shook her head again. "I don't think so."

He stood then and began pacing around the table.

"Maybe you can't think so because you don't want to. You're punishing yourself because you hurt Mark. I get that. But you can't do that forever, Corrie. We made love, you feel guilty. I get that. But we also made a baby. You can't take that guilt out on her, or on me."

Corrie let a tear slide unchecked down her cheek.

"I'm sorry," she whispered.

Daniel sat down beside her and took her hands again.

"Just let it be for a while," he said. "Don't rule it out. Don't just rule it out, okay? Wait and see how you feel after the baby is born."

She smiled at him, her cheeks reddening.

"You really are wonderful," she said finally. "I didn't see before how much you've changed, how much you've grown up."

"Yeah, you can nominate me for sainthood anytime."

She laughed then, rose, and began gathering dishes.

"Let me help." Daniel took the dishes from her and kissed her forehead. "Just let me help you a little bit."

"I'll try."

That evening, they sat in Bob's living room, watching Cody and Micah build with Legos. Bryn curled on the couch next to Bob. Daniel sat on the floor, making suggestions on building design.

Corrie watched them from the rocking chair, marveling at how normal, how domestic it felt to be here with these people, her surrogate family.

She smiled at Daniel, intently sorting colorful tiny blocks. He looked completely at home with the boys.

Who could have known just six months ago that we'd be here like this? Bryn and me both pregnant. Bryn and Bob dating. Daniel here at all. Who could possibly have known?

She shook her head and sipped her tea, allowing herself to simply enjoy the evening.

The phone in her purse trilled impatiently. She looked at the caller ID and sighed, then answered.

"Hello?"

"Coriander, it's Mom." Patrice's voice carried into the room.

Bryn sat up and shook her head. "Hang up!" she hissed.

"You need to come," Patrice said. "It's Maya. She's been in an accident."

"What kind of accident?" Corrie rose. "Is she okay?"

"She's in the hospital, in San Francisco. She got run off the road by a drunk driver." Patrice's voice shook. "It's bad, Coriander."

"Are you at home?"

"Yes, but I have to get out there to be with her."

"I'm on my way."

❧ 54 ❧

Daniel drove fast, Corrie clinging to the armrest of the rental car. He skidded to a stop in the driveway.

"Thank you," Corrie said. She opened the car door.

"I'm coming in with you." Daniel got out of the car and walked around to take her arm.

"No," she said. "I don't think that's a good idea. My mom is pretty mad at you, and you . . . you don't know how mean she can be."

He didn't argue, just walked with her to the front porch. Her hands were shaking so she couldn't get the key into the lock. Daniel took the key from her and unlocked the door, then held it open for her.

"Mom?" Corrie scanned the living room, filthy with magazines and unopened mail and fast food containers.

"Oh Coriander!" Patrice ran from the kitchen, her housecoat flapping open, a tumbler in her hand. She grabbed Corrie and pulled her into a tight embrace.

"We have to go to San Francisco. Right now! We need to go to the airport. Caerl can drive us."

Corrie pulled back to see her younger brother standing in the doorway, clearly high.

"I don't think Caerl is going to drive anywhere," she said. "Daniel can drive us."

Patrice looked up and saw Daniel standing at Corrie's back. Her eyes widened, her nostrils flared, her cheeks reddened.

"That man is not driving us anywhere!" she shrieked. The tumbler she'd been clutching fell to the ground and shattered.

"You bastard!" she screamed, lunging toward Daniel. "You ruined everything!"

"Mom!" Corrie grabbed Patrice by the arm. "Stop it!"

Caerl smirked at them.

"So, Daniel, long time no see, man."

"Caerl." Daniel nodded at him, never taking his eyes from Patrice.

"So, I hear you're gonna be Corrie's baby daddy."

"Shut up, Caerl!" Corrie spun to face him.

"Perfect little Corrie, the perpetual, eternal *good* girl." He laughed at her. "No better than the rest of us now, huh? Quite the little slut, my sister."

Corrie didn't see Daniel move, didn't see him draw back his arm and swing. She only saw her brother fall to the floor.

"You bastard!" Patrice screamed again, pulling away from Corrie's grasp. "You selfish bastard! Look what you've done!"

She dropped onto the floor beside Caerl. "Are you okay?" she crooned. Blood spurted from Caerl's nose.

Corrie stood frozen for an instant, then took Daniel's hand.

"What hospital is she in?" she demanded.

Patrice looked up in confusion.

"Maya!" Corrie yelled. "Maya, your daughter—what hospital is she in?"

Patrice simply gazed at her for a moment, then whispered, "San Francisco General."

"Come on!" Corrie pulled Daniel toward the door.

"Coriander Bliss!" Patrice yelled. "Wait!"

But Corrie didn't stop. She ran to the car and slammed the door behind her. Daniel got in the driver's side.

"Let's go," she said.

They drove in silence for a minute, then Corrie said, "Where are we going? The airport's north!"

"We need to stop and get my stuff," he answered calmly. "Then we'll stop at your place and pick up what you'll need. It will only take a few minutes," he said, grasping her hand. "Trust me, you don't want to go to San Francisco without a toothbrush and a change of clothes."

She leaned back in the seat and let him drive, first to Bob's, where he threw his things in a bag and she promised Bryn she'd call when they got to California. Then they drove to her house, where Daniel packed a bag for her while she sat on her bed, numbly watching. Finally, they were on the road north, to Indianapolis, to the airport.

"I don't know how I'm going to pay for a flight," she said suddenly. "Mark canceled our credit cards."

"I've got it," Daniel said. "Don't worry. Just let me take care of it, okay? My credit is damned near perfect and my Visa is almost empty."

He took the rental car back to the agency and they hopped a shuttle to the terminal. Then Daniel made her sit with her feet up on a suitcase while he stood in line to buy tickets.

"How much were they?" she asked when he returned.

"Don't worry about it."

"Daniel, how much did they cost?" She stood and grabbed his hand. "They had to be expensive, right?"

"Corrie." His voice was soft and firm. "We have a flight in two hours to San Francisco. We need to go to gate number four. I've got it."

"But . . ."

"You said you'd let me help, right?" he reminded her. "So let me help."

Two hours later they were taxiing down the runway. Corrie clutched his hand, feeling sick.

"I hate flying," she whispered through clenched teeth.

"I know." He patted her hand as they gathered speed. "But we need to get to Maya."

Corrie leaned back in the seat and closed her eyes tightly. She never let go of Daniel's hand.

Four hours later, they stumbled into the madhouse of San Francisco International Airport. It was nine o'clock local time, midnight back home. Corrie stared at the crowds passing by in confusion, blinking at the bright lights. Daniel took her hand and guided her toward baggage claim. She followed him, grateful she wasn't doing this alone . . . or worse, with Patrice.

They rented a car and Daniel pulled away from the agency.

"Here," he said, shoving a map at Corrie. "I've been here before, but it will help if you keep track of where we are."

He pulled into the whirlwind of cars and trucks and buses, staring intently at the road ahead.

"Daniel?"

"Yeah?"

"Thank you." Corrie touched his arm softly. "Seriously, I don't think I could have done this without you."

He grinned at her. "It's all good, Corrie-Andy. Just keep your eye on the map and tell me when I'm supposed to exit."

Forty-five minutes later, they pulled into the parking garage at the hospital. Corrie's legs shook beneath her so much that she thought she might fall. Daniel put his arm around her waist and guided her into the lobby.

"Can I help you?" An older Asian woman smiled at them.

"Maya Matthews," Corrie blurted out. "We're looking for my sister, Maya Matthews. She was in a car accident."

They waited a long minute while the woman checked her computer monitor.

"She's in ICU room 1442." The woman pointed toward a bank of elevators and gave instructions, which Corrie didn't follow or understand.

"I'm sorry," she started. But Daniel simply pulled her along.

They boarded a crowded elevator, Daniel's arm still protectively around her. Then he guided her off the elevator and through a maze of hallways, each of which looked exactly the same, until they stood before sliding doors bearing the frightening letters ICU.

"Come on," Daniel whispered, pulling her forward. "Almost there."

They stopped at the nurses' station and Daniel asked for Maya's room. Then they entered the darkened room, where Corrie's sister lay unconscious, her head swathed in bandages, her eyes swollen and blackened, her left leg raised in a rigid cast.

"Oh God!" Corrie sank down beside the bed and took her sister's hand. "Oh Maya! Oh my God!"

"It looks worse than it is," a nurse said softly. "Her leg is fractured and she's got some broken ribs. And she hit her head pretty hard."

Corrie leaned over the bed and cried. "Oh my God," she whispered.

"But she's going to be okay," the nurse continued, patting Corrie's back. "She's got a concussion, but the doctor says there's no internal bleeding. She'll take a while to mend, but she's going to be all right."

"Thank you."

Corrie raised her head to stare at Daniel, so calm, smiling at the nurse.

"Yes, thank you!" she whispered, to the nurse and to Daniel.

The nurse left them. Corrie held Maya's hand and let the tears stream unchecked down her face.

"I can't believe she's all grown up." Daniel sat down in a chair on the other side of the bed. "Last time I saw her, she was only sixteen, just a kid."

"She's a research biologist," Corrie said, gazing down at her sister, touching her cheek. "She's almost got her Ph.D. and everything."

"So both of you came out okay." Daniel smiled at her across Maya's still form. "She's okay because of you, you know."

Corrie shook her head, never taking her eyes from Maya's face.

"It's true, Corrie. You are the one who raised her. You made sure she had what she needed. You pushed her to do well in school."

"She's so smart," Corrie said. "She's always been so smart. And she's so much nicer than me."

She lowered her head to the bed and cried hard.

"I don't think that's possible," Daniel said.

"It's true." Corrie sat up and looked at him. "She's always been nicer than me."

Daniel just smiled and shook his head.

"It's true, and I'll tell you why."

Corrie held Maya's hand tightly, her eyes fixed on her sister's still face.

"When she was seven and ready to start second grade, I took her to buy some clothes for school. I had that paper route, you know? I'd been saving. So I took her to Goodwill. God, Daniel, she was so excited! You can't believe how excited she was. She was so little when my dad died. She'd never been to a store to choose her own clothes. Mostly we just had whatever the church donated.

"So, I took her to Goodwill and I let her choose some things— not much, I only had four dollars. But she chose a couple pairs of pants and some tops and the cutest dress. It was black with red cherries all over it. She loved it.

"And the whole time we were there, this old woman kept following us. She looked like she was homeless, and she smelled. Oh my God, Daniel, she smelled so bad. I thought she might be dangerous, but Maya just smiled at her and showed her what she was buying and talked to her. I couldn't wait to get out of there."

Corrie gazed down at her sister's face, touched her cheek gently.

"So we got to the cashier, and she started ringing things up, and I was seventy-four cents short."

She paused, swallowed hard.

"Corrie, you were just a kid," Daniel said softly.

She stared at him a long minute, then stared back down at the bed.

"I felt so bad," she said. "And I was so mad! I thought I'd counted it up just right. But I guess I didn't. So I told Maya we'd have to put something back. And this *cashier!*" She spit the word out, her cheeks reddening at the memory. "She just kept smacking her gum and staring at me, like she was enjoying it, how bad it was."

Daniel stood and walked around the bed. He put his hand on her shoulder. "You were a kid," he repeated.

"Maya's eyes got so big, and I could see she wanted to cry. But she didn't, Daniel. She didn't cry! She just pulled the dress out of the pile and said she didn't want that dress so much, anyway."

Daniel stood, massaging her shoulder for a long minute.

"Okay," she said finally, looking up at him, "and here's the magic part. That old woman—the one who smelled, the one I thought was probably crazy—she was in line right behind us. And she only had a couple things, I don't even remember what. But she put her hand on my arm and smiled at me. And she held out a dollar."

Corrie leaned her head against Maya's shoulder again, crying.

"She probably didn't have enough to eat that night, but she was giving us a dollar, so Maya could have that dress."

"People are good," Daniel said. "People who have been through hard times, sometimes they're the best."

Corrie stroked her sister's cheek.

"I thought she was crazy, but Maya saw her, I mean really *saw* her. And she wasn't crazy. Or maybe she was, I don't know. But she wanted Maya to have that dress."

"Did you take the dollar?"

Corrie nodded. "I couldn't stand to make her leave that dress."

"So that day, you helped Maya and you helped that old woman."

Corrie raised her head and stared at him. "I didn't help anyone," she said.

Daniel sank to his knees beside her. "Corrie-Andy, why are you always so hard on yourself? You were a kid. How old were you? Twelve? Thirteen? You took a freaking paper route to help support your family. You saved money to get Maya clothes for school. Honey, you taught Maya how to *be* in the world. What would Maya have been without you? What if you hadn't been there, and Maya and Caerl only had Patrice?"

He leaned his head against her and breathed in deeply.

"Do you know when I fell in love with you?" he finally asked.

Corrie didn't answer. She just stared at Maya's small figure in the bed, willing her to get better, to be strong.

"Corrie-Andy!" Daniel's voice broke her concentration. "Do you know when I fell in love with you?"

"Daniel," she said, touching his hair, "it doesn't matter."

"Yes," he said, "it matters. It matters because it's about who you are, who you've always been. And you need to hear this."

He stood and began pacing the hospital room.

"I remember the time we first met," he said. "First day of school, in the cafeteria, with Bryn."

She stared up at him, surprised he'd remembered.

"I thought you were cute."

She laughed, not a pretty laugh.

"You wanted to score." Her voice was harsh, surprising even her.

"I thought you were cute, but not for me." He sat down on the floor beside her, holding her eyes.

"I didn't want to get involved with anyone, let alone a small-town girl from Indiana. I wanted to travel, see the world, *save* the world."

"You made that perfectly clear," Corrie said.

"But then you showed up at the food pantry," Daniel said. "And I saw you weren't just a cute little girl. You'd felt poverty. You knew poverty."

Corrie pushed him away. "You felt sorry for me."

"No!"

His voice was so loud it startled them both.

"No," he repeated more quietly. "I envied you."

"Oh, screw you!" Corrie stood, pushing him away again. "There is nothing to be jealous of about being poor! You have no idea, Daniel! God!"

She walked around the bed and stopped, lowering her voice.

"You think it's *romantic,* somehow, being poor." She spat the words at him. "You think it makes people better somehow, more noble. But you're wrong!"

"Corrie, wait . . ."

"No! You're just wrong, damn it! Being poor isn't noble or romantic or . . . or anything. Being poor sucks! It means wearing clothes your classmates threw away, while they whisper about you behind your back. It means not knowing if there will be dinner on the table that night, and if there is, it's beans and bread or soup or plain rice. It means eating the nasty free lunch at school, and everyone knowing. It's humiliating and . . . and it sucks!"

She sat down in again.

"Look," she said, "I appreciate that you brought me here, Daniel. I do. And I will pay you back for the airplane tickets. But you need to go."

She stopped suddenly, staring at her sister, who had begun moaning softly.

"Get the nurse!"

But Daniel was already out the door, running to the nurses' station. In an instant he was back with a nurse.

"Sounds like she's waking up," the nurse said. She checked the monitors tracking Maya's heartbeat. "That's a good thing." She smiled at Corrie.

Maya's eyes fluttered open briefly and then closed again.

"Maya?" Corrie touched her sister's cheek, held her hand. "Maya, honey? Are you awake?"

"It might take her a while," the nurse said. "She's been heavily sedated."

"Should we do anything?" Daniel asked.

"Just being here helps," the nurse said. "Even if you think she's asleep, she knows you're here."

Corrie sat on the edge of the bed stroking Maya's cheek and crooning to her: "You are my sunshine, my only sunshine. You make me happy when skies are gray."

Maya's eyes opened again and rested briefly on Corrie's face.

"Corrie?" she whispered.

"I'm here, honey. I'm here, and you're okay. You're going to be okay. I'll take care of you."

At midnight, Daniel left to find a hotel room close by. Corrie sat all night by her sister's bed, talking to her, singing the songs she'd sung when Maya was small, holding her hand, and praying.

❧ 55 ❧

The phone woke Corrie from an uneasy sleep. She still sat in the chair by Maya's bed, her neck cramped and sore. She pulled her phone from her purse and answered. "Hello?"

"Coriander, don't hang up!"

"What do you want, Mom?"

"Are you with Maya? Is she all right?"

Corrie looked down at her sister, her chest rising and falling steadily, the monitors beeping regularly.

"She's going to be all right. She woke up for a minute, but she's sleeping now. The nurse says she's stable."

"I need to come out there. You were supposed to take me with you!"

Corrie rose and walked to the window, staring out at the sky just starting to lighten to a steel gray.

"No, Mom," she said, "you need to stay put. I'll take care of Maya."

"But I'm her mother. . . ."

"Mom, do you know why Maya is here? Because some guy decided to drink and drive. Apparently, he already had three DUIs. He was driving without a license and without insurance. He's a career alcoholic, just like you."

"That's not fair!" Patrice was yelling now. "I am not an alcoholic. Do I drink? Yes, I do. Maybe more than I should. But I'm not—"

"Yes, Mom, you are. You're an alcoholic."

"You don't understand." Patrice's voice instantly changed. She was in martyr mode now. "You have no idea what it's like. . . ."

"Really, Mother? I have no idea what it's like to be suddenly alone with a child? To be overwhelmed and scared and responsible for another life? You honestly think I don't understand?"

"Oh, Coriander." Patrice's voice broke. "I'm sorry, honey. I didn't think . . ."

"You never do."

"I need to be there," Patrice said. "I need you to buy me a ticket."

"No, Mom." Corrie spoke softly but firmly. "What you need is to quit drinking. What you need is to act like a mother instead of a child. I'm telling you this, Mom, and I absolutely mean it. Unless you get sober, you will never be a part of my life again. Or of Maya's."

"But—"

"No, seriously! I will not let you expose my baby to your drunk, stupid, selfish behavior. And I won't let you drag Maya down, either."

Corrie ended the call, her hands shaking.

"Good for you."

Corrie turned to see Daniel standing in the doorway, smiling. She tried to smile back, but could only manage a small grimace.

"You look like hell," Daniel said. He held a cup of coffee out to her.

"Well thanks so much," she said, taking the cup.

"I mean it. You need to get some sleep."

Corrie shook her head. "I need to be here when she wakes up again."

"No, you really need some sleep. You're exhausted. It's not good for you or for the baby."

Corrie sank into the chair she'd occupied all night.

"I'm okay."

Daniel took her hands and pulled her back up.

"Here." He put a card into her hand. "This is the address for the hotel. I've got a room. You go downstairs, get a taxi, go to the hotel, and get some sleep."

"But . . ."

"But nothing." His voice was firm. "Here's the key. It's room 824. I'll call you the instant anything changes."

Corrie stood uncertainly, wanting to protest. But her legs could barely hold her weight. Her head throbbed. And then the baby kicked.

"Okay," she said, taking the key. "Just for an hour."

"Good girl." Daniel kissed her forehead. "Do you think you can find your way to the lobby?"

She nodded. He handed her another sheet of paper. "I made you a map."

She smiled at him, let him wrap her in a tight hug.

"Thank you, Daniel."

She stumbled through the maze of hallways, following the map he'd made, silently thanking God that she wasn't there alone.

The taxi deposited her in front of a nondescript hotel. She fumbled with the door key before the door finally swung open to reveal an equally nondescript room. But Corrie didn't notice the faded wallpaper and worn-out carpeting. She only saw the bed, covers neatly turned down. She didn't bother getting undressed. She dropped onto the bed, pulled the covers over her head, and fell into a deep, heavy sleep.

When she woke up, sunlight was streaming in through the window. She stared around herself, unsure at first where she was. Then she sat up, glanced at the clock, and cursed softly. It was almost noon.

She reached for her phone and dialed Daniel's number.

"Hey," he said. "Feeling better?"

"How is she?"

"She's okay, Corrie. She's opened her eyes a couple times and I think she smiled at me once. But mostly she's just been sleeping."

"I can't believe I slept this long. I'll be there in fifteen minutes."

"Take your time." She could hear the smile in his voice. "Take a shower, have something to eat. Maya's not going anywhere, and neither am I."

She hung up and reached for her jacket, then caught sight of herself in the mirror. She did look like hell.

She dropped her jacket and headed to the tiny bathroom for a long, tepid shower.

When the cab dropped her at the hospital, Corrie pulled the map Daniel had drawn from her purse, retracing her steps from the night before.

Outside Maya's room, she stopped and listened intently. That was Maya's voice!

"Hey!" She walked into the room and stopped, staring at her sister's face, now with more color and definitely awake. She sank gratefully into the chair by the bed.

"Hey, yourself." Maya smiled at her. "Look at you, all pregnant and cute."

Corrie kissed Maya's cheek. "How are you feeling?"

"Like I got hit by a train."

"Can I do anything? Should I call the nurse?"

Corrie started to rise, but Maya pulled her back down.

"I'm okay," she said softly. "Sore and pretty pissed that I'm going to miss so much school. But I'm all right. How are you?" She watched Corrie's face carefully.

"I'm good," Corrie said, her cheeks warming. "I'm fine, the baby's fine, everything is fine."

"Yeah, right." Maya smiled at her. "You're in the middle of a divorce, Mom is treating you like crap, you had to move out of your house . . . but you're just fine."

"Hey." Daniel's voice startled Corrie. She'd forgotten he was there.

"I'm going to get some coffee. Do you want anything?"

"No," she said. "Thank you, though."

Corrie watched him leave, then turned back to Maya, who was studying her face.

"What?" Corrie said.

"So . . . Daniel?"

"No," Corrie said. "Not Daniel. I mean, yes, he's the baby's father. And yes, he wants to be involved in her life. But it's not what you're thinking. I slept with him one time, and it was a mistake."

Maya arched her eyebrows, then winced. "Ugh," she said. "That hurt."

"Have you talked to the doctor?" Corrie asked, glancing at the monitors still chirping away behind the bed.

"She left right before you got here," Maya said. "I'm gonna have to be here a few days, but then I can go home. I don't know how I'm going to get to classes with this." She pointed to her broken leg.

"Maybe you should take the semester off. Give yourself time to heal."

Maya shook her head. "This is my last semester," she said. "I only have three more months and classes are done. I can't just quit."

"I didn't say quit. I said take one semester off. Come home and let me take care of you."

"No." Maya let her head fall back onto the pillow. "I'm not coming back to Middlebrook, and you have enough on your plate without taking care of me."

"You can't stay out here by yourself," Corrie said. "You're going to need someone to help you until you get back on your feet."

"I've got friends. And I have Bryan." She smiled up at her sister.

"So . . . Bryan?" Corrie narrowed her eyes.

"Don't go all big sister on me." Maya laughed. "Bryan is great. He'll be here in a bit. You'll get to meet him."

By the time Daniel returned, they had agreed. Corrie would stay a few days. She could sleep at Maya's student apartment and use the bus to get back and forth. Then she would go back to Indiana, and entrust Maya's care to Bryan and various friends. Corrie wasn't completely happy with the arrangement, but Maya would not take no for an answer.

"And you," Maya said, looking at Daniel in the doorway, "you need to get back to Los Angeles before tomorrow. You have that meeting you have to be there for."

"I can reschedule it," he said.

"No, you need to go home. I'll be fine." Maya nodded at him, then winced again.

"Only if you're sure," he said.

"I'm sure."

The nurse came in, pushing a tray of instruments.

"I need to take some blood," she said. "And then let's get you cleaned up."

"We should go," Daniel said.

"No, you go. I'll stay." Corrie stood by the bed, watching the nurse.

"Go," Maya said. "I don't need you to be here for my bath!"

Corrie kissed her sister's cheek and promised she'd be back in an hour. Then she and Daniel walked to the cafeteria and bought sandwiches and sodas.

"Thank you," she said, as they sat down at a table. "I don't know what I'd have done without you here."

"You're welcome." He smiled at her as he unwrapped his sandwich. "I'm just glad you let me come."

"Are you going home today?"

"I guess so." He took a bite and chewed slowly. "But I'm only an hour away if you need me. I mean it, Corrie! They have regular flights all day long between L.A. and San Francisco. You call me for anything, and I will be here."

"Thanks, Daniel. I'll be okay."

"I know you will, Corrie-Andy."

Corrie's phone rang. She checked caller ID and turned off the phone.

"Patrice?"

"Yes. It's the fourth time she's called today."

"You should probably tell her that Maya's okay."

"I will." She sighed. "I just don't want to talk to her right now. But I probably should call Bryn! I forgot to last night."

"I called," he said. "When I left last night I called and talked to Bob. But you should call Bryn if you want to."

She leaned back in her chair and smiled. "You really have been a godsend the last couple days."

"Like I said, you can nominate me for sainthood anytime." He grinned at her and took another bite of his sandwich.

❧ 56 ❧

Corrie spent the next few days shuttling between Maya's studio apartment and the hospital. She stocked Maya's pantry, washed all the bedding, vacuumed the floors, and cleaned the bathroom. When Maya was finally allowed to come home, lying in the backseat of Bryan's ancient Volvo, she gazed around the small apartment and stared reproachfully at her sister.

"You just can't help yourself, can you?"

"I guess not."

"Thanks, Sis. You're the best."

That night, Corrie half slept on the couch, mindful of every small noise coming from the bed at the end of the room. But Maya slept soundly, snoring softly throughout the night.

The next morning, Corrie stood with her suitcase, surveying the schedule Bryan had made with several of Maya's friends. Someone would be in the apartment with her around the clock. Meals would be brought in. Chores would be done. Maya was in good hands.

"Are you sure you want me to go? I can stay a few more days."

"I'm fine, Corrie. You need to go home. You can't take forever off of work."

"I'll miss you." Corrie leaned over the bed, where Maya rested on several pillows, her leg still suspended in a sling.

"I'll miss you more." Maya smiled at her. "You really are the best sister in the world."

"Don't forget, Daniel said to call him anytime. He's only an hour away."

"I've got his number on speed dial."

They hugged for a long minute. Then Corrie took her bag, smiled at Bryan, and turned to go.

"Corrie?"

Corrie turned back toward her sister.

"Daniel really does love you."

Corrie smiled and shook her head. "I'll call you when I get home."

Bryn was at the airport, checking email. Beside her, Cody sat watching impatiently for Corrie.

"There she is! Hi, Corrie!" He ran to her, wrapping his small arms around her legs.

"Hi, Cody!" Corrie knelt down to hug him. "Thanks for picking me up."

"Bryn said we can get ice cream!" Cody grinned at her.

"That sounds great." Corrie rose and hugged Bryn.

"God, look at you!" She stepped back to survey her friend. "You're huge!"

In reality, Bryn was still tiny. She hadn't gained weight anywhere but her belly, which bulged as if she carried a soccer ball under her shirt.

"Thanks a lot!" She smiled at Corrie. "I've gained two pounds since you left. I think that calls for ice cream, don't you?"

"Sure," Corrie said. "Where's Micah?" She looked around the terminal.

"He's at Matt's," Bryn said.

"He said he didn't want ice cream." Cody shook his head and rolled his eyes in disbelief.

"More likely, he didn't want to spend time with me," Bryn said quietly.

"Everything okay?" Corrie asked.

"Yeah," Bryn said. "I think he's just processing stuff."

"Well, he's got a lot to process these days," Corrie said.

Bryn nodded.

"How's Maya?"

They stopped at the Dairy Queen and bought ice cream cones dipped in a chocolate shell, then drove to the house they shared.

"Can I watch TV?" Cody plopped down on the couch.

"Okay, but just for a while. Then we're going back to your house."

Bryn turned the television to the cartoon channel and followed Corrie into the kitchen.

"God, I'm glad to be home." Corrie laid her purse on the counter and gazed around the kitchen. "I mean, it was great to see Maya, and I'm so glad I went. But it's good to be home."

"So what did you think of the boyfriend?" Bryn put the kettle on the stove for tea.

"Bryan? He's nice. Quiet and kind of awkward, but really sweet. He set up this whole schedule with Maya's friends, so they can all help take care of her. She'll be okay, I think."

"Have you talked to your mom?"

"No." Corrie shook her head. "I'll probably call her later. She's called me about a million times, but I just haven't had the strength to answer."

"I still can't believe Daniel punched Caerl. I wish I'd been there to see it!" Bryn giggled.

"It was pretty bad, actually." Corrie sat down at the kitchen table. "Caerl was stoned or high or something. He called me a slut, and Daniel just . . . hit him."

"It's about time someone did." Bryn sat down beside her. "But I'm sure it was awful."

They sat for a moment, listening to the sounds of *SpongeBob SquarePants* from the living room. The teakettle whistled and Bryn rose.

"I'll get it," she said. "Chamomile or mint?"

"Either," Corrie said. "Whatever you're having."

Bryn returned with steaming mugs and set one before Corrie.

"So, I've been patient. This has been me, being patient."

Corrie smiled at her.

"But now I'm done being patient. How was it with Daniel in San Francisco?"

"Actually, it was great." Corrie blew on her tea. "He was really helpful, just took charge and did everything that needed to be done, so all I had to do was be with Maya. Honestly, I don't know what I'd have done without him there."

Bryn sat quietly, watching her. Finally, she leaned forward. "And?"

"And . . . and that's how it was. He was helpful. I'm glad he was there. And I was glad when he went home."

"Really?" Bryn's eyebrows raised.

"Yes, really." Corrie stared down at her tea.

"You didn't miss him after he left?"

"No, not really."

"You don't sound sure about that."

Corrie sighed and set her mug on the table.

"Daniel was great," she said. "But Daniel lives in California. And I live in Indiana. Just because we're having a baby together doesn't mean we should live together or anything."

"Okay," Bryn said. "I just wondered. You guys seemed pretty cozy while he was here. And you know I'm not his biggest fan."

Corrie laughed. "Yes, we've established just how much you love Daniel."

"But it really does seem like he loves you." Bryn spoke softly, watching Corrie's face. "Maybe you guys could work it out this time."

"No," Corrie said, her eyes still on her mug. "I don't think so."

Bryn said nothing for a long minute.

"I don't want to move to California," Corrie said. "This is my home. This is my life. I can't just move to L.A. I don't want to live there!"

"Okay," Bryn crooned. "Maybe he could live here?"

Corrie rolled her eyes. "Yeah, that's never going to happen. And even if he offered to come here, he'd be miserable. No." She rose and carried her mug into the kitchen. "It won't work. It's better this way."

Bryn simply smiled at her back, then stood and carried her own cup into the kitchen to rinse it out.

"Cody," she called. "Time to go."

She hugged Corrie lightly. "Come to Bob's for dinner, okay?"

Corrie nodded.

"I'm glad you're back," Bryn said.

Corrie smiled. "Me too.

❧ 57 ❧

Bryn sat in her car, watching children pour out of the school building, laughing, shouting, lining up in front of the row of school buses. She spotted Cody in the crowd and honked. He waved at her and ran to the car.

"Hey," Bryn said as he climbed into the backseat. "How was school?"

"Good!" Cody grinned at her. "We had macaroni and cheese for lunch!"

"Sounds good." Bryn was scanning the crowd of children for Micah.

Slowly, the crowd on the sidewalk thinned as children boarded buses and buses pulled away. Where was Micah?

Finally, Bryn sighed heavily. "Okay," she said, turning to Cody, "I guess he's still inside. Let's go find him."

She took Cody's hand and they walked into the empty entryway.

"Which way is his classroom?" Bryn asked, looking down the long hallways.

"It's this way. Come on, I'll show you." Cody pulled her along by the hand, stopping in front of a closed door. "This is his room."

Bryn knocked on the door, then opened it to look inside. The room was empty, the lights were out.

"Where could he be?"

"Maybe he's at the principal's office," Cody said. "I'll take you."

They walked back down the hall to the office. A young woman looked up as they arrived.

"I'm looking for Micah Carter," Bryn said.

"We have a dentist appointment," Cody chimed in.

"Did you check his classroom?" the woman asked.

Bryn nodded. "He's not there."

"Well, let me make an announcement." The woman rose and walked into another room. Soon her voice carried over the sound system throughout the school.

"Micah Carter, Micah Carter, please come to the front desk. Your . . . your ride is here."

She returned and sat down.

"Thank you," Bryn said. They waited several long minutes. Micah did not appear.

"Maybe he went home on the bus," Cody said.

"I guess we'll go see." Bryn walked briskly back to her car, still holding Cody's hand. They'd be late for their appointment now.

She drove to Bob's and went inside.

"Micah? Micah, are you here?"

The house was empty.

A cold fear gripped Bryn. *Calm down,* she told herself. *Just calm down and think. Where would he go?*

She turned to Cody. "Do you know how to get to Matt's house?"

Cody nodded.

"Let's go see if he's there."

They walked up the street a block and knocked on a door. A woman a few years older than Bryn opened the door and smiled.

"Hi, Cody," she said. "What's up?"

"Is Micah here?" Bryn asked.

"No," the woman said. "You must be Bryn?"

"Yes," Bryn said. "I'm Bryn and I was supposed to pick the boys up from school for a dentist appointment, but Micah wasn't there and he's not at home." She could hear the panic in her own voice. *Calm down, calm down, just calm down.*

"I'm Christy. Come in," the woman said, holding open the door. "Let me ask Matt if he knows where Micah's gone. Matt!"

"What?"

"Please come in here."

Matt appeared in the doorway. He smiled at Bryn. "Hey, Bryn. Hey, Cody."

"Matt, do you know where Micah is? Bryn was supposed to pick him up from school, but he wasn't there."

Matt shrugged his shoulders. "I don't know," he said.

Bryn's stomach turned upside down. Christy touched her hand and smiled reassuringly. "Let me just call around," she said.

She pulled her cell phone from her pocket and began dialing.

"Mandy, this is Christy. Is Micah Carter at your house? . . . Oh, okay. Well, thanks anyway."

Bryn stood frozen in the kitchen as Christy dialed three more times. Finally, on the fourth call, she breathed.

"Okay, good," Christy was saying. "Keep him there, okay? His babysitter is on her way to pick him up."

She closed the phone and smiled at Bryn. "He's at Dillon Murphy's," she said. "It's around the block on Highland Street."

"I know where it is," Cody said. "I'll show you."

Bryn's knees were shaking and for a minute she couldn't move.

"It's okay," Christy said, patting her hand. "It happened to me last year with my older son, Keith. I went to get him at school and he'd left with a friend. Scared me half to death."

"Thank you so much," Bryn said. "Really, thank you so much."

She followed Cody another block and around the corner to knock on another door.

"Hi," she said. "I'm Bryn, and I'm here for Micah."

The woman who answered simply looked at her.

"I'm Bryn Baxter," Bryn began again. "I was supposed to pick up Micah from school for a dentist appointment."

"Do you have a note from his father?" The woman stood squarely in the doorway, blocking Bryn's view of the inside.

"What? No, I don't have a note. But look, I have Cody and I'm supposed to take him and Micah to the dentist."

The woman didn't move. "I'm sorry," she said firmly. "I don't mean to be rude, but I don't know you and I don't know anything about a dentist appointment. And I can't let you take Micah until I talk to Bob or Wendy."

"Fine," Bryn snapped, pulling her cell phone from her purse. "Let me call Bob."

The phone rang several times before going to voice mail.

"Bob, it's Bryn. I'm at one of Micah's friend's houses, and his mother won't let me take Micah to the dentist. Call me back."

She ended the call and glared at the woman in the doorway.

"Look," she said, "I'm not a child molester or a kidnapper or anything like that. I'm just a friend who's helping Bob out."

The woman took a step back.

"I'm sorry," she said. "Until I talk to Bob, Micah is my responsibility. Cody, do you want to come in and play?"

Cody looked from the woman to Bryn. "No," he said slowly. "I'm going to the dentist with Bryn."

Bryn stood a minute more, staring at the woman in the doorway. Finally, she sighed.

"Fine, I'll tell Bob to pick Micah up on his way home from work."

The woman closed the door and Bryn stood a minute longer, holding Cody's hand.

"Come on, buddy," she said finally. "Let's go home."

"But what about the dentist?" Cody gazed up at her. "You said we were going to the dentist and then to get ice cream."

"Well, we're too late for the dentist now," Bryn snapped. She immediately regretted it.

"But how about this, we'll still get ice cream. Okay?"

Cody grinned at her. "Okay!"

When Bob arrived three hours later with Micah in tow, Bryn didn't look up from the chicken-and-noodles casserole she was stirring.

"Hey," Bob said softly, kissing her cheek. "I'm so sorry about today."

"It's okay," she said, still not looking up.

"Micah, do you have something to say to Bryn?"

"Sorry."

"I beg your pardon?" Bryn turned from the stove to look down at him.

"I said sorry." Micah's eyes stayed firmly on the floor.

"Okay," Bob said. "Now go clean up for dinner."

Micah ran from the room, Bryn staring after him, her mouth slightly open.

"Are you all right?" Bob looked at her, a puzzled expression on his face.

"Are you kidding?" Bryn threw the wooden spoon she'd been holding into the sink.

"It's all right, Bryn." Bob put his hands on her shoulders. "It was just a mix-up, but it's no problem. I'll just reschedule the appointment."

"You don't get it!" Bryn stepped away from him. "I was scared to death. I didn't know where he was! I went to the school and the secretary looked at me like I was an idiot. And then Matt's mom had to call all the other moms, so they all know I lost your kid. And then, that woman wouldn't let me take him! She stared at me like I was a kidnapper or something and refused to let me take Micah with me. It's not okay!"

"Look, I'm sorry you got scared." Bob's voice was soft and he glanced back into the dining room to make sure they were alone. "But honestly, it was just a mix-up. And Karen just did what she was supposed to do. I mean, think about it, a strange woman shows up to pick up a child. She didn't know who you were. She was just trying to take care of Micah."

"Who was inside the house and who I'm sure heard the entire conversation and could have come out and explained to Karen that he had a dentist appointment. Instead, he let me stand out there and make a complete idiot of myself!"

She turned from him to pick up the casserole dish and shoved it into the oven.

"That will be ready in thirty minutes," she said, taking off the apron she wore and stalking out of the kitchen.

"Wait!" Bob followed her into the living room, where Cody sat on the floor in front of the television, his eyes glued on Bryn.

"Cody, I'll see you later, okay?" Bryn smiled at Cody, hating that he had to hear and see the entire scene. She grabbed her coat and walked out.

"Bryn!" Bob stood on the porch. "Wait! Come on, don't be this way. It was a mix-up, it happens."

Bryn got into her car and pulled out of the driveway fast, then sped down the quiet street, cursing at the top of her lungs.

58

"Okay, calm down." Corrie handed Bryn a tall glass of milk. "Sit down and relax. This isn't good for the baby."

Bryn glowered at her over her milk and sat down at the dining room table.

"This Dillon is the same kid who told Micah that Wendy was a whore," she spat. "Where do you suppose he heard that? From his mother! So what do you suppose she thinks of me? She just looked at me like I was trash!"

"I don't know, honey. Maybe she was just—"

"Just nothing! She was enjoying it, watching me stand there like an idiot. God!"

Bryn took a long drink of milk.

"And Bob!" She slammed the glass down on the table. "He acted like it was nothing! Like she was just fricking Suzy Home-maker, being a good mom!"

Corrie said nothing.

"I *know* it wasn't just a mix-up, either! Micah *never* just goes to a friend's house after school without calling Bob. Never!"

"Maybe he forgot." Corrie's voice was soft.

"No." Bryn shook her head fiercely. "Honestly, Corrie, I love the kid. You know I do. I'm trying so hard to understand and be patient, because God knows he's going through so much. But lately . . ." Her voice trailed away.

"Lately what?" Corrie took a napkin from the holder and wiped up milk that had sloshed onto the table.

"I think he hates me." Bryn said it quietly, her voice quivering slightly. "I mean, he's just hateful most of the time. Last week when I asked him to help clear the table, he looked me right in my face and told me he didn't have to do what I said, because I'm not his mother."

"What did Bob do?" Corrie asked.

"He talked to Micah, made him come and apologize. But Micah didn't mean it. Anyone could see he meant what he said before. I'm not his mom and he just hates me being there while she's not."

"It's got to be hard," Corrie said. "I mean, Micah and Cody are both missing their mom, and Bob's trying to make everything okay, and maybe it's just really hard for him to see Micah in that much pain."

"I know." Bryn slumped in her chair. "I really do know, and I really do love Micah. I'm just so tired of him taking out his anger on me."

Her phone rang.

"Is it Bob?" Corrie asked.

Bryn nodded.

"You should take it."

Bryn considered for a second then sighed and answered the phone. She retreated to her room upstairs, leaving Corrie at the table, worrying. Why did everything have to be so hard? Why couldn't Bob and Bryn just be happy together? Why couldn't Mark forgive her for sleeping with Daniel? How did everything get so messed up?

She rose and rinsed Bryn's cup, then flopped onto the couch to watch television. An hour or so later, Bryn came back downstairs, her eyes red, her skin splotchy.

"Are you okay?" Corrie asked.

Bryn shook her head.

"We decided to slow things down," she said, her voice shaky.

"Micah needs some time to deal with the divorce, and I don't want to make it worse for him."

"Oh, Bryn." Corrie opened her arms and Bryn sank onto the couch beside her. "Don't worry, honey. It'll be all right. You're both just upset, but you'll work it out."

Bryn cried for a while, Corrie crooning to her the way she'd done with Maya in the hospital. Finally, she handed Bryn a box of tissues and Bryn blew her nose hard, shook her head, and sat up.

"I'm okay," she said. "It's fine. Bob needs to focus on the boys. They need to be his priority right now. And I need to just focus on me and my baby." She patted her stomach softly. "All I need is this baby."

She turned to Corrie and hugged her again.

"And you," she said. "I will always need you."

59

"Corrie!" Bryn called from the front porch. "Help!"

Corrie ran to the front door and burst into laughter. Bryn sat on the porch step, groceries spilling from a bag beside her, an ice cream cone upside down on her hugely rounded stomach.

"It's not funny!" Bryn said, trying not to smile. "I can't get up!"

Corrie pulled at Bryn's hands until she stood, then surveyed the mess on the porch.

"What a pair we are," she said, laughing. "One big fat lady pulling another one up!"

"Shut up and help me clean this up." Bryn tried to frown at her, but soon she was laughing, too.

It was a beautiful evening in April, only four weeks from Bryn's due date.

"You know if you keep eating ice cream every night, you're never going to lose that baby weight," Corrie said, mopping at Bryn's stomach.

"Who cares?" Bryn grinned. "I'll just be a fat mama. The baby won't care."

They gathered the scattered groceries and carried them into the kitchen.

"God, my feet hurt!" Bryn sat down and surveyed her swollen feet.

"Just sit there and put your feet up," Corrie said. "I'll put this stuff away."

"Thank you," Bryn said. "You're the best."

"Well, in a few weeks you'll have to do the same for me."

Corrie carried plates of pasta salad into the dining room. They had just begun eating when the doorbell rang.

"I'll go." Corrie rose and walked into the living room. Her own feet were tired, too, and her back ached.

She opened the door. Paul stood on the front porch.

"What do you want?" Corrie stood squarely in the doorway, blocking his entrance.

"I came to talk to Bryn," he said.

"I don't think Bryn wants to talk to you."

"Come on, Corrie. I won't upset her, I promise. I just want to talk to her."

"It's okay." Corrie felt Bryn's hand on her shoulder.

Bryn walked onto the front porch and sat down on the glider.

"Wow!" Paul stared at her stomach. "You're huge!"

"Thanks for the update," she said, her voice flat. "What do you want, Paul?"

Corrie closed the door.

"I just want to talk," he said. "I know it's been a while. And I know you're due pretty soon, right?"

"Four weeks."

"Four weeks, wow. That's coming right up."

"Not soon enough." Bryn shifted uncomfortably in the glider. "So, what do you want to talk about?"

"I'm moving in July," he said, "to Lexington. And . . . well, I'm not going by myself. I thought you might want to hear that from me, instead of from someone else."

"The blond?" Bryn sounded bored.

"Yes, actually." Paul shifted from one foot to another. "Her name is Claire and we've been living together for a while and she's coming with me to Kentucky."

"Good for you, Paul."

"Don't be snide, Bryn."

"I'm not, really. Good for you. I hope you'll be happy."

"Oh well . . . thank you."

"So, now you've told me, and you can go."

Bryn tried to rise from the glider, then gave up and sat back down.

"We need to talk about the baby," Paul said.

Bryn simply glared at him.

"Look," he said. "I know I said before that I wanted to be part of the baby's life. But now, it's complicated."

"Let me guess!" Bryn smiled. "Claire's not so interested in having a baby around?"

"She's young," Paul said. "She just . . ."

"Fine."

"What?"

"Fine." Bryn smiled again. "You don't want to be in the baby's life, that's fine with me."

"I'll pay support or whatever," Paul said. "Whatever you work out with the court. But I can't . . ."

"Paul, listen, it's fine. Go to Kentucky with Claire, start your new life. This baby and I will be just fine without you."

He stared down at her for a long minute, then tried to smile.

"Okay," he said. "Well, good luck to you."

"Good-bye, Paul."

"I'll be in touch," he said, backing down the porch steps. "I won't skip out on child support, Bryn. I'll send you my forwarding address."

He got into his car and pulled away, leaving Bryn alone on the porch.

"Okay, kiddo, she said, arms wrapped over her belly. "It's just you and me now. And we're going to be just fine."

Corrie joined her a minute later, carrying their plates.

"Did you hear?" Bryn asked.

Corrie nodded. "Are you okay?" She handed Bryn a plate.

"Actually," Bryn said, "I'm relieved."

"Good. It's so nice tonight, I thought we'd eat out here."

"Sounds good," Bryn said. "We might as well enjoy the weather now; it's supposed to storm tomorrow."

Corrie called up the stairs the next morning before she left for work. "Hey, keep an eye on the weather today. It looks like we might get some bad storms."

"Okay," Bryn called back. She rolled over, pulled the covers over her head, and went back to sleep.

Three hours later, Corrie sat in her office, rubbing her temples and wishing her headache would go away. She always got headaches when the barometric pressure dropped.

What would it be like in Los Angeles? It was dry there.

"Corrie!" Kenetha opened the door to the office. "The sirens are going off."

"Damn!" Corrie began shutting down her computer.

"Honey, I think we'd better go now!" Kenetha grabbed Corrie's arm and pulled her toward the hallway. "Look at that sky!"

Corrie stood frozen for an instant, staring at the greenish-yellow sky, dark masses of swirling clouds hanging low over the ground. Then she ran after Kenetha toward the stairs.

❧ 60 ❧

"Boys!" Bob yelled, staring at the television screen. "Basement! Now!"

He grabbed Cody and took Micah's hand, running for the basement stairs and slamming the door behind him.

"Is it a tornado, Daddy?" Cody's eyes were wide with fear.

"I'm not sure, buddy. But it looks like it might be."

They crouched in the corner of the basement farthest from the windows. Bob pulled a camping tarp over them and wrapped his arms around the boys. The house shook and a sound like a freight train crashing filled their ears.

"Don't worry," Bob shouted above the noise. "I've got you. Don't be scared!"

Corrie and Kenetha stood in a basement hallway with several other people, holding hands. Above them, they heard glass breaking, things crashing, wind howling. Then, suddenly, silence. It was over in an instant.

A cheer went up and people began walking toward the stairs.

"Are you okay?" Kenetha stared at Corrie as she sank to the floor.

Corrie's face was white, and her hands shook.

"I think my water just broke."

After the noise stopped, Bob cautiously walked up the steps and opened the basement door.

"Daddy! Is it okay?" Micah called from the basement.

"Stay there!" Bob yelled back. "Don't you guys move!"

He stepped tentatively into the kitchen and looked around, then sighed deeply, feeling his muscles relax. The windows had shattered and rain poured in through them. But the house was standing.

Outside the sirens still wailed. Bob looked into the living room. Amazingly, the television was still on. They still had electricity. A newscaster was standing in front of a weather map, showing a huge storm moving north and east, away from Middlebrook.

"Boys," he called downstairs. "It's over. You can come up. But watch out for broken glass."

Cody appeared first, staring in disbelief at the shattered windows. Then Micah came, stepping over glass shards to hug his father tightly.

"It's okay," Bob said, hugging them both to him. "We can fix the windows. The storm is over, and we're safe."

"Is Mommy okay?" Cody asked softly.

"I'm calling her right now," Bob said, pulling his cell phone from his pocket. He dialed Wendy's parents and nearly cried with relief when her mother answered.

"We're fine," she said. "No damage here. How about you? Are the boys all right?"

"We're fine," Bob said. "Broken windows and some minor damage, but—"

"Daddy!" Micah screamed from the living room.

Bob followed his stare to the television screen.

"That's Bryn's street!" Micah sank to the floor, shaking all over.

"I have to go," Bob said into the phone. "I'll call you later."

He sat down on the floor by Micah and wrapped his arms around the child, still staring at the television. The tornado had ripped through the park, twisting trees from the ground and throwing them like so many matchsticks into houses and cars. The camera panned down the street to reveal several houses that weren't there. They had simply been swept away.

"Daddy?" Cody stood behind him. "Is Bryn okay?"

Bob stared at the screen, shaking.

"Daddy?"

"Come on," Bob said, standing and pulling Micah to his feet. "Let's go."

They drove through a scene from a horror movie, turning back from one route to try another. Trees lay across roads and houses, power lines lay sparking in yards, debris scattered everywhere.

"Don't worry, guys," Bob said softly. "It's going to be okay."

In the backseat, Micah sat quietly hunched over, his arms around his knees, his back shaking.

After what felt like a month, Bob finally turned onto the street where Bryn and Corrie lived. A police barricade blocked the street; flashing lights from two patrol cars glared.

Bob parked where he was and got out, staring down the street toward Bryn and Corrie's house.

"Daddy?" Cody stood beside him, staring with wide eyes.

"It's okay, buddy," Bob said. *Please, God, let it be okay.*

Then he saw her, standing in the middle of the street, gazing around herself as if in a daze.

"Bryn!" Bob yelled. "Bryn!"

He edged around the barricade but was immediately blocked by a policeman.

"Sorry, sir. You can't go in there. It's not safe."

Before Bob could argue, a small figure darted under his arm and was running down the street toward Bryn.

"Micah!" Bob yelled after him. "Micah, come back!"

"Is that your kid?" The policeman let go of Bob's arm. "You'd better go after him."

Bob clutched Cody's hand and began jogging after Micah.

"Bryn!" Micah called as he ran. "Bryn!"

She turned at his voice and stood gaping as he threw his small body at her.

"Hey, Micah, it's okay," she said softly, wrapping her arms around his shaking shoulders. "I'm okay, you're okay, everybody is okay."

"I'm sorry I was mean to you." Micah was sobbing into her stomach. "I'm sorry I made you go away."

"It's okay," Bryn crooned. "It's okay."

She raised her eyes to Bob's and smiled. "It's okay," she repeated.

"Are you all right?" Bob panted.

"I'm fine. Just really glad to see you guys."

"Thank God!" Bob wrapped his arms around Bryn and Micah and let the tears of relief stream down his face. "Thank God! We saw your street on the news and we thought . . . God, Bryn, I've never been so scared in my life."

"I'm sorry, folks, but you need to move away from here." The policeman touched Bryn's shoulder. "Are you all right, ma'am? Do you need to see a doctor?"

"I'm fine," Bryn said. "Really, I'm fine."

"I think a doctor is a good idea," Bob said. "Just to make sure everything is okay."

Bryn started to argue, and then stopped. She smiled at him. "All right," she said. "Let's go."

Walking back to the car, Bryn held Micah's hand. Bob carried Cody in one arm, his other around Bryn's waist.

He'd just started the car when his phone beeped.

"It's a text," he said, clicking on the icon. His eyes widened.

"What?" Bryn said. "What is it?"

"It's from Kenetha. She's at the hospital with Corrie."

"Is Corrie okay?" Bryn reached for the phone.

"She's in labor."

"Let's go!"

❧ 61 ❧

They drove toward the hospital, swerving around fallen trees and power lines.

"Almost there," Bob said. "Damn!"

They could see the hospital two blocks in front of them, but another barricade blocked their route. Bob sat still a moment, staring at the road ahead, and then began inching around the cones. Immediately, the police car on the other side of the barricade flashed its lights. A police officer, a woman, got out of the car and walked toward them, waving her hands.

"I'm sorry, you can't come through this way. There's a line down." She pointed to a live wire snaking across the road.

"We have to get to the hospital!" Bob shouted. "My wife . . ."

He pointed toward Bryn, who immediately began puffing and moaning.

"Hurry, please," she said. "The baby's coming."

"Oh, for Christ's sake!" The policewoman walked to the edge of the barricade and waved them around, onto the sidewalk. Bob drove cautiously past the wire, then pulled back onto the road.

"Did you just lie to a cop?" Micah's eyes were wide.

"Well, technically, I guess we did," Bob said.

Micah grinned, then began to laugh.

"That's the best sound I've heard all day!" Bryn laughed, too.

Bob pulled into the parking lot and they ran into the hospital. The lobby was filled with people. Bryn walked straight to the front desk, patted her stomach, and said, "Maternity."

Immediately, a young man arrived with a wheelchair and began pushing her down a hallway toward the elevators. Bob and the boys followed them.

On the fourth floor, they wheeled into the maternity ward. The attendant stopped at the front desk and called, "Here's another!"

He turned to Bryn and smiled. "Someone will be with you in just a minute. It's kind of a madhouse today."

Then he walked back to the elevator. As soon as he'd stepped inside, Bryn got out of the wheelchair. Micah was grinning from ear to ear.

"Can I help you?" A nurse appeared, carrying a clipboard.

"Corrie Philips," Bryn said. "She's in labor, but she's not due for two months."

The nurse looked at Bryn's belly, then at her face. "You look like you're due any minute."

"I'm fine," Bryn said. "I just have to see Corrie Philips."

The nurse checked her chart. "She's in room 416." She pointed down the corridor.

"Thank you!"

Bryn took Bob's hand and squeezed it.

"Maybe you and the boys should wait here."

"Give her our love."

Bryn walked fast down the hallway and into the room where Corrie lay, hooked to monitors and an IV. Kenetha sat beside her, holding her hand.

"Are you trying to give me a heart attack?"

Corrie smiled at her weakly. "I'm sorry," she said. "My water broke and then I started labor. It's too soon, Bryn. It's too soon for this baby to come."

"It'll be okay." Bryn sat on the edge of the bed and took Corrie's free hand. "Are they giving you something to stop the labor?"

Corrie nodded toward the IV.

"Is it working?"

"I think so."

"The contractions aren't as strong or as frequent," Kenetha said, pointing to a monitor.

"Good! Just lie there like a good girl and relax and do what the doctors tell you." Bryn patted Corrie's hand. "You'll be fine."

"I'm really glad you're here." Corrie's face was pale, her hair damp with sweat.

"Me too." Bryn smiled. "Did you get here before the storm hit?"

"No, we were in the basement when I started having contractions."

"How did you get here?" Bryn asked. "It seems like half the streets in town are blocked."

"Kenetha called an ambulance." Corrie smiled at Kenetha. "Thank you."

"Stop thanking me," Kenetha snapped, still staring at the monitor. "I told you you're gonna owe me big-time. Next time I want a day off, I'll remind you of that."

"How did you know I was here?" Corrie asked. "We tried your cell, but you didn't answer."

"Bob got a text from Kenetha."

"Bob's here?"

"Outside with the boys. They came to check on me after the storm."

"Are you all right?" Corrie's eyes widened. "Is our house still standing?"

"Actually, it's kind of a miracle," Bryn said. "The house next door has no roof, and the one behind us is just completely gone. I've never seen anything like it."

"What about ours?" Corrie asked.

"That's the miracle," Bryn said, smiling at her. "Other than some shattered windows, ours is in good shape. I mean, I didn't do an inspection or anything, but it looked fine."

"And Bob is okay? The boys?"

"They're good. They're in the lobby. They'll be glad to know you're okay."

A nurse walked into the room, checked the monitors, and wrote on Corrie's chart.

"You're doing great," she said, smiling at Corrie. "Just relax and let those meds do their work."

She turned to Bryn. "How are you?"

Bryn laughed. "I'm fine. Not due for another four weeks."

"Well, this one"—the nurse nodded at Corrie—"is going to be on absolute bed rest for a while. We'll keep her here until we're sure the contractions have stopped. If we're lucky, she can go home tomorrow, or the day after."

"And if we're not lucky?" Corrie's voice quavered.

"If we can't send you home, then you'll have to be here for the duration."

Corrie dropped her head onto the pillow and squeezed her eyes closed.

"Have you reached your husband?" the nurse asked.

Corrie simply shook her head.

"Do you want me to call him?"

Corrie shook her head again.

"It's okay," Bryn said. "I'll take care of it."

The nurse bustled out of the room and they were quiet for a minute.

"Have you called Daniel?" Bryn asked softly.

"No."

"Do you want me to?"

"No."

"I think you should call him," Bryn said. "He wants to be here when the baby comes, right?"

"That could still be a couple months away," Corrie said. "What is he going to do, stay here for eight weeks?"

"I don't know," Bryn said. "But I think you should let him know what's going on."

As she spoke, Corrie's phone began ringing.

Corrie looked at the caller ID and closed her eyes tightly. Then she answered.

"Hi, Daniel. . . . Yes, I'm fine. We rode it out in the basement. . . . Yeah, they're okay, too. Our house apparently survived, so that's a blessing."

"Tell him," Bryn mouthed.

"Um, Daniel, I am okay, but I'm in the hospital. . . . No, I'm not hurt or anything, I'm just having some contractions and they want me to stay here until they're sure I'm not going to deliver early. . . . No, that's okay, you don't need to come. . . . Really, Daniel, I'm fine. You don't need to . . . well, if that's what you really want to do. But seriously, I'll probably be home and fine by the time you get here. . . . Okay, well, I guess I'll see you soon."

She hung up the phone and closed her eyes again. "He's coming."

"I told you he'd want to be here."

Kenetha rose and stretched. "If you're okay here, I think I'll head home and see if my house is still standing."

She bent over and kissed Corrie's cheek. "You call me if you need anything, all right?"

"Thanks, Kenetha."

They watched Kenetha leave, smiling as she swaggered out of the room.

"She's so great." Bryn smiled. "Now . . . really, how are you? Any pain? Do you need anything?"

"I'm fine," Corrie insisted. "Scared maybe, but fine. I just hope I can go home!"

"Do you want to see Bob and the boys? Or would that be too much right now?"

"I'd like it if they came in," Corrie said.

"I'll go get them."

Bryn walked back to the lobby, where Kenetha was filling Bob in on the situation.

"You want to see her?" Bryn asked.

"Okay," Bob said. "Come on, guys."

Cody grabbed his hand, eager to go along. Micah sat in his chair, looking at the floor.

"Come on, Micah. Don't you want to see Corrie?"

Micah raised his eyes and shook his head.

"Why not?" Bob dropped to one knee by the chair.

Micah shrugged his shoulders.

Bryn dropped into the chair beside him. "You guys go on. I'll stay here with Micah."

Bob and Cody walked toward Corrie's room. Bryn took Micah's hand.

"Pretty scary day," she said.

"Yeah."

"But we're all safe."

"Yeah."

"Do you want to tell me what's wrong?"

Micah stared at the floor. After a long pause, he said, "I thought maybe you died. We saw your street on TV and the houses were all messed up. I thought maybe you died."

"But I didn't," Bryn said, squeezing his hand. "I'm here and I'm fine."

They sat quietly for a minute, then Micah said softly, "I'm glad you're okay. I didn't want you to be dead."

"I'm glad you're okay, too."

"Bryn?" His voice was so low she had to lean down to hear him. "I'm really sorry I went to Dillon's and didn't tell you."

"I know, Micah. Don't worry."

"I didn't want you to be like my mom."

"Oh, honey, I know I'm not your mom. You'll always have your mom. But it's okay to have someone else love you, too. Right?"

"No," he said, shaking his head. "I mean, I didn't want you to be around and then leave, like Mommy did."

Bryn sat a moment to let that sink in. "So it was easier to just push me away. Is that it?"

Micah nodded, not looking at her.

Bryn wrapped her arm around his shoulder. "I'm not going away, Micah. I will always be in your life."

"But if you and Daddy get married, what will happen if you get divorced?"

Bryn sighed. "I don't know if your daddy and I will get married. But I promise you, I *promise* you, I will always be in your life."

"Even after you have a baby of your own?"

"Always, Micah. Always and forever."

He leaned into her then and sighed heavily. She kissed his head and rocked him gently.

≈62≈

Bob drove cautiously back to Bryn's house, where they packed a suitcase for Corrie. Then they drove back to the hospital to drop it off. When they left, Corrie was just dozing off.

"We'd better go home," Bob said. "We left in such a rush, I didn't really check on the house. We'd better see the damage."

They drove to the house, the boys gaping at the storm damage from the backseat. When they pulled into the driveway, Bob breathed a huge sigh.

"It looks okay, right?"

"Except there's a hole in your roof!" Bryn pointed to a gaping hole on one side of the roof.

"Well, except for that." Bob grinned at her and they both began laughing. Once they started, they couldn't stop. They laughed until they cried, staring at the hole in the roof.

"What are you guys laughing at?" Cody demanded from the backseat.

"Oh, buddy," Bob managed. "Sometimes you just have to laugh."

They went inside to survey the damage. Most of the windows were shattered and everything was wet. They climbed the stairs to the attic and stared out the hole to the sky above.

"Wow!" Micah breathed.

"It can be fixed," Bob said firmly. "I'll call the insurance guy tomorrow morning. But it's nothing that can't be fixed."

They walked through the house, picking up debris and glass. Outside, the sky began to darken.

"Why don't you guys stay at my house tonight?" Bryn asked. "You can't stay here. Everything's wet."

"Can we?" Cody's eyes sparkled. "We can camp in the living room!"

"I guess so." Bob sounded tired.

"Come on." Bryn took his arm. "Let's pack up what you need and go home."

The barricade at the corner of Bryn's street was gone, but the street was still blocked by trees and debris. Bob parked around the corner and they picked their way to the house, a tiny beacon of normalcy in a surreal scene.

"I can't believe it," Bob said. "It's like the tornado just hopped right over you guys."

"I know." Bryn smiled. "Good thing, too. I didn't have time to get to the basement."

Bob turned to stare at her. "Where were you?"

"In bed." Bryn pointed to the upstairs window. "I woke up and thought we were having an earthquake. The whole house was shaking, the windows were rattling. It sounded like the end of the world."

Bob wrapped his arms around her tightly. "Thank God you're okay."

Bryn unlocked the door and flipped the light switch, but nothing happened.

"Looks like we don't have electricity," she said. "Hang on, we've got some candles in the kitchen."

She returned with several candles and a large flashlight. They swept the light across the walls. Two windows on the west wall had broken, but the rest were intact. They climbed the stairs and looked through Bryn's room and the nursery. Everything stood just as she'd left it earlier that day.

"Unbelievable," Bob said. He stared out Bryn's bedroom window to the house next door, which had no roof at all.

Bob carried the mattress from Bryn's bed to the living room, then put Corrie's mattress next to it. "There," he said. "You guys can sleep right here."

"Where will you guys sleep?" Micah asked.

"Bryn can sleep on the couch and I'll . . ." Bob looked around. "I'll sleep right here beside you guys on the floor."

They piled pillows and blankets on the floor and sat in the candlelight, quiet for the moment.

"Can we roast marshmallows?" Cody asked. "We can make a fire in the fireplace."

"Sure!" Bryn rose and took a candle to the kitchen.

"I don't think we should use the fireplace until you've had it inspected," Bob said.

"Well, then we'll roast marshmallows over the candles." Bryn returned, carrying a bag of marshmallows and some metal skewers.

"Cool!" Cody threaded a marshmallow and held it over a flame, promptly setting it on fire.

"Cody!" Bob grabbed the skewer and ran with the burning sweet to the kitchen, where he doused it with water in the sink.

"Maybe this isn't a good idea," he said, walking back into the room.

But Bryn had already skewered another marshmallow and was holding Cody's hand, showing him how to hold the candy safely above the fire. Bob leaned against the wall, overwhelmed with gratitude that they were safe, that Bryn was safe, that they were together. He glanced to where Micah sat on the floor, watching his little brother, smiling.

Later that night, after the boys had fallen asleep, Bob and Bryn sat on the couch, staring at the lone candle still burning.

"Thank you," Bob whispered.

"For what?"

"For being you, for being safe, for . . . everything."

She turned to look at him, took his face in her hands, and said, "I love you, Bob Carter."

"I love you, Bryn Baxter."

He kissed her, gently at first and then with more urgency. Behind them, Micah snorted softly in his sleep. Bryn giggled. Everything felt right with the world.

The next morning, Bob called his insurance adjuster and took the boys home to meet with him at the house. Bryn packed a few more things in a bag to take to Corrie.

When she arrived at the hospital, she found Mark sitting at Corrie's bedside, watching her sleep.

"Hey," she said quietly.

"Hey, Bryn." He rose and kissed her cheek. "Wow, look at you."

"Yeah, I know, I'm huge." She smiled and patted her stomach. "What are you doing here?"

"Sarah called and told me Corrie was here. I just wanted to make sure she's okay."

"She's going to be fine, I think. Her water broke during the storm and she started having contractions, so they brought her in. They're giving her meds to stop the contractions."

Mark nodded and looked back down at Corrie, asleep on the bed.

"Our divorce is final next week," he said.

"I know. I'm sorry."

"I should go." He picked up his briefcase, resting on the floor by the chair.

"No, you stay." Bryn set down the small bag she carried. "I was just dropping off some stuff for her. I'll come back later."

She turned to leave.

"Bryn?"

She turned around.

"You look great."

"Thanks, Mark."

A few minutes after Bryn left, Corrie opened her eyes, confused at first about where she was. Then she heard the steady beep-beeping of the monitor behind her. She closed her eyes again, wrapped her arms across her stomach, and whispered, "Hang in there, baby. Please just hang in there for a while longer."

"Hi."

She opened her eyes again to see Mark leaning over her, smiling.

"Hi," she said. "What are you doing here?"

"Sarah told me you were here. I just wanted to come see you, to make sure you're okay. Are you?"

"I hope so." Corrie glanced back at the monitor. "I'll be better when I know this baby is going to stay put for a while."

Mark patted her hand tentatively. "You're really having a baby, aren't you?"

"Yes." Corrie smiled. "I'm really having a baby."

They were quiet for a minute, searching for something to say.

"Did you have any damage from the storm?" Corrie asked.

"No, it missed us."

"How about Sarah and your folks?"

"They're good, everyone's fine."

"Good."

Another long silence ensued.

"Corrie?" Mark leaned forward. "I'm really sorry about everything."

"Me too," she said.

"I wish—"

"I know," she interrupted him. "I wish things were different, too. But they're not."

Mark looked at her for a long minute, then rose. "I guess I'd better go." He leaned over her and kissed her forehead. "You take care, okay?

"I will."

She watched him walk away, wondering at how calm she felt. She hadn't seen him since the day they'd cleared their things out of the house. Since then, so much had happened. Since then, her baby had grown from an idea to a real, living, kicking being. Since then, she'd moved on.

She'd moved on.

She shook her head and said it out loud. "I've moved on."

"Good!" Bryn stood in the doorway smiling at her.

Corrie smiled back.

"How weird is that? Seriously, how weird is it? I think . . . I *know* I've actually moved on. I mean, I still love Mark. I probably always will. But, it's like a whole lifetime ago that we were together, you know? I'm different now than I was then."

"You're stronger." Bryn sat down beside her. "You're not a little girl anymore."

"No." Corrie smiled. "I'm a mom."

"Me too!"

"Did you go home last night?"

"Yeah, Bob and the boys stayed at our house. Theirs has a big hole in the roof."

"Oh my God!"

"It's okay," Bryn reassured her. "It's just a hole. It can be fixed."

"You seem pretty happy with the world." Corrie watched Bryn closely. "I guess things are better with Bob?"

Bryn nodded. "And with Micah. Do you know what he told me yesterday? He said he pushed me away because he was afraid I'd leave. Can you believe how smart he is? Seven years old . . . I'm not kidding, the kid's a genius."

"That's pretty smart," Corrie agreed.

"I told him I love him."

"Who? Micah?"

"No . . . well, yes, him too. But I told Bob I love him."

"And?"

"And he loves me, too."

"I'm glad, Bryn. I'm so happy for you, for both of you."

Corrie leaned back into the pillows and closed her eyes.

"Are you feeling all right?" Bryn asked.

"I'm fine. Just wishing I had someone in my life, too."

"Well you could, if you'd just let yourself."

Corrie's eyes flew open. Daniel stood in the doorway, carrying a huge bunch of roses.

"Hey, you." He leaned over and kissed her cheek. "You scared the hell out of me."

"Sorry." She smiled at him. "I'll try not to do it again."

"Hey, Bryn." Daniel stared at Bryn's belly. "You're as big as a house!"

"Screw you, Daniel." But she smiled at him.

"When are you due?"

"Four weeks."

"Wow! Coming right up. I hope we don't beat you to it."

He turned back to Corrie. "What are they doing for you?"

"Giving me meds to stop the labor. I hope they'll let me go home soon."

"But if she does go home, she's on complete bed rest," Bryn said. "No going back to work, no laundry, no cleaning. Just bed rest."

"Oh my God!" Corrie rolled her eyes. "I might just go crazy."

"It's for the baby," Bryn said, watching the monitor carefully. "Hey, I'm going to get some coffee."

She left the room, leaving Corrie staring behind her.

"Bryn!" she called. But Bryn just kept walking.

"Let her go," Daniel said, settling down into the chair by the bed. "This way I get you all to myself. So seriously, are you okay?"

"I'm fine, Daniel. I keep telling everyone, I'm . . ." Corrie's voice trailed off and she sat in silence, her eyes wide.

"Corrie, what's wrong?"

Before she could answer, a nurse ran into the room, stared at the monitor, and announced, "You'll have to leave now."

Behind Corrie, the monitor beeped frantically.

"Corrie?" Daniel stood uncertainly.

"Sir, you really have to go." The nurse pulled a curtain around the bed, leaving Daniel standing helplessly on the other side.

"Daniel." Bryn stood behind him. "Come on. Let's go to the waiting room. They're just going to check on her. Probably the monitor is just screwing up."

Bryn pulled him back to the lobby and they sat, staring down the hallway toward Corrie's room.

"What's happening?" Daniel asked. His face was gray, ashen, his hands shook.

"I don't know," Bryn said, taking his hand. "I just noticed the monitor was beeping faster than it was before, so I called the nurse."

"But she's going to be okay, right?" He turned to stare at her, his blue eyes wide and scared.

"She'll be fine," Bryn said, squeezing his hand. "She's in the hospital; she's got great doctors and nurses. It's probably just a problem with the monitor."

A nurse ran past them, padding down the hall toward Corrie's room. A minute later, they watched as the nurses wheeled Corrie out of her room.

"Wait!" Daniel ran down the hall toward them. "What's going on?"

He caught sight of Corrie's face, pale and frightened.

"I'm the father!" he yelled. "What's going on?"

A nurse turned to him and put up her hand.

"The baby is in distress," she said softly. "We're going to do a C-section."

"But it's too early!"

"Sir, please just go sit down." The nurse spoke firmly, her hand on his arm. "We'll take care of her."

She turned and ran after the gurney, following through doors that swung shut behind them.

"But . . ." Daniel stood, staring after them.

"Come on." Bryn took his arm, pulling him back toward the lobby. "Let the doctors do their job."

Corrie stared up at the bright lights, willing herself to stay calm.

"Okay, Corrie." Dr. Ping smiled down at her. "I know you're scared, but it's going to be all right. Your baby is ready to be born."

Then he disappeared behind the curtain that draped across her stomach. She couldn't feel anything on the other side of that curtain.

"I want Daniel," she said. Then again, louder. "I want Daniel!"

The nurse standing by her head wiped her forehead. "Is Daniel the father?"

"Yes, and he's here. Please! I want him."

The nurse disappeared, returning after a moment. "He's on his way, honey. You just relax."

A few minutes later, Corrie stared up into Daniel's eyes. His head and mouth were covered. He wore a blue robe and white gloves. But his eyes found hers and smiled.

"I'm here, Corrie-Andy. I'm here and it's going to be all right."

He took her hand and squeezed it hard. "You're going to be fine."

"The baby," she whispered.

"The baby will be fine, too. I promise, Corrie-Andy, it's going to be okay."

Soon, they heard a thin sound, a small mew, like a tiny kitten.

"It's a girl!" Dr. Ping's voice came from behind the curtain.

"Is she okay?" Daniel asked, holding tightly to Corrie's hand.

"She's small," Dr. Ping said, "But she's beautiful."

A nurse appeared, holding the tiniest bundle Corrie had ever seen. For a brief instant, she took in a forehead, a tiny nose, and a wide-open mouth. Then, the baby was gone.

"Where are they taking her?" Corrie's voice shook.

"NICU," the nurse standing beside her said. "It's standard for preemies."

"But she's going to be okay, right?" Daniel held Corrie's hand so tightly it hurt.

"She's got a good, fighting chance," Dr. Ping said. "You did it, Corrie. You brought her safely into the world. Now just relax. It's going to be okay."

In the lobby, Bryn dialed Bob's number again. "Bob, it's me again. Corrie's having the baby. Please call me back."

She put the phone back into her purse, looked up, and saw Bob striding toward her.

She fell into his embrace. "It's too early for the baby to be born. I was watching the monitor and it just went crazy. It's too early, Bob."

He held her close, murmuring into her hair. "It's okay. She's in good hands. She'll be fine."

"But the baby . . ." Bryn looked up at him and finally allowed the tears she'd been fighting to fall unchecked.

"Lots of babies are born early," he said, stroking her hair. "Even earlier than this. I know it's scary, but you have to have faith."

"Hey."

They both looked up at Daniel.

"She's here, she's born."

"Is she okay?" Bryn took his hand. "Is the baby okay?"

"She's in the NICU," he said. "They said she has a good chance."

"How's Corrie?"

He paused. "She's a mess. I don't know how to help her."

"Just your being here helps her," Bob said. "What can we do?"

"Pray," Daniel said, gripping Bob's hand. "Please just pray."

❧ 63 ❧

"Can I see her?" Corrie held Daniel's hand tightly.

"Soon," the nurse promised. "Let me just get your vitals."

She attached a blood-pressure cuff to Corrie's arm and squeezed the rubber bulb. Then she watched the numbers on the monitor.

"All right," she said, smiling. "Let's get you up."

She stood on one side, Daniel on the other, and they lifted her.

Corrie gasped at the pain, but gritted her teeth and squeezed Daniel's arm as they helped her into the wheelchair.

"Okay?" The nurse was watching her carefully.

"I'm fine," Corrie said through clenched teeth. "Let's go."

The nurse wheeled her into a brightly lit room filled with tiny glass bubbles. In each, an incredibly small baby lay, blindfolded and hooked to what seemed like a million monitors.

"It's okay," Daniel whispered. "She's up here, and she's beautiful."

The nurse stopped beside an isolette. "This is your daughter," she said.

Corrie stared through the bubble at the tiny infant inside.

"Can I hold her?"

"No, honey, not yet. But you can touch her. Here . . ." She guided Corrie's hand into what looked like a huge rubber glove.

Corrie reached out one finger and touched the baby's stomach, which was rising and falling rapidly.

"Is she breathing too fast?" She looked up at the nurse, begging for the right answer.

"She's fine," the nurse said. "They all breathe fast like that."

"She's so small."

"But she's perfect." Daniel kissed Corrie's forehead. "Our Emmaline Marie is absolutely perfect."

Corrie leaned into him and cried, cried so hard she felt nauseated.

"Okay," the nurse said briskly. "That's enough for today."

Two days later, Corrie was released from the hospital. Daniel drove her back home as she wept in the passenger seat.

"Eat, honey." Bryn rested a plate of stew on the arm of the couch, where Corrie sat, staring into the dark of the fireplace.

"I'm not hungry."

"You have to eat."

Corrie stared at Bryn's pregnant belly, then turned her head and cried.

"It's okay," Daniel said, his arm around Corrie's shoulders. "You don't have to eat if you're not hungry."

Bryn stood a minute, watching them. Corrie had been home for four days, but she'd hardly been home at all. In the morning, early, Daniel drove her to the hospital. In the evening he brought her home. They both looked like hell.

Bryn glanced into the dining room, where Bob and the boys were quietly eating stew. Then she put her hands on her hips and said firmly, "Coriander Bliss! Eat your damned dinner! How the hell are you going to take care of your baby if you get sick?"

Corrie stared at her, then dropped her eyes.

"I mean it!" Bryn was shouting now. "If I have to force-feed you this stew, I will. You have to eat!"

Corrie sighed heavily, then felt a small body crawl into her lap.

"Aunt Corrie?"

She opened her eyes and saw Cody staring at her, his eyes wide.

"Hey, Cody," she said faintly.

"Don't you want to live?"

Corrie sat a moment, looking into his eyes, his upturned face.

"Honey, of course I want to live," she said. "I'm okay. I'm just not hungry."

"No." The child shook his head in a way that reminded Corrie of Bryn. "You're not okay. You have to eat dinner or you'll get sick. Bryn said so."

Corrie kissed his forehead. "All right," she said finally, "I'll eat dinner."

"Good," Cody said, sliding out of her lap. "Because you have to take care of Emmaline. 'Cause she's kind of like my little sister."

Corrie's eyes filled with tears, and she ate her stew.

"How are you doing?"

Bob massaged Bryn's shoulders in the kitchen.

"I'm okay," she said. "Just . . ."

"You're exhausted. You need to rest."

"I'm really worried about her." Bryn's eyes drifted to the closed door of Corrie's bedroom. In the living room, Daniel sat staring vacantly at the television, blaring cartoons for the boys.

"And I'm worried about you."

Bryn turned and leaned into his chest.

"I don't know what I'd do without you."

"Ditto."

They loaded the dishwasher and sat at the dining room table with tea.

"I talked to the insurance guy today."

"Are they finally going to issue a check?"

"Yeah." Bob smiled. "It's a good check."

"Well, it's about time!"

"We'll get the roof fixed and new windows."

"Good."

"And . . ."

"And what?"

"There's enough to finish the attic." He paused, watching her face.

"I'm going to have the attic finished, so you can have a studio."

She stared at him.

"Seriously, Bryn, it will be a great space for you to work."

"You don't need to . . ."

"Bryn." Bob stood and walked around the table, knelt by her chair. "When everything is settled, I want you to come back."

"I can't leave Corrie," she said.

"I said, when everything is settled. I can wait."

"But what about the boys?"

"They want you back, too."

Bryn smiled and shook her head. "I can't just freeload off you, Bob. I mean, I love you and I love the boys. But . . ."

"I'm not talking about you staying in the guest room!" Bob's voice rose. His cheeks reddened. "When things have settled down, when Corrie and Emmaline are okay, I want you to live with me."

Bryn stared at him again.

"What I'm saying is, marry me, Bryn."

Still she stared.

"You don't have to answer now. Just don't say no. I love you. The boys love you. I want us to be together. Just think about it, okay?"

Bryn leaned forward, wrapped her arms around him, and said softly, "You stupid, stupid man! I don't need to think about it. Yes! Yes! Yes, I will marry you!"

∽ 64 ∾

Corrie donned the blue gown and mask at the nurses' station, then pushed open the door to the NICU. She blinked twice, adjusting her eyes to the bright lights, then blinked again.

"She looks less jaundiced today, doesn't she?" She reached into the incubator to stroke Emmaline's cheek.

"She's making good progress." The nurse standing beside her smiled. "In fact, the doctor said this morning that you can hold her."

Corrie's eyes opened wide.

"I can hold her? You mean now?"

The nurse nodded.

"Here, sit down and I'll get her out. You have to be careful with the monitors and feeding tube."

Corrie sat in the rocker she spent every day in and watched the nurse carefully extract the baby from the incubator. And then Emmaline was in her arms for the first time.

"Oh baby," she whispered. "My Emmaline, my precious little girl."

Daniel knelt by the chair and touched the baby's head with one finger.

"She's so beautiful." His voice cracked.

Corrie looked at him, startled to see tears streaming down his face.

"Are you okay?" she asked.

"I'm better than okay." He smiled at her. "I'm just really . . . happy."

"Me too."

The baby let out a small mew.

"Looks like she's happy, too," Daniel said.

He pulled out his cell phone. "Let me take a picture," he said. "The first time you get to hold your daughter."

He snapped several pictures, then sent one in a text to Bryn, Bob, Maya, and his mother.

"Hey, baby," Corrie crooned. "Hey, Emmaline. I'm your mommy. That's your daddy." She pointed to Daniel, who grinned widely. "We both love you so much."

"That's one lucky little girl!"

Corrie looked up in surprise. Sarah stood behind Daniel, holding a large box wrapped in pink and green.

"Hey, you!" Sarah leaned over and kissed Corrie's forehead.

"Hi," Corrie said, smiling. "I wasn't sure you'd come."

"And miss out on meeting my niece? Fat chance!"

"You remember Daniel?" Corrie looked from Sarah to Daniel, smiling anxiously.

"Hi, Daniel," Sarah said, smiling briefly at him. "Nice to see you again."

"You too," he said. Then he took a step back. "I'm going to get some coffee. Do you need anything?"

"No," Corrie said. "I'm fine."

He left and Sarah crouched down beside the rocker where Corrie sat holding the baby.

"Hello, little one," Sarah cooed, touching Emmaline's forehead. "She's just amazing."

"She is," Corrie agreed.

"I'm so glad she's okay. I was worried sick when I heard she came so early."

"Thanks," Corrie said. "Thanks for coming."

Sarah sat down on the floor and took Corrie's hand.

"I know I haven't been around much . . ." she began.

"Don't worry," Corrie said. "I know it's kind of awkward."

"Yeah." Sarah nodded. "But you are still my best friend, Corrie. I love you and I want you to be happy. And I want Ian and Laurel and Grace to know their cousin . . . even if she isn't officially their cousin. I want them to know her and to love her."

"I'd like that, too." Corrie felt tears fill her eyes. "I've really missed you."

That evening, Corrie ate the first full meal she'd had since the baby's birth. Suddenly, she was starving. Bryn watched in amazement as she downed three pieces of chicken, two huge helpings of potatoes, and several slices of bread.

"God," she said happily, "you're eating the way I do."

Corrie smiled. "I know I've been a witch the last week. I'm sorry. I've just been so worried."

"Don't apologize," Bryn said. "I completely understand."

"What time is Bob coming?"

"He should be here any minute. I can't believe he's going to be my birthing coach."

"I'm sorry I had to bail out on you."

"It's fine. Bob's actually really good at it, since he's done it before."

"Plus, he can get up off the ground to help you up!"

They both laughed, remembering the first class, when neither of them could get up from the floor.

"I'm sorry you didn't get to do the whole natural birth thing."

"It's okay," Corrie said. "The point wasn't to give birth, it was to have a baby."

"I'm so glad she's doing better."

"The nurse said they will probably take her off the respirator in a couple days."

"Yay!" Bryn grinned. "Any estimate yet on when you can bring her home?"

"Probably not for another couple weeks."

"So maybe we'll bring our babies home at the same time!"

The doorbell rang. Bryn waddled to the door and opened it.

"Oh," she said. "Um, hi, Mark."

"Hey, Bryn, how are you?"

"I'm fine."

"Is Corrie in?"

Bryn turned to look at Corrie, sitting on the couch, her mouth open.

"Yes, she's here. Come in." Bryn opened the door wider and Mark walked into the room.

"Hi," he said, smiling at Corrie.

"Hi."

Bryn had just closed the door when the bell rang again. This time it was Bob, carrying two pillows and a candy bar.

"This," he said, grinning and holding the candy above his head, "is for after class, and only if you actually do the breathing this week, instead of just giggling hysterically.

"Hey, Mark, I didn't see you there. How are you?"

"I'm good," Mark said. He stood just inside the living room.

"We'd better get going." Bryn picked up her purse and jacket. "You okay?" she asked Corrie.

"I'm fine," Corrie said. "Go, learn, have fun."

They left, Bryn giggling already.

"Sit down," Corrie said.

He sat on the recliner opposite her.

"How are you?" he asked.

"I'm good," she said.

"You look great."

"Thanks."

They sat a moment, awkwardly silent. Then Mark said, "The divorce was finalized today."

"I know," she said. "My lawyer called."

"It's stupid, but I just wanted to come see you."

"It's okay."

Mark rose and began pacing around the small living room.

"This is a nice little place," he said.

"*Little* being the operative word."

He laughed. "It's a lot smaller than our house was."

"And a lot less expensive," she said.

Another long silence. Mark sat down, rose again, then sat back down.

"Look, Corrie, I know I've been a jerk . . . a real jerk. I was hurt and angry. God, I was so angry. It feels like the last few months have just been a nightmare."

Corrie said nothing.

"When the tornado hit, all I could think about was you, where you were, if you were hurt. Then Sarah called and said you were in the hospital, and I thought maybe I'd lost you forever. It scared me, Corrie. It scared the hell out of me."

He sat down on the couch beside her and took her hand.

"Then today my lawyer called and said it was over, we're divorced. I don't know what I thought I'd feel, but man, it hit me hard. I cried for about an hour straight. And I realized I didn't want to be divorced. I didn't want to lose you forever."

"Mark . . ."

"No, let me finish, okay? Just let me get through this."

She stared at him.

"I still love you, Corrie. I didn't want to. I wanted to just hate you. But I can't. I don't like living alone. I don't like being alone. And . . . and I'm wondering if there's any chance at all that maybe we could try . . . I don't know, just try dating? We can take it as slowly as you want. We can go to counseling, if you want. We can . . . can we just try?"

Corrie sat a long moment in silence, then said softly, "You haven't even asked about the baby."

"What? I'm sorry. I . . . How's the baby?"

"She's tiny. She came almost eight weeks early. She's in the intensive care unit with a respirator and a feeding tube. I only got to hold her for the first time today."

"But she'll be okay, right? I mean, lots of babies are born early. The doctors can do all kinds of things now, right?"

"She's getting stronger every day."

"Good, I'm glad."

"Her name is Emmaline."

"That's pretty."

"She is my life. From the first time I felt her move, she has been my life. She is everything in the world. And you didn't even ask about her."

"God, Corrie! I'm sorry. I'm trying, but it's all so new for me."

"Mark." Corrie's voice was soft, gentle. "I'm so sorry I hurt you. I'm so sorry you're sad. I'm so sorry everything is a mess. But I'm not sorry about Emmaline. I'm not sorry I have her. I'm not sorry that she's my daughter. And . . ."

She took a deep breath and said out loud what she'd known since Emmaline's birth. "And I'm not sorry that Daniel is her father."

Mark let go of her hands, his cheeks a dull red.

"So you guys are . . . together?"

Corrie shook her head. "No. I mean, I don't know. He has a whole life in California. And I'm not leaving Middlebrook. So probably not. But . . . but he's Emmy's father, and he loves her so much, and he's been nothing but good since he found out about her. And I'm really grateful that he's been here."

"And I haven't been."

"No, you haven't been. I understand why you haven't been. I hurt you, I cheated on you. You had every right to be mad. I get that."

"But now . . ."

"Now," she said firmly, "I have a daughter and great friends and a life I'm happy with. And . . . and I'm sorry, but that life is without you. At first that was just so hard, but now, well, now I've gotten used to it. It doesn't hurt anymore. I don't think we can go back to before. I don't think I would want to, even if we could. We can only move forward, Mark."

"But we could go forward together."

"No," she said softly. "We can't."

"I . . . I guess I should go then."

He rose and walked to the front door.

"I hope you're happy, Corrie."

"I hope you're happy, too, Mark."

The door closed behind him and Corrie sat for a long time, staring at the fireplace. And then she called Daniel.

⁓ 65 ⁓

"Hey, what's up?" Daniel sat on the couch beside her. "Are you feeling all right? How is Emmaline?"

"I'm fine," she said, smiling at him. "I assume Emmy is fine. I haven't heard from the hospital since we left."

"Good." He let out an explosive sigh and visibly relaxed.

"So . . . what's up? You said you needed to talk."

"Mark came by earlier."

Corrie could see his shoulders tense. "What did he want?"

"The divorce was finalized today. He just . . . he wanted to talk about it."

"Are you okay?" Daniel watched her closely.

"Actually, yes. I am okay. Mark's not, and I hate that. But I am fine."

"Don't tell me he came over here to tell you he wants you back!"

"Yeah, he did."

"Son of a bitch!" Daniel stood abruptly and paced the same path Mark had paced earlier.

"So, now what? You move back in with him? He raises my daughter? God, Corrie, that's not fair!"

"That's not going to happen." Corrie rose and stood in his path, took his hands.

"I told him that I've moved on. And I have."

He stared at her.

"I hate that he's hurt," Corrie said. "But I can't go back to him. I don't want to. I'm ready to move forward, to live my life with my daughter. And . . ."

"And?"

"I'm thinking maybe there's a place in my life for you."

He stared at her and then grinned.

"Seriously? Are you serious? God, Corrie! That's . . . that's amazing!"

She smiled at him. "It kind of is."

He kissed her then, a long, slow, deliberate kiss. And it felt right, kissing him. It felt absolutely right.

Abruptly, he pulled back, stared into her face, and began talking fast.

"Corrie-Andy, it will be so great, I promise you! You're going to love Pasadena! It's close to the mountains and the beach and the desert. We can take Emmy to the beach every weekend, if you want! There's live theater, Corrie. Live music. And—"

"Daniel." Her voice stopped him cold.

"I'm not moving to California."

"But you said . . ."

"I said there's a place for you in my life. And my life is here."

His grin faded.

"I can't leave the center," he said. "That's my whole world."

"Or, Emmaline and I can be your world. I didn't ask you before, I didn't even tell you when I got pregnant all those years ago, because I couldn't stand the idea of trapping you in a life you didn't want. But now . . .

"Now, Daniel, we have a child, we have Emmy. I don't want to raise her in California, with all that smog and all that crime and all those people. This is my life. This is my world. This is where I am raising our daughter. You have to decide if you want to be part of that."

"That's not fair," he said, running his hand through his hair.

"No," she said. "It's not fair. Nothing about this is fair. But it is what it is. If you want to try and be together, if you want to help me raise our daughter, then you have to choose."

He stared at her for a long minute, then said very softly, "I'm sorry, Corrie. I can't just leave the center. I can't just walk away."

"Okay," she whispered.

"So . . . what does that mean?"

"It means, maybe you should go back to the hotel."

"Corrie, please . . ."

"Go, Daniel. I'll see you tomorrow at the hospital."

He stood a moment, then gathered his keys and jacket and left.

Corrie sank into the couch and laid her head on the armrest. And then she cried.

∼∽66∼∽

Emmaline grew stronger and chubbier every day. Within a week, she was breathing on her own. The next week, they removed the feeding tube and Corrie fed her a bottle for the first time, while Daniel filmed everything.

Finally, three weeks after her birth, Corrie strapped her daughter into her car seat, and Daniel drove them home.

"Slow down!" Corrie said, glancing rapidly from the road ahead to the baby sleeping in the backseat. "It's not a race!"

"I'm going the speed limit," Daniel protested. "Don't worry."

"How can I not worry? She's still so small."

"The doctor wouldn't let us bring her home if he thought she was too small."

He parked in front of the house, behind the construction machinery busily tearing down what was left of the house behind theirs. Then Corrie carefully unbuckled the baby from the car seat and carried Emmaline into the house. They were home.

Inside, Bryn, Bob, and the boys waited. The living room was filled with pink balloons and flowers. A huge teddy bear from Maya sat on the hearth. But all Corrie saw was her baby, safe in her arms, safe in their own house.

She sat on the couch, cradling Emmaline. Micah sat on one side of her, Cody on the other, both cautiously touching the tiny girl's face.

"So what do you think?" Corrie asked, smiling at the boys.

"She's really small," Micah said.

"And she's bald!" Cody chimed in.

Everyone laughed.

Daniel made several trips back and forth from the car, shuttling in the car seat, diapers, and bags.

Bryn had made chicken and noodles. Bob brought salad and a bottle of wine.

"You can have a glass now," he said, grinning at Corrie.

They ate, while Daniel held the baby as she sucked contentedly on his finger. Then Corrie took the baby so Daniel could eat. Her eyes pricked with tears, thinking how right it felt for him to be there, how much it felt like they were a family. Tomorrow, Daniel would fly back to California.

"Bryn?" Bob's voice broke into Corrie's reverie. "What's wrong?"

Bryn leaned against the mantle, one hand on her stomach. She raised her eyes to his and smiled. "I think I'm in labor."

"Oh my God! Sit down. Put your feet up. Do you have a bag packed? We need to get to the hospital." Bob's voice rose with each word.

"I'm fine," Bryn assured him. "The doctor said not to come until the pains are five minutes apart."

"How far apart are they?" Bob put his hand under her elbow and led her to the rocking chair.

"The last two were eight minutes."

"That's close enough. We're going."

"Where are we going?" Cody asked, emerging from the kitchen with a slice of bread.

"I'm taking Bryn to the hospital," Bob said. "You and Micah are going to stay here."

"That's not fair!" Micah said. "We want to go, too!"

"Not this time, buddy." Bob was halfway up the stairs. "Bryn, where's your bag?"

Bryn smiled at Corrie. "You'd think this was his first baby."

"Bryn?" Micah stood before her, eyes wide.

"Yes, honey?"

"Is it going to be okay?"

"Yes, Micah." Bryn wrapped him in a hug, then opened her arm to draw Cody in. "It's going to be perfect!"

Bob ran down the stairs carrying an overnight bag. "Is this everything?"

"Yes, honey. That's everything."

"Okay, let's go!"

Bob scooped his sons into a hug, then took Bryn's hands to pull her from the chair.

"Call us when you know anything!" Corrie held the door open for them, hugging Bryn tightly as they left.

"Probably they'll just send us home," Bryn said, laughing.

"I love you!" Corrie called after her as Bryn and Bob walked down the steps.

"I love you back!"

"You all right?" Bob held her hand tightly as an attendant wheeled Bryn to maternity—the same attendant who'd wheeled her up when Corrie was in labor.

She nodded, clenching her teeth as a contraction tightened her stomach.

"That was a strong one," she said as the contraction eased. "Wow!"

"Breathe, honey. Just breathe."

Four hours later, the doctor arrived. Bryn's contractions came one after the other, while Bob puffed in her face, urging her to breathe through them.

"I can't," she whimpered. "I can't do this."

"Bryn Elaine Baxter!" Bob's voice startled her. "You are the strongest woman I know. If anyone can do this, you can."

He mopped her forehead and kept his eyes trained on the monitor. "Here comes another one. Okay! Breathe with me!" He began puffing away while Bryn tried to follow him.

"All right, Bryn." Dr. Reynolds sat down on a stool between her legs. "This is it. Your baby is ready to be born. The next time you feel a contraction, I want you to bear down and push. Are you ready?"

"Oh my God, Bob. Have you ever seen anything so incredible in all your life?"

Bryn held her daughter to her breast, watching in sheer wonder as the baby searched for and then found her nipple.

"She's amazing." Bob sat on the edge of the bed, smiling like a lunatic.

"She is, isn't she?"

"So is her mom." Bob kissed her forehead.

"You did it," he said softly. "You did it."

"Hello!" A nurse walked into the room and checked the identical plastic bracelets that Bryn and the baby wore. "I just need to fill out the birth certificate."

She smiled at Bryn, touched the baby's head. "She's nursing well."

"She's incredible," Bryn repeated.

"I just need to ask a couple things. Mother's name—your official name, the one on your Social Security card."

"Bryn Elaine Baxter."

The nurse asked about the spelling, then wrote on the form.

"Father's name?"

"Bob Carter. That is, I mean, Robert Carter. Robert Ian Carter."

Bob spoke firmly, clearly. Bryn stared at him, felt her eyes filling with tears.

"Really?" she asked.

"Really." Bob kissed her forehead again. "I love you, Bryn. And I love this baby. She's mine. She's ours."

The nurse paused an instant, then smiled and wrote on the paper again.

"Baby's name?"

Bob looked at Bryn and raised his eyebrows.

"Poplar," Bryn said. "Poplar Margot Carter."

She spelled the name for the nurse.

"I've never heard the name Poplar before." The nurse smiled at them. "It's pretty."

"We'll call her Poppy." Bryn kissed the baby's head. "Like the flower."

"Poppy," Bob repeated. "I love that. Welcome to the world, Poppy Margot."

"Can we see her?" Micah stood in the doorway with Cody, Corrie, and Daniel behind them.

"Sure," Bryn said. "Come in."

Cody sat on Bob's lap, watching the baby nurse. "Why is she biting you?" he asked.

"She's not biting," Bryn said, smiling. "My body is making milk for her. She's just having her first meal."

Micah stood by the bed, studiously avoiding looking at Bryn's breast.

"Micah?" Bryn touched his cheek. "It's okay, honey. I'm just feeding the baby."

His cheeks reddened and he did not look at her, but he smiled.

"Wow." Corrie's voice was soft. "I'm really sorry I didn't get to nurse Emmy."

Daniel wrapped his arm tightly around her shoulders. "Emmaline is doing just fine."

"I know." She swiped her hand across her eyes. "I'm glad you get to do it right, Bryn."

"Where is Emmaline?" Bryn glanced around, as if the baby might be hiding somewhere in the room.

"She's at Sarah's. We dropped her off on the way." Corrie smiled again, then abruptly pulled her phone from her purse. "I'm just going to call and make sure she's okay."

She walked from the room.

Bryn kissed the baby's head again, then looked from Micah to Cody.

"Do you want to know her name?"

"Yeah!" Cody yelled.

"It's Poppy."

"Poppy?" Micah sounded confused. "Is that a real name?"

"It is now," Bob said. "Her full name is Poplar Margot."

"That's beautiful," Daniel said, smiling at Corrie as she walked back into the room. "Did you hear the name? It's Poplar Margot."

Corrie stood a second, phone still in her hand.

"That's lovely, Bryn."

"Your mom would be proud," Bryn said, smiling at her.

"Yes, that's a name right up my mom's alley."

"Everything okay with Emmy?" Daniel asked, taking Corrie's hand.

"Everything's fine." Corrie leaned into him, willing herself not to cry.

Daniel would leave tomorrow.

Six weeks later, Corrie stood in Bob's backyard, holding Emmaline, gazing around at the flowers, tables, candles, and balloons.

"Look, Aunt Corrie!" Cody carried a huge arrangement of roses to the makeshift altar. "I carried it all by myself!"

"Good job, Cody!"

"Well, you couldn't pick it up by yourself." Micah frowned, then laughed. "But you did okay carrying it." He shoved his little brother and grinned at Corrie.

"Hey, guys!" Bob called from the back porch. "Come in here and help me with the cake!"

The boys ran into the house. Corrie sank gratefully into a chair, gazing happily around her. She was so happy for Bryn. So happy for Bob. So glad of a small diversion.

She'd be alone now, just her and Emmaline. Bryn would move in here with Bob and Poppy and the boys, and start her life all over again. And Corrie . . . well, Corrie would start her life for real as a single mother.

Daniel called every morning. Corrie held the phone to Emmy's ear, so she would at least hear her father's voice. She swore that Emmy kicked her feet extra hard when she heard Daniel on the phone.

She kissed Emmy's forehead, still amazed that her daughter was here and fine and growing so fast. Emmaline gazed up at her with wide eyes.

"Corrie!" Bryn called from the porch. "Can you help me with this stupid bow?" She held a sash in the air. "Where the hell is my mother?"

Corrie tied Bryn's sash, while Micah cradled Emmaline under Bob's watchful eye.

"Oh my God!" Corrie breathed. "Bryn, you're beautiful!"

Bryn stood in the guest room of Bob's house, the room she'd lived in for months, the room that would now be Poppy's. The bed she'd slept in was gone, replaced by the crib her mother had bought. The walls were a soft yellow, with a wallpaper border of tiny ducks.

"I'm fat!" Bryn gazed at her reflection in the mirror, hand on her still slightly rounded stomach.

"You just had a baby," Corrie said, wrapping her arms around her friend. "And . . . you're beautiful. A beautiful, beautiful bride."

"I'm here!" Bryn's mother bustled into the room, carrying several large shopping bags. Then she stopped and simply stared at Bryn.

"Honey, oh honey!" She wrapped Bryn in a long hug. "You look wonderful!"

Corrie walked back to the yard, carrying Emmy. She was glad Bryn's mother had arrived, but now she felt . . . useless.

"Corrie!"

She spun around. Daniel stood at the rear door of the house.

"Hey!" she called back.

Daniel was to be Bob's best man. She was Bryn's maid of honor. All Corrie wanted was for this day to be over.

"How is she?" Daniel bent over to kiss the baby's head. "Is it safe for her to be outside like this?"

Corrie smiled at him. "It's fine, Daniel. We go outside almost every day. It's good for her."

"I can't believe how big she's getting." He took Emmaline from Corrie and cradled her, touching her cheek with his finger. "I can't believe how much I've missed her."

Corrie turned away, unwilling to let him see the tears that filled her eyes.

"All right, everyone!" Bryn's mother stood on the back porch. "I think we're ready."

The dozen or so guests sat in white chairs facing the altar. Daniel handed Emmaline to Kenetha, who smiled and cooed at her.

Bryn's parents walked down the aisle, Keri carrying Poppy, while a friend played softly on the guitar. Then Daniel and Corrie walked in together, not looking at each other as they solemnly paced down the aisle.

Finally, Bryn appeared on Bob's arm, her dark hair circled with a ring of white flowers, a radiant smile on her face.

Corrie watched her friends walk toward the altar and blinked back tears. She glanced over at Daniel, but he was looking away. She bit her lip.

The service was short, but the party went on for a long time. They danced in the backyard, grilled ribs and corn, passed babies from lap to lap. Finally, Corrie couldn't take anymore.

"I'm going," she whispered, kissing Bryn's cheek. "Emmy needs to get to bed, and so do I."

"Are you okay?" Bryn hugged her tightly.

"I'm fine."

"If you want to, you and Emmy can stay here tonight. We've got a futon in the attic now."

"How romantic would that be for you and Bob on your wedding night?" Corrie laughed.

"Well, we'll already have the boys. We can just make it a slumber party."

Corrie shook her head and kissed Bryn again. "I am so happy for you."

Bryn smiled. "Me too!"

"Bryn!" Keri was calling from the porch. "I don't know how to work your coffee grinder."

Bryn laughed, hugged Corrie again, and ran toward the house, her skirt scooped over her arm.

Corrie stopped to hug Bob, kissing his cheek and making him promise to be happy. Then she carried Emmaline to the car, strapped her in, and drove back to her house—a quiet house, an empty house.

Emmy fell asleep in the car, and Corrie carefully placed her in her crib, then watched her sleep.

"I'm sorry, baby, that your daddy is so far away," she whispered.

The doorbell rang and Corrie pulled a blanket over the baby and tiptoed out of the room. The next-door neighbors often came by in the evenings, just to check on her. They'd become good friends since the storm.

Corrie opened the front door, ready with a smile—a smile that faltered only briefly when she saw Daniel standing on the porch.

"Hey, you didn't tell me you were leaving the party."

He walked into the house and looked around. "Where's Emmaline?"

"She's asleep." Corrie led him to the nursery, where they stood together in the glow of the nightlight, admiring their tiny daughter.

"She really is perfect," Corrie said.

"Just like her mom." Daniel put his arm around her waist and she stiffened.

"Would you like a cup of tea?" Corrie walked out of the nursery, away from his embrace.

"Sure." Daniel followed her into the kitchen. He watched her as she filled the teakettle and put it on the stove.

"So, how are you?" he asked, his voice gentle.

"I'm good. Busy, but I guess that's to be expected."

"Is it hard being back at work?"

Corrie's maternity leave had ended three weeks earlier.

She nodded. "Some days I just take her in with me. Sometimes I can work from home. But the rest . . . It's hard to leave her."

"She's in good hands with Bryn." Daniel put his hand on her shoulder and squeezed it. "You know Bryn loves her."

Corrie nodded again. "I know. But it's still hard not being with her all the time."

"I know." Daniel's voice was low. "I can't believe how much I miss her when I'm not here. How much I miss you."

He pulled at her shoulder, gently forcing her to turn and face him.

"I can't stand this," he said. "I can't do this. It's just too hard."

She simply looked at him, fighting hard not to cry.

"So . . ." Daniel took her hands in his and smiled. "I'm moving back to Middlebrook."

He watched her face first register surprise, then disbelief.

"But what about the center?" she finally stammered.

"I'll still be on the board," he said. "We'll hire a new director. I'll still go out sometimes, just to check in. But . . . I need to be here, with you and Emmaline."

He tilted her chin up to look into her eyes. "I love you, Corrie-Andy. I love you and I love our daughter, and I want us to be a family, a real family."

"But your job . . ." Her voice trailed away. "I don't want you to feel trapped. I couldn't stand that."

"My job will be here," he said, smiling. "I had my final interview yesterday with the Middlebrook Boys and Girls Club. They offered me the job. I'm the new director."

"And you're . . . you're really going to leave California?"

"I'm coming home, Corrie. I'm coming home to the only home I ever want, with you and Emmy."

Corrie's hands shook in his. "Because you want to?"

"Because I want to and I need to and I have to!"

Corrie stared at him for a long minute, letting the words sink in, letting wave after wave of happiness rush through her. She breathed in deeply, more deeply than she'd done in months. She leaned into his chest and cried, then looked up in surprise when she felt Daniel's tears dripping onto her face.

"I love you, Corrie-Andy." He kissed her forehead, her nose, her cheeks, her mouth. "I love you and I don't ever want to lose you again."

"I love you, too," she said, leaning in to kiss him again, this time harder and more deeply.

She smiled at him shyly, took his hand, and pulled him toward the bedroom. He grinned at her, squeezing her hand.

From the nursery, they heard a rustle and then a cry. They both laughed, leaning into each other, holding each other tightly.

Then they walked into the nursery, where Emmaline was yowling.

Daniel picked her up, shushing her softly. Corrie watched them for a minute, her eyes filling again with tears, then went to heat a bottle in the kitchen.

At last, she was home.

Please turn the page for a very special Q&A
with Sherri Wood Emmons.

Your first two novels were told in the first person, through the eyes of a child narrator. Why did you write this book in third person?

I wanted to try something new. Writing in the third person doesn't come as easily to me as writing in first person, so it was a new challenge. And there are three different stories going on in the book, so third person made more sense.

It seems like everyone in this book is in a state of upheaval.

I think at about thirty, most people go through a time of reexamination. You are ten years out of college, too old to be a protégé, and it's time to take stock of your life and decide if you are on the path you want. My life was in a state of upheaval in my early thirties, and a lot of my friends' lives were, too. I think it's the age.

Why did you title the book The Weight of Small Things*?*

The title reflects the way small decisions we make can add up to change our lives. Every day, each one of us makes choices—or chooses not to make choices—and the weight of those choices ultimately determines who we are. Sometimes the choices are big ones and the implications are obvious. But so often it's the little choices, the ones that seem almost inconsequential, that set us on a new path.

How did you decide on this story?

This is actually the first story I ever started writing, and I began it twenty years ago when I had just turned thirty and my own life was in flux. The story and the characters are fiction, but the situations they are facing and the decisions they are making will feel familiar to many people in that age group, I think. They certainly felt real to me.

Corrie Philips, the main character, begins with a pretty good life—a nice husband and beautiful home, a job she enjoys. Yet she can't seem to simply relax and enjoy her life. At times she seems almost ungrate-

ful for her situation. Why can't she simply appreciate her life and forget about her past?

Corrie carries a huge weight through life—guilt over the abortion she had after college, responsibility for her mother and siblings, and a deep-down belief that she doesn't deserve the marriage and home she has built. At some level, she is always waiting for the other shoe to drop, and that prevents her from owning her own happiness.

What I think is interesting about Corrie is the way she grows into herself. As her pregnancy progresses and she feels her baby moving inside her, she finally allows herself to simply feel joy. And that allows her eventually to accept that she can have happiness, that she deserves happiness, and that she can take care of herself.

Bryn seems an unlikely friend for Corrie. In some ways she is Corrie's opposite—free-spirited, unconcerned with what other people think, and always up for fun. What makes the friendship between Corrie and Bryn believable?

I think each fills a void in the other's life. Bryn helps Corrie to loosen up, see things differently, and think for herself. But Corrie helps Bryn, too. She provides constant and steady friendship and a reliable sounding board, and she is always there to encourage Bryn in her adventures.

The friendship works because they are opposites in many ways. But they are alike in some ways, too. Both are kind, fiercely protective of the people they love, creative, and stubborn. Everyone should have a friend like Bryn!

What are you working on now?

I'm very excited about book number four. It's told in the first person by two narrators, a young girl and her new stepmother, as they travel around the country with a man who is harboring some very dark secrets.

THE WEIGHT
OF SMALL THINGS

Sherri Wood Emmons

ABOUT THIS GUIDE

The suggested questions are included to enhance
your group's reading of Sherri Wood Emmons's
The Weight of Small Things.

DISCUSSION QUESTIONS

1. Corrie Philips seems to have an ideal life. Why can't she let go of the past and enjoy the present?

2. Is Corrie a sympathetic character? Why or why not?

3. Bob insists to Bryn that she tell Paul about her pregnancy. Do you think a man always has the right to know when his partner is pregnant? Are there times when it's okay to keep that information from him?

4. What responsibility, if any, does Corrie have for her mother's situation?

5. Corrie believes that her inability to conceive a baby is punishment for having had an abortion. What does your faith tradition teach about God's judgment? How does that apply to a woman who has terminated a pregnancy?

6. What role does Maya play in the story? How would the story be different without her presence?

7. Corrie accuses Daniel of trying to play God. Is that a fair assessment? Are Daniel's decisions reasonable ones?

8. Bob has taken his wayward wife back twice after her infidelities. Do you think a partner should be given a second chance after an affair?

9. Bryn's relationship with Paul began when she was his student. Is it ever okay for a teacher to be in a romantic relationship with a student? Why or why not?

10. Bob and Bryn begin their relationship very soon after his divorce. Is Bryn right to worry about being a rebound girlfriend? Can their relationship last?

11. Corrie and Daniel's relationship is renewed while she is married to Mark. Is the relationship doomed to fail? Why or why not?

12. What is the significance of the title, *The Weight of Small Things*?